H50314

P9-CLR-534

JEWEL OF THE APOSTLES

Enjoy!.

Barb
Dimech

Also by Barb Dimich

❀

Madeline's Jewel
Superior's Jewel
SEALed Fate
Concealed Judgement

JEWEL OF THE APOSTLES

❀

The Apostles Islands Trilogy

Barb Dimich

iUniverse, Inc.
New York Lincoln Shanghai

Jewel of the Apostles
The Apostles Islands Trilogy

Copyright © 2006 by Barb Dimich

All rights reserved. No part of this book may be used or reproduced by any means, graphic, electronic, or mechanical, including photocopying, recording, taping or by any information storage retrieval system without the written permission of the publisher except in the case of brief quotations embodied in critical articles and reviews.

iUniverse books may be ordered through booksellers or by contacting:

iUniverse
2021 Pine Lake Road, Suite 100
Lincoln, NE 68512
www.iuniverse.com
1-800-Authors (1-800-288-4677)

This is a work of fiction. All of the characters, names, incidents, organizations and dialogue in this novel are either the products of the author's imagination or are used fictitiously.

ISBN-13: 978-0-595-40136-9 (pbk)
ISBN-13: 978-0-595-84516-3 (ebk)
ISBN-10: 0-595-40136-8 (pbk)
ISBN-10: 0-595-84516-9 (ebk)

Printed in the United States of America

For Sue Walker and Anna Williamson

When you have to walk that solitary valley and you have
to walk it by yourself, your friends will be on the valley's edge,
cheering you on, praying for you, pulling for you, intervening on
your behalf, and waiting with open arms at the valley's end.
Sometimes, friends will even break the rules and walk beside you.
or come in and carry you out.
When we began this adventure called womanhood, we had no
idea of the incredible joys or sorrows that lay ahead.
Thank you to you both.
I can't imagine life without either one of you.

Acknowledgments

❈

The origin of the Apostle Islands Trilogy came long after my first visit to La Pointe and Bayfield, Wisconsin. With a desire to put many ideas into one simple story, this trilogy came into focus after a phone call to Lori Hinrichsen of Madeline Island's Chamber of Commerce. Best friends Katharine, Michelle and Nicole emerged as three heroines. Lori without your knowledge and guidance of the area and people, I could not have finished the Apostle Islands Trilogy.

To George Toman of the La Pointe Police Department, after chasing you around fourteen miles of rock, I can't thank you enough for filling in the gaps on Wisconsin law, crime scene investigation, the tours and the intriguing 'inside info'. In many ways, our chat iced the cake for an amazing finish.

I am especially grateful to Nori Newago, President of Madeline Island Historic Preservation Association for your assistance in locating the owner of "Song of The Pioneers" by Elvera Myhre. A special thanks to Elvera's granddaughter, Virginia Lofrano, for permission to use the song that your grandmother wrote. As the story emerged, each verse in Song of the Pioneers became an integral part of the trilogy.

A gracious thank you to the Reiman Family and their friends for bailing my car out of one muddy mess then inviting me into your magnificent retreat overlooking 'the big lake'.

Special thanks to Alice Cadotte for the historical facts and reference materials, and to Linda Ohlandt who shared more cultural tidbits.

Thank you to Roger Lenz for your gun expertise and the patient explanations, and to Rudy Sterbenk for detailing the necessary boat info that I needed throughout the stories. *I hope that I got it right.* Your help was extremely useful but your friendships will always be invaluable.

Prologue

❀

Three days before Christmas

"You have sinned!"
Rage spurted through the serial killer like a storm tossing a fishing boat.

An icy winter gale swirled, battered and beat repulsively outside and against the four walls. The killer's despair was peaking high, and forced the worn out sense of inadequacy.

It was time to worship the ending.

The killer looked at the little tramp. It was so easy to snare them. Like the others, Stacy had accepted the gratis offer of drugs and alcohol. Every one of them gobbled up the self abuse with greed until it sedated them, until it made the task of getting them to the communion table for redemption effortless. At first, they all thought it was a game. Stacy laughed and giggled like the others who came before her. She didn't fight and thrash about when her hands and feet were bound, at least not until she woke muzzy and dazed and realized death wasn't a game. Then she began her struggle. She made a great effort to free herself the way the others did but it was too late. Death had already begun. Death always began in the first canonical hour of the righteous ceremony. The slow slipping away of life lasted seven wonderful days. It took seven days for reverence, prayer, and suffering to receive forgiveness.

But Seven days also provided a corporeal climax, a sought after excitement. That needed excitement began with their tear shed, their hope of receiving sympathy. Emotions rarely fazed the serial killer. But watching them die slowly did. Fleshy pores swelled with erotic beads of moisture. Wild, unrestrained excitement liquefied the soul when each screamed in hopes that someone could help them. But when no one came to their rescue, when no one came to save Stacy, she writhed and thrashed about, spit out the holy water mixture, wept on and off with those large panicked eyes they all used to obtain whatever they wanted from whomever they felt like using. When that didn't work, she cried harder and begged for released, promised what she couldn't deliver. They were all defiled creatures of wicked habits. Stacy had pleaded for release like the others who came before her until ulcerations appeared inside her mouth and throat.

Death is the way of life. Death is a firecracker. The loud pop startles. It's frightful and coarse, halting one's breath, before the brittle silence follows those demonic words of death. It lasts mere moments before shock tags and paralyzes the body, raping the soul of life. The quiet silence of death numbs its grievers. The haunting vibes left in the wake of death becomes an intimate loss. It is long-lasting and intense. The horror of death is an utter loss of hope with now way out for the little tramps.

At that moment, Stacy could no longer scream, or beg, and her brows furrowed deeply, as deep and tight as her fear. It was then, like all sinful teens, Stacy prayed it over. Abdominal pain followed. The mess of diarrhea tagged along before a fever set. Stacy peed an unusual color of blue all over herself. At the end of the fifth day, she convulsed harshly. Respiratory difficulty set in with the destruction of her lungs. Stacy's bright-with-life face had fallen dark with agony. Her pleading brown eyes dilated to a fixed position. Eventually, somewhere in her confused state of mind, she realized death always wins and pleading always loses. Stacy's shallow breath indicated the moment had arrived for her to pass over. She would never again tempt man into her clandestine affairs. She would never again filch what did not belong to her.

The killer put on a pair of gloves, turned and faced the teenage girl. Wispy bangs had molded to her forehead from the sweat of her own fear. Her neatly combed hair was the beauty of a black starless night. Bronze flesh glowed beneath the milky whiteness of her frock. The lacy flawless collar was perfect. It must be impeccable. It must be presentable.

"Lacy Stacy White, you were so easy. You're not so pure and now I'm going to save you from your sinful life for sure. I have the power in my hands to take all of you."

Meticulously placing the sacred rosary pea bracelet on Stacy's wrist, the killer anointed her bronze flesh with the holy water one last time. The chant of the morning prayer to the Divine Creator commenced.

"Almighty One, I offer this cleansed flesh to you.
To replace the death of the babe in the woods,
to absolve Stacy White of her sinful transgressions.
Commitment to the cause be pure and white.
Repugnance for the past be foul and black.
Come forth Almighty One to receive this sacrifice.
Come forth and close the gates of my hell forever."

Kneeling at the altar beneath Stacy White, the killer hummed then repeated the chant melodiously.

"Almighty One, I offer this cleansed flesh to you.
To replace the death of the babe in the woods,
to absolve Stacy White of her sinful transgressions.
Commitment to the cause be pure and white.
Repugnance for the past be foul and black.
Come forth Almighty One to receive this sacrifice.
Come forth and close the gates of my hell—"

"Sinner! Be damned to hell for your impurity!"

The killer flinched, looked up. The voice was harsh and mean. It was the Evil Spirit consumed with ruthless rage—a constant reminder of the wickedness of the world. The killer swallowed hard and began humming, hummed louder, chanted, chanted louder to block the wicked words.

"Almighty One! I'm offering this cleansed flesh to you!
To replace the death of the babe in the woods.
To absolve Stacy White of her sinful transgressions.
Commitment to the cause be pure and white.
Repugnance for the past be foul and black.
Come forth Almighty One to receive this sacrifice.
Come forth now! Close the gates of my hell forever!"

"You must pay—you will pay for your sins!"

The killer shouted, "No! You try to draw my life into your devious portal. They will pay! Not me! They will all pay!"

"You must pay for your sins."

"I have paid. Now they will pay!" the killer shouted. "Evil Spirit you don't understand death is eternity's only survivor for sin."

"You have sinned!"

"I have been redeemed. I cannot die!"

"You overflow with sin!"

Enraged, the killer shouted. "The Almighty One preaches I must continue the sacred vows in order to dispose of you, Evil Spirit. I must perform the ritual to deplete the heavy burden of your hatred. I know the terror you feel. I supply your terror by tapping into your fear."

"You must pay!"

"It's magnificent to watch fright mount in your face. I know because I have lived with the same fear and now I have recreated it in the name of vengeance. My reward is death to all—not my own death. They must suffer the same debilitation I have suffered. It is justified. It provides me with absolution."

When Stacy wheezed out her last breath, the killer had triumphed once more. The Evil Spirit dissolved. Four more days would pass before Stacy's soul could move from earth to heaven. Then her adorned body would lie pompously for only *one* to discover. The *one* who had caused the pain. The *one* who would be the next sacrifice. *Her* death would come at the commencement of the New Year. The act of manipulating *her* into capture would be a worthy challenge. Poison wasn't good enough for *her*. *She* must feel the terror. *She* must know the intensity of the haunting vibes left in the wake of death. After *she* confessed the ultimate truth, only then will Nicole Jarvis understand this has always been about passion's revenge. The brazen slut with her honey-gold hair will relinquish her soul to the Almighty One at the commencement of the New Year. The sacrifice for the damage she has caused will be righteous.

It is deserved.

Song of the Pioneers
by Elvera Myhre

The blue water of Lake Superior, the fresh air
you can't compare. Friendly seagulls and the
swallows, here to greet you ev'rywhere.
O the tall trees and pretty flowers to enjoy
where'er you go. Beautiful deer by the
roadside with their little babies too.

O there is no other island so dear to me as thou art.
Mad'line Island, Beautiful Island,
I love the name with all my heart.

CHAPTER 1

❀

December 20th

"Nicole, these sketches are marvelous! We cater to the rich throughout the world and you have the eccentric gift I'm looking for."

"Thank you, Ms. Mackinaw."

"I give women what they want and high-tech is currently vogue. Excuse me again," Chantilly Mackinaw apologized with the sound of a faint tap at the office door. "Come in."

The assistant interrupted the interview for the fifth time in fifteen minutes—*top model Samantha Tobias complained the Cartier jewelry was an obnoxious match to her…, the outfit makes her look fat…*

Nicole waited patiently in the oval windowed office. Her palms were sweaty with excitement. The moment she entered the lobby and faced the attractive receptionist inside Mackinaw Designs, she discovered her dream to design clothes was a fast-paced world of chaos. Phones rang non-stop, artists barked out orders while stylists hustled in preparation for the latest show mid January.

Nicole had hoped her designs would thrill the voluptuous woman sitting across from her. She gazed out the skyscraper window past the owner who accepted intrusions as typical. With a personal need to restrain her internal jitters, she lassoed self doubts congesting her mind and forced herself to guess the designer's age. Chantilly Mackinaw had to be at least sixty, nearing sixty-five but didn't look a day over fifty. Well preserved skin disguised age and she wondered if facial tucking and plastic surgeries were the reasons. The experienced fashioner also articulated her words in a plummy voice.

"Sam wears what I tell her to or she's out."

High-tech clothing might be the latest fashion craze, but this retired model's subtle, classy suit was a Ralph Lauren. Chantilly didn't wear her personal label. Mackinaw styles were intentionally chic for the younger crowd. Nicole glanced downward at her own work of art. The loose-draped, lavender satin blouse complimented a tweed cocoa jacket and coordinated mini-skirt, none of which bore a sought after brand name. Instead, the label was Nicole Louise Jarvis of La Pointe, Wisconsin and very apropos for the cause.

"Becca, give me five minutes without another interruption," Chantilly instructed.

The dressed down assistant left and the illustrious model picked up where she left off.

"You have no previous experience but I like your artistry, Nicole. Your drawings expose a stylish flair. An à la mode if you will. I've been searching for someone with modish verve, but I am curious. You're thirty-two and I wonder why the late start."

Since the call had come requesting this interview, Nicole had thought long and hard about the answer. A major career change on her mind for several years, it was too late to fulfill her childhood dream of modeling. Nevertheless, her deep love for clothes and fashion pushed her to take a correspondence course that taught her the world of styles. She had watched the vacillating rages her entire life. Upon completion of the designer course, she finally discovered the courage to submit letters and resumes along with her secret designs back in early June. Now, here she sat in downtown Los Angeles with Chantilly Mackinaw who wanted to know why the late start. "Choices," she answered. "I passed up my chance to model. This is an opportunity to carry out the other half of a childhood dream."

A rather long, visual examination from the voluptuous woman skyrocketed Nicole's excitement.

"You have sinfully gorgeous skin. You would have swept continents in your youth. Why didn't you model?"

"Perhaps you're right, but my current desire is to draw and design sleek, jaunty styles and provide me the opportunity to contribute to the one thing I enjoy the most."

"Experience counts. What makes you think you understand this business? What makes you think you will succeed?"

It's all or nothing Nicole's heart whispered. "Self-confidence and positive attitude play a role in a woman's self-fulfillment as do intimacy and inner strength. Pablo Manson, creative director for Elizabeth Arden once said, 'beauty is an attitude'."

As her words began to flow, Nicole gathered steam and straightened. "There's a psychology behind attractiveness. Beauty means looking good and turning it into a woman's individual charm. Appeal, charisma, romance. All women want it. They need to know they own it with every breath they take. I am quite confident I can help women seek out their best charm with my ideas and well designed clothes."

"That's quite an assessment. How will you feel knowing your name isn't on the garments you know you created?"

"Ms. Mackinaw, I've never been a jealous person. I love fashion and designing. The reward comes from doing what I love."

"I see," Chantilly responded, shuffling papers. "Today's retail industry is an extremely competitive business. We work long hours combining glamour and femininity to meet the competitive prices, superior quality and greatest availability. I travel a lot and so will you. I expect deadlines to be met. I do not tolerate tardiness, slack or cheating. I've built Mackinaw Designs from the ground up and I will not permit my employees or my models to drag me under by sharing our secrets with the opposition. If you draw for me, I own the design. You play by my rules or you do not work for me."

"Unless I have to advertise the product, none of what you're telling me is a problem."

"I have an entire floor dedicated to satisfying my audience. They also know their primary function is to suitably present the product—*my* designs."

Nicole waited as Chantilly flipped through her sketches again. The door opened a sixth time and the dowdy-looking assistant entered.

"Excuse me. Samantha—"

"Nicole, what I see here thrills me. How long would it take you to move to L.A.?"

Nicole's stomach fluttered excitedly. She vibrated internally, but didn't miss the stunned look from the assistant. "Are you offering me the job?"

"I believe that you are the one I'm looking for. I'll be in touch with you after our January show."

Was that a yes or a no? Recognizing her time up, Nicole uncrossed her legs, hid her enthusiasm and stood. She avoided looking directly at the frumpy assistant who gaped in shock at her now. "Thank you, Ms. Mackinaw. I look forward to hearing from you."

Led out of the office by the currently silent assistant, Nicole felt the urge to sing and dance out of the famous name-bearing skyscraper. Her practiced smile in place, she held back and walked with grace. A month ago, Chantilly Mackinaw, world renowned with offices in Paris, Los Angeles and Rome had responded positively to her query with a request for a detailed portfolio of her ideas before she telephoned to schedule this interview. The news came quickly and walloped Nicole in the chest with a kick-bang surprise. She never expected the famous model turned fashion designer to have the slightest interest in the sketches of Nicole Louise Jarvis. *Louise is a stupid name,* she had subconsciously decided more than once. Despite hard efforts to spend her free time studying and drawing, she always felt the smallest recognition would have tended her ego very well. Chantilly Mackinaw was huge!

The elevator stopped, the doors opened. Nicole took a deep breath. Exhilarated by the marvelous world of fashion, she exited the rising structure stretching out of sight in L.A.'s sunny haze with a strut of excitement. Only five days until Christmas, downtown Los Angeles bustled over with frenzied people and heavy traffic. Several failed attempts to hail a taxi, Nicole did what she heard everyone else doing—she whistled. A cab pulled up curbside and she opened the door, sliding in.

"Luxe Hotel in Beverly Hills," she told the driver. She'd chosen the Luxe over the Regent Beverly Wilshire since it was unbelievably less in price, though money didn't matter.

Glancing at her watch now, the actual interview had lasted a mere fifteen minutes, including interruptions. Becca, the bedraggled assistant, gave her a tour before the interview. Retail and advertising occupied several floors. Another floor housed thousands of disarrayed and scattered material bolts of every texture, style and color desperately and all needing someone's creative mind to design the fabric into gorgeous women's garments. A factory on a separate floor was where the designs came together. Additional floors made up office cubicles with owners who had purpose—the vision to make new and exciting trends both functional and elegant. Models and the clothing they wore had to mimic Paris, Rome and London and adapt to New York boardwalks while holding the interest of the Midwest took up yet another entire floor.

What would it be like to live in a large city after spending her entire life on a remote island in Lake Superior? With a hidden desire to travel overseas, she rarely dwelled on when she might venture that far, but today everything had changed. It was a day with more ado than she'd felt in a very long time. Appreciation of her work from the retired model had stirred up her adrenaline until her heart pounded and she couldn't breathe. *Great balls of fire*, her heart felt out of breath though she officially hadn't received an offer. Unofficially, the job sounded like a sure thing. How long *would* it take her to move from La Pointe to L.A.? And where would she live?

"Luxe Hotel," the driver said, bringing the cab to a stop.

Nicole paid the cabby as a hotel attendant appeared to open the taxi door for her. She could quickly accustom herself to being waited on instead of serving others. "Thank you," she said, slipping a tip to the uniformed doorman.

"You're welcome, Ms. Jarvis."

She hesitated, provided him with a winning smile. The way she did it, told him she loved the way everyone at the Luxe greeted her by name. Their rule of thumb—expect the best. She wasn't used to it but entered when he opened the door to the lobby of the intimate boutique hotel with the ultra chic aura. Polished mahogany, plush textures and limestone floors sparkled. Arriving at LAX last night, she checked in and had dinner in the Luxe's charming Bistro. The food superb, the service excellent, the décor and smallest touches designed to compliment and enhance personal enjoyment.

She planned to spend the rest of today shopping. Tonight she would take in the nightlife. Maybe stay out all night before her six A.M. flight left in the morning. This second, she couldn't wait to discover Beverly Hills' prestigious shopping street—Rodeo Drive. The only place to find womenswear, menswear, special boutiques from ultra elegant to classy casual, a place where one could window shop or splurge until their heart completely satisfied. Nicole hurried to her room, changed into a stylish pantsuit and headed out on foot.

Black fancy streetlights lined the streets. Christmas fringe decorated palm trees lining the boulevard. It grabbed one's attention especially one who had lived in Wisconsin's winter wonderland all her life. BMW's and Porsches zoomed by with male drivers while personal chauffeurs taxied women in Rolls Royces. Nicole thought she spotted Goldie Hawn in one such vehicle and remembered Brad Pitt and Jennifer Anniston had once visited Madeline Island. Gage had mentioned it to her and sure enough, the two celebrities showed up at the Red Rock Tavern for dinner. Too bad they weren't together anymore. They once made a rather charming couple.

Walking past Christian Díor, Chanel, Gucci, Polo, and José Eber Nicole's heart pumped to an all-time high. The near-baroque style stores and salons lined the famous street by the dozens. This was a serious shopper's paradise. The famous Rodeo Drive might just be able to fulfill all her needs and desire. Then as if the atmosphere of the holidays grabbed hold of her, Nicole decided, screw sensibility and entered Yves Saint Laurent. She was going to buy something memorable and walked out an hour later with more than a keepsake. Accessories were a necessity to go with her new luscious and very rich outfit. By five in the afternoon, she found an irresistible matching pair of heels she swore held magic like the famous glass slippers. The height alone bestowed her with the power to seduce anyone. She found a gold bracelet from Cartier and a Coach purse to complete the ensemble.

All jacked-up on self-indulgence, and famished, Nicole decided on Planet Hollywood. She wanted to compare the food to the one at the Mall of America in Minnesota. She also wanted to see Grauman's Chinese Mann Theatre—the walk of fame where movie stars graced the public with their cemented signatures and footprints. She needed to ride a trolley, too, debating the amount of activity she could squeeze in before she had to board a 747 for the flight back. A flight she didn't think she wanted to take now, but refused to dwell on a mundane life and tedious work at the Red Rock Tavern. She focused on the sites and sounds of Beverly Hills, silently praying Chantilly Mackinaw meant what she said. Tonight belonged to her to be served like royalty.

The time had come for a new life.

How can my need to change be wrong?

CHAPTER 2

❀

Nicole arrived on Madeline Island an hour before her shift started, changed clothes and rushed over to the Red Rock Tavern. She didn't live far from it and always walked. Universal green and red trimmings decorated the entire tavern inside and out, lighting up everything with a different kind of holiday warmth. A monumental balsam devoured a corner of the lounge. Holly boughs strung throughout were simple compared to the glitter and gold of Beverly Hills. Sweet aromas of pine and Jacques's special of the night scented the air. Christmas Carols hummed from unseen speakers.

Waitresses Angie and Carla moved quicker than shooting stars in the packed dining room of most all of La Pointe's residents tonight. Wilbur and Iola Tibbs, the gift shop owners, were finishing a meal across from Mrs. Chernak and her fussy relatives up from the south. Mrs. Chernak then went south for the winter but planned to stick around for the grand opening. Widow, Adeline Girard along with her healthy brood of boys had stopped in for a pre-Christmas feast, too. Those who preferred the quiet dining to the rowdy lounge sat sipping their favorite holiday drink in pre-celebration. Even Jacque the chef had a gleam in his eye pulling extra duty between the lounge and dining. Fittingly groomed in a white double-breasted cooking smock, Jacque's aureole goatee, mustache and French hairstyle suggested a certain notability to his skill and ingenuity. Although the kitchen was at the back, he generally made several appearances throughout the night. He thrived on watching patrons devour his specialties, smiled at her as she passed through back to the lounge to get to her office on the second floor.

Buoyant static and male testosterone electrified the lounge's atmosphere from a copious crowd of male town folk and construction crews. Men hooting with laughter and energy that would last til closing had reached a plentiful roar the night before Christmas Eve.

Dog breeder, Jim Berger was bellied up to the bar smoking a cigar with several of the regulars. Their mouth and brains possessed the gutter, and the group whooped rowdily at another Ben McEvoy dirty Christmas joke. Ben owned the Upland Cottage and made his living renting it out. Jim and Ben were the main attraction in the circle.

Nicole's favorite bartender, Hayden Dobbin poured peppermint schnapps for Marlene Evans while filling a frosty mug with tap for one of the guys swaying like a willow tree at the bar. Nicole liked the fortyish barkeeper and enjoyed his cheerful whistling. Tonight his tunes, notable of any lively crowd, matched the festive music. He nodded at her then to Sheila calling for more drinks over the crowd. Additional orders came at him from Gypsy and Beth who provided infectious chatter with the patrons. This group of servers preferred the lounge to the dining room. Nicole didn't care who did what as long as the customers had the most amazing time the moment they stepped inside the Tavern. Her competent employees wore neat ensembles, a white blouse and black slacks or skirts. Although she thought the outfits had the dullness of ditch water, Marlene's husband Ted, owner of the bar, kept telling her the outfits were good for business.

Scanning the lounge, Nicole counterfeited a smile to disguise her confused thoughts. During the flight back from L.A., she promised herself she wouldn't wait with baited breath for the designer's call. It was difficult *not* to dwell on the pending expectations, and until this moment, she hadn't realized how hard it would be to walk away from the guaranteed security. Regardless, she needed to go. She had deep desire for change.

Nicole glanced across the room when newcomers arrived. Carter Taylor, La Pointe's Town Board Chairman, entered with his wife. They joined the Tavern's owner at a table near the floor-to-ceiling stone fireplace. Ed Harris, editor at the Island Blazer in his corduroy writing jacket sat at a nearby table alongside a gaunt-looking redhead sitting rigid and erect. Nicole had never seen her before and whoever the woman was, she appeared duller than the waitress outfits and lifeless. The Island's trio of designated drunks retained center stage with tables pulled together and were well into their evening practice. Of the three drinking brothers, Mark Stewart was the meekest. Kevin, the obnoxious one, smacked his lips and catcalled to Gypsy. Not much longer Curt, the eldest, would begin hurtling offensive words at his wife, Josie, in what had become their nightly routine. Nicole scorned any issues that created dissension between people.

Didn't matter if those issues were between drunken patrons she didn't like, this business appealed to the patrons. Personal feelings had no place here, which was why she couldn't bring herself to sign a restraining order against the Stewart clan like Mac and Gage wanted her to do.

Surrounded by the holiday cheer from the large and noisy bunch, Nicole never felt more alone. The people who mattered the most to her were at home enjoying the company of each other. Mac and Katharine had finally moved into their new home with twins on the way. Michelle and Travis Baines, two weeks into marriage, would also celebrate their first Christmas together. She'd never been happier for her two best friends when they discovered the "L" word. Especially after the brutal killings. Even La Pointe folks had resettled a bit when Michelle's ex, Derek Gunderson or rather Guthrie was arrested and charged. A fleeting look at the new mirror behind the bar, Travis Baines did well after Derek ran amok smashing liquor bottles against it and shattering the smoke-gray glass into a gazillion pieces. The entire back bar, which originally came from the Hotel Saratoga in Superior, Wisconsin, was early nineteenth century. Wide double trim oak and delicate cable molding surrounded the outer edges. Travis unearthed an identical glass replacement and his crews installed it. If they hadn't heard, folks would never know murder mania had taken place a few weeks earlier or that the mirror wasn't the original. The cleanup was swift. Nicole didn't know, forbid herself to ask if Guthrie had rendered the damage before or after he murdered the Ashland woman inside the incomplete ballroom. When she heard *gruesome* used to describe the inside, she was thankful not to have discovered the ugliness herself. Shuddering internally, she quickly flushed the viciousness from her mind.

She'd always loved the folksy Tavern and admirable antique features. Four-panel oak doors flaunting tubular brass hinges and glass panes opened to Jacque's kitchen. Early nineteenth century pictures hung either side of the mirror with wood frames featuring burgundy velvet trimmed inside. A frosted glass partition separated the lounge from dining. Chandeliers with three frosted globes hung over the wood enamel bar and gave off subtle golden light. She smiled thoughtfully taking it all in—had to make the memories last and thought the frosted globes were clones to the hardhats Travis' construction crew wore. She sighed softly. The tavern had always been home, evidently, she mused, by the hours she spent here. Did she really want to leave La Pointe, never live on beautiful Madeline Island again near Lake Superior's south shore, trade it in for travel and prestige? How would she explain the necessity to change to her two best friends?

"Hey, gorgeous. What's on your mind?"

Nicole blinked. A mechanized smile filled her face. "Hi, Mike. Just reveling in everyone's holiday cheer."

"Cupcake, you and that nice software of yours were miles away."

So true in some ways the rhythm of her heartbeat told her brain. Mike Constantini was one of Travis' musclemen working on the nearly finished ballroom. This man derived sheer joy from playful come-ons Nicole swore triggered primal needs in all male species. He used his drowsy lids in a slow calculating way to send Gypsy and Sheila beyond clouds of sweetened desire. Unfortunately, none of this package of pure male sex and challenging smiles was her choice for energy exertion. Oh, she loved the man's observations of her—couldn't live without it. *But she wasn't a floozy.* Over the years, she'd thwarted numerous male advances from tourists without insult. Somehow, she thought Mike showed true interest and had found a way to let him down gently a few weeks back.

"You're not your normal talking self tonight. How come, Nicole? You thinkin' about runnin' away with me?"

She gently chuckled. "You'd only break my heart."

"Cupcake, you got that backward. Can't blame a guy for chasing a woman who'll never leave his mind. When you get tired of waiting for who ever it is you're waiting for, give me a call."

Her breath caught. An automatic grin screened private thoughts while she studied him. Behind Mike, the insult flinging between Josie and Curt started up. "How much longer until you guys finish up the ballroom?"

"The rest is all cosmetic and cleanup. Should be done mid January."

"I certainly hope so. You guys know I'm planning a fifty-year wedding anniversary for Travis' grandparents on January twenty-ninth."

"Yo, Mike! Quit flirting with Nicole and get our damn drinks over here."

"I think that's your cue the gang's thirsty," Nicole said in her practiced hearty voice.

Mike countered with a grin and a wink, and when she didn't respond, he picked up the assortment of drinks sidestepping tables back to his buddies. Nicole did one more walk through then snuck upstairs to her office. Her muscles screamed with strain as she sunk into her desk chair.

She detested Christmas.

This year, all her fa-la-la had been zapped right out of her. The false holiday pretenses she trained herself to display were a heavy load with two very good reasons why it felt below par to previous years. A motherless three-year-old named Caitlin had somewhat stolen her heart. Another one of Guthrie's victims after he murdered her mother, Caitlin Graham had been robbed of family. The child temporarily resided at Paula LeNoir's house, a designated State Foster care home. They'd had the child ever since that horrible night.

A framed picture of Caitlin with Santa smiled back from her desk. *Damn kid has wormed her way into my heart.* She'd taken Caitlin to see the jolly man in red, something the child had never done, and had the photographer take several keepsake shots. She would have enjoyed spending the entire holiday with Caitlin, but like always, invitations to the LeNoir house were for Christmas Day. Paula and Frank never opened gifts on Christmas Eve and opted to serve dinner at their house for everyone the same way they did at Thanksgiving. By dinnertime, the holiday excitement would be over. There would be no memories of tucking Caitlin into bed with *Twas The Night Before Christmas* or watching her eager blue eyes light up with toys from Santa and presents from others.

"Just like when I was growing up," Nicole muttered, signing off on Hayden's order for New Year's Eve liquor.

Glancing at the photo a second time, she vowed long ago not to dwell on her own barren childhood. Passed from nanny to nanny by parents she hardly knew, Conrad and Erica Jarvis had no time for their only child. They were much too busy touring continents with adventures of their own. Archeological finds were something Nicole knew nothing about—out of spite would never show any interest in digging up old bones. The twosome went from crumbling walls, to ancient foundations to only God knew where. They'd had no desire to stay at home and even less to raise a daughter. Some days Nicole wondered if Erica Jarvis entered the tavern, would she recognize her own mother who had provided for her financially but nothing more. The foster care system would become Caitlin's home. Thinking more than she cared too about the motherless child, Nicole doubted she could send any three-year-old to an institution and wondered how Gage could.

The second motive for holiday desolation was the famous designer who gave her a reason to believe in a dream. She should be excited, but Chantilly hadn't actually said 'the job is yours'. "You also told yourself you weren't going to think about it."

Nicole grabbed the bar-to-office phone. "What is it, Hayden?"

"They're at it again."

Nicole groaned, stood up. "I'll be out in a minute." Slamming the receiver, she grumbled, "Damn drunks."

She entered the lounge in time to see Kevin Stewart cold-cock Mike. The six-foot plus, two-hundred pounds went down faster than Lake Superior's Edmund Fitzgerald did. The bar fell silent. Each person gaped at a lifeless Mike lying in the middle of the floor. A couple of Mike's buddies were on Kevin with the speed of quick lightning as Hayden picked up the phone.

"All of you knock it off!" Nicole shouted, rushing to Mike. "Greg, Mitch, back off. Kevin and Curt, park it. Now!"

She stooped and said, "Hayden, get the ambulance. He's out."

She reached to lift Mike's head—

"Don't move him," Greg told her. "He hit his head on a table going down."

"C-Curt, we're leaving."

Nicole stood up chucking her composed anger and faced Josie Stewart. Ted sauntered over to the nightly routine from his table in the corner to inspect the scene. In charge of disputes, Nicole despised this part of her job. "None of you are going anywhere until Mac talks to everyone about what just happened here."

"You witch! You can't keep us here."

Nicole threw Josie Stewart a look that uttered 'I'm fed up with your shit' and the little bitch tossed it right back. Although she and Josie had been enemies since grade school, Nicole thought it odd that tonight the idiot blonde appeared more nervous than she did intoxicated. "I most certainly can and I will."

"I never did anything," Josie argued.

"Then sit down and shut-up. You can tell it to Mac when he gets here."

"You little hussy! You can't tell me what to do or keep me here."

"She can't, but I can. *Sit down* now, Josie."

They all swung around to look. The police chief's stood there with irritated blue slits instead of the dangerous black ones Nicole expected. Paramedics were only twenty paces behind Gage LeNoir and went straight to Mike lying on the floor. "What happened, Nikki?" Gage asked.

"Hayden called me out because the Stewarts were getting into another heated discussion. I saw Kevin punch Mike. Other than that, I didn't see or hear what started it."

Brief, troubled, his lip twisted with disapproval. The lively blue in his eyes, recently extinguished, unquestionably came from the increased crime consuming the island and the blame that came with it. Gage faced the crowd and Nicole slithered backward to observe. Queen of the man handlers, she had never had a handle on this one—didn't care to. Gage was more stubborn than a grizzly. Since their argument a few months back when he stung her with the words, 'the only regret I have is how you yap pointlessly at me about nothing and flaunt yourself in front of me every chance you get,' she had avoided La Pointe's police chief the same way she avoided cod-liver oil. True, she was chatty and verbose. It covered up her personal insecurities, but the accusations he made of her character were required in the business. It didn't mean she *flaunted* herself in front of any man, let alone this one. It hurt he thought she had, hurt so much she told him to go straight to hell. And that disturbed her more. It left her little choice but to increase the distance between them, keep their contact radically professional.

Nicole slid back further and sunk onto a barstool. She couldn't dispute the fact Gage was handsome. Nor could she argue she was always swindling looks at the sturdy hunk with ruffled, sunset-colored hair. Like right now, she wasn't the only female watching him calm the moment. He handled the crowd and the Stewarts with emotional steadiness. He didn't panic under Josie's scornful tongue either. Diplomatic and tactful with everyone, he never had wide dips and swings. Women said he was relentlessly sexy, irresistibly exciting. They were right. Dusty brown flecks fondled his face at the peak of summer. Mile-wide shoulders made him authoritative and lawful, and age had only enhanced his power. All good traits, but it didn't change his bete noire arrogance. Nor did it change the truth. The two of them had forever pitched nasty words and a swing or two at each other.

Nicole stood and quietly slipped away to her office. Exhausted, she dropped to her desk chair and sighed. She would never marry because she knew men committed for only one reason. To spawn their genes. She never had a mother to explain such things, to explain anything, but it no longer mattered. What she really wanted to know was why she was even thinking about the "M" word now when her door swung open. Nicole didn't turn and look. She didn't have to. She recognized his scent without looking the minute he entered her office. American male, potent and vibrant, she couldn't pinpoint why or how Gage kindled rage in her vital fluid of life. When he didn't speak, she swiveled around, stopped short and gulped. He had stopped just inside the door, latching his thumbs atop his gun belt. She scrutinized the meaning behind the anger and frustration in his pale blue eyes.

"Is Mike okay? Or do you need something else?"

"He's fine. Said it was a stupid argument. He's refusing to press charges against Kevin."

"Well, then. I'm glad everything turned out."

"Nikki, why won't you sign a restraining order to keep the Stewarts out of here?"

"This is a business that caters to the public. If not the Stewarts, it would be someone else. Now, if you'll excuse me I have work to do. Unless there was something else you needed," she said, purposely turning to the paperwork on her desk.

There sure as hell was! "How long you gonna keep avoiding me?"

"I'm not avoiding you," she retorted without looking back.

"Yeah, you are. How many times do I have to apologize?"

The damage had been done and if things worked out, she would be leaving Madeline Island for good. "Gage, just let it go. It doesn't really matter anyway."

"Yes, it does. It matters to me. Nikki, we've been friends since you and Pipsqueak could walk and talk."

Friends?

"I'm sorry for what I said and the way I said it."

"And I've told you, you're forgiven," she muttered.

"But you don't really mean it. You've made that clear by not coming over to the station every day with Jacque's famous lunches."

Nicole whirled around full force in her chair. "Is that what this is about, Gage? You not getting three squares a day? Well, fine! I'll see to it that your needs are met."

"Nicole, you know that's not what I meant!"

She eyed him coldly. "So you've said."

He tossed an irritated stare at her then caved. "Nikki, I'm sorry. I never meant what I said and I never should have said it. I'd never hurt you."

Yeah, right, she thought, deciding now as good a time as any to tell him and folded her hands into her lap. "Gage, I had a job interview in L.A. yesterday. If everything works out, I'll be moving to Los Angeles permanently."

Gage gaped at her. Just stood there as if shot and waiting to fall. "For what? To do what? Manage some over-priced nightclub!"

The man knew exactly how to push her buttons. "You just proved what great friends we really are! You have no idea what I want to do with my life and this conversation is as pointless as my yapping!"

Gage's mouth curled with that familiar doubt she could always read on him. Nicole clamped her lips tightly in retaliation and glared back at his blue eyes piercing the distance between them. "Who with?" he finally asked.

"Chantilly Mackinaw, the famous fashion designer."

"Fashion designer? Don't you need some kind of training or education to do that?"

Smugness hung in the air and Nicole laughed bitterly. She wasn't about to divulge to him that he was the first to learn of her plans. "I've been doing what I need to do for two years. I submitted resumes and my designs to several of the big ones. Chantilly Mackinaw is the first one to express an interest in my work. Besides, I've reached the top here at the tavern. There's nowhere else for me to go."

"I suppose Katharine and Michelle already know about this?"

Nicole shrugged.

"Just like that!" The words sprang out of him. "You're gonna leave Madeline Island? Your family and friends, a job you love—*Caitlin*!"

Whenever they spoke, one of them always erupted resulting in a contest of wills where someone's resistance always lost. "Perhaps it's escaped your attentive eye Mr. Police Man, but I don't have a family! My two best friends are happily starting new lives. It's time I did the same. As far as Caitlin…well, it's just better I stay away."

"So we aren't good enough for you anymore?"

"Oh that's mighty damn rich of you!"

"Mom, Dad, Katharine. We've always been your family, Nikki. I thought you loved your success at the tavern by the hours you put in here."

She blinked, felt her insides flinch. Desperation flooded the tone of his voice. "You've said it yourself. The hassles of unsatisfied customers, the Stewart drunks. As much as this has been more of a home than the one I live in, this is not what I want to do for the rest of my life."

"How can you leave Caitlin? She looks to you as a replacement for the mother she lost."

"That's BS and you know it. Besides, she doesn't belong to me and she'll be long gone, placed into the system before I move out west."

"So it's final then?"

She looked away, unable to reply. She was suddenly anxious to escape his disturbing presence, fussed with the clutter in front of her.

"Fine. Are you coming for Christmas dinner? Caitlin will be crushed if you don't."

The beat of her heart sped up and felt like it would amputate the organ from her chest. The man she had fought with since they were in diapers had no interest in her, yet here he stood this moment begging her to come for Christmas dinner. It made little sense when he had never extended the invitation in previous years. Certainly not for the sake of the child, he had rescued. "It's also just as well Caitlin learn about despair early. She won't grow up believing in foolish things that will never happen."

"You don't really believe that."

"Yes. I do." Nicole swiveled around, faced the computer behind her a second time.

"When are you leaving?"

She couldn't very well answer that when she didn't know herself. "If there's nothing else to discuss about the incident tonight, I have work to do."

"Nikki, don't do this. At least come over to the house on Christmas day."

"Why, Gage?"

"Everyone's gonna be there. You've always been—" he stopped.

A faint sound, a moan or a cry, echoed throughout the office. Automatically, he glanced left then right. Nikki looked around and swiveled to face him.

"What the hell is that?"

"The building. It's old and creaky. 'Been doing it a lot since Travis started the ballroom."

With a little quick nod, he asked, "Is your mind made up?"

"About what?"

"Christmas."

Nicole shrugged. "I do have something for Caitlin and will drop it off."

When the building groaned some more, Gage scanned the room with a fleeting look then opened the door and walked out with the most elaborate nonchalance Nicole had ever seen in him.

CHAPTER 3

❀

Nikki's news fueled the rage that had dragged him to the Red Rock Tavern in the first place. Gage now understood why she disappeared for two months back a couple of years ago. Upon her return, Nikki had told everyone she needed a vacation—wouldn't say where she went. He just figured out that vacation featured Technicolor details to do whatever she needed to do to make her move to California. He didn't know how to tell her the lunches weren't what he enjoyed the most and kicked the tire of the squad car parked out front of the tavern.

He wasn't aggressive—most of the time. In fact, he'd been hearing his entire life of his paramount weakness and lack of initiative. He put things off and avoided facing problems his dad said many times. When he needed to think he went fishing and he couldn't very well do that on a cold night just before Christmas. A bit too independent, he hated asking anyone for help. Neither was he efficient as his mother always said. He never ever wanted to think about his appearance, either. In school, kids had taunted him relentlessly—*carrot top, carrot top, you're nothing but a carrot top.* Skin, bones and freckles growing up, he was a clumsy oaf until he went out for football. At least the freckles faded from a hooknose during winter but never from the rest of his body.

What's more, he didn't have what most men could brag about—an accomplished record with women. He'd been around the block a few times, but even if he were the bragging kind, it wasn't anything he chose to blow his own horn about. Besides, women of Nikki's caliber always chose the other guy. He also knew his father's irritation with him went beyond his ability to solve the serial killings. When Pipsqueak came home, he told her he was pleased with himself.

He wondered why he'd said anything at all when he'd been covering up failures and bad mistakes for more than half his life.

How could she do this?

Nikki loved her job. She loved Madeline Island more. Thriving on people and friendly encounters, she went from pigtails and scarred knees to a bundle of tempting flesh his sophomore year. He remembered the changeover like it was yesterday. Her incredibly long legs got longer as the rest of her filled out. He always thought she was hot just because she had a way of snatching his breath right out of him. She'd been breathing in his air since they were kids as if she owned it. And everywhere he went he could smell her perfumed flesh. Her office walls weren't the only physical structures absorbing and soaking up her scent like a sponge. The sweetened fragrance lingered far, near and wide and dizzied him into a quake that jarred his middle ear. That honey-colored hair of hers was a blasted curse, too. It made him crazy the way it streamed like liquid gold around her into elongated waves. Those round seductive eyes were big and whiskey brown like her favorite drink. They could flash as cold as ice or suck him up like the heat of the whiskey itself. She was a disturbingly beautiful woman he loved to hate and he decided a long time ago Nikki Jarvis possessed a look of loving to pamper no one but herself.

Damn her the way they clashed and clawed with each other regularly.

He never considered the obsession she had with clothes was part of any plan to earn an income much less make a career out of it. But then he couldn't decide whether she spent more on creating or purchasing the clothes he thought she had more than enough of. In fact, she had so many clothes and shoes, the woman could open her own fricking store!

She cried easily—always had. She would remain forever faithful to her friends. She worked hard and long for other people, too hard, he thought, giving more than she ever got back from anyone. When she was young, he used to worry a lot about her because her parents left her with strangers. Under criminal law that, to him, was construed as abandonment. Maybe not officially since his mother told him Nikki's folks provided the necessities—"My ass!" he spat.

No ifs ands or buts about it. Leaving your child in someone else's care was inadequate parenting in his book.

Mizz Social Butterfly hated sports, but she loved dancing and action packed movies. Smart, intelligent, and thriving on oral disputes with him, Nikki had a powerful will that kept him under some god-forsaken prickly spell. She loved kids! So what the hell did Los Angeles have that Madeline Island didn't? He couldn't answer it.

Submerged with shock upon her announcement, his erratic heartbeat had pounded in his temples around thoughts dripping like a bad sinus infection. He supposed he deserved the biting sarcasm she flung at him. *But,* she had no right telling him he didn't know a damn thing about her! He knew everything about her. He even knew he was the one wearing the badge, yet she did all the intimidating. He wasn't stone-blind either. Realized a long time ago how all men overdosed on Nicole Jarvis. She could have any guy she wanted. Choked by his uniformed necktie, it wasn't jealousy eating him up. If she left, whom would he wage a verbal war with when the job went back to boring?

The three best friends shared everything. He'd demand Pipsqueak cough up what he wanted to know maybe plead with his sister to change Nikki's mind. Squealing the tires of his squad away from the tavern, he yelled at the windshield, "To hell with her!"

He had a bigger precedent with worse ramifications, to catch a serial killer.

CHAPTER 4

Twenty-four hours later, Gage worked the same shift as the previous evening. He parked his squad at home and went inside to eat. His parent's house was quiet for the first time since Caitlin Graham began staying with them. His folks had taken the orphan to Christmas Eve Mass. In fact, anyone still left on the island should be there. Didn't bother him to work Christmas Eve since he'd done it most of his career. A few years back when his father retired, he continued the routine since the family always celebrated Christmas day—gave his ex-sergeant the night off to spend the time with his family. Tonight he volunteered to work so his new brother-in-law and Katharine could spend their first Christmas together. Mac Dobarchon had replaced his previous sergeant when Joe Hamlin decided on another college stint to study forensics, his newly claimed forte.

Thankful for the alone time, Gage hadn't had a decent night's sleep since the end of July and blamed Nikki for it last night. He'd been thinking increasingly about Nikki Jarvis. Now, when he already had enough on his mind, she went and ripped another hole inside of him. He also blamed their unknown serial killer for the lack of sleep. December twenty-seventh loomed closely. If the serial killer continued his spree, it meant they'd have another body in three days. He and Mac were no further ahead than at the discovery of the first victim in Green Bay where Mac first worked the case almost three years ago. The serial killings had moved from Green Bay onto Madeline Island last July. Some psychotic lunatic who found vicious pleasure in killing sixteen-year-old Native American girls with a deadly chemical was still on the loose.

Evidence provided nothing for them to make an arrest. The first, a finger-print identifying David Patriot at the scene of Green Bay's sixth victim, Clarissa Noma who was Mac's niece, turned out to be a fluke, maybe a screw up. Regardless, in August, Katharine shot the owner of that fingerprint, and the only suspect they had. The continuing murders just proved David Patriot was not the real serial killer. Killer yes, serial killer no. Since the case began in La Pointe, Gage believed Patriot had murdered only two of the now ten total serial killing victims. Four took place—rather four victims were discovered on Madeline and Michigan Islands, the other six took place in Green Bay.

When Michelle's ex husband Gunderson, real name Derek Guthrie, returned to La Pointe, he threw a monkey wrench into the entire case with his vicious killings of two more, but they were adult women. Substance abuse and gambling debts were to blame for Guthrie's crimes. The dirtbag also reneged on his original confession, but the County Attorney had charged him with first-degree intentional homicide, Class A felony with no plea bargains. A trial date hadn't been set. The prosecuting attorney also believed Guthrie's taped confession along with the evidence would make for a short trial. Even now, six murders on the island in five short months earned Gage relentless harassment from the Town Board and too much anger from La Pointe residents.

Only three days left until the killer strikes again, he mused.

Gage slapped together two BLT's, poured a glass of milk and hoisted his gun belt before sitting at the kitchen table. Everybody had their hands in this case, from Green Bay to Ashland County to the Park Rangers to Madeline Island. But the next clue he discovered was the deadly chemical used to do the killing. Someone had stolen six gallons of a toxic substance known as paraquat, and not readily available to the public, from the Ashland County garage over on the mainland. Since learning of the County's theft, Gage believed it was a key to this case. The County used paraquat to kill off roadside weeds. Forensics proved the killer mixed the chemical with Johnny Walker Black, an overly priced liquor. Forced to swallow the deadly combination, the victims suffered a week-long agonizing death with their bodies ravaged from the inside out.

Mac's ex partner, Cole Gilroy used the senior yearbook from Gage's graduating class along with booking photos as a lineup to show pictures of the Stewart brothers, along with Guthrie and Patriot to County employees. He thought someone would remember a face without knowing a name. It might also tell them who had been hanging around the County garage during the time of the theft. To date, sixty employees had examined the photos but none of those folks ID'd anyone except Curt Stewart, who worked there. If someone didn't pick out somebody soon, Gilroy would go back to taping statements from employees about a two-year old theft.

A bracelet displayed on each victim was the next piece of evidence. His ex-sergeant figured out the wrist ornaments were made with hand strung rosary peas by Native Americans who distributed the bangle throughout the entire area. Two of the La Pointe victims had actually died from a poison called abrin found inside the rosary pea. The fact the killer may have changed MO's birthed new questions and problems when they discovered remnants of a tarp under-neath the victims who died of abrin. The rosary pea decoration, which held its poison inside a shell, also appeared to be significant evidence they believed the killer used ceremoniously in what were beginning to look like sacrificial kill-ings.

The last piece of evidence was the liquor bottle. Regardless of which poison the killer used to kill the victims, an empty Johnny Walker Black bottle was always left at the crime scene. Autopsies revealed the alcohol in each victim, but the empty bottles lacked any fingerprints.

Inconclusive evidence came when Katharine uncovered information appearing significant but lacking proof. Wedding dates of the Cadotte women, not the fairytale ghosts Sully rambled on about but the real Cadotte daughters, matched the discovery dates of the victims. The blurred historical facts made confirmation of which daughters impossible—proving the connection would be improbable. Then Michelle plugged Katharine's theory with holes when she informed them the dates also matched births of several members in the family.

Frustrated with a lack of suspects, Curt Stewart had been Gage's first sus-pect. The oldest of the three Stewart's, Curt worked for Ashland County and was married to Josie Hanson. Back in high school, Gage assumed arguments between Josie and her friends with his sister and her friends was a female thing. And though his classmate had adequate alibis for every murder, Gage found it too coincidental that Curt just happened to drink Johnny Walker and worked for the County where the paraquat was stolen.

Curt's incorrigible brother, Kevin was an obvious suspect as well. Too obvi-ous Gage thought. The most problematic Stewart brother had lied about his whereabouts each time they hauled him in for questioning. The truth finally came out upon learning Janice Anderson lived in Green Bay. What he and Mac couldn't figure out was why no one bothered to mention the extracurricular activities going on between Kevin and Janice Anderson who just happened to be Josie's cousin. If someone was trying to frame Kevin for the serial killings, the evidence they had meant other facts had to be inferred. Not good in front of a jury.

Then there was the unassuming Mark, youngest, and follower of his older brothers. His alibis checked out very well. Nevertheless, all three loved their alcohol and occasionally all drank Johnny Walker Black. Curt more so which is why Gage suspected him first. When Mac informed him about Patriot's fingerprint, Gage mindfully dismissed all the Stewart brothers as suspects.

Any way he looked at it, nothing added up yet the killing continued. Mac called it a whole lotta premeditation and still suspected Curt and or Kevin. Even though supposition and a badge didn't give them rights to verge on the edge of serious harassment of the Stewarts, Gage was rethinking his choice of a suspect. The lack of same is what forced him to, but he couldn't prove shit—that wasn't good inside a courtroom either.

Gage finished his first BLT, guzzled the milk and glanced at his watch. Ten minutes had passed bringing him closer to the deadly date. With exception of Jessica Henderson, every victim came from Green Bay or Ashland. Jessica belonged to La Pointe and Patriot murdered her with his choice poison from the abrus precatorius plant. The evidence did prove that. The abrin toxin came from seeds the plant produced. They learned Patriot had the seeds shipped from Florida after stealing a vehicle to purchase the plants with stolen checks. Stripping the pods from the plants, he shipped them to a PO Box in Green Bay. He forced both his victims to eat the seeds they found in a glass basin mixed with peanuts near Jessica's body. Gage repeatedly debated why Patriot went to the trouble of committing a felony theft in Florida when the pea was readily available here by way of the hand strung bracelet. But then nothing in this case made sense, except his adamant belief Patriot knew the real serial killer. He and Mac had had several discussions on the subject of Patriot being a copycat or accomplice. The FBI Profiler who assisted Green Bay PD believed David Patriot was a hostile copycat who sought dominance. Katharine and Mac leaned toward accomplice. Cole Gilroy had no opinion either way.

He finished his second BLT, poured more milk and swiped a couple of Christmas cookies. On and off he thought about getting a place of his own. He knew how to cook and clean, wash clothes and take care of himself. So, why didn't he? He already knew the answer without giving it much thought. Born efficient but totally dependent would be his epitaph. Michelle and Travis were building a house. They'd be moving. Maybe she'd let him rent hers for awhile or buy if they wanted to sell. With Katharine and Mac in their new home, he could always rent Joe's house—whatever, he needed to get his own place. Gage cleaned up the kitchen and locked the house. Hopefully, Christmas Eve would stay quiet. His intent was to reread every page of the reports.

First, he needed to shelf the green-eyed monster burrowing inside of him. Rarely did anger dunk him, but last night when Nikki implied they had a meaningless friendship, his insides unglued themselves. He knew plenty about Nikki and it was time she found it out.

CHAPTER 5

The last one to leave the tavern on Christmas Eve, Nicole locked up. She wasn't up for Mass in the historical church and walked home encircled by quiet peace. Soothing snowflakes, the large dribbling kind, bathed the silent holy night making La Pointe exceptionally pretty and white. Exceptional in that island snow didn't generally expose layers of gray-black dirt. Not the way it did elsewhere. Snow plows didn't salt the roads, and plentiful dollops of lake snow and ice fog crystallized everything to cover what sprinkled down from the branches. Whether folks noticed or not, spring meltdown would expose the falling tree crud.

Folks had already placed bets on when the big lake would form the first layer of ice with the warmer than normal winter season. When and if the water froze, there would be a waiting period for Superior to solidify before a plowed road stretched from Bayfield to Madeline across the ice. Wind sleds would haul students back and forth to the mainland for high school classes. Nicole remembered those days—brutally cold and full of life.

Enjoying the downy white night, a large flake hit her nose and Nicole tilted her head back to catch descending flurries on her face. She loved walking in the utter stillness of La Pointe. Many times on walks like this, she continued to plan for her big, life-altering event. Now on the verge of having her dream career, she found herself squelching the excitement to compare their little jewel in the Apostles with Beverly Hills. It was apples and oranges.

She would have thought last night's loaded words between her and Gage would have helped throttle her enthusiasm more. Less happy with him today when Katharine and Michelle hunted her down, she knew the minute they flounced into the tavern he had blabbed. Didn't want to deal with them or their reactions let alone her renewed anger. True to form, they demanded answers.

When the hell did you decide this? Katharine charged in her police voice.

Why didn't you tell us?

Are you crazy? Los Angeles?

What could you possibly be thinking? Michelle pleaded.

Nicole ushered both women into her office. The delayed explanation had reached the end. 'Life changes but it does go on' she replied to their questions. They had new lives and the time had come for her to pursue new avenues. She guaranteed Michelle she'd stay for the anniversary party, reassured Katharine she would return for the twin's birth in the spring. Agonized expressions signaled their disappointment as she tried to convince them changes were a necessity. Both insisted her presence on Christmas day was necessary and Nicole finally agreed as long as they didn't tell anyone else the news.

Arriving at the house she called home, Secunda greeted her excitedly the way he did most nights. Adeline Girard let the overgrown moose of a dog run at will around La Pointe. His freedom bothered some folks, but he was company for her. She pet the pooch and felt foolish wishing him a Merry Christmas. She was as starved for attention as the golden lab, she thought unlocking the door to her parent's house. She'd started bolting the doors when the murders began, hesitated briefly before entering the empty domicile. Four walls with a ceiling and floor weren't your typical abode. She hated loneliness as much as she cursed the holidays. She hadn't made her comment to Gage about the tavern being more of a home to get his attention or debate the issue with him even when the look on his face implied skepticism.

The man was clueless—always had been. Closing the door and leaning against it, a cynical half-laugh seeped out. Gage didn't know as much about her as he thought he did. He had no rights in the friendship department especially when it forced her to waste half of last night debating his sudden concern for their friendship. It wasn't actually concern she concluded. She couldn't express the exact word to describe his look of bewilderment, but his facial expression exposed some hidden meaning that hammered away at her all night long.

Nicole untied and yanked off her granny boots beneath a gored wool skirt. She tossed her duster coat and pleated cloche hat. A hot sudsy bath and a facial indulgence would lift her spirits but gifts stacked on the dining room table caught her eye enlarging a permanent dull ache. With no one to share the holiday with in this house, it was a waste of time to put up and decorate a tree. The potential for a new job enticed her to buy presents for everyone, including

Travis and Michelle's families. She went on a shopping marathon buying modest gifts with meaning. She fretted repeatedly whether she should have spent as much as she did on Caitlin. Worried more why she spent as much as she did on Gage. Too late for second thoughts, Nicole chalked her actions under vicarious something or other as she readied herself to relieve her stress.

Her long thick hair secured in a wave clip, Nicole patted her skin dry and studied her face in the mirror. Ochroid rich flesh, caramel brown eyes and amber waves definitely made her a warm shade according to the charts. Chantilly called her skin sinful, but beauty had nothing to do with body shapes, the latest fashions, or sinfully gorgeous flesh. A beautiful woman had a bounce in her step, gleam in her eye and a sparkle in her smile. The basics revolved around the simplest ideas, skin and hair care, makeup and health. It didn't matter what the body looked like if the right style covered it. One could discover an attractive face no matter what the shape or flaw.

Told many times how lucky she was to have been born beautiful, Nicole doubted anyone understood the time and years it took to uncover such attractiveness. Her long legs and large breasts were typical characteristics men drooled over, but they were foolish creatures of habit and hormones. Her eyes were too large for a narrow face and pug nose. Her hips too boxy without any waist, her octopus arms were impossible to fit. Her hair, well, if she went any where near a blow-dryer, the long loose curls frizzed right up inciting an age-old cliché about electrical sockets. At five-nine, she loved heels when she could find them to fit her size ten feet.

How beautiful are big feet?

Nicole ran the bath water, dribbling in a delicate splash of her favorite scent. She fancied Yves Saint Laurent who made *Paris* fragrance in every essential accessory. It took very little of the arousing sweet aroma to turn her body into subtle seduction. It lasted forever and should at eighty-seven dollars for a two-ounce glass vessel. Discovering the product, she made it part of her budget like the garments she wore all the way down to her smooth satin flesh.

She dropped her chenille robe to the floor and gracefully sank into the lukewarm water. Each vain effort endured one's whims, most of the time. Lying back in the tub, all she needed to satisfy her fancy was a glass of wine, wished the idea had occurred sooner. Like everything else, she learned to be chief provider for her own happiness and eventually discovered how good the gratification made her feel. Oh indeed, it was all worth it. For in the end she felt like the beauty queen she never was. She didn't anguish over the lack of natural beauty for she'd learned the secrets, but she did suffer excitement deficiency. The lack of it had a way of dragging her down. It was at the root of her survival. Perhaps her need for stimulation was just an excuse to cover a distant heartache, one she couldn't explain—*heartache*…the thought of it left her empty.

Nicole pushed it aside and sponged off. Studying her manicured nails, she preferred a round tip to French style, used soft suggestive colors to go with her overall appeal rather than wild exotic shades. Splashy colors were for special occasions and a last Christmas with friends required red. The new Beverly Hills outfit might be inappropriate, but she'd feel good about herself wearing it.

Out of the tub, dried off and barely wrapped in her teal-green robe, a determined thud sounded against the front door. Occasionally, Secunda returned for a dog biscuit. She kept them around and he was probably waiting since she didn't give him one upon coming home. Before she reached the kitchen to get a biscuit, the doorbell followed the bold pounding. She, stopped, looked and shuffled over wondering who would attempt to drag her out.

She opened the door. Gage grunted as he moved quickly through the doorway slamming the door.

"We need to talk."

"About what? We've said more than we ever should have."

"Maybe you've said everything you have to say, but I haven't!"

When he lessened the space between them in a threatening manner Nicole muttered, "Let the games begin."

"This isn't a game. I know fast and rugged exhilarates you. I know you love rough characters in rambunctious movies. You don't read unless it's to ogle over the latest fashions. You have a heart as big as the universe but you keep it locked tighter than Fort Knox the same way you conceal your sadness from your friends. You take long walks at night instead of the day. Your favorite spot to daydream is the lagoon and you haven't been there since Travis discovered Caitlin's dead mother."

Nicole stood motionless glaring at him.

"I also know you'd like to censure country western anything but if a customer loves it you let them think you do too. *You* prefer rock and roll and think classical and jazz could clear a room faster than a skunk. As a kid, you acted like a tomboy to gain attention. Now you do it with tantalizing clothes, perfected beauty aids, which by the way crowd the hell out of me, and just the right touch of jewelry. I don't know how you do it but you use the scent of your flesh to agitate, arouse and inflame me all at the same time until I think senility has a firm grip on me. That's to your advantage. Then there's pride. Oh how obvious it is that you pride yourself on pleasing others—"

"Gage! What's your damn point?"

"And you're ornery too. Those big dark eyes of yours always show it first. I used to hate the obstinacy that flashes out of them."

"Then it's a good thing my flaws won't be around for you to criticize much longer."

A thin-lipped smile cased his mouth. Gage planted his feet and crossed his arms. "My point is this. I know everything about you except for the secrets you've kept hidden in your heart. You've never mentioned any desire to design clothes in L.A. to Katharine or Michelle. They were just as surprised as I was."

"S-so?"

"So, what I'm telling you, *Nicole*, is that you have no right to disclaim our friendship because of secrets you've kept from all of us. And this is the last time I'm going to say it because I'm damn positive your idiotic decision has something to do with me."

When Gage had finally gained ground over her, Nicole had no idea why he relinquished it. But like any fool, he uncrossed his arms latching his thumbs atop his gun belt. She knew immediately the control had slipped back to her.

"Nikki, I'm sorry I hurt you. I never meant it. If I could erase the insult of my words, I would. None of us…including me want you to leave."

Maybe not. "Damn you," she whispered.

"You are not spending Christmas alone. That obstinate streak of yours is not going to keep you from coming over to the house tomorrow. You're part of our family, Nikki, and you belong with us on Christmas. Besides, Caitlin already told me it'd be my fault if you don't come. She won't talk to me until I give her a guarantee."

Even if Nicole wanted to speak, Gage forbade her with a raised hand.

"I won't take no for an answer and to make sure you do show up, I'm coming over to get you at eight in the morning."

"Gage LeNoir, you are such a jerk."

"I know," he said, reaching over to brush away tears spilling down her cheeks. "Am I forgiven?"

Nicole couldn't defend herself against the magnetic push and pull that had always been between them, combatant opposites always attracting back through enticement, temptation and unmerciful taunting. But for the first time in her life, she lacked any response, could only shrug. Her own body heat mingled with the cool winter air from his gear. The smell of leather from his belt mixed with the scent of her bath. He leaned closer, she moved slightly, he angled his head, she leveled hers then he touched her mouth with his.

She drew back. "What do you think you're doing?"

"Trying to find out if the taste of that savory mouth is the same. I've never forgotten the candy-coated surprise."

Nicole gaped at him, remembering. He'd stolen his first kiss from her at the innocent age of thirteen. She felt positive he did it to shut her up.

"No one has ever come close to duplicating or replacing the perception of a young boy's carelessness. I want to know if that sweet surprise has matured the way the rest of you did."

He didn't wait for her to answer. Pulling her into his arms, his mouth converged with hers. Panic rioted within her. Her hands were jammed between her breasts and his bulletproof covered chest. Every inch of her touched him between uniform and robe. The equipment on his belt cut into her ribs. His boots were rooted near her bare feet. But he managed to smother her curses with searing kisses and bruising strokes. The sensation rattled her all the way down to her toes as she lost complete control somewhere between fury and shock. Then drop by tiny precious drop her own lips softened around her anger. He sampled until eventually she stopped opposing him all together, and he seized her mouth in a thirsting kiss. It detonated the turbulence inside of her, bucked her into the next century before he crushed her body closer. Fisting his hand into her hair, he freed it from its bonds and took all she thought he could get from her. As their mouths clung, her body trembled. His mouth was hot and she dove without a care. The more he monopolized her, the more she took. The more he drove, the more she bewitched him.

His needs were hotter as the menacing surprise of sweetness and sex came back to him—*damn, he'd go to hell for betrayal!*

Gage let go and jerked backward. His heart thumped hard and quick. He stared at those damp, whiskey-brown eyes and remembered the misery. His thoughts raced faster than a nervous twitch on a trigger, but he had to know. "Does it still feel the same?"

Her face heated up, her chest ached and her knees felt like rubber bands. *She was twelve.* They'd had a verbal clash as they frequently did. She'd say it was a beautiful sunny day and he'd dispute it by telling her it would rain, yank hard on her hair and run. He always said things were black and white and she would tell him to pay attention to the shades of gray. One day they had an all out fist-clenching, hair-pulling, nail-scratching scramble. Their shouts were heard all the way to Chequamegon Point his mother told them when she broke their clamped hands free of the other. Scolding them, Paula told them to behave and act like the young adults they were or she'd give them both something to think about. Gage immediately replaced pulling her pigtails with a mouth-watering kiss before he took off running. That kiss had perplexed her. This kiss had weakened her to a trembling idiot.

"You're a damn jerk and I hate your breathing guts."

"So you've said. I'm not sorry—" he started, stopped, noticing the presents stacked on her table. "You never really planned on staying away tomorrow. Did you?"

Nicole glanced, shrugged again.

"Be ready at eight! And one more thing. Before you leave the island, we are going to talk about that night!"

He yanked the door open, left Nikki standing with her mouth open when he slammed it shut behind him. He needed distance. A lot of it. If he didn't put space between them, he would never leave. His nostrils flaring, he stomped away from her house. No matter how hard he tried to forget Brian Callihan, he couldn't forget his best friend. Worse, he was still competing with a dead man. Just as he yanked the squad door open, the same moan that bounced off Nikki's office walls last night floated around him like a UFO. Glancing around, he knew he had to get some sleep and it had better be fast.

CHAPTER 6

❁

The worn wingback chair absorbed her.

Nicole sucked back the crude ache in her chest when Caitlin squealed delightfully, cottony blond curls dancing around her morning-fresh rosy cheeks as if unwrapping presents was a first for her.

The only family Nicole ever knew along with the newest members were lucky to have each other. Mac and Katharine kicked back on the couch while Paula and Frank perched themselves on the edge of recliners. Gage had the center floor and taunted Michelle's black furball with torn Christmas wrap and ribbons. Keeker the cat stayed at the house for Caitlin to play with after the three best friends split up and went back to their respective homes following the capture of Michelle's ex. A safety issue Nicole couldn't dispute, everyone believed Derek would come after anyone close to Michelle. When Travis and Michelle married and took a short honeymoon, Paula didn't object to caring for the cat indefinitely. Besides, the latest newlyweds were taking an extended honeymoon after the anniversary party Travis had planned for his grandparents. They couldn't very well leave Keeker to fend for himself, so he, too, was a new member in this household.

When Gage glanced up and winked at her, Nicole blinked. He'd obviously forgotten the morning event. Last night after he left, she stubbornly loaded up her car then drove herself to the house this morning. Exiting the house when she pulled in, Gage snarled a few expletives at her to which she fired off her own four-letter words.

Nicole refocused on Caitlin. She wasn't the only one who went overboard buying gifts for the homeless ragamuffin. Santa Gage bought a pink and blue tricycle Paula told her when she arrived. Deep down she understood her reason for the toy overload—Caitlin had no one else. But why had Gage felt the need to do it? It would only lead to disappointment in the child's eyes when they shipped her off to wherever. The kid certainly didn't need more pain in her life.

Her thoughts took a tawdry route to the previous evening, blurring the conversation between the others. After Gage's grand entrance and exit, Nicole didn't sleep a wink for the second night in a row. The dark hours were spent reliving one fiery kiss—like she hadn't known or felt Gage's anger—hell! She encouraged it more often then not but their actions had fired them both up into fervent clinging. She went from shock to rage to desperate needing. The big question was why he kissed her when he had never exposed an interest in her except to ridicule. She really needed to get a grip on her tears when she cried long and hard after loading the car.

Gage tapped her foot now. Nicole looked down at him and watched, her insides screaming nervously while he unwrapped the gift she bought him. Many conversations with the experts to explain his fishing habits, she had *Bogey* handcraft a custom rod for him. They guaranteed their designs provided action and power. Since she knew his favorite fish was bass, they also hand painted a replica right on the rod. *Talk about overboard.* She spent an astronomical figure on a stick of wood that she thought could break. The moment he tore off the paper, his expression went from mildly amused to utter disbelief.

"Nikki!" he blurted, gaping from the rod to her.

"Is it right?"

He groped the custom design in his hand and cautiously feigned casting it over Caitlin's head. "It's perfect." *Like you,* he mouthed.

Her heart did that little flipping thing when Gage proudly showed the fishing rod to his dad and Mac then reached under the tree and handed her a present.

"This is for you. I hope you like it."

Nicole took the gift. Many past Christmas' spent with the LeNoir's Gage generally wrapped his own presents. However, this one had professionalism written all over it. Carefully removing the paper, she lifted the cover of a white embossed box. "Great balls of fire!"

An exquisite piece of Venetian gold and glass necklace conveyed edge-of-the-Orient colors. Nicole fondled the hand-twisted coils in twenty-four-karat gold wire. Glass beads of burnt amber, old copper and white gold matched earrings of single amber beads filled with gold leaf and detailed in gold wire. They would drop approximately an inch off her lobes. She knew the exact outfits to wear the set with and cast Gage her own stunned expression. His bright eyes filled with satisfaction and a new tingle ventured fiercely into the core of her bones.

"You like it?"

"It's absolutely stunning. I love it! Thank you."

"When I saw the necklace, it reminded me of you."

All eyes on the two of them, Nicole shifted uncomfortably. Mac helped a pregnant-with-twins Katharine off the sofa. She eagerly lumbered through strewn Christmas wrap toward them.

"What is it? He said I had to wait to see what he got you."

Nicole stood and met her half way. She handed Katharine the box, brushing new tears off her cheeks. "It's Venetian gold and glass."

"You know what it is?" Gage asked, joining them.

"Of course, I know what is. Just like you recognized the fishing rod."

"What's all the fuss about," Katharine muttered skimming her fingers over the beaded necklace.

"Hon, Michelle and I never could teach you the finer things in life."

"It's a string of beads and a fishing pole. It's not like neither of you don't already have this junk," Katharine said, passing the box back.

Spontaneously, Nicole and Gage glanced at each other with a look that lasted but an instant. Exchanging gifts all their lives, but never of this caliber Gage had actually planned this gift the way she had planned his. Nicole undid the clasp nervously and Gage snatched the strand and draped it around her neck.

"Pipsqueak," he said, fastening the necklace while Nicole clumped and held her hair, "I wonder if Mac realizes how lucky he is."

"Meaning what?"

Stepping over toys and paper, Mac said, "Princess, I think your brother's being diplomatic. He's trying to tell you I'm a cheapskate because I don't buy you expensive baubles and trinkets."

"You're a smart man, Dobarchon." Then facing Gage, Katharine said, "Bro, hope you're not calling my husband cheap."

Picking up his *Bogey*, he chuckled. "Lighten up, Sis. I believe the word I used was lucky."

"I've got things to take care of in the kitchen before the next crowd gets here," Paula announced. "Would you guys clean up for me?"

"I'll help in the kitchen," Nicole volunteered eagerly.

Gage was quick, grabbed her wrist, pulled her aside and stole a kiss. "I don't think I said thank you for the rod."

Her nerves already raw, the reserve of self-restraint liquefied.

"You shouldn't have spent this much money. Especially when your intent was to spend Christmas alone."

Fondling the glass beads around her neck, Nicole moistened her lips. His expression said he enjoyed her struggle. "It's no big deal," she muttered. "I wanted to—"

"Be alone?" he interjected.

"Talk about spending money. You didn't really believe I wouldn't know what these are or how much *you* spent, did you?"

"What they are is a perfect match to all of you." Fondling her wrist he then said, "Is it the jewelry or me exciting you right now?"

"I don't like what you did or said last night. How—"

"Babe, once you stopped resisting your reaction makes your words difficult to believe."

Confidence bloomed out of him through a cocky grin. Her heart thumped harder than the fist on the front door. "The jewelry," she retorted to his earlier question.

"That's even harder to believe when the throb in your wrist is contradicting you."

Speechless as Gage laughed at her, the confounded whining Nicole had been hearing for several weeks buzzed through her head. Gage let go of her wrist and swung around to face Mac tapping him on the shoulder.

"What?"

"That phone call. It was Sanders."

When Nikki turned and bolted for the kitchen he asked, "What call? What'd he want?"

"They're missing another sixteen-year-old. A Stacy White. The parents didn't report it until yesterday. She went missing over a week ago. They thought they had to wait twenty-four hours to report their kid's disappearance."

Dread twisted Gage's insides.

"The parents were out of town for a couple of weeks and didn't come back until the twenty-third. At first, they thought Stacy was with friends until they checked and learned the last time any of her friends saw her was before school let out for the Christmas holiday."

Katharine had opened the door letting Michelle and Travis in along with Michelle's sister, Sylvie, her husband, Harvey, and the kids. Brendan and Shalee saw Caitlin with new toys and headed in that direction. Gage finally asked, "Does Sander's think she's here?"

"He doesn't know what to think. Just wants us to be aware since the girl's half Native American."

"Is Cole coming over today?"

"No. He's spending Christmas with Mona. I paged him to call me."

Moments later, his mother summoned Mac to the phone, which Gage assumed would be Cole calling back. The teenager had been gone more than a week and they knew it took seven days for paraquat to kill. The bodies were never discovered until four to five days after death. All his fears quickly confirmed, some luckless man, woman, or child would come across Stacy White before the New Year. Gage shelved the thoughts and focused on the kids. "Hey. Don't I get any hugs today?"

Brendan and Shalee stood, rushed toward him hailing, "Merry Christmas, Gage."

Scooping the children off the floor and giving them whisker hugs, both giggled. "Right back at yah. Did Santa bring you what you wished for?"

"I got Hot Wheels, in-line skates, and a Packers' football and helmet and a remote control Tomcat fighter jet!" Brendan blurted first.

"Did you bring the Tomcat with you?"

"Uh-huh," he bobbed his head eagerly. "But Dad said I had to leave it in the truck."

"I think we need to try out that fighter jet and make sure it works. What'd you get Shalee?"

"Santa brought me Scooter Samantha, a Barbie Grand Hotel and a Barbie remote-controlled horse and carriage. But Mom said I had to leave them home."

"Did you see Caitlin's new Barbie doll and radio-controlled Ferrari?"

"Yup. We're gonna ask Mom if we can play together with my hotel during Christmas break."

"Good idea. Guess what?"

"What?" both children asked in unison.

"I think there might be a couple more presents under the tree for you two."

"Really? What?" Brendan asked excitedly.

"Let's check it out." Gage set them down. "Caitlin, didn't Santa leave something under the tree for Brendan and Shalee?"

"There's a whole bunch still there."

"We got something for Caitlin, didn't we Brendan."

"Then I think we need to finish opening Christmas presents. Because I bet if you check, Nikki has something for both of you and I do, too. Brendan go get everyone out of the kitchen and tell them we're gonna open more presents."

"Cool!" he said and took off running.

Michelle entered the living room first and whispered in Gage's ear. Grinning, he said, "We'll go out there after we finish in here. How's that?"

"No problem. I'm not sure I'll be able to get Travis, Phillip, Ronson, or my dad in here though. They had a blast playing with them all week and wore out the batteries. Phillip either had them recharged or bought new ones."

Brendan led the women from the kitchen, saying, "Auntie Michelle, I can't find Uncle Travis or Grandpa."

"They'll be here in a minute dumplin'."

"Where'd they go?"

"Travis is getting something for me. Go sit with Caitlin and Shalee."

Michelle then whispered to Gage, "I'll go drag the big boys inside." She returned leading her husband, Phillip, Ronson, Frank, and her father into the living room.

After the adults exchanged gifts with each other and watched the children open theirs, Travis told the kids, "I ran into Santa Claus just before we got here. He said this was his last stop and I'm supposed to tell Brendan, Shalee and Caitlin to get their coats on and check out the garage."

Caitlin squealed, "Santa came twice?"

"He sure did. Said he forgot something and had to come back."

"How come he didn't come in and have milk and cookies?" Shalee asked.

"He was out all night delivering toys around the world and his reindeer were tired and thirsty. He told me to wish everyone a Merry Christmas for him," Travis said.

"What'd he forget?" Brendan asked.

"Get your jackets on and go see," Travis told him.

Three eager kids scuttled quickly putting on winter clothing. Adults followed as the children rushed anxiously into the garage.

"A Desert Challenger motorcycle!" Brendan shouted running over and hopping on.

Caitlin and Shalee squealed as each climbed into Barbie Sport's Jeeps—one for each. Gage yelled over the noise. "Rev 'em up, guys!"

"Lordy! We'll never get them back inside now," Paula told Sylvie.

"Good thing we brought the pick-up today," Sylvie said.

While Travis and Phillip explained the vehicle's operation, Aidan and Frank stood by ready with battery chargers. Nicole noticed the garage had previously been cleared for the event. Caitlin's face was vibrant with excitement. When Gage moved to her side she asked, "Gage, where'd those come from?"

"Michelle said Travis and his family went together on them." He shoved his hands into his pockets. "You'd never be able to tell by watching her that she'd ever dealt with any kind of tragedy."

Nicole cocked her head sideways and followed his gaze to Caitlin, looked back at him. His expression transformed to serious, and once more, she caught the presence of uncanny awareness that went beyond the obvious. "Without knowing what they did for her, you saw to it that she'd enjoy today, didn't you?"

"Nikki, you gonna stand there and tell me you didn't have the same thoughts? You bought her enough clothes for her to open her own store!"

"A girl needs lots of clothes."

"Why? So she can put herself on display?"

She readied to retort when Paula shouted over the sound of hummed up engines, "I've got a dinner to get on." Paula went inside, followed by Rosemary and Julia who were complaining the noise too much. Katharine's back ached. With their fill of racket, Michelle and Sylvie accompanied the others inside, too. Frank passed drinks to the men who stood aside of the machines watching the children brutally gun the engines. Mac told Gage he was going to check in with dispatch and went into the house next.

"What do you say when those batteries wear down, we take the kids outside and build a snowman."

"Why the games, Gage?"

"I promised Caitlin I'd show her how it's done."

"That's not what I mean by games," Nicole said.

"It's Christmas, Nikki. Can we put our differences aside for one day out of the year?"

"Fine. I have a better idea. Guys against the gals. You build yours and we'll design ours. The elders can judge who really knows how to make a *snow man*."

"You're on."

"We get the back yard. You can have the front."

"No fair. There's more snow in the back yard because it's twice the size."

"Too bad. I already called it and *I'll* show Caitlin and Shalee how to make a real snowman."

"We'll just see about that," Gage tossed over his shoulder.

Nicole returned to the house consumed by the thrill of competition and the kick-bang of excitement inside her chest. It took little to convince both Michelle and Sylvie to participate. Katharine caved after deliberating rest for her back or beating the crap out of the guys.

"Katharine, hon, if this gets too hard, you can stand guard. I gotta feeling those wimps are gonna try and steal our snow."

"I think we should make a muscleman," Michelle offered.

Sylvie giggled. "Good idea, Sis."

"We'll need to dress him up," Katharine said. "And I know exactly where to find what we need. Shalee, Caitlin, you're learning from the best. Watch closely. I'll be right back."

Nicole, Michelle and Sylvie went to work rolling up balls of snow while explaining to Caitlin and Shalee defeating man was a woman's purpose in life. Katharine returned with ice cream pails filled with water, the necessary ingredient to make it work.

"I'm still hunting down what I need. I'll be back as soon as I can get my hands on them."

"While you're at it, Katharine, check out the front. See if my husband went over and got a truck load of snow with one of his big toys."

"Travis wouldn't dare!" Sylvie exclaimed.

"Oh, he'd dare all right. But we have the edge with artistic talent."

"Got that right," Nicole laughed. "If it doesn't come with screws, bolts and a set of pictured instructions men can't put anything together."

"Why not?" Caitlin asked.

"Because, sweetie. Men don't read and they refuse to ask directions to anything. They think they know it all and will never admit they can't figure out women."

"I wonder why manufacturers bother with instructions," Sylvie sighed.

"Caitlin, Mom always says if you want something done right you're supposed to ask a woman to do it. Right mom?" Shalee asked.

"That's *my* niece," Michelle hooted.

Mother Sylvie stood gaping at her youngest. "I keep forgetting my honeybunch is always within earshot. Shalee, tell mommy what else you've heard me say."

"Nothing," she said, licking snow off her mitten.

Laughing infectiously, the women rolled snow into well-shaped tri's, bi's, abs, whatever, and piled them high.

"Mom, how we gonna put the snowman together?"

"With water."

Speaking of which, where'd Katharine go?" Nicole stood. "I think it's time to check the enemy camp. Make sure they didn't kidnap our spy. I'll be right back."

"Can I go?" Caitlin begged.

"Sure can. But we have to move as silently as a stealth and sneak up on them. We don't want to get caught."

Taking Caitlin's mittened hand, they quietly lurked alongside the LeNoir house. Peeking around the corner, Nicole didn't know what she expected, but what she saw didn't resemble a snowman.

"What're they doing?"

"I dunno, sweetie. But let's go report—"

"Busted!"

They spun around and were smacked with snowballs. Nicole slid back a few steps, shrieking. Gage not only threatened, he bombarded them again with a pre-made pile.

"You're not going anywhere."

"Gage Andrew LeNoir! What're you—"

A blob of snow smacked her square in the chest. Gage lurched, grabbed Caitlin by the waist and tucked her under his arm. Nicole shoved him backward into a snow mound, snatched Caitlin back and tried to run. He was faster, grabbed her ankles and dropped both of them in the same snow bank. Through Caitlin's giggled squeals, Gage filled a gloved hand with a white pile. His bright blue eyes threatened diabolically.

"Seems you ladies were sneaking up on us. I'm taking you both prisoner."

"You think!" Nicole flung a clump of snow at him coating his devilish smirk. He flinched enough for her to shovel Caitlin out of the snow, dumping another handful of fresh white stuff on his head. "Run, Caitlin—get help!"

"That's it!" Gage pinned a snow-suited Caitlin, wrestling Nicole at the same time. He scrubbed both their faces with fistfuls of more white fluff. "You ain't goin nowhere except to our ice cave."

"Shalee!" Caitlin yelled. "Help! The cookie monster got us. Shalee, help!"

"Hush, squirt. Or I'll tickle you. Like this," he said prickling her belly and sides.

"Nooooo!" she squealed between giggles. "Shalee, help us!"

Gage scrambled to his feet keeping Caitlin pinned under a boot. He picked up Nicole and tossed her over a shoulder then yanked Caitlin up by the seat of her snow pants and hauled them both to the newly constructed ice cave in front of the house.

"You overgrown Brobdingnagian!" Nicole yelled, slugging Gage in the back. "Put us down now!"

"Good word, babe, but you're busted. Hey guys, look what I caught snooping around. Three down, three to go."

The men cheered and Nicole twisted and look up. Without the best vantage point, she just figured out what happened to Katharine.

Patting Nikki's rear, Gage said, "This one's a fighter," and bouncing Caitlin, he added, "this one's a squealer."

"Lock 'em up with the princess," Mac ordered.

"I can't believe you bozos have to pick on a pregnant woman and a child to win a contest!" Nicole blustered. "And this is not a snowman."

"Well, you're no dummy," Travis taunted with a wicked grin. "Inside our fortress damsels."

"Nicole, what's a dazzle?" Caitlin asked wiggling under Gage's grip.

"Sweetie, it's dam-zel. It's a beautiful lady, like—ouch!" Nicole yelped when Gage dropped her.

"That pregnant woman you're talking about stole my—never mind. Pipsqueak can't be trusted. Move it, before I take advantage of you like I did last night."

Nicole stood hastily and Katharine peeked out. "I think we can take 'em, Nicole."

"You're hormones are outta whack."

Gage pushed her inside, Nicole slipped, fell a second time and Caitlin landed on top of her. Lying flat on her back Nicole burst into peals of laughter, observing two waist-high walls. Righting Caitlin and herself, she asked, "Katharine, what did you steal?"

"Pipsqueak, shut-up," Gage hollered.

"Thought our muscleman would look cute wearing a pair of Gage's boxers, but before I could turn them over to you guys, Mac caught me red-handed."

"And you call yourself a cop," Nicole said, earning a laugh from Mac. "So, what do we do now?"

"Milady, her sister and offspring will be joining you shortly," Travis said, Harvey nodding agreement.

"All right you overgrown kids," Paula called from the front door. "Inside and wash up before dinner.

"Just in time, my back's killing me," Katharine complained.

A twinge of envy ran through Nicole's veins when Mac swooped Katharine off her feet, kissed her and carried her into the house.

CHAPTER 7

Nicole sashayed into the Tavern the day after Christmas displaying her Venetian beads against an ivory angora sweater. A chocolate brown leather skirt hugged the shape of her hips. With her wealth of waves scooped upward, individual curls caressed her face to expose the companion earrings on her lobes. Her leather knee-high heeled boots clicked across the wooden floor in time with hammers inside the ballroom. As heads turned to look, she thought not even the Stewarts could upset her tonight or destroy the enthusiasm consuming her since Christmas day.

"Hi, Hayden. How's it goin?"

"Hey, Nicole." Looking up, he stopped what he was doing. "Holy carumba! I swear you get more beautiful every time I look at you. If I leave my wife right now would you run away with me?"

"Thanks. But not on your life, sweet thing."

Hayden shrugged. "Not my lucky day. Or yours either. Gypsy called in sick again."

"No problem. I'll cover for her. I've got a few things to take care of in the office. Call me out if it picks up before her shift starts."

"Nicole."

She turned when Travis exited the ballroom. "How's Mike? Is he okay?" she asked.

"I sent him to a doctor when he told me about the incident. He's fine."

"I'm really glad to hear that."

"You look happy today. Gage must have done right by his gift."

Baffled by his knowledge, Nicole just asked, "How's it coming in there?"

"Great. Come in and look. We should be done with plenty of time to spare. How are the plans for the party?"

"Really good. I've done my homework on the 1930's. Everything will be formal and identical to back then. I've booked a twenty-five-piece orchestra that will resemble the Glen Miller era music. I have most of the invites mailed but I still need a final list. I want the rest mailed before January third to give folks plenty of time to R.S.V.P."

"I'll have my mother stop by in the morning. I'm guessing with La Pointe residents and invitations we'll hit around four hundred total. I invited my guys, too. I told them this was a celebration and they have to dress up which caused some groans. They'll let you know."

"Jacque and Hayden keep bugging me for a number so I'll give them that for now," Nicole replied walking with Travis toward the ballroom's entryway. They weren't just treating this as an anniversary party but a grand opening ball as well.

"Have we decided on a dinner then?"

"I'm still working on that one, but your mother and I are thinking a sit down dinner is the best way to go."

"You're a gem to handle everything for me. Will you have enough help to serve a sit down—never mind. I trust you. Now take a look and tell me what you think."

"Great balls of fire! Oh, Travis, it's exquisite! And big!" Nicole exclaimed.

Jerry, the general contractor, Mike and several others called out greetings as Nicole stood inside the entranceway. Every piece of molding, trim and cable molding matched the lounge's bar back. The walls papered in muted colors above wainscoting matched the dining room. Large ornate brass chandeliers hung from a very high alcove ceiling.

"Julia and Ronson are going to love this. It's absolutely beautiful."

"My beloved Grandma-ma," he grinned, "has been ordered to stay out until the twenty-ninth. Nicole, I'm counting on you to keep her at bay. She'll be very determined."

"Not to worry. Everyone's been put on alert. What about the car? Have you figured out how you're going to get it in here?"

"My right hand man Billy Abbott and my dad are handling the details."

"When's the floor going in?"

"Hardwood gleaming floors should be here next week. Then we'll begin installation once we make sure everything else is in place."

"Travis, you've done an amazing job. Especially with everything that's happened around here."

"Thanks, but I get my tenacity from Grandma-ma and that little lady right over there," he pointed. "She's the best thing that ever happened to me."

Nicole shifted, looked across the great room. "Geez. I didn't recognize Michelle in scrubs and a hardhat. You might not believe it, but you're the best thing that ever happened to her. Oh, I almost forgot. What kind of cake do you want for your grandmother? Tier, sheet, marble, white, or maybe you have another idea?"

His face glazed over and Nicole chuckled. "Never mind, I'll let Jacque decide and I'll deal with the rest."

"Nicole, the interior décor will be arriving within the week as well as the ballroom tables and other equipment. Ted said you should decide where to hang pictures and set up the tables."

"Like everything else," she muttered under her breath. "I have work to do before the night rush picks up. One of my waitresses called in sick and I'm covering for her."

"I'll call my mother for you."

"Thanks. Keep up the great work."

Walking through the lounge where Hayden had several at the bar under control, Nicole headed for the back to speak with Jacque. The kitchen aromas were scents of comfort she logged in her memory to forever worship. Travis' crews had worked fast to complete the remodeling of the dining room and kitchen. Both rooms had been enlarged by half their original size to accommodate summer tourists.

"Sweet meatballs! You look good enough to take a bite out of, chérie."

"Get in line, lover boy," Nicole said. "Hayden's ready to divorce his wife. I'm not sure why anyone thinks I look any different today than other days."

"Chérie, someone who looks as seductive as you do everyday of the week is known to the French as défendu amour."

"Meaning?"

"Forbidden love, chérie." He sighed, repeating it, "Forbidden love. What can I do for you tonight?"

"I just spoke to Travis and I'll confirm with Rosemary tomorrow, but I'm almost positive we're going with a sit-down dinner for the twenty-ninth. The guests will be close to four hundred. I'll let you decide the menu, as well as the style, design and type of cake."

"Merci beaucoup. A wise choice and I'll get right on the menu and give you an order."

"I'll tell Hayden and then I'll be in my office until business picks up. I'm covering for Gypsy tonight."

"Again? Chérie, that one does you no good the way she misses more hours than she works."

"I know, Jacque. But she's good at what she does."

"Nicole, what she does is make you work longer and harder. You've had one vacation since I started here. What you need is to take that red-haired man by the horns and force him to sink his hands into that God-given sexy flesh of yours."

Nicole stumbled, felt her face fill with flaming heat and nearly collapsed from his candid words. "Jacque!"

"Ahh, Chérie, you keep your feelings hidden well but your eyes glow with longing in Gage's presence."

"*Gage?* I thought you were talking about Mike."

"Mike doesn't have red hair, Chérie."

"Now I know you're nuttier than the caramel rolls you bake."

"His eyes are filled with remorse when he looks at you."

"Remorse? For what?"

"I couldn't say. His sorrow is embedded deeply. Perhaps somewhere in the past."

Nicole had locked away many things from the past, one as recent as two years ago. Another she was only seventeen. *Lord!* She hadn't thought about that weekend in as long either, until Gage said he wanted to talk about that night.

"You're blind and need glasses, Jacque."

"These are trained eyes of love and I'm inclined to believe what they see. Not to worry. Hayden might suspect, but the others," he waved his hand in the air, "they're too busy with themselves to notice."

The six-panel door swung open just in time and they both looked at Hayden. "Here you are. Travis and his men finished early and things are picking up."

"Okay, I'm coming."

Nicole turned quickly and followed Hayden into the lounge to avoid further discussion with Jacque. Patrons were stacked two deep at the bar. Mike, Greg and Mitch along with the other workers had moved tables together. The Stewart brothers were the nucleus of the room and already guzzling pitchers of beer. Sitting in the corner near the fireplace, Gage smiled and winked when he caught her eye. It had to be the silly season making everyone insane. Either that or Gage was drunk. But he rarely came in here and when he did, he only had one or two drafts. Michelle sat opposite him and Travis was at the bar getting their drinks.

Her mind on Jacque's bombshell and Travis' observations, she wavered before taking the tray Hayden handed her.

"What's wrong, Nicole?"

"Nothing." She went to Mike's table first. "What can I get you fellas?"

"We'll take our usual, cupcake. Then I'm gonna just kickback and watch that backfield of yours in motion tonight."

"Look is all you get to do," Nicole smirked.

"She's gotcha there, slug," Mitch said, laughing. "Nicole's making plans with me."

Another said, "I gotta better chance with her than either one of ya."

"None of you know how to treat a lady," Greg said standing and circling her shoulder with an arm. "This beauty queen is mine."

"Boys! I don't belong to anyone—never have, never will. The sooner you learn that, the sooner you're hearts will recover. Will a couple of pitchers do it for you?"

Nicole felt other eyes upon her and glanced toward the corner. Gage was frigid and his previous smile a frown. He looked the other way, as if to discard her when she moved to the Stewart table.

"Can I get any of you a refill?"

"Yah, one of these. Then maybe you'll lemme remove those C-F-M-B's for you."

Kevin drooled on himself while he ogled her like a stalking panther. Dumb ass that she was had to ask. "C-F-M-B's?"

"Come fuck me boots."

"One more crack like that jerkoff and you're out of here."

❧   ❧   ❧

His jaw muscle twitched so hard Gage thought he would need a root implant. He had all he could do not to go over and beat the shit out of Kevin Stewart. Then asked himself why he sat here making notation on every jack-off in the bar watching Nikki.

Damn buffoons!

The hostile glares from the chosen few were obvious when he entered the tavern. Did they think he hadn't heard their verbal undertones of rage after they pretentiously greeted him? Or not know where the wrath stemmed from. But their anger didn't bother him nearly as much as the way some leered at and treated Nikki. He rooted his eyes back on her, loathing all of them and maybe even her a little. There should be a law. He'd write a couple dozen tickets for indiscretion and toss the rest in lock-up. In fact, he'd make sure and write a couple parking tickets on his way out. Just cuz they're working on the ballroom doesn't exempt them from violations. As far as the middle Stewart brother, well, he had other ideas for the 'jerkoff'.

"Gage, does your mom want me to come and get Keeker yet?"

"Caitlin likes the cat," he said without looking at Michelle. "It's up to you."

"It's harmless," she then said to him.

He scowled and shifted uncomfortably as his mood veered sharply to his own anger. "Several think they have a verbal license to harass Nikki and I don't like it."

"Gage, how long have you felt this way?"

He glanced mechanically across the table at Michelle. Nikki's light little laugh and infectious chatter carried throughout the room and he glanced back at her. Nikki's alluring conduct had nailed everyone's attention in the room now. The woman stirred his blood more than one way. And dammit all to hell, her hip movement was a vexing proposition to every man—*including him*. He couldn't very well arrest every peckerhead in the lounge just because they watched her prink her way toward the bar.

"Gage," Michelle repeated. "How long?"

A moment later he leaned back, exercising an impatient shrug. "Does she always go for the mouthy-tongued types?"

"Omigod! You really *are* in love with her."

The incident of a young boy, which Michelle knew nothing about, made him realize he always had feelings for Nikki. He kept his eyes fixed on the bar, unwilling to share the event with Michelle. Nikki was twelve when the initiation via kiss became a daily drill of cat and mouse between him and her.

"I think you're wrong about Nicole and what she prefers."

He eyed Michelle frugally as another haunting memory came back to him. That one involved Nikki, too. He was eighteen, she was seventeen. Though he loved Michelle like a sister, he would never find the courage to explain to her why Brian's accident was his fault. Neither could he explain to her how he knew that Nikki had been in love with her brother. He had lived with both dreadful thoughts for fifteen years. Another fifty years wouldn't kill him but it hurt like hell to look at the woman sitting across from him because he'd sent his best friend and her brother to his grave. By choice, he had never talked about Brian's accident to anyone. Allowing the regret of that entire weekend to gnaw on his insides, he glanced at Nikki again. His reply was angry. "If I'm so wrong why's she going to Los Angeles?"

"A better question would be why didn't she pursue the modeling career she desperately wanted after high school? Along with why haven't you done anything about your feelings for her?"

That wasn't what he wanted to hear and carelessly shrugged again.

"Have you heard Nicolina crying yet?"

Gage came forward almost hissing at Michelle and was a little surprised she didn't flinch and back away in her seat. What he had heard always came from the summer tourists. They would stop him just to ask where they should look for the buried Cadotte treasures and play twenty questions with the three ghosts who haunted the islands.

"Well? Have you heard Sully's ghost, Nicolina, or haven't you?"

"Thought you told me you didn't believe in fairytales or ghosts, Michelle."

"I didn't." Michelle looked across the room at Travis. "Until that man made me a believer. Just like Mac and Katharine became believers. Gage, you can't fight it. It's going to happen."

"Michelle, are you insane or does marriage do this to all of you?"

Giggling, she told him, "That's what I kept telling Travis when he said he'd dreamt about me and told me he heard Mikala long before he ever met me. Mikala's actually the one who brought Travis here. Katrina and fate brought Mac and Katharine together. Out of all four of us, Travis is the only one who actually believed any of it. Judging by your facial expression, I'm positive you're hearing Nicolina."

He did not believe in ghosts! He just needed a good night's sleep. On that list of violations he was conjuring up, Gage added Sully's name. He'd get one verbal warning for spreading that stupid sham. Thankfully, Travis returned with their drinks setting them on the table.

"What are we talking about?"

Gage grabbed his draft and slugged back a huge gulp. Over the rim, he watched the same sick look pass between Michelle and Travis that he observed between Mac and Katharine. It was disgusting to watch men crumble to women. Didn't matter if he liked these particular two, it was just revolting to watch a man implode with sappiness.

Michelle lifted her iced tea, grinning. "The Cadotte ghosts. Like I didn't, Gage doesn't believe either."

"Doesn't believe in ghosts or doesn't believe what he's hearing?" Travis asked with a foxy grin.

Gage tossed a glare at him. If he once had any inkling for friendliness, that sunk his mood to the bottom of the big lake. Nicole's laughter distracted him and he slugged back the remains of his beer. Slamming the glass on the table, he said, "You're both as crazy as Mac and Pipsqueak."

"Maybe you shouldn't fight it, but join us," Travis pushed.

Digging out a couple of bills, Gage tossed them on the table and stood. Ready to fire off a comeback, he changed his mind. "I'm outta here."

Travis glanced over his shoulder. "Mike's using the same brassy words on Nicole that he uses on every woman. Milady, this could get worse before it gets better."

"Travis, we have to do something."

"Why?"

"Because they're in love with each other."

"Tell me something I don't already know."

"Katharine and I have been sworn to secrecy about Nicole's future."

"Future what?"

She leaned in, speaking softly. "Nicole interviewed in L.A. last week with a fashion designer. She's leaving Madeline Island."

"Who was the interview with?"

"One of the top designers in the world," Michelle whispered, "Chantilly Mackinaw."

"Really?"

Backsliding, Michelle blinked at her husband. "Travis, you know her?"

He nodded. "Designed her office buildings in Paris and Rome."

"Well, we have to do something."

"Oh no!" He set his julep down. This was one time he didn't want to look at his eager wife, but caved. Waving a halting hand, he said, "Milady, don't even go there. I love you more than anyone in the world, but Gage and Nicole have to work this out between themselves."

As Mike and Nicole laughed louder, Travis said, "But, I could deter *that* from going any further."

She glanced over Travis' shoulder and sighed. "No, you're right. We just have to let everything take its course and trust Nicolina to handle them both.

After all, once you and Mikala got your hooks in me it didn't take long before I came around."

"Too long." He leaned in toward his green-eyed lover. "Let's get outta here. I've been waiting all day to take you home and ravish you."

"Travis Baines, I still think you're insane but I love you for what you just offered to do."

"Milady, I hope that's not the only reason you love me," he said leaning closer to her.

Their mouths met in a deep kiss as Nicole watched from the bar. Travis and Michelle got up and walked out arm-in-arm. Gage had left hurriedly and she never had a chance to make it over to their table. So much for chipper spirits. Sheila had arrived, and with her spirits sinking miserably, Nicole decided to take the rest of the night off. Glancing around, she hated this job more since her return from L.A., now wondered if others assumed what Jacque or Travis did. Before leaving the Tavern, she gave Hayden the details for the Perry anniversary party and told him to submit his order.

Outside, the crisp night air refreshed. Since Christmas, La Pointe had been saturated with several more inches of snow. But the temps were still above normal. Not used to people milling in the streets or the noises so early in the evening and burdened with many things, Nicole moved in an oxen-gaited manner. Gage was angry when he left the Tavern. She recognized the offensive authority he possessed. Made her thoughts spin rapidly to embedded secrets and she quickly averted her thoughts. She wasn't jealous of Katharine or Michelle. Nevertheless, both pairs of lovebirds had a way of gnawing the hell out of her lately. She couldn't explain it to anyone, let alone herself. Oh, she cherished each one and was thrilled for her two best friend's happiness, but envy filled her heart. Since the interview, her humdrum life more than convinced her she needed the California job.

Nicole trudged up the front steps of the rambler. She would have to contact her parents about the house before she moved out west. They'd most likely choose to sell it. Four or five years, maybe ten, had passed since Conrad and Erica Jarvis were last here. They stopped over for less than a day enroute to uncover some place where prehistoric man camped, worked and played. They hadn't called in advance. She was working when they stopped for dinner at the tavern and left the same night. She never understood their excitement to dig up dead people.

Unlocking the front door, Nicole slipped inside and mumbled gloomily, "So much for parents."

Removing her outerwear, she realized a long time ago how Paula LeNoir became more of a mother to her than Erica Jarvis had ever been. The munchkin size woman with auburn hair scolded her at a young age, listened to her troubles and bandaged bruised elbows and knees as well as consoled her heart. The ringing phone interrupted her thoughts and Nicole padded over in her nylons to answer. With no one on the other end, she hung up noting several hang-up calls in the past month. She assumed embarrassment the reason for the caller not to admit they misdialed and headed for the kitchen to throw in her favorite frozen pizza. The elaborate wall clock, a gift from out-of-sight parents, closed in on ten PM. She had walked further and longer around town than normal. Yanking out a chef's surprise, she also knew Jacque would hand over a tongue-lashing if he knew of her indulgence in processed food. Setting the oven, Gage's words 'secrets you keep hidden in your heart' alongside Jacque's earlier claim danced in her head.

Nicole glanced around the superficial kitchen to distract her from their statements. The newest wave in appliances, compliments of parents who chose to send gifts for every occasion, stocked the updated room in cold silver. Their love always came in the form of gifts, the latest, thirteen inches of color TV she flicked on with the remote to catch the news. Needing nothing in the materialistic department, she wondered about her own taste in décor since those parents she wouldn't recognize had furnished the entire house. She debated through a teaser to the upcoming news why she hadn't trashed the crap they sent.

The built-in oven beeped it had preheated and Nicole nudged the pizza in and peeked out the window at a barking Secunda in the backyard. Unusual for him not to greet her, his barking sounded like a warning. When his woof turned to a growl, she grabbed a biscuit, flipped on the outside light and stuck her head out the back door.

"Secunda, what's the matter with you tonight?"

The lab pup ran to her steps barking wildly as white slime slithered like shoestrings down the sides of his jaws. The dog had never ignored a biscuit in her hand. He ran toward the property line and back to the steps growling—running—barking.

"What's the matter, boy?"

Nicole retrieved slippers, slipped them on and went down the steps.

"What's gotten into you?" she asked accompanying the overgrown hound to see what had him riled up. Secunda jumped in front of her and snarled viciously at a body lying in the snow. Fearful and horrified Nicole cut loose a blood-curdling scream. Secunda jumped about barking savagely.

CHAPTER 8

❀

Reactionary to scream, several minutes passed, or so it felt, while Secunda's persistent bark at the dead girl kept time with Nicole's gushing adrenaline. Shivering uncontrollably without a coat, she jerked suddenly and ran back into the house. Her teeth clattering more from fear, she grabbed the phone and dialed 911. Couldn't blame the dispatcher for not understanding or believing her, but the woman said she would send a squad.

Moments later, Nicole heard a car out front, rushed to the door yanking it open and dashed outside to meet Mac. "M-Mac, it's a-awful. S-she's in t-the b-b-back. Sssecunda—"

"Nicole!" Mac took her hands. "You're skin is like ice and you're freezing."

Ushering her inside, he said, "Gage is on his way. You wait here." He grabbed her coat hanging near the door and wrapped it around her.

"What's burning?"

Her eyes widened. "T-the uuuven."

Mac rushed to the kitchen and switched it off, grabbed a towel and yanked the appliance door waving at smoke. He moved swiftly, opening two windows. "Whatever it is, it's toast."

Gage stormed into the kitchen, flapping smelly fumes from his face like the gesture would clear the room. He heard the dog barking when he pulled up, and demanded, "What's going on? The call didn't come out as a fire."

Nicole's entire body shook uncontrollably as she peered at him. "Ssscunda's in the b-b-b-back—was b-barking. I w-w-went—"

"Gage, she told me there's a body out there. She ran out in her stocking feet to meet me and I think she was in the back the same way. I'll go check it out. Whatever she put in the oven was burning when I got here."

"Mac, get that blasted dog out of there before he destroys all the evidence. I'll be out in a minute," Gage ordered.

Mac went out the back door and Gage went off half-cocked. "For chrissake!" he shouted ruthlessly. "What the hell were you thinking? Are you trying to catch your death of cold? This is about the stupidest thing you've ever done, Nicole! What if the killer had still been out there when you decided to prance your ass outside? You do this in L.A. and you won't live to see your next goddamn birthday!"

His nostrils flared with fury. If her body would just cooperate, she'd rip him a new asshole and yank those icy blue slits right out of his head. He glowered at her with a sardonic expression that sent her temper soaring and her blood boiling. When she could finally speak, he whirled around and charged out the back door.

"What've we got?"

"A mess. The damn dog's been all over the yard and I finally corralled him and cuffed him to Nicole's step railing. I'm gonna drive the squad around to get more light on the scene. I saw the body with my flashlight."

"Get Del and Gus over here!"

As Mac went through the house, Gage's blood pressure soared. Footprints led from the steps to the back of Nicole's property. "Damn her!"

He sucked the cold night air deeply into his lungs. He should've had more control, but she should have been smarter. He never should've cut loose the way he did, but she had a way of provoking the shit out of him. When Dispatch aired the call, his insides electrified and filled with fear. Of all the people on the island, why did Nikki have to find the next victim? Why was this dead girl in her backyard? He was damn positive this was Stacy White. Dead at the hand of the Green Bay Serial Killer.

Secunda barked some more when Mac parked the squad near the scene to expose the entire yard with both spotlights.

"Shut up dog!" Gage yelled.

They didn't need to inch closer to recognize that the body was a young female. Secunda's tracks danced all around where Nikki's had stopped. Still something was definitely different. If it were in fact Stacy White, she was laid out too perfectly. White clothing graced her figure with dark hair feathering a blanket of fresh-fallen snow. She wasn't just dumped as the others were. She laid there in apparent offering as part of some unknown ceremonial sacrifice. He and Mac exchanged knowledgeable looks.

"Dammit, dog! I said shut up!"

"Gage, I think our killer just upped the ante." Mac glanced at the house and back to Gage. "This is significant to Nicole some way. Maybe a warning?"

"My thoughts exactly. But to what and why? The position of the body seems almost as important as the kill itself."

"You were pretty harsh on her."

Mac threw it at him casually. "I panicked when I heard the call," he responded lamely. Exhaling, he said, "Wait here. I'll be right back."

Gage stomped back into the house, slamming doors and windows shut. It still stunk of whatever she burned but she could just live with it. She wasn't anywhere, the TV was off and he hesitated, finally calling out, "Nikki."

Her voice was muffled and he approached the closed bathroom door. "Nikki, are you okay?"

"Kiss off asshole! Get out of my house and leave me alone."

He clenched his teeth. "Nikki! Mac and I knew there was gonna be another murder. His captain called Christmas day and told us another girl had disappeared from Green Bay."

He stopped, waiting for her to come out. His impatience returning, Gage sucked down the hostility. "Nikki, we're sure it's her out there. Her name was Stacy White."

He waited again, heard the faint splash of water. After several minutes when she didn't open the door, he smacked it hard with his hand and walked away.

"Gage."

He shifted about. She wore slippers and a green robe. Her hair was shoved up and his earrings were pale compared to her dark fear-filled eyes. That's when his heart took a toppling dive. He moved swiftly and stopped short of pulling her into his arms. "I'm sorry, Nikki."

"You doorknob!"

From an asshole to a doorknob in a matter of minutes, he mused. Probably the only guy on Madeline to graduate from a damn jerk to an asshole doorknob all in the same week.

"How do you think I felt? Secunda went crazy. It was natural to go out and see what he was barking at. I wasn't thinking. Secunda always greets me when I come home every night. Yes, I went out there. Yes, maybe it was stupid but it doesn't give you the right to verbally abuse me!"

Her words were electric and rapid. Even in the course of fear, the woman talked a blue streak. He took her hand, but she yanked it back. "Come 'ere and sit down. Please? I need to tell you something."

Following him, she sat on the leather sofa. "What?"

Stay calm he told himself. Don't retort to sarcasm. "Nikki, we aren't going to know until the crime lab goes over the scene and the ME does an autopsy. Mac and I are positive of who she is and that she died at the hand of the Green Bay Serial Killer."

"Okay," Nicole said skeptically.

"There's something's different this time. The victim is laid out ceremoniously, like she's being offered. We think it's related to you somehow."

"What? Have you flipped?"

Yeah, he'd flipped all right. And she always controlled when and where he flipped. "Nikki, we believe she was put in your yard so only you would find her."

"That's crazy! How could you possibly know that?"

"Dammit, I'm a cop! I do know a thing or two!" he blasted back, watching her flinch and crumble.

Inhaling and exhaling the frustration, he put aside his anger and took both her hands to halt her shaking. He believed her whiskey-gold eyes always had a way of looking right into his soul and reading his innermost thoughts. He knew she couldn't otherwise she'd make it easier for him to be with her. Rubbing his thumbs over the back of her hands, he wrestled with the idea to kiss away the quiver in her bottom lip but didn't. "Nikki, I don't know anything for sure. Whatever is going on, I'm not taking any chances."

"First Katharine then Michelle. Now you think this maniac is going to come after me? Why?"

"We don't know. Gus and Del have to get here first and it's gonna take awhile to get this cleaned up once they do. Mac will be here with me. If I call Pipsqueak, will you stay with her tonight?"

"Why can't I stay here?"

A pleading look he'd never been able to resist filled her face. He sure as hell didn't feel like arguing with her anymore. "One condition."

"What's that?"

"We stop fighting with each other."

"You're not getting off that easy, Gage LeNoir."

"What's that supposed to mean?"

"I'm still mad at you…oh never mind."

"What?" he asked, truly curious.

"Gage, there's a dead body in my backyard. Let's talk about it later."

"Would you do us a favor and make some coffee? We're gonna need it. Please?"

"Yeah, I will. Tell Mac to come inside. I'm sure he's freezing."

Standing, he said, "He's probably sitting in the squad. I have to go. I don't want you out there. I'll come back for the coffee."

"Gage?"

"What?"

"Why *do* we keep fighting with each other?"

He latched his thumbs on his trouser pockets and studied her for a long moment. Innocence is what he saw and thought about things a man never asked a woman. "One way or the other, Nikki, we are going to talk about that night."

Gage went out the back door without saying another word. Nikki knew what he meant. He found Mac right where he figured he'd be.

"Everything okay?" Mac asked.

Not truly knowing, Gage shoved a hand through his hair wondering what excuse Nikki would use to avoid the subject this time. "She'll make coffee."

"That's all you have to say is 'she'll make coffee.'"

"Butt out, Mac."

"Fine. I've been studying the scene without going over there. Take a look and tell me what you see."

Gage shifted and examined the dead girl. "From here, she looks young, Native American. I can see the bracelet on her wrist—the bottle is placed near the top of her head. That's new. The white dress is different as well as the way her hair is combed out over the snow. She's not covered with snow either, so she had to have been put here some time since noon today."

"Look at how her hands are crossed over her chest, the braceleted wrist on top and her legs are spread just so. Her bare feet are turned, almost like the killer tried to push them downward."

He saw it, responding, "Like down, for going to hell maybe?"

"Uh-huh. It's almost like the white signifies an angel. The body or girl is praying for forgiveness, and whatever the reason, she doesn't quite make it. Hence, the position of her feet. Who do you know that thinks Nicole has sinned and should go to hell?"

"Better question. What does she have to do with the other victims and why change the MO now?" Gage looked at Mac. "Except for the date, race and obvious age, everything is different."

"Yeah. My question is why weren't the other two December twenty-seventh victims displayed like this?"

"That's exactly what worries me, Mac. I'm more convinced than ever that this guy has it in for Nikki. We don't know who he is or why he'd go after her let alone where he's from. There's something else."

"What's that?"

"Nikki didn't leave for work until four. The Stewarts were at the Tavern around the same time I met up with Michelle and Travis. I was there until nearly seven tonight. That means whoever killed this girl had to place the body here after four today."

"You're saying the chances are that none of the Stewart brothers would have had time because you're they're alibi."

"You got it."

"I thought Nicole worked until closing."

"She does normally. Why?"

"What's she doing home at ten at night?"

His brow furrowed.

"We just narrowed our time down to within six hours of the body being dumped. That's a first, Gage."

"I think that coffee should be done. I'll go get us some."

Gage turned and headed back inside.

"Good timing, it just finished," Nicole said. "I'll pour you two thermal-covered mugs to keep it hot."

He waited, expecting her to slam him with some flippant remark about the last thing he said before he walked out. Instead, like always, they covered up, pretended nothing ever happened. He inhaled and exhaled in silent frustration. "Nikki, what time did you get off work tonight?"

"I left a little before eight and walked around for awhile before coming home. Why?"

"You didn't see anything out there before you left today did you?"

"No."

She gawked first, set the mugs on the table. "You think he put her there after I went to work? I remember coming in the house a little before ten. Went and turned the kitchen TV on to catch the news after getting a pizza out of the freezer. I started the oven and put it in—that's what burned. I don't think the news had started but about the time is when I heard Secunda outside barking."

Gage inched nearer as she dropped to a kitchen chair. Her face went stark white quicker than a transformer.

"You were right. He *was* out there."

"Nikki, we don't know that."

"You were right," she repeated. "Secunda never growls. He's playful and barks a lot but I've never heard him growl at anyone."

A distasteful note of envy in her voice, Gage realized the absurdity of their battle over right and wrong. He glanced at his watch, not for the current time, but believing Mac would have the call time as would dispatch. He thought the call came out just after ten. "Why did you come home early tonight?"

Nicole looked up. "I was tired and had a headache. After you guys left, things slowed down and I called Sheila to come in. Why?"

"It's nothing for you to worry about. Mac and I are trying to pinpoint the time frame she was left in your yard."

Believing Nicole might break down any minute, Gage wanted to stay with her except he had to get back outside. "Will you call Katharine and have her come over here until we're done?"

"She's probably in bed."

"She's a night person," he said, half smiling. "Always waits up for Mac."

"Maybe, I'll do that."

"I'll call her for you." He moved quickly to the telephone, doing exactly that. "She's on her way."

"Fine. Good. Whatever."

Gage watched her and waited a moment, shook his head regretfully, picked up the mugs and went outside, passing one through the car door window to Mac. "She came home around ten. Katharine's coming over to stay with her. Mac, check with dispatch for the time the call came out."

He did and the woman aired, "...time of call, twenty-two-o-three. Time now, twenty-three forty-five. The ME and crime lab are enroute from Bayfield. They'll need transport to your location. ETA, twenty minutes."

Mac acknowledged the dispatcher then looked at Gage. "So whoever probably knows Nicole works until closing never expected her to find the body until tomorrow. Chances are the killer did this after dark—"

"Which could be anytime after four-thirty, five."

"It also means the killer most likely missed the last ferry outta here at four-thirty."

"My squad's out front. Finish your coffee and go get Gus and Del. We'll check with the neighbors to see if they heard or saw anything when you get back."

"What about the dog?" Mac nodded in the animal's direction.

Gage glanced over where Secunda quietly sat on full alert. Contemplating a stern chat with Adeline Girard about letting the dog run loose, the idea hit him like a semi. Secunda probably kept Nikki from harm. "Leave him just in case he's got evidence on him."

His pregnant sister came out the back door and Gage stepped aside letting Mac exit the squad. He waited for their hugs and kisses to end noting Katharine wore her nine secured in a shoulder holster under one of Mac's jackets. He knew these two people belonged together. They gave each other strength for what each had endured. His sister didn't fall apart when she saw the dead girl. Tonight was one year since Mac's niece was found dead at the hand of the same killer. His reason for calling Katharine had been twofold. Upon Mac convincing her he was okay she carefully swiveled around in the snow to examine the backyard.

"This one's different," she stated.

"We noticed," Mac replied. "We're keeping our distance until the crime lab gets here. Secunda's already disturbed the surrounding area."

"How long you think she's been here?"

"Nikki left for work just before four and came home around ten." Then Gage told Katharine their opinions on the layout of the victim.

"I dunno. If the killer wanted any significance to hell, wouldn't the body be lying face down? Why is the liquor bottle placed perfectly at the top of her head with the neck pointing up? It looks as if she's an offering to God, or praying to God, for possibly a sin she's committed. In fact, this one looks excessively neat. Almost perfect. Like the act had to be faultless. Off the top of my head, I'd say start looking for a perfectionist who believes he's committed some sin of sorts. Instead of a confession, maybe he's offering a virgin gift—assuming she still is like the others."

"Or it could be someone who thinks Nikki is perfect."

"Except for one thing, Bro. Nicole's not a perfectionist, but it is obvious this was meant for her. And now with my take on it, it's too cold out here. I'll be inside."

Katharine exchanged a second kiss with Mac and left.

"Gi'me your keys and I'll be back in a few minutes."

When Mac walked off, Gage slid in behind the steering wheel. Katharine was right. Nicole might be perfect in his eyes and she worked hard to achieve, but she was far from being a perfectionist by nature. He thought it extremely interesting how his sister's perception of the dead girl was entirely opposite of what he and Mac thought. 'Excessively neat. The act had to be faultless. Start looking for a perfectionist who's committed a sin'. That, Gage mused, would be someone who believed they were above the standards of common people.

Someone who believed they were better than anyone else. Just a bit on the psychotic side perhaps even schizophrenic, as well as a serial killer. He began reading about character traits of murder styles after La Pointe's second homicide. Without training and education on the subject, too many things overlapped creating grave amounts of confusion. If supposition could hold up in court, his would eliminate the Stewart brothers as suspects instantly.

It was time to bring the profiler here.

They had to stop the killer.

Looking over his shoulder, Mac, Gus Rankin and two others from the crime lab, along with Del Cadavor *with an 'o'* he remembered, exited Nikki's back door. Glancing at the time, Gage exited the squad at half past midnight to brief the four men with what he knew.

The medical examiner spoke first. "Gage, at the rate you're sending us business, Gus and I are ready to set up shop on the island. Which case is this one related to?"

"Green Bay Serial Killer." Media came up with that one he recalled. "I may be job hunting in the near future if you guys don't find me new evidence that leads us to the killer. See what you can dig up."

Gus noted the time, studied the scene, and spoke. "This is as clean and neat as the way my wife keeps house. Let's hope we find something."

Gage blinked—recalled a theory—looked pointedly at Gus who had started toward the dead girl. "You gonna have enough light to get pictures?"

The investigator stopped, looked at him. "Gage, that's the least of my problems. We'll be here most of the night. This minute I'm wishing, with the temp falling as fast as this new snow, that I had a nine-to-five job in doors. It was bloody f'ing cold coming across in the boat. You're lucky water's still moving."

"If I were lucky, none of this would be happening, Gus. Contrary to popular belief, crime doesn't work nine-to-five. Even here."

"Got that right," Gus muttered.

"You want Mac and me to talk to the neighbors?"

"Hold off until I see what we got here."

They did and hung back with Del as snow fell heavily now. Gus snapped off pictures of the body from every angle while the other two men scoured the surrounding area with high-powered handheld flashlights.

"Well, well. What have we got here?"

"What is it?" Gage asked.

Gus didn't answer him at first and used a long pair of tweezers to pull a piece of paper from under the girl's hands. He bagged and tagged whatever he found.

"Gage, come 'ere and take a look."

Mac and Del followed and Gage took the evidence bag, reading the paper inside as Mac held his flashlight on the paper.

> *Do you know*
> *How a long time ago*
> *One poor little child*
> *Whose name I do know*
> *Was stolen away*
> *On a fine summer's day*
> *And left in a wood*
> *As I've heard people say.*
> *And when it was night*
> *So sad was her plight*
> *And the moon gave no light!*
> *She sobbed, and she sighed!*
> *No one bitterly cried*
> *And the poor little thing*
> *Lay down and died!*
> *And when she was dead*
> *The robins so red*
> *Brought Rosary Peas*
> *And over her spread*
> *And all the day long*
> *They sang her this song:*
> *Poor babe in the wood, Poor babe in the wood!*
> *And don't you remember the babe in the wood?*
> *Oh, so young a parent to be when history repeats.*

Gage looked at Gus. "What the hell is it?

"You asked me for new evidence. It appears to be a poem."

"What do you think it means?"

"Reads like a nursery rhyme. We'll check latents for you and find out whether it was done on a typewriter or a computer. There's something else."

"What?"

"The body hasn't frozen yet and Del will probably backup she's been dead about seventy-two hours."

"Which means," Gage said, "wherever she died it was inside somewhere."

"You got it."

They went back to work and at zero-five-thirty Gus finished processing the entire backyard and cleared the scene. A few hours earlier, they called for an ambulance routine so Del could take the body to his boat and over to the mainland. Mac went with to assist and would take the first ferry back at seven-thirty A.M. Del advised he'd call with his findings. Gage drove the crime lab team back to their boat after stopping at the station to photocopy the nursery rhyme.

"I'll have my report for you in a day or two."

"The sooner the better. Mac and I agreed. We're calling in the profiler who was working on the Green Bay case. She'll want to see everything ASAP."

"I'll do my best," Gus said and left.

Gage had turned off Nikki's coffeepot and locked the house before they left. She and Pipsqueak had fallen asleep in the living room and he didn't want to wake them—didn't want to argue with Nikki. With roughly an hour before Mac returned, he headed home to grab a hot shower and his umpteenth cup of coffee. He'd have to make it himself to avoid his dad's pee water.

❦   ❦   ❦

Gage climbed the foldaway ladder into the attic of his parent's house. Yanking the string hanging from the ceiling, a dim light cast cowardly shadows across the room. A layer of dust and cobwebs covered old furniture and boxes scattered and placed disorderly. Prints marred a layer of otherwise undisturbed thickness on a forgotten dresser Pipsqueak had removed her paint supplies from last summer.

Books.

He was looking for books with nursery rhymes his mother used to read to them as kids. Some he remembered some he didn't. Making his way around tables, chairs and floor lamps to a pile of boxes, his mouth curved upward. His mother, pack rack of all time, couldn't throw anything away. She kept precious childhood memorabilia, clothes, toys, school projects all secured in cardboard.

Gage began shifting boxes identified with his or Pipsqueak's name, age and the school year looking for the books. The tenth box stopped him. Boldly printed on the top in black marker like the others was Nikki's name. Nosey, he flipped the lapels expecting similar memories and art projects from her school years.

What lay inside heightened his curiosity and he picked up a handful of envelopes. The first was a birthday card then a mother's day and another for Christmas that Nikki had given his mother. Each, expressing sentimental thoughts and thanks for being there. More of the same accompanied a plaster imprint of Nikki's hand from kindergarten. His mouth curved a second time. The pudgy cast didn't hold a lighted candle next to her sleek slender hands of today. Unfolding pictures she had painted and drawn throughout elementary school, each was of female models wearing elaborate fashions. Looking through them first surprised then sorrow almost sold him out. She didn't draw the standard backyard scenes of family picnics and siblings because she never had either except what his family had offered.

Stuffing the remembrances back into the box, a smaller envelope dropped to the floor from between the cards he held. He tossed the rest inside and picked up the envelope, noting postage with no return address. He didn't know why he felt the urge to read it, but removed the card and stared at the writing.

∾

Dear Precious Paula,

Words will never describe your caring during this trying time in my life. This was the hardest thing for me to do, yet in the middle of it all you were there for me. Your love and comfort means the world to me. I think of you as the mother I never had. I'll always love you. Thank you for all your love and support before and during my recovery.

Love you forever, Nicole

A hard punch smacked Gage in the middle of his chest. Caught off guard, *recovery from what?* He flipped the envelope and noted the postage date before he reread the card a second time. His insides tumbled out in gushes as his mind conjured up several scenarios. He examined the climactic words, deeply feeling the solitude of Nikki's loneliness.

He needed to find out what had happened to her and remembering his mission, stuffed the card and envelope into his uniform shirt pocket. Gage closed the box and moved it with the others continuing his search for old books. At almost eight-thirty in the morning, he looked up and saw a bookshelf in a back corner. He dodged more junk and hurriedly scanned shelves eventually spotting the book of nursery rhymes on the bottom. Grabbing it, he doused the light, hurried out of the house and drove to the station. Mac had called from his cell phone having the same idea he had to warm up—a shower.

Gage arrived at Town Hall and made fresh coffee before sitting down to look through the worn and yellowed book. The Xeroxed rhyme lay next to it. Since the verse emphasized a baby dying and or being lost in the woods, he searched endlessly. Leafing through pages in the book on no sleep, he finally found what he was looking for.

The Babes in the Wood nursery rhyme spoke of two children dying in the woods and he highlighted each divergent line on one of the copies, writing in the correct words along with additional notations. The killer's poem had been typed and written with reference to only one child. Two lines, *brought rosary peas,* and, *oh, so young a parent to be when history repeats,* were not part of the real poem. Another idea struck him and he scribbled more notes as the station door swung open and his father entered.

"Gage! I just heard. Who was she?"

Closing the book, he covered the copied rhyme. He purposely escaped from the house before his dad came downstairs for coffee, knowing they would only agitate each other. "Who told you? Except Katharine and Nikki, nobody else knew."

"Carter called. The neighbors weren't too happy about being dragged out of bed in the middle of the night."

"Too bad."

"Folks are getting riled—"

"You know what, Dad? I'm fed up with everybody's anger over these murdered girls when no one's willing to help. I'm also sick of you insinuating that I had something to do with their deaths! You could at least give me a little credit."

"Carter thinks, and I agree. We want the FBI to handle this."

The last thing Gage would divulge was his plan, or his thoughts. Only six pertinent people knew of the nursery rhyme and it would stay that way considering it was a brand new clue.

"Carter doesn't know shit! The *only* thing he cares about is folks calling him in the middle of the night. I'm well aware of the complaints about me but I'll persist until they tell me what they know. Carter, you, the whole damn town will have to deal with the harassment, Dad."

Mac entered the station and his father swung around.

"Mac, try to talk some sense into this knothead. You need to get the FBI involved in these serial killings."

"Frank, Gage is the police chief. Using me as a go between isn't gonna solve the real problem between the two of you. I'll do what he says, not what you or anyone else on this island wants."

"Fine. We'll just take matters into our own hands."

"Be my guest, Frank. You already decided that long before you ever walked in here."

A common scowl formed on his father's face just before it hardened. Then his dad stormed out.

"Mac—"

"Forget it. We'll be seeing a lot more of that and I'm definitely familiar with repercussions. By the way, I got a hold of Claire Huntington early this morning. I told her what we had and she'll be here sometime this afternoon. I called Cole as well. He wants to know if you want him to continue with statements or help here. Sanders gave him carte blanche."

"Has he uncovered anything?"

"Nada."

"Call him and tell him to come back. Mac, I have a hunch we've all been going about this the wrong way. I want to run it by this profiler—what'd you say her name was?"

"Claire Huntington."

"I wanna talk to her before I say anything and screw myself even more. Take a look at what I was working on."

Taking the book and piece of paper from him, Mac scanned the handwritten notes. The way his sergeant shot him an astonished look hit him with a physical impact.

"Damn, Gage! We eliminated the possibility with the first dead victim. Do you think?"

He nodded. "Just keep it between us for now."

CHAPTER 9

❀

"Maw, that boy of yours is mule stubborn...,"

Paula denied her husband her full attention this morning and pitched memorized ingredients into a bowl. Lord knew they had plenty of treats in the house with the holidays. But she always went overboard baking when she needed time alone in her head. Today her mind was certainly on other things besides her family's favorite applesauce cookies and her husband's complaints. After thirty-five years, she could whip the cookies up in her sleep. Over the years, she'd learned how to block out Frank's blathering, too.

No, she mused, more importantly was the idea that had been egging her on for weeks. As she mixed up her hubby's favorite cookie, she inched closer to him one step at a time. She needed to persuade the man she loved more than life itself. A rigid thinking, close-minded, confident, stubborn, controlling man. Many days slipped by with her debating why she put up with all his faults, except she knew very well she had a few of her own bad habits. The same way she knew God never dished out more than she could handle. The good Lord had granted her with everything she had ever dreamt of needing, too. She reckoned it was time she gave back.

The plotting going on in her mind wasn't for herself. It was for her first born. Every now and then kids needed a kick in the backside without knowledge that they were being shoved toward something they couldn't do themselves. Paula smiled to herself. Travis' grandma-ma, Julia Perry, such a spirited woman she was, agreed. She liked the Baines and the Perrys. Polite Michelle being such a kind-hearted woman deserved Travis for what life had dealt her troubled family. Normally an impartial onlooker, Paula's heart ruptured when Katharine explained the horrific events Michelle had suffered in that awful first marriage. And Elizabeth and Aidan with all their misfortunes. So sad, Elizabeth living only to mourn her son. Just didn't seem fair to any of them, including Michelle's mother who had once been such a delightful person. Paula didn't quite understand how anyone could ignore those two adorable grandchildren either, but then she never lost a child.

Her dear, dear Nicole. Well, she might just as well be an orphan like Caitlin with parents prancing on every side of the world not devotedly attached to their only child. Whether it was legitimate or not, Nicole felt like her very own daughter—*was* her adopted child in some ways. For crying out loud, she'd known forever the significance of those sparked emotions between her son and the girl she felt she raised herself. If she didn't nudge them now, those two were gonna keep on sparring words until the end of time.

Indeed, she alertly observed Nicole's instant affection for Caitlin. For that matter, Caitlin had latched onto her son as well as Nicole, but then Gage never could resist a child, especially one who needed his help. Paula felt as sure as her heart beat life into her old bones God brought these three people together purposely. She interpreted years ago how stuff happens for a reason. Her doubts were slim that God would boot her out of the church for interfering this once. Nope. We were put here to help others and it was time she made her contribution. Indeed, she was going to meddle.

"…Paula, are you listening to me?"

"Honestly, Frank. You're being over dramatic. He can fight his way out of the same wet paper sack you had to. Why is it that the kids always belong to me when you've had words with them? What was it this time?"

"How's he gonna catch a killer? He should be calling the FBI to solve these murders."

Paula reached for the eggs. She also knew without Frank speaking his mind what he thought of their son's sexuality. That was at the core of her husband's real frustration, not how Gage did his job. She didn't dare bring that up when she wanted something from him. He threw a fit if she talked openly about sex. Paula almost chuckled aloud. So frisky, and so narrow-minded. If Frank would just open his eyes, he could see what was as big as the old girl that surrounded their rock. Gage was straight as a pin.

"You're jealous because it's not you working on these murders, Frank. You know very well, Carter always harassed you the same way he's harassing Gage. Let *our* son do his job, Frank. He knows what he's doing. After all, you trained him."

She heard the newspaper rustle and without looking, knew that dear sour-puss man of hers was gawking at her with his mouth open. "Frank, I've been thinking about Caitlin. She's doing very well here. Uprooting her to send her off to another foster home would be very difficult when she's suffered so much at such a young age."

"What are you saying?"

Paula shifted about. "What I'm saying is that we should keep Caitlin here with us."

His jaw dropped. "You want to adopt her?"

Exasperated, she sighed. "No, Frank. I just want her to stay with us until someone does adopt her. She's a good child and no bother at all."

"Paula, you'll get attached like you've always done. It'll break your heart when she has to leave."

"I'll deal with that when it happens. I want her to stay with us, Frank. Please, it means a lot to me." She knew he didn't understand when they had twin grandchildren on the way, but he always gave into her wishes.

"Fine. I'll call and make the arrangements."

Elated, Paula nudged up against him and kissed the top of his balding head. "Thank you, my precious."

🍁   🍁   🍁

She hadn't slept but Nicole did dream—wild chaos and a crying woman haunted her semi-conscious. The telephone drew her from the nightmare first, followed by a frivolous tap touching the front door. Nicole stumbled over and answered the phone then hung up as Katharine shuffled toward the door. It only took an instant for her to recall the previous night's events.

"Katharine, I just heard. How's Nicole?" Michelle asked proceeding inside.

"Long night, but I think she'll survive. Who called, Nicole?"

"Another hang up. I need coffee."

Massaging an immense kink from her neck, she plodded into the kitchen and brushed slips of falling hair off her face. Burned pizza lingered in the air. Cranky and irritable, she snuck a peek through the window. The only remains from last night were yellow crime scene tape and the abrupt imprint of the girl's body beneath another new layer of snow.

"What hang-ups?" Katharine followed. "What're you talking about?"

Nicole came to a sudden stop, connecting with the piercing blue eyes Katharine shared with Gage. Brother and sister had the same look when angry or inquiring. "A wrong number," she stated grimly. "A misdial. How hard can it be to understand?"

Michelle had joined them and Katharine persisted, "How long have you been getting them?"

The kink in her neck quickly churned into a raw headache. She finished the coffee ritual and flipped the on switch. "A month or so. Why? It's just some mortified idiot afraid to admit they dialed wrong."

"Nicole, you need to tell Gage."

Both her friends were standing there with doubtful twists around their mouths. With a sideways glance out of the corner of her eye, she saw it and betrayed nothing of her annoyance. "Why?"

"It might be related to last night."

"You can't be serious," Michelle blurted. "How are the murders related to Nicole?"

As Katharine quickly explained what she observed in the backyard, Nicole scorned the fact it confirmed what Gage had told her. She had no clear understanding or reason how or why she could be on the serial killer's list of intended victims. Why would this nimrod want to come after her?

"Nicole, if you don't tell Gage, I will."

The annoyance increasing, her patience sinking, her back stiffened rigidly, Nicole intersected her arms. "For chrissake, Katharine! I'm not some poor bastard who needs your pistol packin' protection. I've been taking care of myself my entire life. I don't need you or your brother saving my ass."

"Those quick, sharp remarks aren't gonna keep that ass of yours from being the next victim, Nicole."

Erecting her posture more, she had no argument but was definitely in the mood to fight with somebody. Katharine's squared-off jaw was the silent signal the battle was about to begin. Nicole took a quick deep breath.

"I have an idea," Michelle interrupted. "Let's work on the details for the baby shower today."

"I can't," Nicole snapped, maintaining the stare-down with Katharine.

"Well, then let us help you finish the plans for the party," she pleaded.

"Rosemary and I are meeting to finalize those today."

"I'm sure Rosemary would happily come here and we could all help," Michelle urged.

Shifting, Nicole blew out, "I have to finish the invites, make reservations for the orchestra, go over the menu with Jacque and meet with Ted. Can you do all that, Michelle? Can you get everything ready that has to be done for New Year's Eve? You wanna help?"

Michelle nodded.

"Fine. Tell Sylvie she's invited to the party."

"I can—"

"Niminy-piminy! You're all becoming ultimate nutjobs over this. Just get the hell out of here and leave me alone."

Whirling around, Nicole poured a premature mug of piping hot coffee, tightening her hand around the cup.

"Nicole, stop trying to blame Michelle for the anger and frustration you're feeling. We're only trying to help you."

She swung around shooting daggers at both of them. "Why? Because you all feel a need to pamper me. Because I'm the motherless bitch who doesn't know any better. I don't need help from either one of you and I don't need your patronizing sympathy."

Michelle let out a startled gasp. Katharine gawked in disbelief at her. What she just said to the two people who meant the most left her humiliated and deflated.

And where did the motherless bitch comment come from anyway?

Nicole gulped hot coffee from the mug. It burned but the punishment didn't dissolve the feelings welling inside of her. Strangling out the words, she muttered, "I have to get ready for work."

"Nicole, all you've been doing is working. As I recall, you gave me a similar speech not long ago. You need to slow down. Besides, there's something I need to talk to both of you about."

Nicole was already leaving the kitchen, but the sound of Michelle's voice compelled her to stop. She did work long hours to ignore personal grief. She faced both women silently wishing she hadn't said what she did, really did want to be alone with her haggard thoughts. Neither would understand a blasted thing, especially Michelle. Nonetheless, Michelle's pleading eyes coaxed her to listen.

"Michelle, what's wrong?" Katharine asked.

"Well, my dad called last night. He and my mother are getting a divorce."

A momentary flicker of pain skipped through Michelle's green eyes as guilt clunked Nicole in the chest. She didn't need this added on top of everything else. For some reason though, Michelle's news reminded her of Tommy Johnson and their first teen dance. They were thirteen and in seventh grade. They thought they were so smart back then. Infatuated with the nincompoop,

Michelle floated on clouds after he asked her onto the dance floor. Giddy delirium followed in Michelle's wake that entire evening, until later, when she witnessed Tommy in a caliginous corner with his hands inside Mary Sue Potter's sweater. The look on Michelle's face right now reminded Nicole of that disappointing evening.

The recollection and Michelle's trusting face sunk her and Nicole stumbled, opening her arms while tears slithered down her cheeks. "Oh, hon, I'm really sorry. Are they sure they can't work it out?" she asked more to rid herself of past blame and squeezed Michelle close.

"Dad said he and Mom had a bad argument about betrayal and responsibility. She's not willing to take responsibility for what she did and he feels betrayed. My dad told her he wants the divorce. I guess Mom's moving out of the house."

"Honey, I am so sorry." Nicole let go and wiped moisture away when Katharine inched closer.

"How are you holding up?" Katharine asked.

"It shocked me, but it doesn't hurt. Not like what she did. I suppose it was bound to happen under the circumstances. Travis is the amazing one. He just keeps giving."

"Why does that surprise you?" Nicole asked in a more sober voice.

"It doesn't really. I'm just not used to it. Nicole, you were right all along about him. I'm sorry I once took out my frustration on you." Michelle looked at Katharine. "Both of you."

"Michelle, we've used each other for punching bags and support through the bad and the good," Katharine told her. "That's what friends are for."

"You guys are the best," she responded hugging both. "Now," she said looking at Nicole, "if what Katharine says has any truth, please, please don't be as foolish as I was."

"She's got a point, Nicole. We're both here to help no matter what kind of grumpy-ass rat you turn into."

"I'm sorry," she muttered.

"Now, you might be motherless, but you're definitely not a bitch."

Nicole swallowed hard, biting back tears. "I never meant any of what I said. I just don't understand why this crazed killer might be after me."

"I don't want to upset either one of you, but, Nicole, the fact the killer is still out there and has changed his MO makes us all suspicious. Whether our fear is real or not, none of us want anything to happen to you."

"Omigod, if anything happened to you, I don't know what I'd do. Nicole, please do what they ask."

"But what does it have to do with me?"

"We don't know yet," Katharine told both of them. "It could be someone with a personal vendetta against you."

Nicole's eyes splayed.

"It could also be some slimeball who ventured into the tavern and has a fetish for you. The important thing is to tell Mac and Gage about anything and everything, like the hang-up phone calls. There's ways of protecting you but not if you don't keep them informed. Nicole, we do love you and I'm sorry to make you worry, but I'd rather have you alert with fear than walking around oblivious to the problem."

"Katharine's right. The biggest mistakes we make are to pretend that it can't happen to us. I thought that."

"Why are you going in early today?" Katharine asked. "Is it really necessary?"

"I wasn't lying. I have a ton of things to do. Besides, I don't want to be here, in this house. I hate this stupid place and everything it stands for."

Large amounts of gut-wrenching sadness absorbed their eyes. In that moment, a flash of wild grief ripped through Nicole because she kept a whole lotta crap from her two best friends. She should have left La Pointe years ago. None of this would be happening to her now—to them. "I have to get ready," she said, turned and fled.

Michelle and Katharine exchanged worried expressions.

"What're we gonna do?"

"There's not much we can do, Michelle. We both know how she feels. I'm just wondering what she's not telling us."

"You mean about her and Gage?" Michelle asked.

"No, their fights make it obvious to everyone but them. I mean there's *something* she's not telling us. Whether it has to do with the dead girls, or what, Nicole is definitely keeping something from us. You've been around her since college. What's she been doing besides waiting for Gage to hang his belt on her bedpost?"

"Katharine Dobarchon, I keep forgetting we can't keep anything from you. This coffee aroma is getting to me," Michelle said, pouring herself a small cup. "I'm afraid I'm guilty of not noticing until recently."

"My guilt comes from the fact that I haven't been here. We're not the best kind of friends to have are we?"

Taking a sip, Michelle winced at the strength and the question, set the cup aside. "If you hadn't come back here this summer and brought us together like you always did, Nicole and I were on the verge of growing further apart. You think she'll really leave the island and move out to the West Coast?"

Katharine found orange juice in the fridge and poured herself a glass after dropping bread in the toaster.

"I did tell Travis about it—"

"So much for faithful friendships," Katharine grimaced. "I told Mac. You know it'll kill my brother if she does move, and knowing Nicole, she'll do it out of spite."

"Travis knows this Chantilly Mackinaw. He said he designed two buildings for her. My new husband definitely has me figured out. He promptly refused any involvement that would keep Nicole from getting the job. Oh, and although Gage wouldn't admit it, I'm pretty sure he's been hearing Nicolina."

"How do you know that?"

"Last night at the Tavern. He was with us for a short time until all the male attention Nicole gets drove him out."

Michelle quickly explained their entire conversation to Katharine along with Gage's abrupt departure. "Don't forget the comment she made the day of my wedding."

"What was that?"

"In your bedroom when we started giving her a bad time about Nicolina, she blew us off because she didn't need to be rescued."

"Michelle, I don't want to worry you but this is really starting to look more and more like the killer's ultimate goal is her."

"I was afraid you were going to say that. I don't want to believe it. I mean why?"

"I didn't want to believe it either."

"Who do you think is after her?"

"I dunno."

"Katharine, are you aware she and Gage have been in love with each other forever?"

"Well, now I am but what makes you so sure when all they've ever done is verbally abuse each other?"

"I saw it in their faces Thanksgiving Day at your mother's house. Gage wouldn't confirm it the other night when I asked him, however he didn't deny it either."

Katharine located a new jar of grape jam, opened it and smeared it on her toast. She pulled out a chair at the kitchen table plopping down. "Interesting. I admit when I first came back, I suspected something, but then well, everything happened at once. I wonder why they haven't acted on their feelings—" Katharine groaned and rubbed her tummy.

"What is it?"

"These little guys are kicking up a storm this morning. I'm sure it's just a preview of the fights they'll have with each other growing up."

Michelle smiled. "You're so lucky to be having twins. Do you want boys or girls?"

"A boy for me, a girl for Mac. He asked if one is a girl, could her middle name be Clarissa after his niece. I told him he could name her Clarissa if he wanted to but he thought it would be difficult for his sister."

"Have you picked out any boy names yet?"

"Not really. I forgot to tell you that Iola called me the other day. She said she's gonna keep the shop one more year. I still have a job and first dibs on buying if Mac and I want it."

"Really? That's wonderful! It'll give you a chance to adjust with the babies."

"Well, I don't know anymore. That plan changed when we found out I was pregnant. Right now, I'm more inclined to want to stay at home."

"Katharine, would you be willing to work from home?"

"Yeah. But doing what?"

"I've been putting off hiring someone. I can't continue much longer. Saundra called to tell me how pleased she was with your fence designs for her yard. I haven't worked out any details, but how would you like to work for me? If you did, it would save me having to find an office and we can set you up with a computer at your house."

"Are you serious? I'm not real efficient on a computer."

"We've got all winter to teach you. I'm after your talent, and maybe we could sell your sketches as well. I've wanted to expand the business to the mainland, but can't offer benefits yet and really need help. Are you interested?"

"You've definitely kindled my interest."

"Great, then—"

Both women lurched when Nicole let out a scream. Katharine pulled her weapon and led as they bolted for the bedroom. She stopped in the hallway, signaled Michelle to wait and crept closer to the open door.

"Jesus," she muttered, re-holstering her nine.

"What is it?" Michelle asked nervously, stepping forward.

"...*babies gone, Brian's gone—Gage!...can't stop...I killed 'em.*"

"What's she saying?"

"I don't know, but we better wake her outta that nightmare."

Before they made it over to the bed, Nicole screamed a second time. She screamed so loud Michelle sucked in wind and Katharine felt an incredibly all too familiar fear deep within her stomach. She took a deep breath and moved to Nicole's side sitting on the edge of the bed. "Nicole. Nicole, it's a bad dream. Wake up."

Her eyes flew open.

"Are you okay? You were having a nightmare," Katharine said.

She licked her lips and swallowed dryly as the two women stared at her. Chained events were arousing the old memories, the uncertainties. Nicole sat up and shouldered herself flat with the headboard. She felt trapped by their penetrating eyes and thought for sure both were reading the thoughts in her mind.

"Stop looking at us like we're devil spawn, Nicole. You started screaming and we came running in here. Are you okay?"

"I thought you two left. I must've fallen asleep."

"Sweetie, you're sopping wet with sweat. What were you dreaming about?" Michelle asked. "Never mind. I know how stuff in one's life can torture the subconscious."

"I need a shower," Nicole muttered.

She scrambled off the bed and walked around both of them as if they owned a contagious disease. "Please, don't be here when I come out."

Michelle looked at Katharine after Nicole slammed the bathroom door. "You know she's always been there for us. We can't let her down, Katharine. But you're right. She's definitely keeping something from us."

"Come on, let's leave her be for now."

CHAPTER 10

❁

Claire Huntington looked FBI. She made a lot of eye contact, had an erect and powerful posture. The unity of her tailored suit only added to the head-to-toe authority of her PhD. She even had an orderly face with equal distances from a dark hairline to brow to nose to chin, and electric blue eyes. Attractive, but well regulated Gage mused.

The moment she entered their insignificant office in Town Hall he knew her. He'd done his homework. Regardless, no one came to Madeline Island looking this formal or stiff, and Gage rose from his chair.

"I'm here to see Gage LeNoir and Mac Dobarchon."

"I'm Gage. Mac's catching forty in the back."

"Claire Huntington," she said as they exchanged handshakes. "I expected someone older."

"Two years earlier you would've gotten someone older. Have a seat, Ms. Huntington. You want some coffee?"

"Claire. Thanks, I'll pass," she said, pulling up a chair.

"Fine." Gage sat after refilling his mug. "We'll have the crime lab reports on last night's victim later today or tomorrow for you. In the meantime, there's a few things I'd like you to clarify for me."

"Such as?"

"The difference between murder styles and their characteristics."

"Been doing the groundwork, Chief?"

He dipped his head over the cup brim. "Seems to me, a murderer's quirks can all overlap."

"Absolutely. First, let me explain. People can be very normal in some situations and completely disturbed in others. The key is what motivates the behavior. Is it love, greed, or pain? There's a class of personalities that prompt murder. The motive and common denominator are always self-interest. The justification for the act comes from irrational emotions."

"A killer sees no difference between a need to kill and their desire to commit the brutal act?" Gage asked.

"That's right. Understanding people is endlessly engaging. It's like peeling away the layers of their skin to get to the center of the psychological puzzle that makes the individual what he or she is. Another key is to know there is no sharp line between normal and pathological behavior."

Leaning back, he asked, "How do you peel away the skin when you don't know who the individual is?"

"Traits cluster together but are rarely exclusive to one personality. There are twenty adult styles. Although the positive or negative traits of those styles may differ, they may also be alike. Extraordinary circumstances will expose certain traits."

"Making your profile."

"Yes. Certain characteristics also tell us things. Periods of life will create predictable issues as well. Teens often need to have identity so they color their hair purple and wear a nose or tongue ring. It's similar to the way a midlife man or woman identifies with their own mortality. A happily married man may turn forty and see his life going down the tubes. He believes he needs to revitalize his youth and seeks out an affair with a twenty-year-old, or he goes out and buys a sports car."

"Uh-huh. What about people who commit murder?"

"Most aren't career criminals and no one style exists."

"Tell me how you came about labeling this particular murderer a psychotic serial killer?"

"I never officially labeled him psychotic. I said he probably has schizophrenic tendencies and most likely lives out a deep-seeded fantasy with killing. Murder is an attempt to fulfill his fantasy. With each murder, he becomes better, more ritualized. The ritual gives meaning to the killer."

"Sounds psychotic to me."

"The psychosis of a murderer is a mental disorder characterized by symptoms of delusion or hallucinations and indicative of their impaired contact with reality. A serial offender picks strangers for victims. The fact your victims are all Native American females, sixteen, and each scene is identical suggests the ritual, which probably means the killer is psychotic. He doesn't know the victims personally. He may hear voices telling him to kill. The delusions could suggest persecution, or that the killer thinks he's someone else with a job to do. He or she may also believe an evil force is pursuing them. I believe Green Bay PD and Mac suggested all of those scenarios. They labeled him psychotic. Without medical documentation, I can't officially confirm it."

"Well," Gage snarled, "aren't all serial killers psychotic?" He caught the flicker in her eyes indicating her displeasure with his sarcasm.

"Chief, we don't know that Patriot suffered delusions or that he was out of touch with reality. There are no records to indicate he'd ever been hospitalized. His background strongly suggests he needed professional help. The truth is, mentally ill people are not generally violent criminals. However, violent criminals are often mentally ill. Serial killing simply means sequential."

Whether from forty-seven hours without sleep, or Claire Huntington's long winded explanations, Gage's brain cells were taking a nosedive. She did seem to know her stuff and he willed himself to stay in the game. "Do you really believe Patriot was a copycat versus being psychotic?"

"What I believe and what I can back up aren't always the same, Chief."

"Do you believe he knew the real serial killer?"

"Possibly. A serial killer sometimes will take a trophy of their victim like a ring or body part. In this case each scene is identical, the bracelet and bottle of liquor. Those two items are symbolic to your killer for some reason. Like a trophy, they make a strong statement. Patriot used the liquor but he didn't kill his victims with paraquat. Instead, he actually used the bean inside the rosary pea. Why? Symbolic to him in some way, the same way the bracelet left on the wrists of the dead girls is symbolic to the killer who uses paraquat to kill. If Patriot knew the real killer, I suggested his search for dominance came from choosing his own method. Why he copied, we'll never know. It could have been for recognition in the public eye or caused from maltreatment by his father. His search for identification. Regardless, we need to figure out the significance of that specific liquor and the bracelet."

The more she told him the more questions he logged but needed sleep in order for her answers to make sense. "Then you're convinced he copied versus being an accomplice?"

"I can only speculate but generally I'm accurate. Yes, I believe that. Why?"

He wasn't ready yet to bounce his new theory off Claire Huntington. "Mac tell you about last night's victim?"

"Yes. It was very well planned suggesting the search for recognition through perfection, and or an offering to fulfill a misdeed or lack of perfection. Possibly, it's leading to an even greater ultimate sacrifice. Either way, Chief, your killer is working his way up to the perfect murder. Why the perfect murder? is the question of the hour."

"So what you're telling me is that all these styles can overlap, invariably creating confusion for us."

"Some, not all, will overlap with others. It's not completely confusing when one has been taught and trained."

Her reply wasn't intended as insult and Gage didn't take it as such. "Is it possible we could have ourselves a psychotic simmering style murderer repeatedly committing the offense to lead up to, say, the perfected sacrament?"

"A simmering style would suggest accumulative hostility, history of frustration, incapability of working out conflict, or feelings of abrupt rejection. The killer could be seeking revenge for perceived wrong, which definitely means multiple victims. Yes, it's very possible."

"Murdering would be a relief for them. They would see it as restitution?"

"Yes. Because they can't deal with the increasing tension murder causes."

"Can the act be precipitated by anger or jealousy enhancing the need for perfection?"

Claire nodded.

What the hell, he thought. He was on a roll now and continued. "What about the time delay in exposing the dead victims? Paraquat takes roughly seven days to kill. However, eight of nine victims weren't discovered until rigor mortis set in. Stacy White hadn't been dead long enough to freeze before discovery, but we think the killer kept her inside before exposing her because rigor was there."

"She was also discovered on private property, not public, correct?"

Gage nodded this time.

"Mac said the person who found her wasn't expected home at that time. The location signifies a private battle. It also indicates that the killer wanted the owner of the property to find the body. The killer wanted only this person to find the girl, but at a precise time. Those facts also suggest this homicide was personal. The property owner could very possibly be the ultimate sacrifice and the next victim."

He did not like where this conversation was going and remembered what Katharine said. "So anyone could be jealous of the owner or angry with her then?"

"Her?" Claire asked.

"Nicole Jarvis is the owner of the property and found the dead girl. Well, technically her parents own the property but they don't live here. The eighth victim who died of paraquat poisoning was also discovered at her place of business."

"Simmering style fits with those well thought out plans. Mac said you discovered the theft of the poison."

Gage acknowledged.

"The theft and use of that specific chemical also implies the murders are well planned. It fits with the length of time the killer possibly wants the victim to suffer. Say maybe for some personal suffering the killer has had to deal with. I believe that sacrifice may be the Jarvis wom—"

"Why?" Gage erupted. "Why her?"

"A jealous ex-lover or boyfriend. Someone who's angry with her for something she may have done to the killer. It could even be a perceived wrong. I'm making an assumption she's Native American. What does she do for a living?"

The woman was as mechanical as a robot and just became extremely unpopular with him for assuming Nikki had lovers. He smirked. "She's as white as you and I and manages the local tavern."

"Perhaps she innocently insulted a patron, even a tourist who doesn't live here."

"But why would the killer have begun his or her spree in Green Bay first? Why not just do them all here if the plan were to kill Nicole from the very beginning?"

Claire studied the police chief for a moment. "Why did you just refer to the killer as *her*?"

"I said his or her. As in you also mentioned, 'he or she' may believe an evil force is pursuing them," he replied, realizing his brain *was* keeping up.

Claire nodded reluctantly. "I can't answer those questions. Perhaps the killer is a vacationer from Green Bay. Regardless, I definitely want to see the evidence from last night's crime scene. I also want to speak with the Jarvis woman. There has to be some connection between her and the dead girls. Perhaps between her and the killer and the dead girls."

Gage despised it, but Claire Huntington might be right. He decided the question of the current hour was what was the link between Nikki and the murdered Native American teenage girls? Girls she didn't even know. He handed a clean copy of the nursery rhyme to Claire. "Whaddaya make of this? We found it between the folded hands and chest of last night's victim."

She read it over and glanced up as Mac crept slowly into the office from the back room.

"Claire, thanks for coming," he said, advancing and extending his hand.

"Hi, Mac," she responded, rising. "How are you doing?"

"Not bad, except for a severe lack of sleep."

"Your Chief and I were having a similar conversation to the one you and I had."

"Did Gage tell you about his theory yet?"

"I think we were just getting to that."

"Gage, let's take Claire over to the tavern for supper tonight. Cole should be here by then."

Yawning, he answered, "Sure. Have you checked into a room yet?" he asked the FBI agent.

"No, I came here first."

"You wanna get checked in?"

She nodded.

"Good," Gage said. "Right now my brain has malfunctioned. I'm going home to grab a couple hours. We'll meet back here at six."

CHAPTER 11

❀

Rosemary Baines left the Tavern after the anniversary party's fine points were finely tuned to completion. Jacque would determine the menu for a sit down dinner of four hundred twenty-five guests. It was customary to have more versus coming up short. La Pointe's couple hundred residents were responding enthusiastically, however, the already mailed invitations were slow to confirm. Nicole corroborated hotel reservations for the orchestra as well. Doing everything humanly possible to make this special for Travis and his grandparents involved lengthy hours of meticulous details, and money, which Travis had plenty.

Nicole pulled out her compact mirror. With only three hours of troubled sleep this morning, mothball-type pouches had been constructed under her eyes. Makeup disguised those puffy sacks. Too bad cosmetics couldn't disintegrate the insecurities of the slow agonized torture eroding her insides. Nicole dropped the compact back into her desk drawer.

The latest murder submerged her brain in deep fry faster than a northeast gale could whisk punishment across their island. They were all nuts for even thinking the murdered girls had anything to do with her. She'd never met any of them except for poor Jessica. Had never heard of the others. Sealing the last formal invitation, she decided her mind all screwed up. Having beaten a self-imposed deadline to mail the note cards by almost a week, she would mail the monogrammed envelopes on her way out. The New Year's Eve liquor had arrived. She confirmed the live music for New Year's Eve and made reservations for the orchestra in January an hour ago. Leaning back, she blew out an indrawn breath.

Jacque whirled more bad news at her first thing this morning. Nick, their second chef, gave his resignation. She had one other distasteful task to deal with before the day ended, then Ted wanted to see her.

All day she re-speculated on the belief that the murders had anything to do with her in between the trials of managing the tavern. She didn't readily make enemies and strongly doubted what Katharine said. However, her once peaceful life had hastily been saturated with ugliness. Maybe the linked events that began in July had unlocked her subconscious. Or that disturbing nightmare this morning. Might be a man's kiss opening old wounds that caused her reflections to flip hurriedly. Having forgotten the first time Gage kissed her, she hadn't lied to him. His second kiss left her sucking wind backward and confusing logic with renewed passion. The emotions mingled with one single day fifteen years ago—a lifetime—stored guilt now dawning.

If she'd never done what she had, Brian Callihan would still be alive. Michelle would still have a mother and brother who loved her. And Aidan and Elizabeth Callihan wouldn't be divorcing. As if those flipping thoughts traded place with the present, she drifted backward right along with them.

Spending hours in front of a vanity mirror engaged in the art of putting on appearances wasn't abject. On the contrary, it raised Nicole's spirits immensely. Loving long walks, a day at the beach triggered a need for capturing healthy doses of sunshine along Madeline's shore, so off she went.

A new way of looking, a new way of feeling created a captivating image. After all, she just read in her favorite teen magazine, Seventeen, how they describe themselves as 'Where the girl ends and the woman begins'. Being the same age, wasn't she striving to be a woman? In many ways she already was. She prepared herself daily using femaleness, charm, and dying attempts to illuminate her popularity all on her own.

Everyone, except her parents and a blond witch named Josie Hanson, liked her. Nicole didn't like her classmate on principle. The floozy was a natural without a clue of how to enhance her God-given beauty. She used hideous color on her badly manicured fingernails, doused her pretty face with too much makeup then dressed for obvious flaunting to get a handful of man. The fact she taunted daddy's money in every girl's face had little bearing on her lack of intelligence where beauty was concerned.

Nicole didn't care. She didn't have to.

But every girl had a dream to move from adolescence into womanhood. She supposed Josie did too. She had another—modeling—world recognition. She studied fashion magazines every free minute she, Katharine and Michelle weren't together. Today her two best friends were working summer jobs. The fact she didn't have to work like they did dunked her confidence. She really had no knowledge whether her parents were wealthy, however, they arranged for her to be taken care of and money was no object.

The last time they called, Nicole refused to mention her career decision to Erica. Aching with inner pain of loneliness, she suspected her mother wouldn't care what she did with her life after high school. This time, her parents were in Egypt for at least six months digging up the remains of whomever. Why? she had no idea. Unfortunately, the mistake her parents made was left behind with the most recent houseguest. A pert little caretaker named Lilly. Lilly performed her responsibility with little enthusiasm and it really bit. It wasn't bad enough to have parents trekking the world. These days this seventeen-year-old had a thirty-year-old babysitter with little knowledge of housekeeping and a very hungry appetite to nurture cravings for election of the Island's flirt. She even thought about introducing Lilly to Josie.

Though having a babysitter left her with inexplicable feelings of emptiness, she had learned young how to be responsible. She didn't need anyone to take care of her. She also despised Lilly as much as every holiday spent without family. Getting no help from the help, she had already discovered most things on her own, and Lilly was a waste of time and money. Thanks to parental guilt and financial proviso, Paula LeNoir filled the motherly roll and Frank saw to her passing the required tests to get her drivers license. Then mummy and daddie provided a new set of wheels—disgusting, she mused. Having reached a conclusion years earlier, when she married, her kids would never know the destitute feeling of loneliness.

"Hi-ya, sweetcakes."

She recognized the voice and where Brian Callihan was, so would be Gage LeNoir. The two had been best buds for as long as their sisters were best friends with her. Like a swan, she gracefully turned and flashed her practiced, brilliant smile.

Her heart sank. Dark hair and a twinkle in his pale green eyes, this smooth-talking hunk stood alone. He didn't have the machismo to make her young innocent heart go flippity flop. Although the word was he loved women, he loved cars more. A NASCAR t-shirt stretched tight across fiber and flesh. His souped up Mustang, 'Stanger' Brian called it, wasn't enough to budge Madeline Island under her feet. At least not in anyway the gorgeous sunset-haired man who saw everything as black and white did.

"Hi, Bri. Where's Gage?"

"Working. For college this fall."

Her question caused disappointment in Brian that he tried to conceal.

Nicole also knew her own maturity exceeded her years more than her long-legged height exceeded most kids. She excelled past girls Brian's age at every-thing—not that his being a year older made too much difference—but height did. Being taller than every girl in school, most boys too, all legs was positively revolt-ing. Suffering an overnight burst from a boyish outline to boobs, she finally filled out and the saliva dribbling opposite sex suddenly became interested. They were too engrossed in the obvious to pay further attention to her height. As their eyes traveled, she fully comprehended the meaning behind their gawking stares. Brian tried real hard not to look now.

It was one more of many reasons Nicole had set her sights and heart on Gage LeNoir. If he looked at all, his erotic blue eyes revealed nothing. In fact, the only interest he had was to quibble with her, which they'd been doing since time began. Now, that sexy, easy-going man of her dreams would be running off to college. Everyone knew Gage was pursuing a cop career like his father. He had hopes of returning one day and filling his dad's shoes.

"Are you going to college?" she asked.

"Haven't decided. I'd really like to race. Maybe NASCAR or the Indy. But the folks want me to get a degree."

She felt the constant pang of jealousy not having parents to tell her what she should or shouldn't do. "Would you race the Mustang?"

An insignificant eye roll told her that was a stupid question.

"Naw, the Stanger's a classic and not meant for racing."

"Oh," she responded, liking the way Brian didn't verbally ridicule.

Suddenly, he blurted, "Nicole, would you go out with me Saturday night?"

Thinking it over, she had tried everything to get Gage to ask that question. Nicole tilted her head slightly, letting her golden mane billow. What the hell, she thought, Friday's were spent with girlfriends and Saturday's were date night. Maybe Brian would take her dancing to rock and roll. She loved dancing and rarely dictated to the boys who did ask her out what she preferred. It was a test, sort of, to ascertain if a boy's interest was on her breasts or brains.

"Sure," she answered.

"Really?!"

She held back a giggle. "Yes, really."

"Great! I'll pick you up at six. We'll go over to Ashland."

"'kay," she said and flashed an award-winning smile.

Then Brian left. Always the same she mused. They asked her out and left, having no desire to hang out. Maybe this one was different because they'd always been part of each other's lives. She could only hope, but deep down she knew better.

Walking along the shore, Nicole heard the grating giggles before the low, throaty moans began. She kept walking and searching, and came to a halt so hard sand underfoot went flying. Exposed for the world to view there on the rocks Josie Hanson was braless and groping Terry Hunter's exposed and very big dick. Terry was preoccupied with a full mouth of Josie's boobs as his hands moved like pistons ripping off her skimpy shorts. Then he slid his knobby fingers between her thighs, she screeched out a sick cry and he choked on those milk-white balloons.

Not completely sure why, but Nicole's feet wouldn't move on. She watched in total shock as Josie wailed, "Fuck me now!" Terry sucked madly on her tits, grabbed Josie's hips mounting her atop his lap and shoved himself inside while her red-hot steaming thighs wrenched around his waist.

Gasping loudly and without thinking, Nicole blew out the words, "Great balls of fire!" Never realizing the words would stay with her forever.

Their sweaty bodies were quickly severed. Terry gaped at her, his face turning as crimson as the marks he left on Josie's pale breasts. He scrambled upward clothing his bare ass, leaving Josie buck-naked. Disgraced, Josie screamed, fixed a sinister glare on Terry before draping a skimpy strapless something-or-other across her front.

Nicole stifled her giggles with a deliberate hand gesture as Josie's chest heaved and swelled in additional rage. Unable to hold back, she roared with laughter, and the little slut shot her a doomed look as hard and brittle as glass.

"Getting our daily workout?" Nicole snickered more.

"What're you doing sneaking around here you motherless bitch?"

Pitching her wrath, Nicole sneered back, "This is public property. I would think with your daddy having a motel, you'd be using one of his rooms for your indiscretions."

"You prissy, motherless bitch!"

"Better than a slut," Nicole tossed back repugnantly and spun on her heal. Laughing aloud, she definitely had to tell Katharine and Michelle. In fact, she couldn't wait to expose Josie Hanson—pun intended.

Waiting for a Saturday night date wasn't nearly as difficult as waiting to spread gossip. Her original plan for the previous was a prescription for inciting jealousy with Gage. After contemplating several scenarios though, Nicole decided it wouldn't be grown-up. Besides, she and Gage already argued enough over her social calendar. Whether he and Brian were best friends or not, Gage had a way of making her feel, well, like what she thought of Josie Hanson. Furthermore, keeping the knowledge of her date with Michelle's brother from her two best friends became very complicated.

So, on a warm summer's eve Brian picked her up promptly at six in the blue Mustang. He brought a single yellow rose—friendship—she fleetingly thought, complimented her newest outfit as Lilly tried in vain to snatch his attention. They caught a ferry over to Bayfield and were off to Ashland.

She heard stories of Brian's wild dates, and asked, "Where you taking me?"

"Thought we'd catch a movie after grabbing a pizza?"

"Cool." She answered, liking both.

The evening flew by smoothly and Brian played the roll of a perfect gentleman, keeping his hands to himself. The only comedown had been his movie choice—a western called 'Draw' just out with Kirk Douglas and James Coburn. She absolutely cursed anything related to cowboys, but she wouldn't hurt Brian's feelings.

Neither did she mind that he brought her home at a decent hour or gave her a kiss goodnight. What really bothered her was getting her first taste of rejecting a decent guy in what would become a long list over years to come. She let him down tenderly when Brian asked her out a second time. As he shoved his hands into the front pockets of his jacket, she saw the hurt in his eyes. They conveyed a sad understanding making her explanation wretched.

"So why'd you go out with me?"

"Brian, I'm sorry. I like you and I'd think you were a decent guy even if you weren't my best friend's brother. I enjoyed the evening but I can't lead you on."

"It's Gage, isn't it?"

"You know?" she shrieked in that juvenile surprise she detested.

"Strongly suspected." He slowly smiled. Under the porch light, he studied her face then said, "You're a beautiful woman, Nicole Jarvis. I hope Gage realizes what a lucky guy he is. I'll see what I can do."

With that, Brian gave her a hug with a peck on the cheek and left upon seeing her safely inside. The idea that someone thought of her as beautiful at a young age, and without trying to feel her up, made her day and night. It made her whole week.

Nicole hadn't been in the house more than five minutes when she heard the shouting out front. Swinging the door wide, Gage was toe-to-toe with Brian.

"Christ! You're my best friend! How could you?"

Nicole couldn't get out fast enough before Gage clenched his fist and swung, knocking Brian to the ground.

"*Gage!*" *Nicole screamed, tossing him a hostile glare.* "*What the hell are you doing?*"

"*Protecting your ass, Nikki!*"

"*Excuse me!*" *Goading him further, Nicole ripped back,* "*Gage Andrew LeNoir! My ass, or whom I go out with, is none of your damn business—*"

"*Guys, wait!*" *Brian heaved out.*

"*Butt out of my life, Gage!*" *Nicole shouted.*

"*You know what, Nikki. You're just as bad as the ones he's bedded.*"

The words and tone in Gage's voice unleashed with vehemence cut deeply. Nicole glared back but an instant before attacking, "*You slimy snake. I hate you, Gage LeNoir!*"

His face dark with a grisly frown, rage crackled in his eyes. He stomped off furiously, Brian scrambling to his feet. "*Nicole, I'm sorry. I'll talk to him.*"

Brian sprinted after Gage but he was faster. The tires of his Chevy pickup sprayed dust and tiny rocks as he raced away on the dirt road with Brian now running. Nicole's eyes no longer burned with crazed rage. They were drenched with tears.

The next day became the worst when Katharine called. "*Nicole! Michelle needs us,*" *came her distraught voice.*

"*Why? What's wrong?*"

"*It's Brian. He's been in an accident—the boat. My dad was there…he's gone, Nicole.*"

"*Gone?*" *Her heart thrashed savagely inside her chest.* "*Katharine, what do you mean, gone?*"

"*They couldn't save him, Nicole.*"

"*What? How?*" *Horrid regrets overwhelmed her. What had she done?* "*What happened? What do you mean?*"

"*I called Michelle the minute I heard. She said Brian was upset about something. You know he always took the boat out when he needed to think. I don't have any details right now, but Michelle's hysterical—we have to get over there.*"

Katharine's strained voice came through loud and clear. But Nicole's ache was internal suffering and as silent as the tears streaming rivers down her cheeks. Brian went out on the boat to think over her rejection and Gage's anger

"*I'm on my way. I'll pick you up in five,*" *she said disconnecting. With no one to comfort her, Nicole burst into lonely sobs.*

The week that followed, Gage shut himself off from the world. He avoided and refused to speak to any of them. She and Katharine crumbled right alongside

Michelle and Sylvie, the youngest of the Callihan children. Michelle's parents, Aidan and Elizabeth were devastated beyond repair.

But, those precious months following that fatal Sunday turned more dismal, murky, as the tragic summer had altered the bond between the three best friends. Michelle had lost a brother, the others a good friend. Completely avoiding her before he did so, Gage went off to college without a word. It worsened her grief. The three best friends whizzed through twelfth grade and high school graduation with less than normal fanfare. The final year when one should cherish priceless memories was lost.

Following graduation, Nicole gave up all hope of happiness and took her first job waiting tables at the Red Rock Tavern. She didn't need money, nevertheless, the busy summer kept her mind occupied—she didn't have time to think about her culpability.

Katharine's plans and desires never deviated. She also followed her father's example and off she went to Stout University in Southern Wisconsin. Normally meticulous and detailed, Michelle changed her mind a dozen times, finally settling on college as well. Everyone who meant anything to her was gone, along with all the—

A tap on her office door summoned Nicole back to the present. She never forgot Gage's return four years—neither had dared to bring up the night that preempted Brian's life, until now. Or, at least that's what she thought he meant when he said they were going to talk about that night. Although she forever felt the powerful emotion internally, she had forgotten the reason she despised Gage as much as she did. Josie's beach exhibition elapsed somewhere between tragedy and time that summer. The motherless bitch comment no longer a mystery, telling Michelle and Katharine about the nude exhibition had completely slipped Nicole's mind along with everything else. She had blocked the manacle of events from her sight and brain right along with the entire weekend. Only because what happened that summer had broke her heart. Remembering now, her heart damn near shattered all over again.

"What is it?" Hastily she swiped at her cheeks and Gypsy entered.

"You wanted to see me?"

"Yes. Come in."

"Nicole, I heard what happened last night. I'm sorry."

"For what?"

"That you had to be the one to find another dead girl. We're all scared out of our minds over this. I just don't understand what's taking Gage so long to catch this parasite."

Taking a breath ready to respond, Nicole decided against saying anything. If her eyes were any sign, words would only provide unnecessary gossip to spread across the island quickly. Reliving the past had crystallized many things today and she'd deal with her thoughts later. Right now, she had to deal with the problem. Her most adequate waitress, uniformed and ready to work had a gold heart. Young, she was a demure little thing, yes sir, yes ma'am. Never instigated stuff between the women employees the way a few of them did. Her name didn't give anyone a clue as to her appearance or background either. She wasn't some vagabond drifting ashore. No, in fact, Gypsy was one of a slew of descendants. Distant cousin to one of the Cadotte's. Michelle knew which.

Always nicely attired, Gypsy quickly mastered the little details that provided success for the tavern. Filling glasses from the side of a pitcher so ice came with it. Not to mention how the twenty-year-old conversed without intrusion and didn't dwell too long with a customer. She had also memorized the menu and daily specials, as well as pertinent ingredients to unusual drinks. Frosting glasses as a way to keep drinks cold wasn't a guarded secret, but the kid always remembered to place mugs in the freezer. Removing the customer's dinner plate too soon was a sore spot with most. It's like Gypsy could read their minds on that one. Yet, her best server had a flaw, and Nicole needed to overcome her sour mood and shoulder up to the managerial task.

"Thank you for caring. Have a seat, would you?" Nicole said needing to find a way to reenergize life back into her body and tortured soul.

"Gypsy, you're very good at what you do here. My problem is the amount of sick days you take. Officially, I can't deny sick leave nor can I ask what's wrong, but I can request a doctor's written excuse. I'm afraid I'm going to have to ask to see one on any future sick days you request. The other servers and I cannot keep filling in for you. I need someone that I know is going to show up once I've put their name on the schedule. Now, I can offer to rearrange your hours or days, but I need to know that you're going to be here once the schedule is finalized."

"That's a relief."

Nicole leaned back. "What's a relief?"

"I thought for sure you were going to fire me."

"Fire—*Gypsy*. You're one of my best. I don't want to lose you. Would it help if we cut back on your hours? Maybe changed them?"

"Well, actually I need more hours to make up for lost time. The problem is my hours overlap with Chuck's and they're going to do so indefinitely. It's really hard to find a sitter for our son."

"Overlap how?"

"He doesn't get home until an hour after I start. We're seriously thinking about moving to the mainland because his job pays more than mine."

"Which means we'd lose you all together and you may still have to find another job." Gypsy nodded as Nicole reached for the schedule. "Working days wouldn't do it for you?"

"No, it wouldn't help at all. I know calling in sick isn't fair to anyone."

"Gypsy, what I need from you today is a guarantee that you'll be here Friday night for New Year's Eve and the Perry Anniversary party on Saturday, January twenty-ninth. I have a meeting with Ted today, and perhaps we can make some schedule changes. Can you give me your word?"

"Yes. Chuck will be home early on New Year's Eve. He knows I have to work that night. He's off on Saturday's which helps."

"Okay. Let me see what I can work out and I'll get back to you."

"Nicole, I sure would appreciate whatever you can do to help me out. I do not want to move off Madeline."

"All right. I have a meeting with Ted, so get to work and I'll see what I can do."

After Gypsy left the office, Nicole wondered if any other employees had scheduling problems. Whenever revisions became necessary, winter was best for tryouts of those changes.

"Nicole, you got time now?"

She looked up. "Ted, I was just coming to see you."

"Here is fine," he said, entering the office and plunking down in a chair. "How are the plans coming for the anniversary party?"

The Red Rock Tavern owner was sixtyish and slight framed making one believe he was a wimp. It contradicted his lively personality. Since being shot in August, his maple-faced coloring had returned weeks ago. Nicole believed those pinkish blotches filled in due to the excitement of the ballroom's start and near completion.

"The plans are set," she answered. "Rosemary was here and we finalized everything. They prefer a dinner and she's okay with Jacque planning the menu. Have you talked to him today?"

"No. Why?"

"Nick gave his notice, but he did promise to stick it out until after the party."

"Nick did?"

She nodded. Although Ted gave her full charge of the servers, she ran everything by him. "I'm also contemplating making some schedule changes or we may be hiring more than a replacement chef."

"Why's that?"

"Gypsy has schedule conflicts at home. Hubby works past her start time, the baby. Normal stuff. I told her I'd see what we could do about rearranging her hours. I don't want to lose her."

"How much will it cost me to keep you here?"

Her brows shot up, her eyes widened with surprise.

"Nicole, I've suspected for awhile you're unhappy. It's rare for you to take three days off in a row. What's it gonna cost me to keep you from accepting another job?"

She pushed herself to a standing position and faced a window. "Nothing. Money's not the issue."

"Then your mind's made up?"

It was pointless to deny what Ted knew and she figured one of three people had told him. She managed a shrug. "I haven't been offered the job yet. Well, not officially."

"Where at?"

"L.A. Designing fashions for Chantilly Mackinaw. I interviewed with her last week."

"I hope finding another dead girl in your backyard isn't the reason you're leaving. Carter, Ben, Frank and I have been talking. We all agree the FBI needs to be handling these murders since Gage can't seem to get the job done."

Nicole disguised her annoyance with serious thought. She detested the way everyone blamed Gage, and wondered if his dad had incited this planned attack against him. Ted certainly couldn't blame Gage for his being shot. Could he? Discreetly glancing at the time, she wanted to be gone by now. "Ted, whatever decision I make has nothing to do with that. I'll let you know the minute I've made up my mind."

"I can't stop you from leaving, but I'd hate to have to replace you." Rising, he asked, "We all set for Friday night?"

She responded with an impersonal nod. "What do you want to do about Nick?"

"Go ahead and run an ad then arrange the interviews with Jacque."

Ted sauntered out of the office without closing the door. She fell into her chair plopping her head in her arms on the desk. The blasted building wailed loudly only serving to increase the headache she woke up with this morning.

How could anyone be convinced Gage wasn't doing everything in his power to catch the Green Bay Serial Killer? How she ever forgot what he said to her that night was another good question. Was that what he wanted to talk to her about? She couldn't stop the courtship of neurotic dreams with the phone calls that Katharine thought might be related to the murders. What about the way Gage had kissed her. Why now? Numbness weighed her down and she was sinking fast. All these years so much hate between so many—her sixth sense broke her thoughts and her head flew up.

He stood in the threshold wearing his uniformed white shirt with jeans and bloodshot eyes. His chin and jaw were masked with a layer of golden stubble. His blue eyes were almost white against a sea of red.

"Nikki, are you okay?"

Looking at him standing there, he looked worse than she felt. Did his wanting to talk about *that* night come from wanting to do a round of debate so many years later? When was the last time he slept or ate a decent meal? "Just tired," she answered.

"How late you working tonight?"

"I'm not. I've been here since early this morning."

When he moved into her office and closed the door, her nerves jangled a little more.

"Nikki, we're gonna have to get a formal statement from you. There's also someone who wants to talk to you."

"Who? About what?"

"She's an FBI agent who's been profiling this case. Mac called her and she's downstairs. We came over here to grab something to eat."

"I'm glad you contacted the FBI."

"I—" he stopped, emphatically asking, "why are you glad?"

She exhaled a deep sigh unwilling to end the day the way it began. "Gage, that wasn't an insinuation. Ted was just here. He knows about my job interview and—"

"I didn't tell him!" he butt in ferociously.

"But you told Katharine and Michelle," she hurled back and rose arming herself for their battle of words.

"I told Katharine. I sure as hell did not tell Ted!"

"Why'd you have to tell anyone at all?" she shouted.

"If you wanted it kept secret, you should've bagged it along with everything else you won't talk about!"

"What's that supposed to—" she froze where she stood. "*Jesus!* You can't possibly know."

"Can't possibly know what?"

"Things aren't as black and white as you always think they are, Gage. Or as simple. I'm sorry. I wasn't accusing you of anything. I think the Town Board is ganging up on you."

She turned away to screen further expressions from him and straightened her desk. He'd struck a chord buried deep inside of her and she was apologizing to him, for what she didn't know.

"How can you possibly believe that I don't know what's going on in this town? Nikki, my dad came by this morning none too happy. They've been ganging up on me since Joe discovered the first body."

Understanding, she tossed a sympathetic look over her shoulder now. "Did you want me to talk to that Profiler tonight?"

"No, too public here. Can you come by the station tomorrow at ten? We'll take your statement and she can talk to you then."

"Yeah, I'll be there."

"Nikki, whether you want to admit it or not, we both know why we keep fighting."

"Gage, don't."

"We've been sidestepping what happened for too many years and it's time to get it out in the open."

"Why, Gage?"

"We can do it now or later, but one way or the other we are going to talk about it."

"Why? The damage is done." He was studying her long and hard, his gestures implied the mounting fury.

"Okay later. But tell me something. Did the paralyzed look I just saw on your face have anything to do with that night?" Then pulling the envelope from his shirt pocket, he asked, "Or does it have something to do with this? You gonna tell me what happened to you?"

She couldn't move when he tossed the envelope atop her desk. She literally could not move any part of her body. She knew where the envelope came from. Could only stand there, gaping wordlessly at piled up paperwork surrounding the card, under the card, near the card, everywhere but at the carded envelope. With her heart pumping hard inside her chest, that stage of her life came back with full force, too.

"O-B-G-Y-N."

The word followed each ringing phone at a reception desk in the center of a supposed-to-be soothing room décor. Hah! The word soothing challenged her wit and confidence Nicole thought as she secretly watched husbands fuss over their wives. First born children were scattered near a toy box while waiting for mom to finish her appointment. It was disgusting to watch and she absolutely did not belong here—anyway not for the reason she was here.

Shifting miserably on a chair presumably made for comfort, Nicole did a time check. Apprehension clouded her mind. Chewing her bottom lip, she decided a long time ago that waiting was the desperate want of things that couldn't be. With another wrist twist, only sixty seconds had ticked away since the last check. She'd been sitting here for more than an hour. When an emergency called Dr. Jamison away, they said she could wait or reschedule.

Re-focusing her gaze through the large window, a bare parking lot increased the hidden fears grating on her nerves. I already know the outcome. It's a prognosis I do not need any doctor to confirm. I can sense the things that go on inside of my body. Especially with this constant sharp pain, but the physical hurt is unparalleled to the agony in my heart. How will I—

"Miss Jarvis, you can come back now."

Nicole looked at the nurse standing in a doorway. A knot in her stomach felt ripe and ready to rupture. She picked up her purse, stood and followed the woman.

"How are you today?" the nurse asked.

"Fine," she replied. An ever-present smell of antibiotics and drugs hit Nicole head-on as she passed through door.

The nurse ushered her into an exam room, and said, "Dr. Jamison will be in shortly." She exited and closed the door.

No removing of the clothes or checking the vitals? That fertile witch knows the diagnosis, Nicole mused and sunk to the chair. She yanked a magazine from a pile on the desk-top table. How to diagnose your child's personality was not exactly what she wanted to read. Neither did she like the baby's big blue eyes staring at her off the front cover. After thumbing the pages cover to cover, she dropped the glossy-paged advice back on the stack, drummed her polished nails on the Formica top, crossed and uncrossed her legs.

Moments later, the door opened a second time and Dr. Jamison entered. She was tall, slender and neat, conservatively dressed. A gold wedding band graced clean hands and short manicured nails.

"Hi Nicole. I apologize for the wait."

"No problem," she muttered out the lie when the doctor gracefully sat on her little wheeled stool then scanned her medical chart.

The physician displayed no outward signs of the emergency that had called her away. No doubt, another birth Nicole decided and squirmed in her chair wondering how many kids she had herself.

"Nicole, your laparoscopy was informative. You're full of endometriosis and both ovaries are a solid mass of cysts. We took a biopsy which came back negative, but I want you to get a second opinion."

"For what? Just give it to me straight," she demanded harsher than she meant.

"You need to have a complete hysterectomy."

Wild grief ripped through Nicole. Her insides erupted with alarming spasms. The prognosis finally spoken aloud, the horror of it screamed harshly near the center of her soul. It was permanent sorrow. That knot in her stomach raced up to her heart and clenched it tight and hard. She looked away, fighting back tears. She had expected—had hoped for some miracle cure to change everything. It's not fair! I'm only thirty!

Swallowing the lump lodged in her throat, Nicole looked back at Dr. Jamison. The poised professional calmly sat waiting for a response. An appropriate amount of required compassion coated the doc's disgustingly pretty face.

"I'd like you to have a second opinion so you are well informed and feel comfortable with your decision. Nicole, you can't put this off for more than a couple of months."

Stiffening, Nicole sat upright. "Why? What else?"

"You're an extremely high risk for uterine cancer. It's not life threatening today, but you can't delay your decision any longer than necessary."

This isn't my decision. It's a do or die choice by a demon monster demolishing everything I have ever wanted. A new flash of loneliness seared Nicole's heart. She wanted to bawl but the tears were trapped between death and future hope.

"Nicole, there's no way you will ever be able to conceive," the doctor gently said.

Those final words bounced off the walls in a loud echo. Their clarity didn't need repeating. The thought of death knocking shot chills up her spine. The doctor prodded with a sympathetic look. The baby on the magazine smiled cutely. What did it matter? She didn't need a second opinion and gulped back the damned lump of solitude while silently cursing her runaway parents. This was their fault. They'd never been around to talk over anything and it was easy to blame them. Easy to hate them, too. All the same, she was on her own and had two alternatives. Lose giving life to one of those, she thought now glaring angrily at the baby on the cover, or lose her own life. Some choice!

Michelle and Derek's wedding was next weekend. They would be off to Jamaica for their honeymoon. Katharine would return to Minneapolis. No one would ever know and she wouldn't have to conceal her deficiencies from either.

Straightening, Nicole eyed Dr. Jamison. The uncertainty of the situation made her voice harsh, demanding. "How long would I be off work?"

"Seven weeks."

Nicole winced, shifted awkwardly from the round-the-clock pain. With detached inevitability, she said, "I don't need a second opinion. Schedule the surgery for two weeks from today."

CHAPTER 12

❀

Light footsteps alerted him. Pudgy hands fisted and rubbed her slothful eyes. Caitlin's blond feathery cluster of hair reminded Gage of baby fledglings, a pajamaed bundle of pink in footed fleece.

"Hey, squirt."

Scuffing her padded feet across the kitchen floor, she crawled into his lap. He didn't know if the weird comfort came from her nuzzling against his chest, or the simplicity of *Johnson's*. The pink woolly bundle snuggling near him reeked of the universal aroma. Without giving it much thought, Gage decided this ball of sweetness was the closest thing he ever felt to satisfaction. The unusual contentment wouldn't last because Caitlin would be gone soon.

Her breathing evened out when she nudged a thumb into her mouth. The opposite hand played with his hair. Brushing plumy strands of hair off her face, Gage kissed the top of Caitlin's head. The behavior was automatic. Taking a swig of coffee, he went back to reading reports Gus had faxed to the office late last night.

The rhyme fixed to Stacy White had been printed with a computer's inkjet. Typewriters, electric or manual, left trademark impressions on paper. No fingerprints on the paper or the liquor bottle, but liquid remnants inside the jug were identified as a mixture of fermentation alcohol and toxic herbicide. Gus recorded the chemistry numbers for each, which meant nothing to him. But then he didn't need numbers to tell him the deadly combo was a smooth blend of scotch and whiskey mixed with the chemical paraquat.

The rosary pea bracelet was identical to the others and handmade throughout the area by Native Americans. Carefully drilling the outer shell so not to disturb the poison bean inside, the lab figured out the Natives used sturdy nylon to string the beads then sold the trinket to gift shops.

Thanks to his last sergeant, he also knew rosary peas were grown in and out of the country. They were imported from Canada on necklaces and other decorative items as well. The attractive shiny red and black seeds came from the abrus precatorius plant, a twisting perennial vine grown naturally in tropical climates. Part of the legume family, the pea had several superstitious names besides rosary pea—precatory beans, crab's eye and jequirity bean to name a few. What Gage didn't know was the significance of the bracelet to the murders.

The killer was smart. The toxicity rating of one bean could kill. But the seed swallowed whole didn't necessarily cause poisoning unless that little pellet on the inside broke through the shell coating. The seed could actually pass through the body without harm or incident. Patriot had exhaustively cracked each shell then mixed the inner pea with peanuts and fed them to his victims.

Interesting, he mused draining his coffee cup. The killer used an extremely adequate poison for symbolic decoration, yet committed a felony theft to obtain a toxic chemical. He deliberated a moment over one more question. Was the homicidal maniac buying, stealing, or making the bracelets?

Believe what is, not what you think. It had been years, but the professor's words came back loud and clear. *Always expect the unexpected* he preached to a class of anxious rookies.

Gage didn't know what to expect other than he needed to expose and prove the truth. Not to mention jurisdiction needed to be established since the location of the paraquat homicides remained a mystery. That point could become a technicality that freed criminals if they didn't figure it out.

Gus' notations on the white dress the latest victim wore were interesting, too. The material was a fiber blend of polyester, cotton and silk, possibly expensive. Material content meant nothing to Gage other than for creature comfort. The crime scene in Nikki's backyard hinted of faultlessness. Katharine called it perfection. Gus said cleanliness. The Profiler said the killer was working up to the perfect murder. Simple and plain, un-fancy, he thought the white dress Stacy wore indicated pureness, innocence, maybe perfection. But what was the significance? He'd bet a paycheck the dead girl was a virgin—perfectly unsoiled. He hoped to have the autopsy results from Del today.

Had there been a perfect wedding spoiled by a child's death he wondered, rethinking the nursery rhyme. If a child or baby had died in this area, he'd have known about it. They monitored all pregnant women because babies came at the most inconvenient times. No hospital on the island, and the big lake in between, they were always prepared. With exception to Katharine and Michelle, there hadn't been any recent weddings either. What the hell was the connection to Nikki?

Those weren't the only things he haggled over in his mind. He'd been suspicious of the unexpected for some time. Nikki's abrupt reaction yesterday came unexpectedly and blew him away. Tossing that card on her desk, she grabbed her coat and purse and fled without a word. He thought she might know something about the brand name on the dress and wanted to ask her about it. Now it gave him an excuse to go over and talk to her.

Shifting Caitlin, Gage stood and poured a caffeine refill. The little tyke snuggled closer. "What brought you downstairs before seven this morning, squirt?"

When she didn't respond, he gave her temple a peck. It didn't take long for him to connect with kids. He fell for this one at the moment of rescue. Left alone in the motel, she was huddled protectively in bedding when he and Mac barged in. If Caitlin's mother hadn't already been dead, he would have hauled her in for child neglect and endangerment. Later he discovered Caitlin Graham had no living relatives. Maryann Graham's mother had been a druggie who prostituted to feed her habit. Caitlin's mother hadn't been any better. Maryann may have been a product of immorality and crime, but she had choices. Everyone had choices. She chose degradation. No one who offered an innocent baby the evil side of life deserved children. It was that simple.

Caitlin whimpered. Gage leaned back in the kitchen chair and massaged her back soothingly. "You're okay, sweet thing."

His juggled thoughts brought him to the tarp. There'd been no dragging marks up to Stacy's body. That meant the killer carried her and deliberately placed the victim. Stacy's arms left imprints before they were put in a crossed position across her chest. New fallen snow didn't help once Secunda demolished the impressions and foot tracks left by the killer. Damn dog had done the damage before they arrived. It wouldn't have mattered since it appeared the killer marred and twisted them anyway. The lack of tarp threads meant this killer didn't use a tarp—didn't have to.

"Mreow."

Gage glanced down. Michelle's cat rubbed against his pant leg. The feeding bowls his mother had set on the floor were bare and dry. "Hey, Keeker. Bet you want breakfast."

"Mreow. Mreow."

"Hold on."

Recently weaved into part of his morning routine, Gage rose a second time with a sleeping Caitlin in one arm, found the cat food and squatted to fill the dish. The cat pushed against his hand letting out a boisterous half cry entwined with a noisy purr.

"Well, isn't this a blessed sight and so natural, too."

Her powder freshness filled the kitchen. "What's that supposed to mean?" he questioned without looking at his mother.

He then moved quickly and flipped the report over screening the contents before he re-sat. Shuffling toward the fridge in a drab robe she'd worn since the beginning of time, she had a small frame, pleasantly full from thickening with age. The faded blue robe did nothing to enhance her lovely auburn hair. She was preoccupied, too. He recognized the plotting in her soft blue eyes.

"What'd you do, get Caitlin out of bed?"

And when she didn't want to answer a question, she asked one. "Nope. Came down on her own, climbed into my lap and went back to sleep."

"Honey, you want some breakfast this morning?" Paula asked.

"No thanks. I have to get over to the station. Nikki's coming in to give her statement."

"The poor thing finding that girl in her backyard. How's she doing? Gage, you tell Nicole if she needs anything to call me."

"Already have, Mom. I have to get going. You want Caitlin back in bed?"

"Gage, you should know we've decided to keep Caitlin with us until they can find a good home for her."

The announcement didn't surprise him. His mother loved kids running in and out when they were younger. He asked anyway. "How come?"

"She's no trouble and doesn't need to deal with additional upheaval. It's horrid for a child to be passed from home to home having no one to love her. At least here I'll know she's loved and cared for even if it means she's with us until she's eighteen, or they find a loving family for her next week."

That last comment kicked him hard where the sun didn't shine. Caitlin became part of the family household immediately. He never considered what he'd feel when she left. "Dad agreed?" he asked with more gusto than he meant to. "Speaking of which. Where is he?"

"Sleeping in. Your father won't admit it, but he spends half the night wandering the house. Never have understood why that man can't sleep when the rest of us do. Worries himself too much."

"I'd say it has more to do with his doubts concerning my capabilities."

"Nonsense. He just envies you right now."

"Yeah, right. Envies my lack of initiative. He's made it perfectly clear Mac and the FBI are more capable of handling this case."

"Gage, I've taught you better. It's what you believe that's important. Just because you and your father do things differently, doesn't mean you lack initiative. You've got your father's independence and my patience."

"Yeah, Mom. You've been telling me my whole life how efficient I am. Has it ever occurred to you that although I'm the police chief, I can't claim responsibility for the capture of Guthrie or Patriot?"

"You've never had an ounce of greedy recognition in you. Why now?"

He hated when she initiated conversations then turned her back on him. He hated when she was right, too. If he hadn't been holding Caitlin, he would have stormed out of the house. "This has nothing to do with greed or recognition, Mom. Our island is going to hell right in front of me."

"If you say so."

"Dad doesn't trust me. He's always believed I'm weak and lack confidence—" Gage stopped. "What do you mean if I say so?"

"You're only half right, honey."

He wasn't in the mood for decoding cryptic comments today. "Dad thinks I avoid facing issues and confronting things head-on the way he does. Well, I'm not like him."

"Perhaps, but lower your voice so you don't wake him."

"It's never mattered what I did, I've never been good enough for him. He hates the idea that Carter Taylor can't control me the way he was monopolized when he had this job. He thinks I don't know what he's thinking about my—" *sexuality* is what he was going to say to his mother. Felt that twinge of embarrassing guilt. "I have to go. You want me to put Caitlin back in bed?" he asked again.

"Gage," she said, turning to face him. "The only lack of confidence you have is with one woman you've been dodging since the first time you kissed her."

Now things surprised him, occasionally, but never had his mother startled him. "How'd you—"

"A mother sees all," she said quietly. "And knows all. I practically raised that child myself. She's in love with you but she's been waiting for you to make the first move."

Mom, she hates me he wanted to shout. He didn't know which he felt more; disloyalty to a dead friend or embarrassment his mother had seen the kiss.

Heaving upward, he handed Caitlin to her. "Since I know you're talking about Nikki, it doesn't matter anyway. She's moving to Los Angeles."

Her jaw fell hard. Gage knew further discussions were warranted, but bailed on the conversation, headed for the crime scene. He needed to go over it in daylight. Just an excuse to see her his conscience berated.

❦   ❦   ❦

Remarkable described how time allowed one to forget stuff until something triggered memories. Nicole had forgotten how she acquired instant rancor toward Gage that summer. With Brian's fatal accident, and him leaving for college, she completely neglected the reason for abhorring him the way she did.

The thank-you card he tossed on her desk spurred additional morbid thoughts of an undoable circumstance. Although Paula had been with her every step of the way, his mother never would have told him about her surgery. So, how did he get his paws on that card? What assumptions did he make from the words she wrote? What *had* she written? Brooding away the entire night, she'd have to thwart off all the questions he raised before she left town.

An hour until the meeting at the station, she realized that long ago weekend had been bulldozed deep into her subconscious. Kept under lock and key, until yesterday, it came to life in her mind. Though hints of the past had been rearing their ugly head, yesterday was the first time she relived the gory details in blazing color. Now after fifteen years, Gage decides he wants to talk about it. How could she possibly explain after all the years? *I went out with your best friend to make you jealous. You punched him to protect me and Brian's dead because we both hurt and deceived him. Now you want to discuss the loathing grudge I have for you?*

Yep, she could hear the entire argument. A living hell is what it would be. Maybe an angry punch or two thrown in for good measure.

The incident with Josie and Terry on the rocks the day Brian asked her out had slipped her mind as well. Why hadn't she remembered the bold incident when she, Katharine and Michelle took Frank's boat over to Michigan Island this summer? After all, the subject did come up. Remembering would have triggered things that required her thinking about them. And she did trip over a corpse.

Nicole shuddered and clamped her arms tightly in front of her.

Whatever happened between Terry and Josie had slid away with the years. She always assumed those two would end up together until Josie's surprise engagement to Curt Stewart covered a half page in the Island Blazer. *That* she remembered. Michelle said Terry bailed on the relationship. Michelle also thought Clyde didn't look anything like Curt. Not that it mattered, but thinking about that beach scene, Nicole wondered now whatever happened to Terry. She thought he was a couple years older.

In transit, mug in hand, she answered the ringing phone. The hang-ups were occurring more frequently. Two last night three this morning, she slammed the receiver down. Coffee sloshed out. Maybe Katharine was right. Grabbing a towel to wipe her hand, she automatically peeked out the kitchen window.

A bit long, a little unkempt, his sunset-colored hair protruded and covered the navy blue collar of his uniform jacket. Gage was squatting, examining something near the indentation where the girl's body had once lain.

Nicole slipped on a pair of loafers and her leather, fleece-lined jacket, went out the backdoor and approached. Winter was upon them as she stepped carefully atop new-fallen snow. A fresh layer glittered with intense brightness under a brilliant sun. Their well-known northeast bluster felt moist and cold. Nicole shoved bare hands into her jacket pockets to conceal nervous jitters and took short cautious steps. Inching along, fearful of stepping in dead body or some other god-awful muck, she asked, "Gage, what're you doing?"

Her scented flesh overtook his senses long before he looked. Those huge round eyes were dark and inquisitive. The rest of her—what could he say about the control he was losing. Not a damn thing. He didn't know how to extinguish personal torment knowing the love of his life had always loved someone else. Oh hell! Was he really in love with her? His heart never could say no to her. Looking incredibly sexy in a pair of ratty jeans and a faded sweater, she seldom wore pants of any kind. He enjoyed measuring up those drawn-out legs covered in intimate mystery. Erecting himself, he said, "Not gonna run on me like you did yesterday."

"What are you doing in my backyard?"

"Wanted to see it in daylight. See if we missed anything."

"Did you?" she asked in a voice that sounded as if she didn't care.

"Nikki, would you get me a baggie—"

"What else did you find?" she asked shifting her feet nervously, when he glanced behind him and back to her.

"Looks like a fingernail. You're gonna hate me for asking, but I have to see your hands."

Nicole was too flabbergasted by his suggestion to offer any objection. He guarded his deepest thoughts as she complied by jabbing her hands in front of him. "All intact, and you're right! I do hate you for asking," she flouted.

Before he could offer her an explanation, she spun on her heel, slipped, regained her stance and hurried back to the house. Sixty seconds hadn't passed when she huffed back outside balancing awkwardly in the snow. She flung the little plastic bag at him letting it fall.

Gage grabbed it, exhaling, "Nikki, I know you don't understand. When we nail the killer, every piece of evidence has to be detailed before we go into court. You're involved just because threads from your shorts were found on the girl you tripped over this summer on Michigan Island. One girl was discovered at your place of business, and now this. A defense attorney will rip you to shreds if we don't have the right answers and documentation to back up every piece of evidence."

"Oh! I never realized—"

"Maybe if we spent less time disputing every topic in the universe—never mind," he finally huffed. "Nikki, you're in this up to your eyeballs."

She eyed him skeptically then insisted, "Gage, lemme see it."

"Why?"

"Because you nitwit—"

"So, we're back to my intelligence."

"I'm wondering how you found a sliver of a fingernail lying in the snow, not questioning your I-Q. Unless it's polished with a bold-color, it would be very tough to see. Did it?"

"Not that I can tell! But then it's not a sliver," he told her.

Carefully stepping, she reluctantly accepted his offered hand. She bent to look at the spot where he indicated.

"Gage, it's a fake that fell off and it's polished with clear shine." Nicole straightened, snatching her hand out of his. "F-Y-I, there's not one damn thing about me that's fake. It's not mine."

"I know. Nikki, if you're ready to go, I'll take you over to the station to start your statement before the Profiler talks to you. There's something I'd like to learn, if you can help us out with it."

"What?" she responded eagerly, considering accommodating him.

"The white dress the girl was wearing. Where did it come from? Whether it was expensive or not?"

"Who's the designer?"

"Can't remember off the top of my head. Some woman's name. I've got the info back at the station. If you're ready, I'll take you now."

He stooped and with a pen from his pocket nudged the fingernail into the baggie as she told him, "I'll get my purse."

He followed her into the house. She locked the doors and they arrived at the station a few minutes later.

"You want some coffee?"

"Hun-uh. I'm caffeined out. Where's Mac?"

"He'll be in shortly," he answered thumbing through papers. "Here it is. The fabric content is a blend of polyester, cotton and silk. The label is Susan Bristol." Gage looked up. "Have you heard of her?"

"Sure have. Susan Bristol is the genre of showy cardigans and sweaters. Very expensive. She does design other styles of clothing as well. Generally, her designs are sold in specialty shops."

"Specialty?"

"She's not featured in outlet malls. Sometimes you can find her in a major department store. But Susan Bristol fashions are for boutiques and specialty stores. They're unaffordable to the average person."

"Why's that? Unaffordable, I mean."

"Because a lot of her designs are unique. They're also casual, a touch of informal business with a flair for romance. Her dresses are delicate in nature."

"Delicate?" he inquired.

"They're designed to attract." When he handed her one of his puzzled looks, she said with added inflection, "Sex, Gage. They're designed to physically catch the male eye in a subtle way so that he has no idea what hit him."

"So, how expensive are you talking?"

Her last explanation hadn't dazed him in the least and Nicole was beginning to wonder what it would take for the right woman, any woman, to dismantle that brick wall of his. She also wondered if a woman could.

"Her cardigans start at around a hundred and forty bucks. On-line you can find dresses varying in prices. In store, I haven't found a dress for less than eighty, even on sale."

Gage sat, nursed his coffee. "What's considered affordable for the average woman?"

"That depends. Some wouldn't spend fifty let alone eighty if they were going to wear an outfit only once. For some, twenty can be high."

"Where would I look for these specialty shops you mentioned?"

"Here in Wisconsin?"

He nodded.

"There's around forty shops that feature Susan Bristol. Not all in the same town or city. The closest is a small shop in Spooner. But then I'm sure Duluth would have some as well."

"How do you know all this?"

What was she gonna tell him? I spend all my spare time shopping—why just last week I dropped over two grand on Rodeo Drive. She didn't think so! "I just know," she answered.

"Then this white dress could have been purchased anywhere?"

"Afraid so—wait. You said white? As in lightweight for summer?"

"Yeah, I guess. Why?"

"Gage, this is December."

"So?"

"So, winter lines start appearing in July and August. The summer lines don't hit the stores until January, maybe late December. If the dress is a summer design, it means someone most likely bought it off a sale rack from last season's merchandise. Assuming it was recently purchased."

"How does knowing that help me?"

"Stores don't have floor space to keep everything that doesn't sell. For that reason there's sales. Profit and cleanup, otherwise it goes back to the manufacturer. The smaller shops—"

He sprung forward. "Your specialty shop has even less space and sends it back. Do you know if it's a summer or winter dress?"

"Well that's the key. If it's true white, its standard practice by some that white is worn between Memorial and Labor Day. Nowadays, people wear any color anytime, but anyone with an ounce of vogue knowledge knows the difference between winter white and summer white."

"All I have to do is narrow the gap down from forty shops and hope the killer bought this dress with a credit card."

"The dress could have sold out immediately in some areas. The down side is it could have been purchased by anyone at anytime since first being displayed. More likely a woman would buy it unless it was a gift from her significant other."

"The up side would be it didn't sell at all. Hence, the store might remember the buyer. Is this designer the most expensive one available?"

"No, far from it. There's Ralph Lauren suits. Cache does evening and prom gowns and both are extremely expensive. Price-wise, Susan Bristol is less."

"So even the victim could have purchased the dress herself?"

"Gage, anyone with money could have bought the dress. But it's unlikely a sixteen-year-old would have the kind of money we're talking about unless she came from wealth. There's far more affordable fashions for teenagers since designers and manufacturers cater to that crowd."

"I'm guessing these Susan Bristol shops would be in Green Bay also?"

"I know there's at least one there who carries her name."

The station door swung open and Mac walked in yawning. "Sorry about being late. My loving wife had a restless night and thinks I have to suffer with her."

Alertly, Gage asked, "Is she okay?"

"Yeah. Katharine's emphatic it's my fault she's breeding boxers."

Gage bared a quick grin, and said, "Listen, Mac. I checked out Nikki's backyard a second time and found this." Showing the bagged and tagged fingernail to Mac, he continued. "I'm gonna take it over to the crime lab after I log it."

"I can see how Gus missed it in the dark and snow."

"Hindrance or help to our case, I wouldn't have seen it either, considering. And finding this almost thirty-six hours later can destroy us if I don't take care of it."

"Gage, you think—"

"Mac, don't say it," he eyed his sergeant. "Would you get Nikki's statement and take care of her talking to Claire?"

Mac nodded.

"I'm gonna call Del to find out when he'll have the autopsy done."

"Gage," Nicole began, "I could call those shops about the dress—"

"No!" he said sharply. "Absolutely not!"

"Why not?" she clamored defensively. "I at least know what to ask and could save you time. What harm is it gonna do if I call and find out if they stocked the dress?"

He glared rigidly at her. "I said no!"

"Talk about stubborn! Gage, you're so cocksure of everything, you can't see the obvious. If this is about me, like you've so adequately pointed out, I have every right to be involved."

"No you don't, Nicole!"

Ripping the evidence from Mac's hand, Gage skirted the desk and slammed the office door leading into Town Hall.

CHAPTER 13

✿

New Year's Eve morning, Nicole awoke to a crying woman. Opening one eye, she expected a fossilized countess wearing a white sheet to be floating near her bed ready to nudge her from comfort. No doubt, some prehistoric idiot her parents sent gift-wrapped. The persistent cry sounded more like an animal than a weeping woman. Annoying is what the clamor was now and she burrowed under the blankets with a groan, covering her head with a pillow.

Some million years ago when Sully started telling his ludicrous ghost story none of them believed it. But years later, both Katharine and Michelle had been converted. Too early for her brain to engage Nicole never would give credence to its truth.

After several minutes of continuous wailing, Nicole threw back the covers in a huff. "Nicolina, you are really torquing my ass this morning!"

Climbing out, she ranted, "Just great, Jarvis. Now you're talking to a ghost you can't even see."

Robing herself, Nicole shuffled out to the kitchen to nurse her temper with caffeine. Assuredly, she couldn't see Nicolina, but she definitely heard what her two best friends kept talking about. Another new practice that turned into morning habit was the hurried peek at her backyard through the kitchen window. Snow now fell in heavy doses camouflaging the morbid images.

Pouring a cup of coffee, she muttered, "Some life. Dead girls in your backyard and crying ghosts in your head."

Nicole shuffled into the bathroom for a long, brain-unclogging shower. The plan to go into work at two changed with the latest disturbance. The tavern would fill quickly today with islanders partying in a New Year. The fright in folks' eyes mingled with hushed gossip they were going to party like it was their last. Their worry, she thought, was legitimate speculation of who would be the next murder victim.

Hot water poured over her head as her thoughts logged things done and yet to be completed. She spent the last several days working on a different schedule to begin in January. Speaking with all the waitresses, she discovered others had similar problems to Gypsy's and she rejiggered everyone's time. Hopefully the new hours would work thus eliminating shortages. Next week ads would come out for a replacement chef.

Stepping out of the shower and patting her skin dry, Nicole applied liberal amounts of lotion. Jacque would handle hiring Nick's replacement unless he needed her assistance. The Perry's anniversary party had to be perfect and she couldn't overlook a single detail.

Applying her makeup first, then forking her hair, she went into the bedroom to dress. After a dozen changes, Nicole studied her reflection in the mirror. A gracefully fitted wool purple jacket and tailored black slacks were chosen out of orneriness. Originally planning an outfit to match Gage's gift, another dispute put her well-known streak in high gear. She was just as stubborn as he was and chose a silver pin with complimentary earrings.

She wondered now what Gage thought of the profiler. Priggish and starched, the FBI woman Claire Huntington had questioned her to death. She was one of those women every other loved to hate with her flawless flesh and perfect proportions everywhere. Locking the door and walking to the Tavern, Nicole brooded. They were crazy to think she knew anything that could help them nab a homicidal maniac. The only way she could assist, Gage patented pigheadedness and refused her involvement. What he didn't know wouldn't hurt. She began calling Wisconsin shops to learn what she could about the white dress. Unfortunately, she hadn't ascertained any info let alone pertinent.

A few cars in front of the Tavern already had premo spots for the day and night. Cleared once, the step's entrance was hastily cloaked with additional fuzzy flakes. Nicole proceeded cautiously inside the foyer, stomped her boots and shook snow from her hair. Tim, another back-up tapster was behind the bar serving the few who always started early. Hayden would be in later. The fact Sully was seated on a barstool at one end had to be an omen. Although he lived on Madeline, he rarely came in for drink or this early in the day when he did come for a meal. His preference was a pepper Jack burger with sautéed onions and a side order of Jacque's deep friend jalapeno poppers, breaded and stuffed with cream cheese.

Looking up, his practiced eye reflected out of the smoke-glass mirror. He looked directly at her with an invitation to join him. His grayed beard had scruffy seasonal growth and sagged to cover a wrinkled neck. He uniformly wore a tattered, navy blue beret with a crown and peak brim that now lay on the polished bar alongside his well-used pipe. Both were his mark of character. Those buff-colored eyes pleaded earnestly with her.

Nicole didn't resist, went over, pulled up a barstool and plopped down alongside the skipper. "Haven't seen you in here for awhile. How are you, Sully?"

"Aye, lass, tis been awhile. I'm good. You?"

"You seem to know everything before it happens so I'm almost positive you know how I'm doing."

He tittered softly and went back to his meal.

"Are you coming to the grand opening of the ballroom?"

"Haven't decided, lassie."

While he continued to eat, details of the frequently told ghost story came back. Madeline Cadotte, daughter of Chief White Crane and wife to French fur trader, Michel Cadotte, had three beautiful daughters together. More than three children, Michelle had corrected numerous times. That point didn't matter as far as Sully was concerned. He narrated the fairytale with complete affirmation. Said the loving parents adored each child, Katrina, Nicolina and Mikala. Michelle argued their names, too. Sully's mystical ways convinced tourists each child was graced with jeweled eyes—jewels that were supposed to have been gifts centuries ago. His legend narrated to passengers and vacationers told how the daughters were each murdered by medicine men the night preceding their wedding vows. Pledging the daughter's jeweled eyes, as the story went, was supposed to be a sacramental gift from the medicine man to his divine creator. For what Nicole didn't know. Didn't care either.

As misfortune has it, according to Sully Tanner, part time captain of the Island Princess, the daughters were each murdered the night before they took their promise to love, honor and obey. Murdered by the medicine man who swore to have the jeweled eyes. Following the death of her third and last daughter, the Native American wife went into seclusion on the largest of the Apostle Islands, Madeline. Not true according to Michelle and another story in and of itself. Nevertheless, in the make-believe tale, the goofy skipper sitting next to her told all that Madeline C. hid out here, never to be seen or heard from again. If any part of that were true, Nicole assumed it was a mother's way of mourning her loss. But according to Sully, Madeline C. died within a year of her third daughter's death. It was then the ghosts of those three beautiful young women began appearing—rather crying on various islands throughout the Apostles for about the past hundred years or so.

Tourists were forever twisting the bridal gift into a large treasure of gold-bearing medallions and coins the French fur trader brought with him from France. Hence, those same tourists were constantly in search of dreams that didn't exist. Besides, Nicole thought, Cadotte traded *furs* with the Indians, not gold. But Sully swore on his ship's log the three ghosts were going to weep loudly haunting the Apostles until that lost dowry of jewels was located. How can eyes be jeweled, let alone made into a dowry? Three women must unite in island marriages to their soul mate and only then, according to Sully, would the Cadotte ghosts come to rest for good. The story didn't make sense to her as a kid and made less sense to her now.

And Lord, forgive her. She mustn't leave out the part where Sully always said she, Katharine and Michelle were the three women who had the power to calm ghosts because of *their* jeweled eyes.

She might be the queen of man handlers, but she sure as hell didn't have jeweled eyes nor would she attempt to calm a ghost. Even if she did believe, which she didn't, exchanging those sacred vows certainly didn't mean a promise of love to the very dying end either. She peered sideways while Sully finished the last of his meal, thinking, what a crock.

"Yer eyes are doubtful, lass. Yer needin' more proof than Katharine or Michelle."

"What I need is for our island to go back to the way it was. Quiet and serene."

"Sometimes, tis change happening fer reasons beyond our knowledge. Tis why it's taken so long fer ya ta hear Nicolina's cries."

"Sully Tanner, I won't give you the satisfaction of knowing either way whether I've heard your ghost or not."

Lighting his pipe, the skipper released a spirited laugh. "I already know."

"Sully Tanner, don't you make me call you a fool. Don't make me!"

Chuckling, he said, "There's a great deal more doubt in yer jeweled eyes, lassie. Fer different reasons."

He gazed at her long and slow and Nicole debated who was more insane. Silently questioned her reasons for even giving this man the time of day.

"Yer the last one, lassie."

"Oh bull."

"Nicolina must be calmed and put to rest. Tis only you who can do that."

"Another nut job," she muttered.

"Lassie, yer dodging and hiding in the past. It does no good fer ya ta dwell on things ya can't change. Yer as kindhearted as the seagulls and the swallows dwelling here, Nicole. Ya must let regret go. Forgive yerself fer what ya had no control of. Twasn't yer fault."

"What wasn't my fault?"

"Tis been how long now? Fourteen years?"

"Fifteen," she muttered then gaped at him, knowing full-well what he was talking about. "Sully, you don't understand."

"More than ya know, lassie. Tis time fer you and Gage ta get on with yer lives together. He wanted it that way."

"Who wanted it that way?"

"Lassie, stop blaming yourselves fer what happened to Brian."

She choked on a quick breath of utter shock. Unspeakable words and questions were wedged in her throat. Sully stood and winked his standard goodbye.

"When yer open ta hear the truth, you and Gage stop by and see me."

"Truth?" squeaked out. What truth? Nicole shivered with panic as Sully drifted out of the tavern before her tongue could engage.

❦   ❦   ❦

Gage sat behind his desk reading the ME's report while Mac patrolled the island. New Year's Eve would most likely cough up a few disturbances and he told Mac to call if he needed help.

The ninth serial killing victim identified as Stacy White from Green Bay had turned sixteen in November. She was still a virgin and like the others had marijuana and whiskey in her system. No one could determine whether she was a runner or not since her parents had been out of town at the time Stacy disappeared. Gage fixed on the typewritten words, *cause of death-respiratory distress from paraquat poisoning.* He didn't want to read the rest of the gory details knowing the poison's process. But he had to. Del had found traces of vomit in her mouth. Stacy's esophagus and tongue were corroded with ulcers. She had fatal lung damage. Toxicity had developed in her liver and kidneys showing jaundice and oliguria—scantiness of urine due to diminished secretion. He shuddered internally.

Cause of death was identical to the other eight victims who died from paraquat poisoning. The fake fingernail he found in Nikki's backyard also belonged to their ninth victim. Both Gus and Del figured it fell off when they bagged the body. The bothersome point was the fact rigor was into seventy-two hours and their victim's body hadn't frozen.

Gage studied the list of names more or less to ease his own conscience. Nine girls were dead from paraquat poisoning and he felt as responsible as anyone that had ever been involved in the case. Amelia Rainbird had been the first, followed by Emma Coldbath and Marcia Racine when the homicides began three years ago. The next year Danielle Aitkins was murdered first succeeded by Natalie Hunter and Clarissa Noma. This year their serial killer waited until the end of July—*why?*—instead of the beginning to kill Jennifer Wicket and changed the discovery location by leaving her body on Madeline. Sharon Marquette their eighth victim was discovered on Michigan Island. Now number nine, Stacy White. With the exception of Jennifer Wicket being from Ashland, all the girls were from Green Bay.

Oddly, Jennifer Wickett and Sherry Martin were the only two from Ashland, best friends, and runners together. The Martin girl was not a virgin, Jennifer was. Jennifer died from paraquat and Martin died from abrin. Another weird piece to the puzzle was the first six were found within a mile radius of the same trashy biker bar Mac had told him. The only connection to the Apostle murders thus far was Nikki. It wasn't even a sound one, but it nagged his conscience there was any connection at all.

How did two girls who ran away together from Ashland end up dying two different ways by two different killers? Why was a tarp used to haul two and not the others? Why was Stacy White the only dead girl displayed majestically? What about the correlation being made to the Stewart brothers?

The dowdy old professor's words *'you can't be caught up in the emotion, you must remain focused'* chanted in his head with Claire Huntington's words *'the bracelet and bottle of liquor are symbolic to the killer, like taking a trophy'*.

The more he thought about it, the more he believed the real serial killer was setting up Kevin Stewart, maybe even Curt. It meant their murderer knew them both. Maybe had a vendetta for them. Professor Burough always told them to believe what is, not what you think. Always expect the unexpected he said many times.

A thought occurred to Gage and he dug through mountains of paper to find the detailed events of the day Katharine spotted Patriot's car in the ferry parking lot in Bayfield. The tabs on Patriot's car had been stolen off the car that belonged to Natalie Hunter's dad. The Hunter girl connected Patriot to the real serial killer. But how? Hunter rang a name too, but he couldn't place it. Clarissa Noma connected Patriot to the killer from his fingerprint Green Bay PD discovered. From the beginning, that point had convinced him Patriot knew the real serial killer.

They needed to find the original crime scene as in the place where the victims spent their last seven days. There was a lot of territory between Madeline Island and Green Bay. Without that location, they were screwed and tattooed. But Stacy White's unfrozen corpse did prove the location of death had to be inside somewhere.

Gage yanked the nursery rhyme out from another layer of reports, leaned back in his chair and examined his notes. He had a link. All he had to do was uncover solid evidence to prove a theory. Since Green Bay seemed to hold the key, it was time to pay Josie's cousin, Janice Anderson a surprise visit. Going to Green Bay himself would give him a chance to check out the specialty shop Nikki told him about. Some how he felt positive that Stacy White's dress came from that shop.

Mac had called and confirmed T. Kohl's LTD still existed and was east of the Fox River on Monroe Street. He'd find out if they sold the white dress to anyone. With luck, they might be able to tell him who bought it. Maybe he was expecting a lot, but following a hunch solved many cases and Mac got Anderson's address for him as well.

At that moment, his sergeant entered. "All quiet?"

"A little too quiet."

"Not to worry, it'll pick up after midnight. If you're bored, you wanna run checks on Janice Anderson for me? See what you can dig up? I think it's time I went to Green Bay and checked her out myself."

"When you plan on doing that?"

"Day after tomorrow, unless you wanna drive down there."

"Not a chance."

Gage glanced at his wrist. "Have you eaten?"

"Not yet. Came by to see if you wanna grab something at the tavern before all hell breaks loose."

"Sounds like a winner, but you tellin' me you think we won't survive the drunks?" Mac shrugged and Gage stood, putting on his jacket. "Let's go eat. We've got bigger concerns than what happens at midnight."

They each drove their squads and parked in front of the building. Enroute, Gage decided to ask Nikki if she wanted to go to Green Bay with him. She was right about one thing. She would undoubtedly ask a sale's clerk the right questions. Five hours in a car would give them time to discuss that summer night without her being able to flee. It would make him feel a whole lot better knowing Nikki was safe, too. These days he wasn't taking any chances. Neither was he sure she'd accept yet another apology from him.

Maybe he'd lost it altogether. Their arguments were occurring with more frequency to the point the clamor echoed daily in his head. Clearing out the past might hopefully end the verbal disputes he despised and the insufferable whining he kept hearing. He thought about his conversation with Michelle—

"Mac, get a table. I'll be back in a minute."

The instant they entered the lounge Gage sensed Nikki's uneasiness. She glanced his way from behind the bar. Her enlarged eyes overflowed with panic. Her face bared blatant wiped-out exhaustion around stark fear.

He headed toward her as Nikki rushed out from behind the bar to him. "What's wrong?"

"I have to talk to you."

She didn't wait for a response and Gage followed her upstairs to her office. Nikki thrust the door shut behind him and worked off nervous energy marching in front of him. Her hands went from her hips, to crossing, to wringing her fingers together.

"Nikki, what's wrong?"

"Gage, Sully was in here earlier today trying to convince me Nicolina's ghost really exists."

"Not you, too?"

"I don't believe in ghosts! Neither can I get her damn cries out of my head. Everywhere I go, I hear her wailing loudly. But that's not what I need to tell you."

She was worse than Pipsqueak, and he wondered if she was losing her mind. "Then what?"

"Gage," she said facing him now, "Sully said he knows something."

"About what?"

"Brian's accident."

"*What?*"

"He obviously talked to Brian and made it sound like there was more to it. He told me to stop blaming myself for what happened."

"What do you mean Sully talked to Brian?" *Was everyone going crazy?* "When? Nikki, what are you talking about?"

Biting her lip, she looked away. Tears trembled near her eyelids and quickly turned to choking sobs.

"Nikki—"

"I can't take it anymore! Katharine said Brian went out on the boat that day to think. It's my fault Brian's dead. I betrayed him. I killed my best friend's brother! Michelle will never forgive me if she knew what I did."

"*What* are you saying?"

She caved to the compulsive sobs shaking her. Gage moved swiftly, pulling her into his arms. "Sssh. Don't cry. You didn't kill Brian. It's not your fault."

Holding her snug, the heavy burden ached inside of him. How could he tell Nikki she was wrong to blame herself? How would he explain to her that Brian's death was his fault? What the hell did Sully know about it to upset Nikki this much? Between her intensified sobs and crying against his chest, Gage now wondered if what she was talking about had been the reason she'd been avoiding having this discussion with him.

"Oh, Gage!" she cried. "I've regretted my mistake ever since. I-I owe you a-an, an apology."

That little twist of the unknown wrenched his gut. He pushed her to arm's length. "What're you saying? That it wasn't an accident? Are you telling me you and Sully know something?"

"I don't know what Sully meant," she said swiping tears. "All I know is I went out with Brian on an innocent date to make you jealous then changed my mind. I hurt him badly—"

"What! You and Brian—I thought the two of you—" before he could stop, rage consumed him and his words came out bitter and cold. "You slept with Brian that night to make me jealous? Why? Why the hell would you do that, Nicole?"

Her vision may have been blurred but her hearing worked fine. "You bastard! It was innocent!"

He let go of her, yelling back, "Nicole! Brian's dates were never innocent and sleeping with him isn't either! Why'd you do it?"

The words were loaded with ridicule. His eyes went icy cold, inflexible. "Damn you all to hell!" she screeched. "I did not have sex with Brian that night or any other time! All these years you've thought—" she stopped. "You don't really know me at all."

As if having deep desires to hurt him, Nicole hurled, "Brian was a perfect gentleman! We went to Ashland for pizza and a movie and he never laid a hand on me. You're such a big dumb jerk! It wasn't him I wanted to be with, it was you! I had just told him that when you showed up at my house!"

Gage blinked, stumbled backward and stared at her completely startled. "*Ashland?*"

Her teenage feelings and fifteen years of spite exploded right out of her. "Yes! You idiot! Why would you think that we had sex? Brian was trying to talk to you, but you went ballistic on him."

"If what you're telling me is true, why'd you ever agree to go out with him?"

"Because you never asked me!" she shrieked.

Stunned into silence, he gaped at her. He permanently blocked that entire weekend out of his mind. It took less than a second for the events to come back in agonizing color. He'd worked until nine and afterward went over to the hangout on the north end of the island. Like they still do, kids were partying. With little intent of sticking around, he walked through talking to several. Then he ran into Josie and Terry, and Margie with some dipstick she picked up. The four of them were soused to the gills and he made the mistake of asking if they'd seen Brian anywhere.

He quickly remembered the vindictive look in Josie's eyes and thought it odd at the time. Just a bit too fast, she volunteered how Brian was hot and heavy on Nikki and they'd gone off somewhere, to score a homerun Josie told him. He fell apart. Refused to believe it until he saw them at her front door kissing.

"You and Brian weren't at the hangout that night?"

"Not even close," she sniveled. "Gage, I've only gone there once in my life and it certainly wasn't that Saturday night. Ask your mother if you don't believe me. Where'd you ever get an idea like that?"

Nikki's eyes were overflowing with new hurt he caused then and now. She'd never once lied to him. She might not divulge everything, but if he asked, she always answered. That much he knew.

Christ! What I said to her and did to Brian that night is unforgivable. No wonder she hates me.

Gage washed his hands over his face and shuffled off taut steps. Suddenly things were making sense, yet he never felt more confused. Although ruled accidental, he always wondered if Brian had flipped his boat deliberately. *Did Sully see it happen?*

"Gage, what is it? What are you thinking?"

He turned to face her. "Nikki, I've never felt more regret and blame than I do right now. Josie led me to believe Brian hit on you and you guys left together—"

"Josie!" she detonated. "That rancorous bitch! I have no idea how she found out that Brian asked me out. I did not tell anyone. Michelle and Katharine didn't even know. They still don't. Brian and I never went to the hangout either. The same day he asked me out, I saw Terry screwing Josie's brains out north of the beach. They were naked on the rocks and I was too shocked to sneak away without them seeing me. We exchanged bitter words and after everything else that happened that weekend…well, I forgot it until a few days ago. Gage, I never breathed a word to anyone about the date or what I saw until now."

Lately nothing surprised him. Why would this? "Why do Katharine and Michelle have a beef with her?"

"Don't you remember?"

He shook his head.

Nicole dabbed her eyes. "She always flaunted daddy's money in everyone's face. The last straw was in sixth grade when Josie told Mrs. Grambs that Katharine and Michelle were cheating on a math test. They did not cheat and none of us knew why Josie lied about it. Anyway, Mrs. Grambs called yours and Michelle's folks. Michelle was more upset about the incident than Katharine was. I don't remember how it all resolved itself but afterward the three of us made a pact to make Josie's life a living hell. Which we did."

"Nikki, if Brian's accident was anyone's fault, it's mine. But I don't understand what Sully meant. Tell me exactly what he said to you."

"Well, he told me to stop regretting something I had no control of. I'm positive he was talking about Brian. About that weekend."

She studied him for the longest time. He recognized the debating thoughts. "What else?"

She took a deep breath and told him. "He said you and I were supposed to get on with our lives. Together because Brian wanted it that way. Sully told me when we were both open to learn the truth we were supposed to go see him."

"The truth? Nikki, Brian was speeding! He hit a sandbar with the boat and flipped it."

"I know, Gage. But if I hadn't gone out with him in the first place he never would have been out on Superior thinking, like Katharine said."

Or if I hadn't beat the shit out of him, Gage miserably relived. The one thing that had always bothered him about the accident was Brian fished when he needed to think, like he did. Although wild with women, Brian handled his toys with extreme caution. He never would have been speeding under the circumstances. As much as he wanted to race the Indy, Brian played it safe with machinery. Verbatim, Nikki was telling him what Brian tried to explain the night before. The green monster of jealousy had eaten him up. He wouldn't listen—didn't believe his best friend.

"Nikki, I'm the one who was wrong. Brian wasn't out there thinking about you. He was nursing emotional and physical wounds I had caused."

She inched toward him and he stopped her with a raised hand. He hadn't exactly planned it this way, but he needed to clear his conscience—if *that* were even possible anymore.

"Nikki, after what happened at your house that night, Brian chased me down and caught up to me. It started with angry words and escalated to an all out fist fight between us."

Gage cringed recalling how rage had choked him. He worked off nervous energy now by mimicking Pipsqueak and stopped in front of the window behind Nikki's desk. He stared into the darkness remembering every detail.

"I'd give anything if I could have that night back—if I hadn't gone to the hangout—if I hadn't listened to Josie." He looked at her, "If I hadn't said what I did to you. God, Nikki. Brian was my best friend. I didn't care that he slept with everything in a skirt until he went after you. I had feelings for you." Quietly he added, "I still do. But it was hard for me to tell you how I felt when you practically lived in our house from day one. My own mother looks at you as her daughter because you never had your parents. I always felt sorry for you being alone. Never having anyone to go home to or to love you. I always thought he was the one you were in love with when I saw you kissing him that night."

"Oh, Gage."

Tears welled in her eyes until she bit her lip to control the stifled sobs.

"I beat him up pretty bad. He tried to tell me everything you just said but I wouldn't listen to him. I told him to get lost. I never wanted to see him again."

Relieving every second of that horrific weekend, Gage felt his insides detonating all over again. He sucked in a deep breath and told her what he'd kept buried through the years. "Nikki, I wished him dead and the next day he was."

She choked.

"Every time I look at Michelle or think of her parents, I die a little more inside." He strangled back the burning lump in his throat. "I feel responsible for what Michelle's ex did to her because he reminded all of them of Brian. And what I did to Aidan and Elizabeth—I can't even go there."

Nicole's heart swelled so sharply it hurt. She sensed the emotional guilt coiled within his body and couldn't keep herself from him. She skirted the desk and went to him with open arms. Simultaneously, they clung to each other. Nicole bawled until she was physically drained. Gage embraced her tightly, she felt sure he was trying to relieve himself of fifteen years of buried pain.

Stroking her hair, he whispered, "Baby, I've never been sorrier for everything I did to you—to Brian."

Gage took her face between his hands and for a long moment looked at her. Her eyes told him everything and he bent lightly kissing her mouth. He brushed kisses along her stained cheeks and jaw, grazed morsels along her ear and neck. The hollow at the base of her throat pulsed fleetingly and he feathered her flesh inhaling the sweetness engrained in his memory.

The wails of a woman echoed through the office and Gage stopped. He glanced up and around Nikki's office.

"Damn her," Nicole muttered.

"Thought you said that was the building creaking."

"I thought it was until I started hearing the same sound everywhere I go."

"Me too," he told her.

She looked up at the ceiling. "Nicolina, give it up!" Then looking at Gage asked with surprise, "You're hearing her. too?"

Holding Nikki close, he told her, "Michelle says we can't fight this."

His eyes had softened and she gazed into an almost hopeful glint. "I think I've got another confession to make first. And I'm pretty positive you'll be p-po'd at me."

He half smiled. "What did you do now?"

"Weeell, I sorta started calling those specialty shops to find out what I could about that dress."

He scowled. His back went ramrod straight.

"I wanted to help!" she blurted defensively. "Everyone's talking about how you can't catch the Green Bay Serial Killer."

Keenly aware she'd be determined to get involved, he blew out a breath. "I know they are and I figured you might pull something like that. I also figure the only way I'm gonna know you're safe is to keep you within eyesight."

"Do you really believe this demented nutcase is after me?"

A moment of silence loomed between them, before he confessed. "Yes, and I'm not taking any chances. I'm going to Green Bay on Sunday. Come along and I'll let you talk to the sales clerks at that shop, unless you've already called that one, too."

"No, I mean yes. I mean, no I haven't called any shops in Green Bay and yes I want to go with you."

"Good. At least we don't have to argue about that. I'll let you know what time we're leaving. There's two more things."

"What?"

"If there's missing facts from what may or may not have caused Brian's accident I *am* going to find out what they are. We'll go talk to Sully when we get back, but for now we need to keep this between us. No one else needs to be hurt by something none of us can change."

"Gage, I'm still partially responsible and there's no way I could tell anyone. What's the second?"

"This."

He leaned forward applying his mouth to hers and traced her lips with open kisses. "Baby, I promise I'm going to try and do right. I promise I'll make things better between us."

Then he covered her mouth hungrily, swallowing her up and giving strength to his pledge. Her arms folded around his neck and he gathered her close and tight. Their bodies melted into one, both aching too long for the moment.

CHAPTER 14

❀

The year had arrived without incident. Nicole needed to tap into her reserves New Year's Eve fighting off human instinct to go over and rip Josie's eyeballs out of her head. The tavern had stayed lively beyond closing, and yesterday Nicole slept not wanting to consciously picture or think about the past. Finally dragging herself out of bed around noon, New Years day held too many long hours with questions that had no answers.

She lost sight of the direction of her desires, and had coveted secret hope of seeing Caitlin until she called and Paula let Caitlin go to Bayfield to spend a night with Shalee and Brendan. Time with Caitlin might've created the major distraction she desperately needed. Instead, she wasted a shitload of energy on guilt and anger. The two emotions had mangled each other throughout fifteen years of blame she and Gage had placed on themselves for Brian's death and the blond bitch lying about something that didn't concern her. Although she had intentionally instigated animosity, the bottom line was it didn't matter with the lingering, irrefutable facts. Brian was dead and nothing could bring him back.

Packed with an overnight bag for Green Bay, Gage said he would get two rooms. Since Superior still hadn't frozen solid, the ferries were still running and they wouldn't be back in time for the last ferry to Madeline. Nicole wondered if going with him was the right thing to do. He'd arrive any minute to pick her up and she mustered out a paltry sigh.

With little hope of resolve, the ache in her heart was different now. He said he had feelings for her, promised he was going to make things right. How? Eliminate the blame? Arrest Josie for lying? Caught between silk euphoria, doubt and wanting revenge, Nicole blotted out the mocking voice replaying the questions—she was leaving La Pointe soon. None of the hidden elation or wanting of innocence could scratch out what she now understood they both did to Brian. Neither was Josie's vindictiveness an excuse. Leaving was just a way of escaping the blame, and her monumental doubts that Michelle would never forgive her or Gage if she learned the truth.

The combination of poignant emotions mingled with Sully's words. If Sully knew some important detail about that day, why hadn't he come forward back then? Regardless of whatever he claimed to know, it didn't change anything.

The doorbell sounded as the telephone rang. Nicole opened the door, letting Gage in then snatched the receiver. She hung up quickly and faced him.

Lord!

His rugged appearance made her insides twitter with old excitement. A concealed weapon draped between a leather jacket and navy blue sweater only made him more potent, attractive. The sweater's darkness drew out the erotic eye color in his eyes, not to mention what the entire package was doing to her.

"You look really good, Nikki."

Her heart jolted with her racing pulse. She was left wordless. She'd dressed in ivory-sleek, twill slacks with a matching ribbed turtleneck. A sumptuous, taupe basketweave jacket with a double shawl collar completed the outfit while his necklace and earrings added the perfect hint of color.

He moved in haste, encircling her in his arms. The voracious kiss he laid on her shattered what little calm she had left and rippled through her body. Her obliging response filled her with greed. An aching gurgle seeped out of her when he nibbled her ear.

"Who's calling this early?" he probed with another kiss.

Katharine's comments came back. She stepped back and let out a long audible breath. "I've been getting hang-ups for a month."

"Nikki, why didn't you say something?"

"I didn't think much of it. The morning after I found…they called while Katharine was here. They called the night before, too. She wanted me to tell you but I still thought they were just wrong numbers. I'm getting several a day. I always hear the click after I say hello."

"We have to put a trace on your phone."

"A trace? What will that do?"

"It'll tell us who's harassing you then Mac and I can haul 'em in and find out why."

"Gage, it's an irritant, not harassment."

"It's harassment and a crime if they're doing it with intent." He hadn't forgotten Claire Huntington's words, and added, "If it is related to the dead girls, you could be the killer's next target."

Restless, she watched him. He was too serious but she supposed with good reason. "I'm having a hard time believing anyone's after me when I'm considerably older than the victims."

"Please, Nikki." It bothered him, too. "For once, don't argue with me. Just do what I tell you."

His face had filled with sober determination while his eyes pleaded with her. He blocked another blow up between them with a quirking lip. Giving in, she said, "All right. Tell me what I have to do?"

"Call the phone company, explain what's going on, and tell them you want a trace put on your phone. They'll ask you several questions including if you've made a police report. Tell them yes. I'll get you a case number in a minute for you to give them. Once the trace is in place, they'll relay info only to Mac or me. Then I want you to document the time and dates every hang-up comes in and give it to us."

"You want me to call now?"

He nodded dialing a number. Disconnecting moments later, he tore the paper from his pocket notepad and handed it to her. "Here's the phone and case number. Call and I'll put your bag in the truck. When you're done, we'll leave."

She did and thirty minutes later, they drove onto the ferry. Docking in Bayfield, they headed south to Green Bay.

❦   ❦   ❦

Pummeling aggressively with two fists clenched to the handle, the claw hammer ruptured the glass pane with a loud crash. Fragments of jagged glass shattered and fell from the window alongside the house. The killer ducked, wavered then stared at the broken shards lying defunct on the ground. They were irregular and symbolic to life's defects. Blemishes of imperfection that could never be obliterated or forgiven.

"You have sinned! You'll be damned to hell for your impurities."

"Bring me one more and the gates of your hellish torture shall close forever."

The voices and cries were confusing, inconsistent. They rose in overwhelming conflict, triggered desperate actions. Where once a single tongue spoke, several now united into one. The Divine Creator, the crying baby, dead girls, father. The dying girls whimpered as each drew in their last breath, and father's was righteously the worst. Too many voices induced additional dispute and suffering. The sounds tormented and hailed annoyingly at the killer until a burden to annihilate the non-innocent stopped their shouts.

The Divine Creator promised murder was a permissible solution to end the personal suffering. He preached rejection fed power. Taught necessity for revenge. He said death was a beautiful dance of moonbeams along the golden water. Then he summoned for the jeweled brown eyes of the bodacious bitch. He ordered a sacrificial ceremony even before the killer could offer the slut freely.

It wasn't his idea.

Her faultless life and her perfection were maddening.

"She's my enemy! She believes she's indestructible! She thinks her insides rotting out won't kill her! But a knife through her heart will slay her."

Bloody messes were ugly and despicable. Stacy had been presented beautifully. She died so well with the mist of fear encasing her eyes.

But the real rush came with the others reveling in their confusion and flying blind without knowledge. Watching the panic fulfilled secret desires and replaced the loss. The killer blinked and twitched, cleared the broken spears from the sill, grasped the window ledge then climbed into the Jarvis house. It was time to commence the New Year offering. Only seven days until that bitch was marred, dead, and gone forever.

Sneaking quietly, the atmosphere inside appeared sedate. It was clean, organized, and too damn perfect. Brandishing a fillet knife found in the kitchen, the killer moved from room to room chanting, "Nikki-wikki, where are you? Come out come out wherever you are. Your time is up."

Negative energy increased until each vacant room unveiled no one. With the house empty, the killer maliciously yanked clothes from closets. In flailing assaultive strikes, the outfits were shredded into nothingness, piece by piece, thread by thread until wrath depleted the killer's energy. Sweat beaded in small dewy droplets across the killer's forehead.

"Nikki-wikki! Come out, come out and I won't have to hurt you!"

The killer's anger boiled into a rampant fire of hatred. Brandishing the knife, the killer took stabs at the air before ripping linen and blankets from the bed and mutilating each piece. Drawers were emptied of personal possessions and tossed across the room. Glass vessels of perfume were slammed against the walls shattering and spraying the scented liquid. Panting with breathless rage, the killer stomped over the mounds of cut-up garments, stabbed the mattress until out of breath. Knuckles white from squeezing the knife's handle, vicious emotions rose higher in the killer with each new attack, charging every room, destroying every tangible piece of property.

"Nikki-wikki you bitch! Come out Nikki-wikki and others won't have to die anymore!"

Drained of physical exertion, more countless hours would be spent finding ways to ruin her. It was no longer enough to feel the sensation of sweet revenge through poison.

Too slow.

Too monotonous.

Patience sinking, rage rising, the killer paced and waved the knife in a staccato manner. "She must die painfully! The worse possible way to go."

Think!

"She was supposed to be here today—the schedule said so—the phone call proved it."

Death was part of living. Love was part of hate. Pain was part of pleasure. She would suffer in some unique and agonizing way. More than the little bitches who came before her, but slowly. Hearing them beg for life was intense passion. It was a craving greater than any sexual appetite. Larger than any raging storm. It was almost as tremendous as the acclaimed title, *Green Bay Serial Killer.*

"That bitch has to die! Must die! Will die! She will feel the ache of my suffering. She will exhale her last breath of my rejection. They will all die for what they did to me."

Exhausted, the killer stopped in the middle of one room, let the knife slip out and descend silently to the carpet.

❧   ❧   ❧

When he left Nikki's office on New Year's Eve, Gage immediately put a call into Tom Coville with the Park Rangers. Although long before Tom's time, they had handled Brian's accident. He wanted a copy of the report but had no idea if Tom could get his hands on the fifteen-year-old paperwork. Later that same night, like too many others, he laid awake wondering what Sully meant. What he knew? The rest of his sleepless hours he thought about Nikki and the familiar scent of her fragrant flesh. The way his insides burned when she kissed him back. Like one of those rockets taking off for the moon. He also compared the past hurt he inflicted to the bedeviling way she goaded him. He dwelled on the tormenting hell he rendered to those who meant everything to him. In between, he struggled with ways he would learn what recovery Nikki went through. What role had his mother played in it? How much time did he have until she left La Pointe for good?

Still speculating, Gage looked across his cab at Nikki with little hope. During the five-hour drive, they stopped once along the way for coffee. Their conversation was casual and both were careful not to mention two things. That weekend, and their feelings. Being enlightened to the new facts was still too fresh for both of them to digest with any real logic. She was probably wondering the same things he was although he didn't know how she could when she'd eagerly carried the conversation for the duration. Telling him about her trip to Beverly Hills and the job offer she was bound to get and accept almost sold him out.

Her emotional excitement had stimulated life back into her. Spunkiness he thrived on. Perhaps even instigated just to get her to wrangle with him on everything. He admired her courage in view of the way she was raised without parents. He looked at her sideways again. Although he couldn't burst the balloon she was sailing on, he felt sick inside thinking of the day she would leave.

Hitting the outskirts of Green Bay, he asked, "You hungry?"

"Yeah, a little. I also need to use the ladies room again."

"We'll stop somewhere and grab lunch. Any place special you want to eat?"

"Mexican sounds really good if you can find one."

He shelved his queasy thoughts and smiled. "Thought pizza was your favorite."

"It is," she confirmed, looked at him, "but late night."

"Mexican it is. After lunch, I want to look up Janice Anderson. Then tomorrow—"

"Who's Janice Anderson?"

Her voice held a tart tinge, and glancing sideways, he wondered if she knew her brows always crested suspiciously when that inflection infiltrated her speech. He debated whether she'd be safer not knowing. "Would that be jealousy I hear?"

She jerked then shifted in her seat. "Jealousy? Gage you are so full of yourself."

"I was hoping," he said with a grin. "I mean considering…,"

"Considering what?"

"Considering the way I seem to affect you."

"And a pint of *Häagen-Dazs* has six servings," Nicole shot back.

His grin deepened into laughter. "Babe, you have all these fascinating little quirks when you try to flaunt yourself at me."

"What quirks?" she flouted, instantly retorting, "I don't flaunt myself at you or anyone else."

"Bet me. The first is this little flex in your left eyebrow," he reached, touched the spot and laughed when she flinched. "Next you clamp your jaw. Yep, there it is. Here comes the arm gesture."

She sent him a brow-arching scowl as she crossed them, making him hoot.

"Last, but my favorite, is your eyes. They get really big. The color changes from golden to chocolate brown when you glare at me."

"So, because you hate my flaunting, which I don't do, you have this dying need to provoke me."

"That's not what I said." He pulled into a parking lot, shut off the engine and exited his truck. "Nikki, what I hate is the way other men look at you."

He closed the door before she could sound off and pocketed his keys. He walked around the front assuming she'd spout off one of her acquired pet names for him. When he opened her door, she was still sitting with an amazingly annoyed look on her face.

Offering a hand, he nodded toward the restaurant. "Will Chi Chi's satisfy your craving?"

She took his hand and slid out of the truck. "You wanna talk about quirks? You have this marvelous crimp near the corner of your mouth when you disapprove or doubt."

She gently touched the corner she was referring to. The gesture caught him off guard. It sent his insides sailing like a surface-to-air-missile.

"To confirm you understand or accept anything, you render a quick nod with your head. Your eyes turn to slits when you're angry. They pale when you're irritated."

"What do they do when I'm thinking about you?" he asked hoarsely.

"How would I know that, much less when you're thinking about me? What I do know is when you have something to say, instead of fidgeting you latch both thumbs on your gun belt." Finger walking along his chest, she said, "But you still haven't answered my question. Who's Janice Anderson and why are we going to see her?"

He stood stone-still collecting the emotional pieces she'd blown across the parking lot. It wasn't the lack of what she said. It was *how* she said it. The old push and pull between them had him all knotted up inside. His next thought was how much he preferred tasting that loquacious mouth of hers. He leaned and didn't hold back. He took her mouth eagerly, descending inside. A primitive sound hummed deep in her throat. It came fast with hot, hungry need. He felt her response all the way down to his toes then regained control by teasing. He sampled more of her now than he did kissing her.

Nicole felt it. Felt every inch of her body against him. Felt the way he thrived on torturing her. She couldn't help herself and savored every stroke he made. Unhurried and deliberate, it sizzled through her bones. Sizzled so, she fought for air, was elated, terrified, and groaned out his name.

"*We* aren't going to see her," Gage finally answered between more kisses. "I am...it's related to the case. Tomorrow we'll stop at that shop...head back in time for the last ferry...,"

He inched his face between her neck and jacket collar, breathed in the scent of her, felt the quiver of her desires as she freed her hand and wound both inside his jacket and around his back.

"Does it still feel the way it did when you were twelve?"

"Hmmm...,"

He slipped his hands around her midriff, brushed her brow, and coaxed her lips. "Do you hate me or love me, Nikki?"

Caught up in the moment he knew he had dumbfounded her, and drew her face to his in a renewed embrace. "I've no objection to standing here persuading you, but guarantee we'll become public spectacles if you don't answer me."

Instantly alert, she stepped back, bumping into the seat of the truck. "If I didn't know better I'd think you were trying to seduce me."

Gage grinned, thought about what it would be like have total control of her. The fact he couldn't control her is what appealed the most to him. Taking her arm, he said, "You'll definitely know I'm seducing you *if and when* I decide to. Those quivers of yours tell me a lot more than you will."

"Those quivers are because I have to pee!"

Laughter floated up from his throat. He locked and closed the door of the cab. Following her, he took in every swooshing hip movement enjoying it. He'd always wondered if she swayed that way deliberately or naturally. Catching up, he opened the restaurant door, prompting, "You still haven't answered *my* question."

Looking, seeing the sign, Nicole was going to head for the bathroom then stopped. "Does it matter?" she asked and walked away.

The voice in his head roared, *Hell, yah, it matters!* Conflicting emotions attacked taking away the control he reaped, replacing it with loss. His heart raced and body fluid bled out of his flesh. Too many years the anticipation of being without her bucked inside of him. He stood motionless believing the loyal struggle would never be fulfilled. His dismantled heart could never take not being set free of her. In that moment of silent suffering, he realized her strength was ten-fold his. Believing one thing all these years, he'd lived with the agony and the hell. Somewhere he resigned himself to accepting comfort in knowing she would always be around. Customers finally nudged him back to earth, out of the entry.

Muttering an apology, he saw Nikki approaching gracefully. She was stunning as she glided through in booted shoes and slacks that murmured of intimate relations. He thought for sure that everything she wore had been created for her alone. Although he loved the short skirts, there was something remarkably stirring about keeping those long legs concealed.

Heads turned to look at her promenading beautifully past all of them. Her long honey-colored hair was fluent with her as if body and mane couldn't be cut apart. She displayed the same bountiful smile she always did working the tavern. Then, Michelle's question flipped through his thoughts.

Why hasn't she pursued the modeling career she wanted?

Practiced and wordless, she acknowledged several greetings from watchers. At that moment, as if she were reading his mind, he was instantly caught unaware. It was in her large amber-brown eyes looking only at him. The answer hit him with a forceful impact.

She's waiting for you to make the first move.

Both her reason for staying and now for leaving were because of him. Because of everything that had occurred years ago. He clearly saw her war with love and hate. Not only had he never asked her out, but he accused her of the worse thing a man could.

"Well, that was a relief. Gage, I have an idea."

"What's that?" he asked somberly.

"Will that be two for lunch, sir?"

He answered the woman with an impersonal nod and touched Nikki's elbow lightly, urging her to go before him. They followed the woman to a table near the back and Gage seated Nikki then pulled out the chair next to her instead of across from her. "What's your idea?"

"Drop me off at that store after we finish eating and you can go find the Anderson woman. Then we could head back to La Pointe in the morning."

He brushed a knuckle across her cheek and challenged, "You anxious to get rid of me?"

"I just thought…,"

Holding her hand now, he kissed the palm. "Nikki, it won't do me any good if I'm not there to hear what they have to say about the dress. Mac hooked me up with a Green Bay detective. I'm meeting with him this afternoon to go over and talk to Josie's cousin. We can check into—"

"Josie's cousin? Gage, Josie doesn't have a cousin."

He dropped her hand like it was hot, and leaned back. "Come again."

"I'm telling you Josie does not have any cousins. Her parents were only children like she is."

"How do you know that?"

"Stuff always comes out as kids growing up. I don't recall, but I'm positive she's cousinless."

"Did you ever hear her mention the name Janice Anderson?" Nikki glanced around the restaurant and back to him.

"I can't say. The name doesn't ring any bells."

Sliding his chair back, he said, "Wait a minute. I have to make a call."

Although he rarely used it, Gage pulled out a cell phone. His mind floundered as suspicion crept through him. Who was Janice Anderson then? Why had all the Stewart's lied to him and Mac about her? He dialed Pipsqueak's number first and spoke to Mac who filled him in. As Mac repeated it, he heard his sister in the background dispute, then recall and confirm what Nikki had just told him. Mac gave him Harry Lindell's number. Gage hung up and called the detective. They spoke for five minutes before he disconnected a second time.

"Everything okay?" she asked him as the waitress stepped up. They ordered coffee.

"Gage, what's going on? Why do you need to talk to this woman?"

"Nikki, we don't have much time," he told her still believing the less she knew the better. "The detective is gonna meet me here. We'll drive over to the hotel, check in then I have to go. If you want, you can take my truck and go shopping or whatever."

"That won't be necessary. I'll just kick back and relax. I brought a swimsuit in case there's a pool."

Perking up a little, he said, "Really? I'd like to see that later."

The waitress returning kept Nikki from responding. Her blushing cheeks gave him the advantage, which increased his adrenaline immensely. Their meals ordered and delivered a short time later, Harry Lindell found him just as they finished. Gage paid the bill and followed the detective to the motel where he checked him and Nikki into separate rooms. He left his truck keys with her just in case she changed her mind.

❦   ❦   ❦

Shy of seven-thirty, Nicole had showered and slipped into her new Beverly Hills silk flared skirt and side-slit belted tunic. Thankfully, Gage would be the first to see her obnoxiously overpriced outfit. As much as she wanted to wear the lovely jewelry he gave her, the set didn't match the forest green.

He'd called not long after he left with the detective to tell her they'd go out for dinner when he returned around seven. She thought she heard him showering in the room next to hers and debated whether to knock on his door. She didn't want to appear anxious.

There's a word!

Anxiety-ridden since returning from L.A., she had no way of identifying which incidents caused the turmoil anymore. In the truck this morning, she was on overdrive sharing her trip to Beverly Hills with him. Then out of the clear blue, it turned into a hundred-degree day smack dab in the middle of winter. She'd had all she could do not to jump his bones right there in the parking lot of Chi Chi's. Grateful the hotel had a pool, she tried to sort out the chaos while swimming laps to slow her racing hormones.

Every time he touched her, looked at her, or feathered her flesh in anyway her insides quaked uncontrollably. 'Quivers' he called them, right after he told her she'd definitely know when he was seducing her. Obviously, the man had no idea it took very little for him to seduce her into anything he wanted. In fact, she was on fire inside wanting to feel his breathy kisses against her flesh. Since they'd talked that night in her office, she'd been overheating like a bad radiator. Was this what he meant by making it all up to her?

Screw sensibility and propriety.

Nicole slipped into the matching heels, grabbed her room key, and shrieked swinging the door open. He stood there readied to knock, his tired eyes brightening as an appreciative smile formed across his face. It took less time to decide he looked too confounded handsome for anyone's good.

"You're exhausted," she blurted.

"You're beautiful," he told her.

"Thank you," she said, smiling. "How'd it go today?"

Shrugging, he said, "If you're ready, Harry gave me the names of a couple good places to eat."

His voice sounded emotionless. Chilling as it made her feel she worried more knowing he hadn't slept. "Gage, you're wound tighter than a wine cork. We don't have to go out for dinner. Come in and I'll order room service."

As if she were flashing subliminal thoughts at him, he took her by the waist backing her into the room. Her hands came up to his shoulders and he touched kisses around her lips, along her jaw. Her mouth burned as the rest of her body obsessed over and argued with her aching need. He kicked the door shut with a foot and covered her mouth demanding a response.

She returned the kiss recklessly parting her lips as tongues intertwined. Driven by his needs she matched the urgency with lusty desires. Nicole slid off his jacket letting it fall to the floor. He removed his holster. She meshed her hands into his hair as he gathered her taut against him.

It was fast and quick. They went from mild to wild, tasting, stroking, touching, and kissing. She gave him love bites on his neck, he nibbled her ear sending Goosey Lucy up and down her flesh. Her fingers twisted through his hair, he wrenched his hands through hers. Wherever she touched him, he took the direct route wanting his hands on her.

She tugged his sweater over his head. He plucked her tunic in one quick jerk. She dashed her tongue over him, he turned to jelly and groaned inhumanly. He cupped, massaged her covered breasts, her knees caved, she moaned louder.

Wildly he ripped away her bra tormenting her swollen buds with heartless open-mouth kisses. She yanked him closer, undid his belt and zipper in a rush. He slid his hands, wrenched her thighs and hips roughly, closer, tighter. She kissed, sampled, enjoyed; he stroked, taunted, controlled. It was hot and stormy, untamed and frantic. She gasped. He panted.

She kicked her shoes off, his boots were next, her skirt flew, his jeans hit the floor. There was no time to gaze or stare before he briskly sheered off her silk stockings.

He explored her flesh in arousing torment, lifted, and carried her to the bed. Her impatience grew to ignitable proportions as he cleverly rocked her world. In an endless search for her pleasure points, she uncovered his.

He tasted and nipped between agonizing moans. He pecked and teased paving her ribs deliberately and then her stomach. He traced her thighs with convincing palms exploring further. The more he stroked, held the reins of power, manipulated her intimately, the more the fire of life and breath raged through them both.

Coiled in liquid fire, the contact between them heated up and bled over. Her heart swelled, her chest tightened, and her head swirled. The more he made her quiver, the more she made him tremble. Each untamed caress stimulating until their bodies vibrated uncivilly. The more he groaned her name, the more she greedily kissed, sampled and relished the fragments of his flesh. He shuddered and she briefly caught his pupils dilating. Never once had she believed she could control him, leave him defenseless as her name rolled off his lips repeatedly.

Those hot tides raged through both of them in raw acts of possessive claims. She wanted and took, he needed and gave, he demanded, and she surrendered. Then he was atop her insatiable and taking. She gasped on soul-drenching air rising to welcome him into her body. Her flesh molded with his and she cried out for release, clutching, embracing herself within him. The hidden fulfillment she'd longed for was absolute. The gusts of her needs ignited, she shook until he took everything she had to give.

Collapsing in sheer exhaustion and selfishness, the energy was powerful. The room lit by a street light, their breathing was the only sound. Gage snuggled alongside Nikki taking in the warmth of her intoxicating flesh. He kissed her lightly and memorized her face.

A deep sensation of peace had reached and touched the tuber of her soul as he caressed the planes of her back. Quite effectively she thought, before she tumbled into a deep slumber.

CHAPTER 15

✿

She woke first from a dreamless sleep and lay under Gage in the early morning hours. His breathing was soft, even, and he occupied three-quarters of the bed. Nicole supposed if she tried, she could slide out from the nonchalant brace of his arm. But, she didn't want to. Not yet.

Everything had changed between them. Completely unexpected.

Amazing didn't exactly describe what had happened between them last night. She couldn't come up with an accurate word to explain their vigor. Slow hands and easy touches held no water next to Gage's superb performance. Nicole looked at the man lying half on her, half beside her. The strained lines in his face were relaxed. They would stay that way until he opened his eyes. She still worried, but at last, he slept.

Recalling the thank-you card she wrote to his mother, tears trembled on her eyelids. If Brian had lived, if they'd never argued a day in her life, if she wasn't leaving, none of it would change the fact that she had never been fertile a day in her life. Although he never mentioned the subject of children, she always knew he wanted kids, a family. His actions always spoke clearly. She didn't love him—no. She *couldn't* love him.

It was too late for that.

Nicole wiped her eyes with a corner of the sheet and glanced at her watch over him. She'd have to wake him shortly if he didn't do it on his own. As much as she enjoyed lying in the discomfort of his flopped-over arms, they needed to leave Green Bay before noon to catch the last ferry to Madeline. Breakfast first, then T. Kohl LTD would undoubtedly open at nine or ten. She figured about fifteen minutes were all she needed to find out what Gage wanted to know. That left her an hour to have her way with him one last time.

Once back on the island, it made no sense to continue the fast exhilarating and most beautiful experience she'd ever had. Nicole slid out from under him and he rolled over. She slipped under the sheet and barely skimmed his abdomen with her lips. Her blood bustled through her veins eagerly. It reminded her of La Pointe's fog that excited and chilled her bones. She kissed his flesh lovingly, scarcely brushing over him with an open mouth.

His eyes flew open and Gage thought he was going to rupture. It was an involuntary reaction for him to groan. But underneath the brain fuzz of morning, Nikki was telling him two things; she liked sex and she liked it with him. He'd be sending her dozens of roses for her generosity, for filling him with the morning sensation.

Last night had been energetic and quick, hot and spicy. Then he slept, and he dreamt of fooling around with her at a leisurely pace. He wanted to fool around now. Control her until she was begging and they were both so hot they had to do it immediately or spontaneously combust. He dragged her up along his body and planted a deep kiss on her mouth.

"Good morning, beautiful," he spoke wearing down her lips. Gazing into her sensual eyes, they glazed over. He wove his hands through her long golden hair, rolled her over sliding them along her arms languidly. It wasn't just the sex he wanted, he'd always wanted—needed her. Wanted to give her his heart and have hers in return.

She arched, moaned softly as he caressed the satiny lines of her belly, her waist, her hips, watching the color in her eyes change amorously. He took a bite as her buds swelled, and he watched the color in her eyes change more. Exploring, he played with the spots that had propelled her last night. She surged with each caress and stuttered out the same low cries. Arousing her stirred him up tremendously. Teasing, he fondled, nuzzled, and kissed long past her pleas. Slow rolling sighs melted off her lips. The sounds she made turned him on more than her touching him did.

He glanced up. Her eyes were varnished in a unique shade of bronze. The scent of her flesh lingered, blurred his brain until his insides blazed. The more he empowered her, the more she weakened him.

"Gage!"

She unharnessed an explosion of his long awaited sensations. He converged gradual, deliberate, and deep, relinquished everything to her, letting her consume his soul.

Freedom would escape him if she left.

Clinging in sultry kisses, they united and he found himself drowning within her. She squirmed beneath him, and he drove himself deeper inside of her. His breath went ragged. He throbbed to implosive proportions. The turbulence of his craving twisted around her, shook him. The urgency to hold her heart and soul the way she'd always possessed his ruptured into burning desire. He felt it deep within the breath of life. In that costly moment, he knew the center of his world would be bound to her until the end of time.

The flare and stimulation of internal excitement made her heart beat until Nicole could barely breathe. It was like a dream. One that never left but couldn't be explained. His mouth heated against hers, he conquered and disabled her. Took, then claimed her, and she'd never been more enlivened by any thing or one.

Was this the heart-pounding, blood-boiling commotion she'd been looking for?

It wasn't love—to love him would hurt him. The idea startled Nicole.

Gage felt the change, tried to ignore it, nevertheless, he came down quickly. Lying motionless, he heaved a sigh heavily into her hair. Their hearts thumped hard against their chests. His words came out irregular, hoarse. "Baby, stay here with me."

"Gage," she whispered, "we'll miss the last ferry."

He rolled off, gazed into her eyes, played with her hair. "That's not what I mean."

She lovingly touched his arm before she sat up. "I can't give you everything you need," she blurted out.

Gage took hold of her arm. "How do you know what I need?"

She closed her eyes, biting back the tears he constantly wanted to sooth. He let go of her arm to drag a hand through her silky hair. "Nikki, what is it? What's wrong?"

She scrambled off the bed, shameless to her nudity and went into the bathroom. He exhaled the familiar frustration and fell against the pillows. When he heard the shower come on, he jumped out of bed scrambling toward the closed door. It opened when he tried and he moved into the lavish room stepping into the tub with her.

"Gage! What are you doing?"

She'd lathered up her hair. Shampoo dribbled down her face and he didn't answer. She was the one at a disadvantage, but the power she had over him was gut-sucking.

"Let me do that."

Depositing his hands into the slick mass, he massaged her head. She took the bar of soap, frothed up her hands and gently cleansed his flesh. If he thought he'd been turned on earlier it was nothing compared to the way she was exciting him now. Purposely she caressed him in places where he never gave any thought to and in places he always thought about. He'd never sucked in this many abrupt deep breaths in his entire life. Simultaneously, he ran his fingers tenderly against her scalp, kneading the back of her neck and head.

"Oh, Lord!" she purred. "That's better than any hairdresser I've ever had."

His hands and body soapy he wrapped himself around her water-slippery flesh, kissing her under the fall of water. "I've heard the best way to a woman's heart is by shampooing her hair."

"You think so," she murmured.

"Might not have gotten to your heart, but your body sure is reacting. Gi'me that soap and let me convince all of you."

"Gage, we—"

He kissed her to shut her up. Sliding the bar out of her hand, he rubbed down her satin flesh. Starting with her back and shoulders, he swashed foamy bubbles up and down her arms, slowed and outlined the circle of her swelling nipples, gradually brushed her hips, knelt to do each leg with lazy deliberate strokes, last her feet.

When she squirted shampoo into his hair and stroked his scalp, the gesture inflamed his insides. *Damn*, an earthquake reverberated inside of him as she kneaded his head and neck erotically. He explored her thighs then moved up, stroking with his fingers until she cried out in appeal. She vice-gripped her hands to the metal handle on the wall, and he said, "Let it go, baby."

Her head fell back. Her breasts swelled and surged. Pleading to him, she filled him. He scrunched into the tub pulling Nikki on top of his hardness. She closed around him, her body and hips vibrating. Her breasts within reach, Nikki held his hands, kept him from touching her. Her eyes darkened recklessly. It changed unexpectedly, shockingly. Through blurred vision Gage looked, saw more than he expected and it stole his breath away. Amidst the tremors flowing between them, her amber eyes exposed her love for him. Nikki was submerged inside the storm-tossed moment and all he could do was follow.

Their dual craving fundamental to the deep necessities of human appetite, he could never let go, never starve again. He freed his hands and took her face. Her arms swathed his neck and he crushed her sleek soapy flesh against his kissing her fiercely, passionately, selfishly.

"Nikki, I'm asking you now. Please stay. Don't go."

Nicole choked. Her body rhythm shut down.

"What's wrong?" he asked hoarsely

"Nothing." Hefting herself up and rinsing off, she told him, "We better get moving or we won't make it back before four-thirty."

They dressed in silence, ate the hotel's Continental breakfast quietly, and drove to T. Kohl LTD without a word between them. Nikki went directly to the store's manager and within minutes, Gage felt like a pair of Packers defense had bulldozed him into the ground. The Susan Bristol white dress Stacy wore had been a huge sell-out. Whoever purchased the dress at the Green Bay location had done so long before fall arrived. The woman had sales receipts. Some were credit card purchases, others paid cash. She did have customers fill out their name and address for sale notification. Gage gave her the station's fax number and she would put together the lists in a day or two.

He and Nikki headed back to La Pointe in awkward reticence. They stopped once to eat before arriving in Bayfield. Outside, the temp had dropped several degrees by the time they boarded the ferry. Inside the cab, body heat soared with spleen. Gripping the wheel relentlessly, he couldn't take another moment of her muteness. Locked, loaded, he finally erupted, "Nikki, what's wrong with you?"

"Nothing."

"This is not nothing," he barked. "Are you upset about last night?"

She shot him a stunned look.

"Because we finally made love to each other the way we've both wanted to all our lives?"

"No."

"Then what? We've both wanted this too damn long. How can you deny what we both feel, Nikki?"

Exhaling, she spoke in a whisper. "Without knowing why, I've hated you for fifteen years. Until this past week I didn't know I'd been waiting for you inside my heart my entire life." Looking at him, she realized her eyes were dried up, recognized the half-truth she was about to drowned him with. "Now, when you finally make a move, it's too late?"

"Too late?" He looked across the cab at her. "How? Why? For what?"

"Because Gage," her voice was calm, motionless, "Chantilly offered me the job two days ago. I accepted. I start February first."

That foundation she tilted blew up. Clamping his jaw, he glared at a faded red trunk of a Pontiac Sunbird in front of them. The color, when new, would have matched his current wrath. Parched eyes, Nikki sat stone still, more silent than he'd ever known her to be, and scrunched against the passenger door ready to challenge it in a one-on-one.

Coercing his anger away, forcing it to dissolve, he followed the red Pontiac off the ferry. Parking five minutes later in front of her house, he jumped out and slammed the door. She didn't wait for him to open the door. He took her bag and trudged behind.

She unlocked, opened the door and screamed. He dropped the bag yanking out his weapon. The inside in total disarray, Gage pulled her behind him inching cautiously into the house.

"Wait here," he ordered.

His heart pumping, sweat frothing his brow, room by room, he snuck through checking behind doors and in closets. His adrenaline fully ignited, he should have called for backup. Everything had been overturned and destroyed. He came back to the living room, stopped, still abundantly alert, and saw the knife for the first time lying in the middle of the floor. It looked like one of her kitchen knives. The scene transformed his guts into torment. How would he solve this? Kicking a chair, he went to Nikki and blocked her entrance. Vivid fear glittered through a round of new tears.

"You won't be staying here tonight," he told her. Holstering his gun, he said, "I need to call the crime lab to process the entire house."

"I want to see it."

"No, goddammit!" He glared a split second before exploding again. "Someone smashed a kitchen window to gain entry! Everything's destroyed!"

The sudden outburst caused her tears to erupt into sobs. Hissing under his breath, Gage gathered her into his arms and held her tight. "Baby, I'm sorry. I'm not gonna let anything happen to you."

"Gage, what did I ever do? Who's after me?" Breaking into feral sobs, she cried, "I'm scared!"

"I know, Nikki. I'll keep you safe. You're staying with Mom and Dad. I'll sleep at the station. I'm gonna call Mac and have someone come and get you."

Clinging to him, Gage comforted her until her sobs diminished. Brushing the stains off her cheeks, he said, "I'm not going to let anything happen to you. I promise."

Sniffling, she told him, "Gage, you don't have to sleep at the station. I won't argue about staying with your folks this time. I'm really terrified."

He was too. "Nikki, nobody's getting anywhere near you." When she nestled against him, he couldn't resist an effortless kiss. "And, Nikki, I didn't put the moves on you last night without having an ulterior motive. This isn't how I planned it, but I've waited too long to tell you I am in love with you. I always have been. Don't move to L.A. Stay here and marry me, raise a family with me."

Nicole choked. Hysteria broke into more uncontrollable weeping. The reaction sent Gage two steps back. A mountain of inconceivable emotions, thoughts, and questions overwhelmed him. He balled his hands into fists with fresh waves of panic.

"Here!" he ordered, trying to analyze too much at once. "Take the keys and go keep warm in my truck."

She took a breath to speak and Gage waved off further arguments. Didn't have the patience left to fight with her. Afraid of his own reaction, he gave her a convincing nudge toward the truck. Once she was seated with the engine running, he went back inside the house, and again used his cell phone to call dispatch.

Was the idea of being married to him that repulsive?

He realized his seething hostility came through in his voice when the dispatcher said, "Having a bad day are we?"

Apologizing, he requested she send Mac and get the crime lab to his location.

"They're not gonna be happy campers," the woman replied in his ear.

"I don't give a goddamn what they are! Just get 'em here and get me an ETA! Now!"

❧   ❧   ❧

Thankfully, Katharine didn't hang around after dropping her off. Paula and Frank were gone with Caitlin—she didn't hear where Katharine said they went. Nicole fell onto Paula's sofa, laying her head back. She needed to be alone with her thoughts. She wanted to be isolated to sort through the events. She certainly had no desire to work, let alone prepare herself for a new job.

She had peeked. Annihilation, the coming of the third world war filled the inside of her house. Gage had said everything was destroyed, and he was right. From what she could see there was nothing left except what she took to Green Bay with her.

What faithless force had deteriorated her life?

He told her he loved her—he always had. *Does that give him the right to throw the big M question at me without warning? To staple on the family thing? If he had stopped at marry me, would I have said yes instead of bursting into pathetic tears. How can I say yes when I can't say those three words back without deception attached to my answer?*

Nicole didn't know how to feel anything after feeling the hurt for so long. Last night had been exquisite, but it was also hormones on overdrive. *It had to be.* Befuddlement curdled around her for the first time. She knew very well what Gage wanted and he just confirmed it. The ache squeezed hard inside her chest. If she could find the courage to explain he would certainly reject her when he discovered she couldn't conceive. Her eyes filled with tears and she wept aloud rocking back and forth until all energy was bludgeoned from her.

Sitting lifeless, numbed, defeated, she was a woman facing the harsh realities of loneliness. In the wake of hapless luck, another opportunity had been tossed her way. It was a dream come true. She knew the choice she had to make. Change is good she mused. Threatening to most, people don't adjust unless pain or conflict forces them into the deed.

"Nikki!"

Caitlin squealed her name bringing her back to the moment. Running, the elated child jumped into her lap. Nicole wrapped her arms with an endless hug around snowsuit and child, and quickly wiped her eyes. "How's my little blond cutie?"

"Good. We went snowmobiling and Frank let me drive. Why are you here? Where's Gage?"

"Working. Did you have fun?"

"Uh-huh. Paula and I got to ride on the sled behind, too."

"Sounds like you had lots of fun. Let's get your snowsuit off and make some hot chocolate."

"Mmmm, hot chocolate," she responded, scrambling off. "Nikki, are you gonna sleep over?"

She slid forward and began unzipping Caitlin's suit. "You betcha. Gage and I agreed I should stay here for awhile. Would you like that?"

Vigorously bobbing her head, Caitlin squealed again. "Yippee! Paula, Nikki's sleeping over!"

Nicole looked over the top of Caitlin. Paula had stopped mid-stream removing her boots. Her eyes girdled over with complex emotions, love shone through all of them. It took only a second for her mind to flood over and not with the good things Paula had done for her. But the not so good came flipping back. The first time she swore and Paula doled up punishment. In ninth grade another blasting speech came when skipping school with Michelle and

Katharine seemed like more fun. None of them had considered the conse-
quences of their choice—more discipline. The summer night they sneaked out
of the house on one of numerous sleepovers to skinny-dip in Superior was a
night none of them would forget. Paula greeted them at the door upon their
return. The first time they tried drinking at the hangout, then smoking, and
anytime she badmouthed Lilly or the other nannies sent to live with her. Every
time she criticized her parents, screwed up in anyway, Paula was there with a
thousand new rules and explanations, and love.

Love as big as the universe stared back at her right now with hope and
belief. With plenty of expectations from the woman who'd actually raised her,
soothed away the tears and fears of a lonely child, and gave her love no matter
what stupid thing she said or did. Could she really walk away from the only
family she knew?

"Caitlin, upstairs with Frank and wash your hands," Paula said, finally prying loose the other boot. "I'll make dinner and you can have hot chocolate
afterward."

"Nikki, come with?"

"Caitlin, Frank's going up with you. Nicole's going to help me in the
kitchen."

She recognized that clear-the-room-we're-gonna-have-a-talk voice. Paula
used it on all of them more than once. She instantly felt the whack inside her
chest as the oh-shit-I've-done-it-now knot pompously filled the inside of her
gut. Slowly lifting herself off the sofa, the cuckoo clucked the evening's sixth
hour from the wall, and Nicole gradually proceeded to the kitchen.

"What would you like me to start on first?" she asked in her expert work
voice hoping to deter a parental lecture although she had no idea what the talk
would be about.

"Frank wants burgers and fries tonight," she answered with her head in the
fridge. Taking out the food, Paula told her, "You can set the table. Will Gage be
joining us tonight?"

"No. At least not for a couple of hours."

She looked up. "What happened, Nicole?"

Looking at the woman who always provided emotional security, she realized Paula rarely wore slacks let alone jeans. Jeans with a double-rolled cuff to
accommodate her baby-keg legs. Gage had her pale pitying eyes and her real
daughter had her smooth satiny complexion. Skin that you saw on young girls
mostly, not old women. Paula wasn't old. Now that she thought about it, she
had no idea the age of this woman who stood several inches beneath her height

with her blended look. Her face always contained affection and commitment as she waited for an answer. "Someone broke into my house while we were gone."

"Oh! Good Lord! Come here, you poor dear," she reached pulling Nicole into her arms. "Thank God you weren't there when it happened. Go sit down. I'll take care of everything. Are you all right?"

She did sit, as her eyes misted over. "I don't know. Everything is getting too crazy for me. I don't understand who could be after me."

"Oh, honey, you need to rest. Gage will take care of everything. You'll see. My born-efficient son will know exactly what to do."

"Paula, you don't even know the half of it."

"Why? What else happened?"

She chewed on her bottom lip and swallowed hard. "He said he's in love with me." Nicole burst with tears and words. "He asked me to marry him and raise a family and you know I can't give him what he wants."

She moved and stood over Nicole with her arms wrapped around her. Thinking, *he certainly didn't waste time—she should have said what she did years ago.* "Honey, you haven't told him, have you?"

She shook out her answer along with the sobs. "How can I?" she managed.

Stepping back, Paula grabbed the box of tissues handing it to Nicole. "Darling, I can't help you with this one. He has to learn about it from you. You must find a way to tell him yourself. His love for you is stronger than you think and I'm positive it will survive."

She stopped, looked up. "Paula, I can't tell him. I don't know how and now I've been offered a job in Los Angeles. I'm leaving after the anniversary party."

Time to kick her plan into action. "Nicole, did Gage tell you we're keeping Caitlin until they can find a good home for her?"

Sniveling and wiping her nose, Paula had moved away from her to begin her supper routine. "No, he never mentioned it."

"She's doing very well here. I thought it would be best. Now dry your eyes, dear, and set the table for me."

She stood up, knowing where everything was in Paula's kitchen and performed the task. Odd how this woman who once filled in for a traveling mother didn't seem to care that she was leaving, or the danger she faced.

"Nikki, can I have some hot chocolate? Can you read me a story like you did before I go to sleep?"

"Did you wash your hands?" Nicole asked the returning child.

"Yes. Can I have some hot chocolate, please?"

"With your meal—"

"I want it now!" Caitlin demanded and dropped to the floor.

Nicole gawked at her for a moment and went about setting the table. Although a wonderful exhibition, it didn't work. Even when Caitlin's tantrum turned to screams.

"I think somebody's tired. Caitlin, you can lay there or help me set the table."

"Hot chocolate!" she screamed loudly and thrashed her hands hard against the floor.

"The sooner we get the table set, the sooner you can have hot chocolate with your meal."

"No!"

"Fine, go without."

Bawling and screaming louder, plentiful tears rolled down Caitlin's cheeks. Nicole went over and lifted her off the floor as Keeker cowered under the table. Caitlin stiffened, kicked and wailed a bit louder, if that were possible. After several moments, even the cat became fed up. He turned disgustingly and sauntered out of the kitchen.

Tightening her hold, Nicole coaxed, "Listen to me, sweetie."

"No! I want Gage!"

"She didn't get a nap today," Paula said over her shoulder.

"No kidding. Caitlin, that's enough. You'll have hot chocolate with your dinner."

"Now!" she screamed.

"At the table with your dinner," Nicole restated.

"I don't like you!"

"You don't have to like me. But I love you and now you sit at the table nicely or you can go to bed. It's your choice."

Caitlin fisted a pudgy hand into her teary eyes.

"Can I have hot chocolate?"

"With your dinner."

Those tear-stained blue eyes studied her for the longest moment as if the choice she was contemplating would be the hardest one she'd ever make in her life. "I'm hungry," she finally decided.

"Good." Nicole put her in a chair and finished what she started. She made hot chocolate as Paula finished hamburgers and waited for the French fries to come out of the oven. Looking at the blue-eyed monster that had replaced her blond cutie, Caitlin's eyes drooped. Within a matter of moments, she could barely hold her head up.

"I doubt we'll get much food into her, Paula."

"It won't be the first or the last time. You handled the situation well."

"You make it sound like I performed a miracle. It was nothing compared to an out-of-control drunken crowd."

"Maybe, but you still did good with her. Now tell me about this dream job you've been offered."

Surprised by Paula's unexpected request, Nicole explained she'd been planning the new career ever since her surgery two years earlier. She studied and practiced, and sketched out dozens of new designs.

"Today you're not sure if it's what you really want to do with your life?"

Nicole had taken a seat next to Caitlin. Sheer exhaustion had forced her blond cutie to deposit her head on the table and fall asleep. Tenderly brushing hair off Caitlin's face, she said, "I guess it is. There's just…things, Paula. Gage found the thank you card I sent you."

"Honey, you can't change yesterday, but you can change today and tomorrow. Look closely around you. Think about what's important before you decide anything."

Nicole looked at Paula. She'd had no reaction to Gage's discovery. "This is one time you're not going to tell me what to do, isn't it?"

"I've never told you what to do, Nicole. I've always given you both sides and let you make up your own mind. With the normal exceptions, you've done very well so far. When things make the least amount of sense is when we should forget our brain and listen to what our heart is telling us. I'm sure you'll do the right thing."

"Paula, I can't decipher between the two."

"You will in time dear child."

CHAPTER 16

Prying the storybook loose from her hands, Gage stood vigilant over Nikki. She slept curled up with her arm sheltering Caitlin. Keeker was nuzzled near her feet. Her breathing was smooth. Her face relaxed. Beneath the ethereal glow of a nightlight, mellowness finally emerged. She was more beautiful each time he looked at her.

Annoyance made it imperative he quickly rid himself of her at the crime scene. Once she left, he had never felt more alone. He needed to see her and that's why he came home the first time. They hadn't heard him come in and he stood in the living room stunned by her words. He heard everything and remembered thinking, *why can't I make her understand that the only thing I want is to spend the rest of my life with her?* After discovering the break-in, he felt sure he was going to lose her again and took a huge risk asking what he did.

Gage absorbed a sharp breath to knock back the aching throb in his throat as he laid the book on the nightstand. It took the lab five hours to go over the inside of her house. They bagged the knife, took latents from everything and he and Mac secured the smashed window.

Someone is out to kill her. How can I protect her from that?

The best thing is for her to leave. The sooner the better. Give up his love for her life. It wasn't debatable. There were no choices. Regardless of what he wanted, Gage swallowed hard. He had to let her go.

"Gage," Caitlin muttered.

"Hey, squirt," he whispered hoarsely, and when she raised her arms, he leaned over and lifted her out of bed. "Sssh, don't wake, Nikki."

"Nikki hates me."

He doubted that. Inching away from the bed, he sat in the rocker his mother had recently moved into Caitlin's room. "Why's that," he asked quietly.

"Cuz I said I didn't like her."

She snuggled against him. "Why'd you do that?"

"She wouldn't give me hot chocolate."

"Before or after supper?" He smiled recalling she was asleep at the table.

"Before," she murmured.

"Caitlin, you own a special place in Nikki's heart. I'm positive she loves you as much as I love her." He'd spoken the words quietly and glanced down. Caitlin was asleep with a thumb in her mouth.

He never once doubted Nikki's parental abilities. She loved kids. He just wasn't sure she knew it. He assumed both she and Caitlin being parentless gave them a unique bond. He looked down at Caitlin a second time, shifting her, adjusted his shoulder holster then stood and walked over laying her down. Knowingly, his mother had left a blanket and pillow near the rocker. Since Nikki was still dressed, he covered them with the spare and bent kissing both. Re-sitting in the rocker, he grabbed the pillow.

He wasn't going anywhere.

Then his heart pitched him a curve ball.

He never noticed before now how much the two of them could pass as mother and daughter. It had to be the blond hair, but even Caitlin was long limbed. She would be lanky and clumsy all arms and legs until she matured. The same way Nikki had been.

He smiled before closing his eyes but it didn't take long to transform into fear. His suspicions were no longer that. Harry Lindell was on the Green Bay Task Force that Mac and Cole had led. Although the detective didn't know the Stewarts, his cop interest increased when they discovered Janice Anderson was not related to Josie. During their meet with her, she confirmed the lack of any relation, said she didn't know Patriot either. She shocked the hell out of him by backing up the hunch he'd been contemplating for several weeks. He didn't know why it surprised him when the Anderson woman confirmed Curt's wife was being unfaithful to him. Of all the sick things. Kevin Stewart was just one of numerous affairs Josie had had. It explained their behaviors the day they booked Josie back a few months ago. Then Janice told them Josie also had an affair with Michelle's ex. That turned his gut inside out. What he didn't understand was Curt's ignorance to it all. How could a man not know? Better yet, how had Josie, Janice and Kevin convinced Curt that Janice Anderson was

Josie's cousin? What about the unassuming Mark? Was he one of Josie's lovers, too?

Gage opened his eyes and rocked forward. Could Curt really be their serial killer? Jealousy of Nicole didn't make sense here. He'd known Curt his entire life. Curt had no reason to go after Nikki he argued in his mind. At least not with the violence he saw inside her house. But, Kevin had reason and so did Michelle's ex. Besides, Curt was at the Tavern the night Nikki discovered Stacy White in her backyard. So was Kevin. Mark had good alibis, too.

When he asked Janice how she and Josie met, he was no longer stupefied. It was at a Green Bay fitness center. Josie had membership and since meeting, they worked out together when Josie was in town. He recalled seeing her jogging frequently around the island and often wondered why. She wasn't that bad on the eyes. He was also curious about the excess money she spent for fitness that far away.

Anyway, the friendship developed. Janice went along with the idea of pretending they were related. Josie had fabricated a long lost cousin story with her husband so she'd have a place to stay during her affairs.

How many were there?

Supposedly, she introduced Kevin to Janice a little over two years ago. Ever since, they'd been an *item* she called it.

Mac was less surprised. Still, none of it made any sense. There was absolutely no connection between Nikki and the victims. The symbolism the killer placed on the bracelet had no connection with Nikki either. Too cheap and gaudy for her. That bracelet also leaned away from the perfection everyone kept noticing, yet, he knew that bracelet was important somehow.

As he lay back shutting his eyes once more, Gage couldn't stop asking himself who was out to kill Nikki. He wasn't seeing something. Something so obvious it would make them all look ridiculous. He had several inconclusive hunches but without solid proof that's all they were. Supposition. He'd have to do some more digging. He'd also have to interview Guthrie in County lock-up. The guy couldn't make bail and was still there. He'd find Sully and have a chat with him as well. Something was definitely amiss there, too. Gus hadn't gotten back to him about Brian's accident report yet. He had a destitute thought before he dozed off. Who would watch Nikki while he went after the *real* serial killer?

❦   ❦   ❦

After thirty-five years of stealthy moves around the house at night, Frank hadn't lost his skill to sneak about. It was the cop in him. Unable to sleep, he'd gotten up at two to sit in the rocker in front of the bedroom window and damn near fell on to the floor. Hearing Gage, he stood in the hallway shadows watching him soothe Caitlin. There sat his son in the rocker he dragged home doing exactly what he'd done to both his kids when they woke in the middle of the night. Then his son's admission to Caitlin damn near knocked him to the floor a second time right here in the hallway.

How many times could a father be wrong about his children?

Taken back, Frank studied Gage now. He didn't lean back like most folks. Nope, the grown man curled up around that pillow and sort of bent himself to one side. He looked terribly uncomfortable sitting there all scrunched up guarding Nicole.

He knew the minute they arrived home and saw Nicole that something horrific had happened to her. She'd been crying—she cried easily. Lord, how many times even he had soothed some of her tears.

Paula was good. She always got the kids to spill their guts. It was later when she told him about the burglary, and without the details. How many years had he been telling her that details were important in a crime? But that was Paula and he didn't bother to ask the routine questions of her.

He must be getting mushy in his old age. Hearing what happened to Nicole actually felt like a heart attack. The ache was very powerful. The pain wouldn't quit. Every time Nicole encountered more suffering and misfortune it squeezed on his chest and heart. The same way it was pinching him now as he watched his son. Although spunky, that girl had strength and character. She always found a way to survive. He pursed his lips shut to halt a chuckle. Nicole had always been dauntless too, inciting many fearless mishaps the girls got into. Now this, he thought.

He looked at the back of Gage's head. *The kid needs a haircut.* His snoring simmered down the way it did when he was a tyke. Frank recalled many nights that he spent comforting this one. Gage always wanted something he couldn't give him.

To be wrong irritated Frank. Nevertheless, he'd been wrong. Men were supposed to solve problems not create them. Seeing his son kiss a woman he felt was his own child convinced him he had created a lollapalooza this time. All these years his loving wife let him think Gage was…odd…different—could he be wrong about his son's capabilities, too? The next thought hit him harder. *His scheming wife was plotting a big one.* And she thought he wouldn't figure it out.

Frank moved quietly and dug out a spare blanket in the hallway closet. Skulking his way back into Caitlin's room, he hovered momentarily. *Kid needs a shave, too.* He shouldn't be wearing his weapon while he sleeps either. Frank smiled. The protector, the way he used to be. He covered his son with the blanket and sneaked out. Frustration kept making these wet pools in his eyes and he didn't like that either.

❧   ❧   ❧

The physical pleasure she felt was fragile and delicate. Nicole opened her eyes. A big-hearted smile and happy blue eyes greeted her cheerfully. Caitlin lay next to her stroking her face tenderly with busy fingers and quiet chatter. Being this innocent was a powerful feeling, she thought. In her own little way Caitlin sheltered and protected without knowing the security she gave.

"Morning, sweetie," she muttered.

"Ssssh," she whispered with a finger to her mouth. "Gage is snoring."

Nicole lifted her head when she pointed. Her heart went out to him. Slumped in the rocker near the bed, a pillow was bunched between his fist and head. A blanket hung more to the floor than covered him. He looked seriously uncomfortable, and very worried even as he slept.

"Nikki, Gage said I'm in your heart."

She examined Caitlin for a moment curious as to what the words meant then said, "Let's not wake him."

When Nicole got up, Caitlin stood on the mattress and leaped into her arms. Shifting about, Gage grabbed her waist. He dragged both onto his lap, wrapped arms around them, and sowed a kiss on her mouth that sucked the air right out of her. His lips hard, searching, until he parted, and gazed into her eyes.

"Good morning, lovely ladies," he finally said, giving Caitlin a peck on the cheek.

Heat flamed fiercely in Nicole's cheeks. "We woke you," she muttered out before he rendered another slow kiss. Surprisingly gentle and just a fleeting thought before she felt the conveyed distress in his mouth. She leaned back to look at him. Vacancy covered his eyes. "What's wrong?"

He lifted them out of his lap, stood and stretched out kinks. "Nothing."

"Nikki, I have to go potty."

She took Caitlin to the bathroom mentally floundering. Too many emotions converged inside of her. Had he discovered another dead girl inside her house? Is that why he didn't want her in there?

"Can I have Fruit Loops?"

Helping Caitlin, she tried dissecting the whole structure of events. Who was after her? She was leaving, why bother to explain something that couldn't be changed? Paula told her to think about what's important before deciding. She'd told Caitlin she loved her. Paula also said when things make the least amount of sense to forget what her brain says and listen to her heart. Gage said he loved her. She looked right through Caitlin contemplating.

"…go sliding…,"

She knew she couldn't change what happened yesterday, but how could she change today and tomorrow. She was frozen in limbo where all decisions and actions seemed impossible.

"Nikki, please."

"Huh?" Nudged out of her thoughts, Caitlin stood half-dressed, pajama bottoms snaking her ankles.

"Help me. Please."

"Oh, sweetie. I'm sorry," she said, tugging the garment upward.

"I want Fruit Loops."

Helping Caitlin wash her hands, Nicole asked, "Is that what you normally eat in the morning?"

"Sometimes," she nodded her head of blond waves.

"Well, let's go check out Paula's kitchen and see what we can find."

"Gage never eats in the morning. Do you?"

"Sometimes," she said as they went downstairs.

"Do you drink coffee like Frank and Gage?"

"You betcha."

"Can I have some?"

"I think orange juice and milk are better for little blond-haired girls. Coffee's for grownups. Now, let's find those Fruit Loops and how about a slice of toast?"

"Okay. Can we go sliding today?"

"Caitlin, I have to work."

Climbing onto a chair, she asked, "How come?"

"I'm planning a big party for Travis' grandparents."

"What's that?"

Finding cereal, Nicole asked, "What's what?"

"What you said."

Milk in hand, she turned and looked at Caitlin. "A party?"

"No, Travis…you know."

"Grandparents?"

"Uh-huh. What is that?"

She shuddered inwardly feeling an acute sense of loss. Moving to Caitlin, she set the stuff on the table and squatted to the child's level. "Oh, sweetie. It's not what, it's who. Grandparents are people. You remember Aidan Callihan."

"Uh-huh."

"Well, Aidan is Shalee and Brendan's grandpa."

"Is he my grandpa?"

Stunned, a new anguish seared her heart. She fought back an emotional outburst. "No, darling, he isn't your grandpa."

"How come I don't have a grandpa or a daddy? Why'd mommy have to die and leave me?"

Hugging her, Nicole's insides cried out for the child. "Oh, Caitlin—"

"Hey squirt, what're you having for breakfast?"

Choking back a hard lump in her throat, Nicole looked up at Gage. An agonizing maelstrom clashed awkwardly inside of her. She wasn't up for coping with Caitlin's questions as Gage's eyes filled with gentle understanding.

"Fruit Loops and toast," Caitlin answered.

"That sounds like a winner. Can I have some with you?"

"Yup," she bounced her head. "Gage, are you going to Nikki's party?"

"Maybe. Why?"

He removed bowls and spoons, and gratefully Nicole figured his interruption had been intentional. He lightly rubbed her shoulder and quietly asked, "You okay?" She nodded.

"Can I go too?" Caitlin asked.

"Well, since it's Nikki's party, you'll have to ask her."

"Nikki, can I come to your party?"

She dropped bread into the toaster while Gage fed Keeker, made coffee then plopped to a chair. She poured cereal for Caitlin, and realized this little girl asked way too many questions. "I bet we can arrange with Paula and Frank for you to come."

"Are Brendan and Shalee coming too?"

Pouring milk on the cereal, Nicole grabbed the toast. "Sweetie, eat your breakfast. We'll talk about the party with Paula later."

Nicole supplied them with mugs of coffee when Frank stepped into the kitchen. Caitlin chattered and she leaned against a counter with her mounting thoughts. She was trapped by the memory of her emotions. Ceaseless inward questions. Who wanted her dead? *Marriage*—he'd asked.

"What time you going into work?"

She blinked when Gage nudged her then recalled the feeling of being held in his arms. Caitlin and Frank had left. "I don't know. I need something else to wear. Why?"

"We'll need another statement from you. I don't want you going back and forth anywhere alone."

"Gage—"

"It'll do no good to argue with me, Nikki. I'll handcuff you if I have to. I'm giving you a ride to work and will pick you up when you're done."

"I wasn't going to argue with you. I was going to ask what else you found in my house."

"Nothing. What makes you think we did?"

"I felt it in your kiss. I saw the look on your face. What aren't you telling me?"

"I should be asking you that question."

Her eyes widened with familiar alarm. She felt it. He observed it.

"Nikki, I came home to talk to you yesterday. I overheard you and Mom."

She stiffened. "You're always sneaking around listening in where you don't belong."

"With you, that's the only way I can learn anything!"

"Did it ever occur to you that maybe it's none of your damn business?"

"Yeah, it occurred to me. But then you've said that to me before. Only fifteen years later, I find out it was my business."

His words hit hard and mean and she glared but a second before blasting him. "You bastard!"

"That's it!" He met her eyes disparagingly. "I'll save your ass from whoever's out to kill you, but I'll be damned if I'm gonna stand here and let you ridicule me! I'm done trying. You go to L.A., Nicole! In fact, I'll buy the fricking ticket for you! Just name the day! Pursue your dream, don't think about us or Caitlin, don't think about me, and don't you dare look back because I won't be here when you unravel the feelings between your brain and heart!"

His broad shoulders were heaving as he breathed. Wearing his uniform, boots, and gear, he towered dangerously above her. She was paralyzed yet she could feel her blood gushing through her veins. Hurt and longing lay naked in his eyes and she had again caused his pain, and his desire.

He waited but a second and barked, "Call the station when you're ready to make your statement."

He glowered menacingly before turning on his heel. Stomping out of the house, he slammed the kitchen door with savage force. Her spirits sank dismally low as she closed her eyes, feeling utterly worthless.

CHAPTER 17

❀

He understood the hate. He understood the fear. He even understood his own anger. What he'd never understand was her reluctance. This moment, he hated himself, feared for her life and was madder than a storm pummeling the island. He needed her to go, but wanted her to stay. He'd never planned it this way.

"Damn it!"

Gage couldn't begin to unravel why it was so difficult for her to explain whatever secret she was keeping from him. Having surgery wasn't necessarily a secret. Being that it was over two years ago, she couldn't possibly be dying. His mother would have said something. She always told him the important stuff.

Parking the squad, he got out, slammed the door and stomped angrily. The desperation swelled inside of him like waxy buildup. Unlocking the station, he was more determined than ever to make this case.

He threw his jacket on the desk, wrenched his fist around the coffeepot, and headed for the conference room. Exasperated with Nikki, he'd like to fire off several magazines from his weapon just to relieve the mounting tension. The office phone rang and he vocalized a round of profanities instead.

Returning, he grabbed it. "Who is it?"

"Gage, Tom Coville here."

He sucked in a deep breath. "What'd you find?"

"It took some doing, but I finally got my hands on that report you wanted. What did you want to know?"

"What caused the crash?"

"Initially it was listed as speeding. Reckless operation. No drugs or alcohol involved."

"Initially?" Gage asked.

"Yeah. Appears the parent's of the deceased insisted on having the boat checked. But the findings don't make any sense. The throttle control malfunctioned."

"What?" Gage blasted into the receiver. "Tom, that's not possible! That boat was kept in mint condition."

"How do you know that?"

"The deceased was my friend. We worked on that boat together. Brian never would have taken it out if he thought there was a mechanical problem."

"What if he didn't know there was a problem?"

Chills spiraled down his back. "What're you saying?"

"Gage, I'm not sure who his parents had check it over, but it's unlikely the throttle control would just malfunction all on it's own. It takes a helluva lot for a cotter key to jiggle loose, it would need a lotta help."

"Are you saying this wasn't accidental?"

"If what you said is true, what I'm telling you is someone maybe jimmied the throttle, loosening the pin. The report says he was speeding, but if the pin fell out of the connection, that would definitely cause the boat's speed to race on it's own. The operator wouldn't have a chance."

"Jesus, Tom!"

"What?"

"Can you fax me everything you got?"

"On its way as we speak."

"Thanks. I owe you for this one."

Gage disconnected and waited for the report.

He hissed first, then shouted. "Son of a bitch!"

When the fax spit out the pages, Gage yanked them out scanning each. The waxy buildup inside of him just went into scalding meltdown. Unable to squelch the tension masticating his insides, he abused the carafe of water by heaving it against the wall. Water and glass shattered and sprayed the wall and floor very nicely.

Years he and Nikki had blamed themselves for Brian's death when the facts actually leaned away from it being accidental. Why hadn't the investigators caught this?

The door driven open, Mac aimed his weapon cautiously entering. "What the hell's going on? I heard a pop. Sounded like a gunshot."

Gage sunk onto the chair behind his desk, report clutched in hand. Mac reholstered his gun. The kink in Gage's neck throbbed unmercifully. He'd had many doubts in his life, but this time he'd never felt more sure of anything. He knew that boat like the back of his hand. He had to talk to Sully. He had to find out what he knew about Brian's death.

"You've got that blazing murderous look in your eye. What happened, Gage?"

"Mac…," he handed over the faxed report and waited for him to read it.

"This was Michelle's brother?"

Standing, Gage nodded. "After fifteen years, facts are coming to light and I'm convinced Brian's death was murder. Nikki's gonna call when she's ready to give her statement. I want you to pick her up and make sure she gets to work safely. About that gunshot you heard, we'll need a new coffeepot."

"Gage, what's going on? Is this related to the serial killings?"

Opening the door, he stopped. "Mac, I'll fill you in as soon as I know. Take care of Nikki for me."

"Gage, where you going? Claire's gonna be here any minute."

"Call the County Jail and make sure Guthrie hasn't made bail. I'm going to see a skipper," he said, slamming the door behind him.

❦   ❦   ❦

Ripping the yellow police tape from across the front door of her house, Nicole inserted a key and opened it. "You guys, thanks for coming with me."

Katharine pulled out her nine. "Nicole, lemme check it out first."

"You mean checking the whatever you called it isn't enough?" Michelle asked.

"Outside perimeter and no it's not good enough. Wait here."

"You can't go in there alone. You're pregnant."

"Michelle, I've got the gun. It'll only take a minute."

"Mac will kill me if anything happens to you," Nicole muttered, "and if he doesn't do it right, Gage will certainly finish me off."

"Listen you two, I'll deny any such thing if you repeat it to Mac, but I kinda miss the action. Now shut-up and wait here," she ordered before entering the house.

Both waited approximately two minutes before Katharine exited holstering her weapon. "All clear. Nicole, you sure you want to see this?"

"Yeah, I'm sure," she said walking inside. "I'm putting the house on the market. I have to get it cleaned up before I can do that."

Following, Michelle said, "When did you—Omigod! This is worse than what happened to my folk's house. Nicole, you're gonna need a lotta help and a dump truck."

"I had an ulterior motive for dragging you two with me," she half smiled. "I also need to see if I can salvage any clothes. To answer your previous question, Michelle, I got the offer a couple days ago. I start February first."

"Thought the house belonged to your parents?"

"It does." She turned to face both. "I got a hold of them New Year's Day after Chantilly called. They don't want to keep it."

"What'd they have to say about your career move?" Katharine asked.

"Same as always, nothing, whatever you want, that's great."

"I wish you wouldn't do this," Michelle muttered. "You belong here with us. With Gage, not out in L.A."

"I've never belonged anywhere and Gage could care less." Nicole tore herself away from their penetrating stares with a choke.

"Sweetie, I'm sorry," Michelle said. "But that's not true. We both know he's in love with you."

The last forty-eight hours flashed through Nicole as wild grief shredded her insides. Tears flowed without cue. "I know. Neither of you understand what I can't explain."

"What don't we understand?" Katharine urged.

"I can't give him what he wants and I've hurt so many people. Neither of you have any idea what I've done."

"Can't give him what he wants? Nicole, the only thing he wants is you," Katharine informed her.

Swallowing hard Nicole sunk onto a table chair. "He wants a family. Can't you see that?"

"Yeah, with you."

"I can't give him babies."

"*What!*" both said with shocked surprise.

"I had my plumbing removed after your first marriage, Michelle."

"A hysterectomy?"

Miserably, she nodded.

"You never told us? Why?"

Nicole felt her palms grow clammy. "Michelle, I couldn't wreck your wedding, which wouldn't have mattered anyway. You were only here for the weekend, Katharine. Michelle went off on her honeymoon and I went into the hospital."

"Why?" was all Michelle asked again.

"I didn't have a choice. My insides were a doctor's nightmare. She said I couldn't wait more than a couple of months. Cancer risk, you know. Katharine, your mother's the only one who knew. My own parents don't even know. Paula was with me through it all."

As both women stood there speechless, Nicole said, "Gage doesn't know either and I can't tell him but I also can't say no."

"To what?" Katharine asked.

"Two days ago, he asked me to marry him to raise a family with him. I can't marry him because I can't deceive him. Besides I already accepted the new job."

"So, un-accept it," Katharine said.

"Now this," Nicole waved her hand at the mess.

Michelle went to her first, wrapping her arms around her. "Sweetie."

"Nicole, what else?"

Both women looked at her. "God, Katharine. You sound just like your brother."

"You said you've hurt a lot of people. Who and how?"

Nicole swallowed hard. "Katharine, this is one time in your life you had best let things go. Forget I ever opened my big mouth. I'm not discussing it with either one of you. Now, I could really use whatever help you can offer me in cleaning out this joint."

"Okay," Michelle said. "Once we do, let's plan the baby shower so we can all be part of it before you leave. I brought buckets and garbage bags. They're in my car."

When Michelle went out the door, Nicole appealed, "Please, don't push this one, Katharine. It's only going to hurt Michelle."

"You have my word. But explain to me one more time why you won't marry Gage."

"Can't, Katharine, not won't."

"You're afraid!"

"I am not!"

"You are too!"

"Am not."

"Are too."

"No I'm not!"

"You're scared shitless, Nicole."

"Kiss off, Katharine."

"Is Gage hearing Nicolina?"

"Yes, dammit!"

"Are you hearing Nicolina?"

"No!"

"Liar. Nicole, you can't fight it. You can waste a lotta money and time moving, but Nicolina's gonna follow you wherever you go. Then you'll just waste more money moving back. It's written all over you. You're in love with him, too."

"Shut-up, Katharine."

"Nicole—"

"I said shut-up. I need a drink."

When Michelle returned, Nicole asked, "You want a beer? I'm making myself a double."

"I'll pass. Let's check out the CD player, see if it still works."

"Katharine, you want anything?"

"Orange juice, if you have it."

Each picked a room. Michelle took the kitchen. Katharine took the living room finally giving up on CD's. Nicole went into her bedroom. For several hours they bagged and tossed all the damaged pillows, stuffing, clothes and linens. It seemed whoever broke in had no mercy on material-covered items. Appliances had been salvaged, but the furniture had been slit to smithereens. Michelle finished first and stopped Katharine from hauling heavy plastic bags out to the garbage. Hunting down the vacuum cleaner, she discovered Nicole crying again.

"Sweetie, what's wrong?"

"Oh, nothing and everything. There's a couple of articles of clothing he missed. But the majority is shredded."

"Have you called the insurance company yet?"

"No. No time. I will…Michelle, you know I'll always love you no matter what."

"Of course, I know." She gave her best friend a hug. "Why would you ever question it?"

"Are you two loafing on the job?"

"No way, sergeant," Michelle teased. "But, I'm getting hungry and I just happened to see a couple of single-serving pizzas in the freezer. How about it?"

Nicole stood. "Yeah, whatever you guys want." Tears streamed down her cheeks once more when she bent and picked up the smashed picture of the three of them from high school. She'd always kept it on her nightstand. Of all destroyed, it was the most sentimental.

She remembered the day like it was yesterday. They were sixteen and it was taken long before Brian's accident. She'd never considered it, but maybe that's why it was her favorite of the three of them. That day came before their lives turned into muck. They were coming back on the Island Queen from shopping. Because of rain, Sully was working the ferry instead of the Island Princess where he expounded his ghost stories. They filled in as his tourists when he told them for the hundredth time the story of the Cadotte ghosts and the jeweled eyes. The picture he'd taken of the three of them was still in one piece. It'd have to be re-framed. As Nicole studied the trio of eyes, Nicolina wailed sadly in her head, and she saw what Sully had always—

"Nicole!"

"Katharine!"

"Michelle!"

They swung around to face three very furious men.

"Damn you three! This crime scene was marked," Gage ejaculated abruptly.

"Nicole needed our help. Besides, I did a perimeter check first and went through it before I let them in here. All clear," she smiled exposing her concealed weapon.

"Princess, if you weren't pregnant I'd flatten you."

"You could try, Dobarchon."

"Do you realize what time it is? Travis came to the station frantic when Michelle didn't come home. When we called your mother—"

"Blah, blah, blah. We're fine, Mac. It's only—whoa!" she exclaimed, looking at her watch. "Ten at night."

"Yikes!" Michelle burst out, looking at Travis. "I'm sorry."

"Milady, next time tell me where you are," he said, hugging her tightly.

"I forgot about my statement," Nicole muttered. "I guess Ted and Hayden aren't gonna be too happy I didn't show up either."

"Sorry," Katharine apologized. "We really did get caught up in the mess here. Gage, we're gonna need your pick-up to haul everything out."

"Not tonight, Pipsqueak."

"Well, duh! Bro, sometimes I really wonder about you. I'm pregnant and I'm not hauling anything. The three of you are doing it tomorrow."

"Dammit, Katharine! I'm in the middle of a murder case. I don't have time for this shit let alone spending hours looking for the three of you! Why can't you all listen just once in your life?"

"A couple of my guys can do it," Travis suggested.

"Good," Katharine said. "Now why don't you three be nice and take us all over to the Tavern to get something to eat. We're starving."

"Just like that!" Gage bellowed. "No I'm sorry we worried you to death?"

"Gage," Katharine sighed. "Lighten up. We already said we're sorry, but we're also starving." Waddling around the men, she said, "You guys coming or not?"

Gage blew out his exasperation and followed all of them then waited while Nikki locked the house.

"They're leaving without me."

"You afraid to ride with me?"

Katharine's taunting came back to her. "No."

"Then what is it, Nikki?"

"Gage—"

"Why are you afraid to talk to me?"

"I—"

"What's so bad that you think it'll hurt me for you to tell me?"

"Gage—"

"Damn it, Nikki!"

"Would you—"

"God, woman! You're driving me crazy!"

She kissed him to shut him up. His arms came around her and they fell against the closed door. It was uncivilized as he pinned her in between. It was the worse kind of hunger—anger—a crushing kiss as his mouth closed over hers. He jarred life back into her and it hurt. Hurt so, she couldn't stop the shock of passion jolting between both of them. Neither could she stop the desperate wanting as she drew him in deeper.

He groaned when she did. He could taste desire in her mouth and pulled her closer, tighter, harder. Everything he was going to say, everything he wanted to say, should've said was lost in a sea of appetite. She was wicked, she was good, she distracted—it was that last thought yanking him out of her spell. His breath was fast and shallow as if he'd swum across the big lake.

"Nikki," he breathed into the scent of her hair. "This isn't going to change anything."

He confused the crap out of her. She remembered her thoughts when they barged into her bedroom. She wanted to tell him, had to tell him. "Gage, I'm sorry I've hurt you. Sully's right. Katharine's right. They're all right."

He thrust himself back and stared into her shadowed face. "Nikki, I don't—I can't—There's been a new development," he finally heaved out.

"What new development?"

He wanted her so badly it bruised his insides. If he touched her again, he'd never let her go and he knew now her leaving was the only way he could keep her alive. He looked left then right. "Let's go inside for a minute."

She studied him a long time until he took the keys from her hands, unlocked the door and nudged her into the house.

Shutting the door, he told her. "Brian's accident wasn't an accident."

"What are you saying?"

He shoved his hands into his pockets for control. Otherwise he'd reach out and pull her in, hold her to stop her quivering. "I'm positive Brian was murdered."

"Oh my God! *No!* How do you know? Who?"

She shook harder. "There was a problem with his boat."

"That's not possible. Brian was a mechanical genius."

"I'm aware. That's how I figured it out."

"When did you talk to Sully? Did he tell you this? What did he say?"

Gage hesitated. "I haven't been able to find Sully."

"Then how do you know? Gage, not only do we have to find Sully, but you and I have to talk about this morning. About everything."

It hurt to think it, let alone say it, but he was right this time. The details were still shadowed, but the situation was as black and white as night and day. He knew someone was out to kill her. Putting aside their verbal sparring, the fright that had set up permanent camp inside of him scared him to death.

He was a bastard the way he let his words slither out emotionless. "There is no *we* anymore. You and I are done, Nicole. Go to L.A."

CHAPTER 18

❀

Gage ate little. He slept less. Since that night at Nikki's house, he hadn't gone home except to shower and change. Mac gave him the keys to Joe Hamlin's place so he wouldn't have to sleep on the station's cot, but it didn't matter when he couldn't sleep. So he worked round the clock.

He was better off not seeing her anyway. He couldn't be angry anymore. He couldn't desire anymore. He couldn't worry. He was drained. The longing inside of him was gone.

Besides, his dad, Mac, everyone was protecting and watching over Nikki for him.

As he drove, a former simplicity flowed back. It had been easy when they were young. Laughing and bantering, teasing and badgering, no cares in the world except anticipated arguments and summers. He'd taken her fishing once. His mouth curved, recalling the moment. As much as Nikki tried to enjoy it, it had been a miserable experience for her. She endured his passion, and because of it, suffered with the smelly fish and slimy worms she called them. Said the worms reminded her of overcooked chow mien noodles. She had sunburned crispy that day—her nose shucked skin for a week.

Gage negotiated the corners, parking in the County Jail's lot. Her Christmas gift told him exactly how much she knew his love of the sport. Bass fishing had become a favorite, though not on Superior since it was uninhabited by the white, large or smallmouth species.

Not entirely true he mused.

Bass could be found in a few lakes off Superior's drainage. They'd been introduced by humans, but were very uncommon. When he had a hankering to catch bass, he crossed over into their neighbor's country—Minnesota—the

Land of Ten Thousand Lakes. The Boundary Waters Canoe Area was heavily populated with smallmouth bass, and made for a great weekend getaway.

Exiting his squad, he heard the crying woman. "Ah, shit! Not today," he muttered.

He entered the foyer and waited for the guard to finish whatever he was doing beyond the locked doors. He'd been looking for Sully for nearly two weeks to no avail. No one had any idea where he went. Old codger was probably burrowed away in his icehouse somewhere on Superior. The temps had dropped drastically, snow fell in barrels, and the water had finally froze solid.

"Can I help you?"

"Police Chief LeNoir to see Derek Guthrie."

The guard buzzed him in next and instructed him where to go. Take the elevator, turn left, walk this hall, turn right, talk to another guard, get directions, lock up his weapon, and finally he sat waiting inside a secured interview room. He'd spoken to the County Attorney before setting up the interview. No deals insinuated, promised, or made with Guthrie. Then he called the public defender to explain his reason for this interview as well. Not being related to the charges, that attorney saw no problem with his being here.

Took another five minutes before a guard brought Derek into the room handcuffed and sat him down. He didn't know if he'd find out what he needed as he noted Derek's appearance.

Ruddy facial pits and weather-beaten skin from substance abuse. Clear, dirt brown eyes indicated he'd been dope-free for awhile—since incarceration. It was the black puffy bags beneath his eyes exposing his previous usage. Underneath all of it, his pale flesh was unhealthy looking. A brutally cold puckish smirk instantly told Gage he'd never make a deal with the slimeball. He didn't understand how anyone could possibly see Brian in this filthy piece of shit.

"Derek, I'm Chief LeNoir. I'm here to ask you a couple of questions. I'm going to record this conversation as well."

"You got a cigarette, man?"

Gage shook his head.

"You know my wife, don't you?"

"This isn't about Michelle or the two women you've been charged with killing."

"Then what?"

"Do you know Janice Anderson from Green Bay?"

"Don't remember. Why?"

"What about Josie Stewart?" His eyes flickered briefly before the pupils shifted right.

"Yeah, I remember her. Whacked, man."

It was pathetic to see the nervous after effects of substance abuse. Jittery, non-trusting. Gage wondered if Derek Guthrie really understood why he'd been arrested—if he even remembered committing the ghastly slayings. He also wondered if the dirtbag was playing a game with him.

"You remember, you and Josie were seeing each other awhile back. In Green Bay."

"Me and Josie?"

"Yeah, you and Josie. Kevin Stewart's sister-in-law. Curt's wife."

"Yeah, I remember Kev. Who'd you say you were again?"

Those beady, petty pupils shifted left this time just before he asked that last question. "How long did you and Josie Stewart continue to see each other."

"About a year. Well," he thought for a moment, "depends on if you're asking before or after my wife."

Although slight, Gage's disgust and reaction was involuntary. "Afterward," he answered.

"Not long. She found someone else."

Eyes shifted left. "Who? Kevin Stewart?"

"Didn't know him."

"Does the name Patriot or Cannon ring any bells?"

"Some guy from Green Bay. Don't remember his name or know those you just said."

"David Patriot was from Green Bay. Did you know David Patriot? Maybe you knew him as Josh Cannon."

And there it was. His pupils flickered but they definitely went left. Remembering, people always looked right. Creating, they always looked left. Profile training taught him the slimeball was lying through his teeth.

"Don't remember either name."

"Who you protecting, Derek?"

"Not protecting nobody."

"Who's Janice Anderson?" The minute he said it, Guthrie's eyes bulged. "When was the last time you saw Janice Anderson or Josie Stewart?"

"Man, that bitch is weird."

"Which, Janice or Josie?"

"Always babbling about voices and crying babies."

When Gunderson focused on the ceiling, Gage did everything within his control not to overreact. "What baby?"

"I dunno, never said."

"Who's baby are you referring to?"

"Did you find the kid? I never touched *her*."

He assumed Gunderson was referring to Caitlin now. But no way was he going to bring her into the conversation. "How and where did you meet Janice Anderson and Josie Stewart?"

His eyes shifted both ways before Guthrie shrugged, leaned back in the chair. Shook his head like he was in another world.

"Where'd you meet them, Derek?"

"Green Bay I think."

"Tell me about the baby that died?"

"Ain't no baby died. Unless you're offering me a deal, I'm done talking."

"No deals. Whose baby was it?"

"I guess we're done."

Gage eyed Gunderson skeptically. Shutting off the recorder, he summoned a guard.

By the time he hit the front doors, Janice Anderson had hit the top of his list of suspects. Driving away from the building, at least he'd gotten something, new doubts, but it was something.

Whacked out—voices—a baby hummed through his mind alongside murder is an attempt to fulfill fantasy. 'Motive and common denominator are always self-interest'.

The self-interest? Perhaps the Anderson woman had lost a child and was seeking revenge for a perceived wrong. 'People don't act without reason, voices in her head telling her to kill'. Maybe. *Why?* 'Doesn't know the victims personally. Every action has motivation and intention'.

A baby dying in the woods? 'The killer thinks they have a job to do.' How would Anderson have stolen the paraquat from the County garage? Why shift the murder location from Green Bay to La Pointe? How and why were the bracelet and the liquor symbolic to Anderson if she was their killer?

Perfection kept looming at him from every angle. Claire said well-planned suggesting the search for recognition through perfection. She also said the dead girls could be an offering of fulfillment for a misdeed or the lack of perfection.

Frustrated, Gage thought the pieces of the puzzles had too many miles between the answers. And it always came back to, what did any of it have to do with Nikki and perfection? Nikki didn't know Janice Anderson. The only answer Claire had given him was jealousy or anger. Neither made sense.

❧   ❧   ❧

"Profiling provides an identity of a killer through a cluster of traits gathered from crime scene evidence. I still believe everything I've given you is accurate."

"Claire, we have no proof the real serial killer is male? It's classic self-tortured rage watching the death of a friend, or child," Gage told her.

"Female murderers generally commit murder with a gun or knife, not poison. They rarely kill strangers, Chief."

"Seven percent of women murderers *do* kill strangers. Aggressive female murderers also kill in the street, alley, or yard. We've never found the actual crime scene where each victim is being held and murdered with the poison. You did say traits cluster together but there's no exclusive on them. Are you telling me it's not possible the killer could be a stewing female?"

"Chief, anything's possible. It's just not likely your killer is a woman."

"Why?"

"The odds. Eighty percent usually kill men who were lovers or friends."

"Which leaves twenty percent who might kill women out of jealous rage, or a million other reasons."

"Women ordinarily kill someone known to them," she argued. "The crime is spontaneous. They're often unemployed. One-third will have a history of violent crimes and one-half already have an arrest record."

"That leaves two-thirds that don't have a past history of violent crime," he returned, "and fifty percent without an arrest record that we may, or may not know of."

"Only if you're assuming the entire female population could be serial killers."

"What makes you so sure it's not a woman?"

"What makes you positive it is?"

"You heard the recording," Gage contended.

"What I heard is a man talking gibberish. In your own words an addict who's been around the system a few times."

Inhaling deeply, he asked, "What time of day do women generally kill?"

"Generally? Between eight P.M. and two A.M. Why?"

"Time of death on all nine victims has been during those hours. I strongly doubt I'm barking up the wrong tree, since no one's been able to find the man responsible for the death of nine girls over a three year period."

"The odds—"

"Fuck the odds!" he finally erupted.

"Claire," Mac jumped in, "I think Gage is onto something that we should strongly look into. With this nursery rhyme left on the latest victim, I'm inclined to agree he may be right."

"I'm not disagreeing with that. But, Mac, the Anderson woman doesn't fit with the evidence or the profile."

"Claire, the last line on this poem says a lot, 'oh so young a mother to be when history repeats'. Its not even part of the original nursery rhyme, but eludes to a mother losing a child."

"Okay. Let's say I agree with you. For a moment, let's assume you're both correct. For the sake of reason, let's also assume a female killer has lost a child. Explain the connection between the Jarvis woman and sixteen-year-old Native American girls. Explain how losing a child would force anyone to kill teenage virgins leading to what I'm positive is the ultimate sacrifice. The Jarvis woman. Not to mention, Janice Anderson *is* employed and *doesn't* have an arrest record that we know of."

"Until Cole gets back to us," Mac said, "we aren't going to know anything. But, I'm inclined to agree with Gage right now."

"If Cole finds out…,"

Only half listening, several details were playing hardball in Gage's mind. He was worried about Sully since he still hadn't located him. The store manager from T. Kohl LTD still hadn't faxed him a list of customers either. They had nothing to prove if Stacy or the killer had bought the dress. That list was important. Cole went back to check out Janice Anderson more thoroughly and would bring the list back. Moreover, they still hadn't located the paraquat or the location of the murders. Another nonsuccess—find the place of death and he'd find the paraquat and the killer.

🍁   🍁   🍁

Everything in the house, except a few boxes, was gone. Nicole stood in the middle of the living room staring at nothing. Somebody once sang, *first you love me, then you hate me, it's a game for fools.* Who, Nicole had no idea, but the composer had hit the nail dead center.

It was here, they'd said their last words to each other. She died that night and had been dying inside ever since. She fell apart that same morning when he blew up in her face. Later, the same day, she finally grasped Sully's meaning. What he'd been telling the three best friends her entire life made sense and she finally scraped up the courage to tell Gage everything—that's why she kissed him outside her front door. Now she couldn't explain it to him because they were done.

He dropped a bomb. Make it plural, two bombs. She crumbled inside the same way he must have felt the night she told him about her new job. Fifteen years she'd spent not liking him and the uncanny realization had come too late. No matter how unfortunate for her, she loved Gage more than she loved anyone. In spite of that, his wants were clear and she couldn't love him without deceiving him.

Tonight was the big anniversary party, her last night at the Tavern. Her last night on the Island. Every resident on Madeline, and then some, bustled excitedly in anticipation of the ballroom's grand opening. Before leaving the LeNoir home tonight, it had been difficult to check her emotions with Caitlin. After tomorrow, she would never see the child again. Nicole wondered why, once Frank had dropped her at the Tavern with her gown, she sneaked back here to look at a place harboring bad memories. She bought the evening dress along with a few other replacements earlier in the busy week. It seemed pointless to replace everything at once and haul it when her life was changing.

Exhaling, Nicole slipped the photo of her and two best friends out of her purse. Looked down, looked around. After replacing the kitchen window, the house she'd spent her entire miserable life alone in was for sale. Prospects weren't hot, especially in late January. Unlikely the place would sell quickly. It was astronomically priced just by location—an island—a piece of rock in the middle of nowhere. She could care less if it sold. It wasn't her responsibility.

The insurance company wasted no time paying her off substantially on the damages once receiving the police report with photos. In fact, they had paid off so well, she decided to cover the cost for Katharine's baby shower, plus a little bonus. They could use the extra cash. Katharine wanted a dual housewarming and shower and Michelle had convinced Travis to wait an extra week before they went off on their official honeymoon. She, on the other hand, was going to miss the party.

Apathy consumed her. With the anniversary party, there hadn't been a moment to spare or to schedule Katharine's party any sooner. They all knew her start date. Still, their miserable demeanors would be burned in her memory forever. Her leaving hurt them. It was best this way. A combo meant everyone would attend. It was bad enough she'd see Gage tonight. She couldn't deal with the shower, too.

Her airline ticket was for tomorrow. Tuesday she started a new job and life.

Sitting alone within the empty room, Nicole debated what the pros would call the poverty she felt inside of her. It was as bleak and barren as the miles of frozen ice and white snow obliterating the fresh blue waters. There'd be no more healthy air or friendly deer with their little babies to greet her on her walks. The trees, well, she could just forget those. From what she had already seen, southern California could never compare to the abundant forests here.

Still clutching the picture, Nicole glanced at her watch. Out of the corner of her eye, she saw a stack of old books atop one box. No expense spared, her parents had provided everything. She picked up one they thought she needed to know about, *The Cadotte History*. Their gesture was ridiculous and Gage was right. The only books or magazines she ever opened contained beauty secrets. Flipping the pages, Nicole wondered if she'd known the outcome and finality of a teenage decision, if she would have done what she did many years ago. Probably not.

Glancing at on open page of the book, Nicole stopped. Panic welled inside of her and she literally freaked. It had to be an apparition as she stared at the two pictures and compared them. With exception of black and white versus color and an outdated ferry, they were identical. Not just the three women, and a ferry, but the eyes in the old photo matched the eyes in her photo. The date—there was no date on the book's page. It was a little too spooky to see three women from the past with identical eyes to three women in the future. Nicole looked up, glanced around. Nicolina was chanting as if to confirm her discovery.

Flexing her wrist again, she had to go. She slid the picture back into her purse, closed the book to take along, and headed out the door for the Tavern. Having decided not to sell her car until the house sold, it would stay parked in the garage. The boxes would stay where she left them. The same day Travis sent two dump trucks and six men to dispose of the parental love, she conned Mike Constantini into driving her to the Duluth airport tomorrow.

Blustery and cold, the air swirled around her now. She stopped when Nicolina cried mournfully. As if the crying would convince her to waste anymore thought on the newest discovery. So Sully was right. So what if the trio of friends had jeweled eyes like the Cadotte daughters. Big deal. She looked skyward almost believing Nicolina was floating over her head.

"It didn't work out old girl. I'm sorry you'll have to cry through eternity."

Nicole snuggled deeper inside her coat to block the wind and her wet eyes. It would be the last time she felt Lake Superior's icy chill and told herself she wouldn't miss it.

Arriving at the Tavern, everything was quiet. Heading to her office to change into the gown, she discovered some idiot had left one bouquet of flowers in the center of her desk.

Hissing under her breath first, she spouted, "Dammit! Who brought these up here? They should've gone in the fridge downstairs until the party starts."

Picking up the box, the label bore her name. From Travis? He thought of everyone. She opened the box and smiled at the long stem red roses, counted twelve. Odd, she thought opening the card and dropped to her chair gaping at the words.

This is best…,
Love you always and forever, Gage

The batter in her heart thrashed wildly then stopped. Why'd he go and do it? She grabbed a tissue, reoriented herself, picked up one rose and inhaled the sweet scent. He was right. It *was* best not to get involved. She changed into her evening gown, shelved the chaos and checked her makeup. There wasn't time to decipher his actions.

Nicole stuffed the book into a bag, picked up the boxed flowers and went to the ballroom. Elegant, classy, an exquisite duplicate to the nineteen thirties, she couldn't have been more pleased. A few members from the twenty-five piece orchestra were tuning up on stage. The 1934 Cabriolet was near the front with spotlights adorning it. She had no idea how Travis got the car inside. How sad that a fifty-year wedding anniversary celebration could create more unwanted moisture in her eyes.

Walking through the formal room, Nicole checked the seating for the guests of honor, Julia and Ronson, their family, Phillip and Rosemary and Travis and Michelle near the front. Closest friends were at three tables nearby. She put Frank and Paula with Suzanne and Garrett LeNoir along with Mac and Katharine next to the head table. Near them, she seated Gage with Caitlin, Aidan Callihan, Sylvie and Harvey, and their two children. There was seating for the orchestra and tables for each family all throughout the room. A table for gifts, a podium in place, along with Hayden's bar, and fabulous decorations. The servers had done an exceptional job and would be arriving any minute. *The new schedule was working for all of them, Nicole subconsciously thought.* A social hour first, dinner would follow. They'd rehearsed all week how to serve and keep the flow moving smoothly. Hayden and Tim were working the bar. Then an honorary tribute and ballroom dance until everyone decided to call it an evening well spent. She hoped everything went off without a hitch and the guests had the most amazing time of their lives.

She had just enough time to check last minute things. Nicole went to the kitchen to see if Jacque needed anything and double-checked corsages for Julia and Ronson. Those arrived this morning along with the largest bouquet of red roses she'd ever seen. Travis was giving his grandma-ma one for every year of marriage. The moment she saw them, she instantly wondered what her own parents did on their anniversary. Next wondered when Conrad and Erica celebrated wedded bliss. Sighing, she shoved her boxed roses into the fridge, and turned to Jacque who appeared from nowhere.

"Ah, chérie. You look ravishing tonight, like always."

"Thanks. Jacque, the cake is beautiful. How's everything else coming?"

"Perfecto. What bother's you, chérie?"

"Jacque, this is my last night. I want to say goodbye now before it gets chaotic back here. I've—"

"You're leaving for good?"

She nodded. "I asked Ted not to say anything, but it's something that's been coming for awhile."

"Ahh, Nicole. You harbor eyes of broken love. What did that man of your dreams do to you? I'll sear him in half—"

"Jacque," she looked at him and giggled at the way he stood there brandishing a butcher knife for hand-to-hand combat. "He didn't do anything."

"You're a liar, chérie. And not a very good one."

Well, that makes two, she thought. "I'm following my dream, Jacque."

"The hell you say. You're dream is here."

"Jacque, I came back to say goodbye to you. I don't have time for counseling sessions from the damn cook!"

His face fell, and Nicole attempted a retraction. "I'm sorry. I didn't mean that," but it was too late. All she did was hurt people and she couldn't wait for tomorrow afternoon.

"You'll be back."

Shaking her head, she turned and left. This was going to be a very difficult ending.

CHAPTER 19

❁

Breathtaking!

The air was emphatically drawn out of his lungs upon entering the tavern's lounge and seeing Nikki. Caitlin bolted from him.

Honey-gold ringlets fell around her face and swooped up hair. She was a goddess in an exquisite, glistening black gown, and seriously tall. All he could do was stand there, like some lovesick geek, gaping at her. She had never looked more beautiful. Detesting sappiness, Gage didn't like the sensation, which was happening a lot lately. The stirred up conflict was initiating too many fires inside of him.

He needed a drink to douse the internal blaze.

He and Caitlin missed the official ribbon cutting because he wanted to elude, somehow thought he could escape what was happening to him now. He maneuvered the crowd, would take the squirt off her hands. Figured he could sneak the kid away without suffering the uneasiness of nothing left to say.

Too late.

Caitlin jumped into Nikki's arms as she greeted several more. Nicole looked right at him and her first breath came quick and fast. Gage inched forward, took her hand—ice cold fingers—gave her cheek a quick kiss. "You're beautiful, Nikki."

"Thank you. Gage…the roses…,"

He squeezed her hand. All sound around them turned unintelligible. Time halted as he gazed into her eyes with longing. He could only see, smell and taste her. His heart was thrashing savagely inside of his chest. He wondered if hers was, too. The squirt said something, jarred him out of the trance. "I meant it."

Nicole's thoughts were jagged, painful. Her throat burned while her sense of loss went beyond tears.

"Nikki, are you sitting at our table?"

Nicole cleared her throat. "No, sweetie. I'm working tonight greeting everyone."

"Come on, squirt. You and I have a date."

"Nikki, can I tell you a secret first?"

"Sure. What is it?"

Gage waited while she whispered in her ear. He couldn't hear what Caitlin said, but saw Nikki's emotional reaction.

"Caitlin, I know you didn't mean it. I love you, too." She hugged Caitlin for a long moment before saying, "Gage, your table is near the front next to the guests of honor. There's names on each."

He nodded, took Caitlin, and remembered what she said about his gesture the day they went to Green Bay. He remembered a lot of things from that trip. The way she gave herself to him. Nevertheless, what he remembered the hardest was she couldn't say she loved him back. Although he felt it from her, he needed her to tell him what he waited for all his life. He needed to *hear* her say she loved him. Ultimately, it backed up the shitty reason he finally told her they were through.

Taking Caitlin, he hesitated. He still wanted to erase the lonely ache he'd always known, always seen in her eyes. Instead, he turned away and moved inside the ballroom. Travis and Michelle were standing with Phillip and Rosemary. A crowd gathered around the guests of honor and the hotrod. He saw Harvey flag him and point to the table while his insides battled with his willpower.

"Hey squirt, have I told you how pretty you look tonight?"

"Yes. Before we came. I wish I had a dress like Nikki's. She's pretty."

With that, he looked back. *Never look back!* They always did it in the movies and regret followed. Yup, they were right.

"Caitlin, look who's sitting at our table."

"Where?"

He pointed and she squealed first. Shalee shrieked second as Brendan twisted to look. Both kids hopped off their chairs and beelined toward him. He stooped, hugging both. It didn't help. Nothing he did replenished the barrenness that had depleted life out of him. Putting Caitlin down, he led them to the table, greeted Sylvie and Harvey then headed for the bar.

"Gage, what'll it be?"

"Scotch rocks. Make it a double, Hayden."

"Nicole's done a fantastic job tonight."

"The ballroom's nice. You got anything cherry flavored for Caitlin?"

"Cherry seven-up."

"That'll work. Give me three," he said tasting his drink. "Brendan and Shalee will want one, too."

"There ya go."

Digging out a ten-spot, Gage looked back again feeling more remorse than the first time. When Hayden set the glasses on the bar, he dropped the bill in a tip glass.

"Enjoy."

"Thanks, Hayden," he said with more confidence than he felt at being able to enjoy anything.

He picked up the glasses and eyed the massive crowd before ambling back to the table. There had to be four hundred people here celebrating fifty years of matrimonial bullshit with Ronson and Julia. This really was the last place he wanted to be under the circumstances. He passed the seven-up to the kids and sat down.

"This is some doing," Harvey said. "You wanna take a look at that street rod?"

"Yeah. Caitlin, wait here with Sylvie. I'll be right back."

"Where you going?"

"To look at that car. You kids stay here."

They walked away as Harvey said, "Must be nice having money."

"And fifty years of marriage," Gage responded.

His parents were sitting with Aunt Suzanne. Didn't want to talk to her he mused. She'd drive him nuts with questions. He saw sweet Saundra Chernak, Ben and Charlene McEvoy, Adeline Girard and her three boys standing around near Ted and Marlene Evans. Kevin and Mark were permanently camped out at the bar alongside Curt and Josie. That's where the designated drunks would spend the night since Travis was footing the bill during social hour. Josie's parents, Bert and Irene Hanson were sitting with Carter Taylor and company. He wondered if Bert had any idea what kind of a daughter he'd raised. Probably not, he decided.

Ed Harris from the Blazer was working. Had a very tall redhead trailing. He thought she was from Bayfield, heard her name was Carol. The guy from the Bayfield Weekly and a Duluth TV station were also camera'd down for photos of the eventful evening.

Wilbur and Iola Tibbs, Jim Berger, even old Jesop had put in an appearance. Merryweather had cleaned up real nice, Gage thought. There were several dozen people he didn't recognize, and assumed they were friends of the Baines and Perrys. Michelle's ex busy body neighbor, Mrs. Hardy was following the Stewart parents into the ballroom. Too bad for them he mused. He saw the guys from Travis' crew gathering near another table. Some had wives or dates, some didn't. It looked like Constantini was with someone he didn't know. Significant others to the working folks had congregated in another circle. Alongside their circle, he saw Charlie Andrews, owner of the motel with his wife and several descendants to the Cadotte family. Yup, he thought, the entire town, except one, had showed up. He still hadn't found Sully, which bothered him. Scanning the ballroom, he had his eye on almost every one of them.

Harvey interrupted his thoughts whistling praise to the '34 Cabriolet. He looked from the crowd to the car.

"Chrome plated windshield, cowl lamps, dual horns and tail lamps. She's a beaut!" Harvey crooned.

"Take a look inside. Taupe leather and a rumble seat," Gage told him.

"Did you know this is the original and the only one of it's kind? Wonder how and where Travis found it."

"Harvey, I didn't know you were a hotrod buff."

"Gentlemen, I searched the world for two years looking for her. You're right, Harvey. It's the only one left."

They turned, "Hey, Travis, Michelle," Gage said exchanging handshakes and kissing Michelle's cheek. "Michelle, you look stunning, and happy."

"Thanks, Gage. I am happy."

"Does the guest of honor like the car, Travis?"

"Grandfather would deny it, but the old softy had a tear in his eye when he saw it. Harvey, glad you made it."

"Wouldn't have missed it. The place looks good and Nicole's done a fantastic job, too."

"That woman, as you folks say around here, 'kicked butt' to make this happen for me. She's one in a million." Putting his arm around Michelle, Travis said, "My lovely wife has informed me I have to make the rounds with all four hundred people. We'll catch up to you guys later. Enjoy."

"I better get back to my wife, too. As patient as Sylvie is, she doesn't like being left with the kids for very long at one of these events."

Following Harvey, it was automatic for Gage to glance toward the entrance. He immediately panicked when he didn't see Nikki, felt the rush to his brain, the kick-bang in his chest. Then she reappeared from inside the lounge. Undeniably, one horrifying fact remained—he didn't want her to leave tomorrow. He couldn't live without her, but always knew he could protect her. His parting words that night clanged loudly now.

"Gage, I'm hungry."

He looked at Caitlin. "It won't be long before we eat."

"Can I have some more pop, please?"

"Sure, squirt. You wanna come with me?"

"Yeah," she said nodding her head

Lifting her into his arms, he sauntered over to the bar opposite of the Stewart's. Josie's megaphonic laugh compelled him to look. She wore expensive-looking clothes that successfully made her unfashionable. Bosomy in an unprepossessing way, Josie almost reminded him of wrestler-type women in desperate need of Cosmetics 101. Thinking 'queen player', he felt sorry for Curt. One day discovering your wife unfaithful would wage a war of suspicious distrust, if not divorce. As offensive as he found Josie's cheating to be, it wasn't the reason he disliked her. He glanced at Nikki. What he thought of Josie wasn't even hate. He did not like her as a human being.

"Gage, are they gonna play?"

Caitlin pointed toward the members of the orchestra. "Yep. You gonna dance with me later?"

"I don't know how."

He grinned. "Then I'll just have to teach you."

"Okay. Will you and Nikki dance?"

He looked again to where she had resumed welcoming. "We'll have to see."

"I think you should."

This child was too young to understand or be telling him what he should do. He took the glass in his other hand and returned to their table. Katharine's pert wiggle was now a portly toddle as she and Mac made their way to the table. "Sis, you look real nice."

"I'm pooched out. My hips are spreading. These none-to-soon ankle biters are fisting it out. My Braxton Hicks are getting stronger and I'm only a few weeks past half way. Gage, I don't need your indulgence about my appearance."

"Princess," Mac said, chuckling. "You're priceless. I love you dearly."

"Dobarchon, you're cruisin' for a bruisin' with all that mushy shit."

"That's why I'm gonna massage your back and legs when we get home tonight," he promised, laying an intimate kiss on her mouth.

He should never have come here tonight. Frustrated, Gage picked up Caitlin. "Come on, squirt. You and I are making the rounds."

"Gage," Katharine said, "wait a minute."

He tossed her a dirty glare.

"I'm sorry, Bro. I'm just not used to carrying around the extra weight."

"Forget it."

"Are you aware that Mike Constantini is driving Nikki to the airport tomorrow?"

"Katharine, I don't care."

"Yeah, you do. How long are you two morons gonna keep up this sham?"

His temper veering to resentment, Gage set Caitlin back in her chair and pulled his sister away from the table. "I really don't see how this is any of your concern."

"Bro, I love you and I care about you. You're making a big mistake if you let her go. You love her and she loves you. Trust me. Nothing else matters."

"It'll be an even bigger mistake if she stays," he muttered out the lie.

"Gage—"

"Katharine. This is not the time or the place." With that he turned, lifted Caitlin and walked away.

He was right about this! Nikki's life was more important than getting what he wanted. He'd never risk it. Then silently asked when he would stop lying to himself. He glanced across the room. Maybe never, but he could stop one thing from happening and headed toward Constantini. Old man Merryweather stopped him first.

"Chief, still got me a problem with the deer."

"How is it your gardens survived winter, Jesop?"

"Now they're eatin' off my bird feeders."

"Only way to deal with that is not put seed out."

"Birds'll starve if I don't. Have ya figured out—"

"*Jesop,*" Gage interrupted, fully aware the old man was going to inquire about the murders. Caitlin didn't need to hear it. "I think you'd all know if I'd figured it out. Furthermore, God's creatures will not starve. They're smarter than humans."

Merryweather chuckled before slugging back the remains in his glass. He hobbled himself around in the direction of the bar. The old man had fallen off the cliffs when he was a kid. Lucky all he did was break a hip, Gage thought as he watched him limp away, cane in hand.

"Hey, Chief."

He turned to face his next encounter, Jim Berger.

"Chief, hate to bring this up at this here event, but have you talked to Adeline yet about that dog o' hers?"

"She's been advised."

"Last thing I need is another brood from one I done give her. I like dogs and all, but had a—"

"Jim," he stopped him. Jim had a mouth that would make blood flow in the dead. "Save it for another time and place?"

"Pretty soon Madeline's gonna have more—," he looked at Caitlin. "Well, you-know-what, than it does islanders."

"I'll have another talk with her."

"You do that so's I won't be taking matters into my own hands."

"I'll handle it," he said on the verge of irritation. Berger then sauntered away. "Squirt, there goes your average complainer."

"Gage, can I have a dog?"

"What about Keeker. Thought you liked cats."

"Keeker is Auntie Michelle's. After mommy went to the angels, she said I could call her auntie and I told her a secret, too."

She was too forthright, but he grinned anyway. "You just got secrets all over the place, don't you, squirt."

"Uh-huh. You wanna know what I wish?" she asked eagerly.

"What do you wish for?"

"Nikki would be my new mommy."

He stopped and stared at her. It was bona fide belief the kid had. She totally thought the idea possible. And, well, hell now. It booted him hard in the backside. Made him forget for a second where he was going. "Is that what you told her tonight?"

"No. Auntie Michelle says they aren't secrets if we don't keep them."

"How will Nikki know what you want if you don't tell her?"

When she didn't respond, he looked at her a second time. Large tears pooled down her cheeks, her bottom lip quivered. "What's wrong, squirt?"

"Nikki's going because I was mean. I don't want her to go," Caitlin cried.

Wrapping her arms around his neck, curveballs rocketed through his stomach.

"She's going because I told her I don't like her."

Her crying increased and trying to soothe her, Gage reassured, "Caitlin, that's not the reason Nikki's leaving us."

He changed direction and headed out of the ballroom. Caught a few, including Nikki, watching them as he exited and beelined around several toward the vacant dining room. "Don't cry, Caitlin. Everything will work out."

When she only cried harder, he tried, "I'm still gonna be here."

"I don't want Nikki to go."

Inside the quiet dining room, he snuggled her in his arms. "I know, sweet thing. Sometimes people do stuff because they have to. Nikki loves you, I heard her tell you tonight," he said, having a helluva time convincing himself of the idea.

Sniveling, Caitlin asked, "But why does she have to go? Can't you make her stay?"

Caitlin wasn't the only one crying. Gage looked upward when the damn ghost magnified his inner turmoil. When in the hell had he started believing? He had no way of explaining to a three-year-old what he'd done, let alone why he did it. Neither could he turn and face Nikki standing behind them. He sensed her immediately—always had.

"I'm sorry, sweet thing, I can't make her stay. She has to want to stay on her own."

❦   ❦   ❦

Nicole knew this evening was going to be difficult. Standing in the foyer to the dining room, she overheard everything both said. She had no idea her little blond cutie would augment the ache in her heart. She didn't want to leave them here alone, but the social hour was almost over.

As heaviness centered in her chest, Nicole made her way into the kitchen first to see how Jacque was doing. Everything right on schedule, taking a deep breath, she donned a counterfeit smile and went to the ballroom to find Travis. Gage had returned to their table with Caitlin. She watched from across the room. Caitlin was snuggled in his lap and had gone from tears to the same happy face that woke her everyday over the past two weeks. However he handled it, he'd done—

"Nicole, are we just about ready?" Travis asked, coming up behind her.

"Yes. Whenever you want to start. Jacque has timed the dinner to coincide perfectly."

"I can't thank you enough for everything you've done. Grandma-ma's face has been a steady beam of pleasure. It's brought back many memories for her. She's working on grandfather to move back."

"Oh! That is something. It's been my pleasure, Travis. I wouldn't have missed it for anything."

"You're very special. If you ever need anything, Nicole, all you have to do is pick up the phone."

She looked directly at him now. In the short time knowing him, she'd seen him happier once. The day he married one of her two best friends. "Thank you. Just take care of Michelle, that's enough for me."

He touched her shoulder in a light gesture. "Nicole, I told my wife I wasn't going to interfere, but I believe you're making a big mistake. I wish you would reconsider your decision."

"I can't, Travis."

Giving her a hug, he spoke quietly. "He might not be the best at showing it or saying it, but he loves you."

"Okay, Travis. Get your butt back to your table before I crumble, smear my makeup, and have to kick it up there for you."

Travis chuckled, sobered. "I mean it, Nicole. If you need anything, you call us."

With that, he headed for the front of the ballroom he was so proud of, stopping to usher the woman he loved more than life itself with him. Nicole averted her attention, when Gage looked her way. If he loved her, why had he changed his mind?

She has to want to stay on her own" echoed in her head. Nicole shifted and fled—had to get dinner served.

Seven waitresses answered up professionally. They flew in and out of Jacque's kitchen serving three hundred ninety-nine guests dinner rolls, house salad with choice dressing and Penne Pasta Chicken, cleared dinner plates, refilled coffee cups, then served anniversary cake. Nicole had never been more proud of the women she had trained.

It was fun to watch the islanders in their best dress, conversing along with mainlanders from near and far. The tête-à-tête carried from one table to the next with embellished compliments of the ballroom and the meal. The mood was festive, the guests lively. But, seeing both honored guests with happy glows sent Nicole's heart into overdrive and was a memory she'd carry with her long afterward. She had done her job and done it well. That's what mattered.

The program was brief as a beaming Travis took the podium. He applauded his grandparents, expressed gratitude to his parents, praised his construction crews for a job very well done, thanked Billy Abbott for finding the Cabriolet, and the Town Board for voting in favor of the ballroom. Then prodding his loving wife to the podium with him, his smile broadened as he finished off his oration by announcing Michelle's pregnancy.

Standing in the back, happiness filled Nicole. Julia and Rosemary were out of their chairs as Ronson and Phillip followed to congratulate both. With nudging from Sylvie and Michelle, Aidan was coerced on stage, too. The rest clapped and cheered.

"You finally did it, girlfriend," Nicole whispered to herself.

Travis spoke into the microphone, "I have one more item before we polish off the evening with the finest music from the nineteen thirties. Nicole, are you back there? I need you to join us up here?"

Stunned, unable to imagine for what, everyone turned and looked at her. *This might be what it would have felt like walking down a platform in a model's showing.* Slowly, she threaded her way around tables with the grace she'd taught herself. All eyes were upon her when Travis met and escorted her to the stage. Michelle had gone off and reappeared, bearing an armload of roses and handing them to her.

"Nicole," Travis began. "Without your support for this project, your wisdom and help to pull this event off tonight, your love of doing it, your patience for dealing with all of us, we could not have pulled this off without you. To show our appreciation and with my family's and my deepest gratitude we've put something together for you."

Michelle had taken a hold of her arm for support. Which didn't matter. Nicole couldn't have moved if she tried—thought she might faint when Travis reached into his Tuxedo pocket.

"Since none of us could agree where to send you, we finally agreed to send you around the world."

Nicole gawked at the packet Travis held out to her. She couldn't move.

"Folks, she's speechless for the first time in her life."

Laughter filled the room before Travis continued. "Grandma-ma liked Rome. My mother loves Paris. I thought Florence, my father and grandfather said Nice and Cannes. Anyway, from all of us with our deepest appreciation and love, we've put together an all expense paid trip to see the whole shebang."

The crowd clapped, cheered, whistled then went silent waiting. Michelle nudged her. Nicole took a deep breath and slowly accepted the envelope. Regaining her composure, she inched forward and spoke into the microphone. "Okay, I want to know how you all kept this from me."

Laughter roared from the guests before silence befell them and all eyes were on her. "I don't know what to say." She looked at Travis and Michelle, his parents, grandparents. "Except, thank you."

Travis stepped forward, kissed her cheek. Ronson and Phillip gave her little pecks, too, and Rosemary and Julia squeezed her tight. Michelle ushered her off stage and she found the words to congratulate her second best friend for her good fortune.

"Oh, hon, I'm so happy and excited for you. When did you find out?"

"Yesterday, but I waited until this morning to tell Travis."

"Just how long have you and Katharine known about this?" Nicole asked, waving the envelope.

"Quite awhile. Sweetie, that comes with a lot of love attached to it. We'll always be here for you no matter what, and now I think I'm gonna start crying. I wish you weren't leaving."

Nicole hugged her giving up on fighting back the day's emotions. "I have to. I love you, Michelle. Both you and Katharine. I think there's a man coming at you for the first dance."

She turned as Travis offered his hand. "Milady, and mother of my child, will you have this dance with me?"

Nicole shifted, wanting to escape and bumped into Gage.

"I promised Caitlin the first dance. Will you promise me the second?" he asked.

"Gage, I—"

"Please?"

It wasn't pleading she saw in his eyes, but determination. "Yes. Just let me go take care of these," she indicated the flowers. "I'll be right back."

He waited, having noted she'd been on her feet the entire night. He then went to the bar, ordered a seven-seven, her favorite drink and met her half way.

"This is for you. Come sit at our table while I teach Caitlin how to waltz."

She let him lead the way and it felt good to sit. Nicole sipped the drink and watched Gage crate Caitlin onto the gleaming wood floor. Caitlin giggled when he swirled her in slow moving circles holding her in his arms. The next song started and he set her down, told her to place her feet on his toes, the same way Frank taught her and Katharine. His moves gradual and refined with their little girl—her thoughts screeched to a halt. Caitlin didn't belong to either one of them.

Averting her eyes from thought and scene, Brendan was dancing with Shalee, Sylvie and Harvey gazed at each other, Ronson held Rosemary, Phillip was with Julia. Couples of all ages were smiling at their partners ready to dance the night away. The lights dimmed, the orchestra was grand. The mood was romantic and fanciful with moonbeam dreams. Nicole's vision went back in time to women's attire, men in uniforms, Glen Miller music filling the air with novel love.

"Nikki, I was waltzing!" Caitlin squealed excitedly before she crawled into her lap.

"Yes, you were, sweetie. You were also the prettiest one out there."

"Gage said I could have pop if I'm good while you waltz with him."

"How many pops have you had tonight?"

"Mmm, I dunno."

"I bet more than you should. Are you having a good time?"

"Uh-huh."

"Did you eat all your dinner?"

"I only had to eat the noodles and my roll."

"And I bet the cake."

"Yup. It was good."

"Here you go, squirt." Gage set the glass on the table and stooped. "Now remember our little secret, and this one you can't tell anybody."

Bobbing her head up and down, she said, "Promise."

Caitlin was smiling like a cat that had just nailed a bird after a wild chase. Gage's grin was even broader. "What're you two cooking up?" she asked.

"Nothing. Go dancing."

"Yes, ma'am," she responded, kissing Caitlin's cheek before placing her on a chair.

It didn't take long for Nicole to realize she had never danced with Gage. But as if they had always done it, he dragged her into his arms. Solid arms that held her tenderly, not too loose, not to tight. His hands were warm and gentle against her exposed flesh and they danced as if they had been paired from centuries past and now into eternity with each other. Floating elegantly across the floor to the harmonious sounds of the thirties romance, they gazed into each other's eyes.

Nothing was ever more perfect.

CHAPTER 20

❀

Magnificent. Impressive and heartfelt. Everyone had had the most amazing time as the last guests jiggled out of the tavern a little past two A.M. Hayden and Tim were almost done with cleaning detail behind the bar, Jacque had left an hour ago, and the servers were taking a direct route to the door.

It only took two drinks for Nicole to feel giddy. The dancing made her light-hearted. The favorable turnout made her happy. But Gage waiting to take her home energized Nicole. She was definitely flying high on those moonbeam dreams.

"Crown that woman with success!" Gypsy said to the others. "Nicole, everyone had a fantastic time tonight."

"You ladies did a superb job. I've never been happier or more proud of all of you. I have something for you." Handing each a sealed envelope, she said, "Thanks, again, ladies."

"What's this? Nicole!" Gypsy shrieked sliding out a hundred-dollar bill.

The others quickly opened theirs. "It's my appreciation for all you did to help make tonight a huge success."

"Do we dare tell her how generous everyone was tonight?" Beth asked.

"They should be the way you gals worked your tails off."

"We wouldn't have missed it," Sheila yawned. "Thank you."

"Does anyone need a ride home?" Nicole asked. When all said no and without thinking, she said, "All right. We'll see you tomorrow."

She locked the door and faced Gage.

"Will they really?"

The roses he gave her were on the bar with the other flowers she had received from Travis. Her change of clothes, coat and bags lay nearby. He'd literally yanked his tie off hours earlier. She watched him shove it in a pocket and tear open his buttoned collar. Straddling a chair backwards, he leaned casually. Suit material pulled taut against every muscle.

Nicole swallowed hard. "Will they really what?"

"Will they really see you tomorrow?"

She sighed. "I guess not. It's a habit."

Gage stood, approached. "You were positively the most beautiful woman tonight, and very tall."

She swallowed hard again. "I'm ready. Hayden will lock up. I've already turned in my keys."

"What time does your plane leave tomorrow?"

"Three." The way he was looking at her set her blood aflame. "Why?"

Broad shouldered, potent, watching her, he was standing near her now. His blue eyes—her destiny to never forget them—blazed with longing. His air of self-confidence and incredible everything had always moved the island under her feet.

"I told Constantini his services weren't needed."

"Gage," she murmured, and unexpectedly was in his arms. That flair and stimulation she wanted banged in her heart until she couldn't breathe. She trembled when he touched her mouth.

"Baby, let me show you how much I love you."

"You said…we…were…,"

She trembled more when his hands skimmed her bare shoulders and whatever he said was forgotten.

"Hold me in your arms tonight," he whispered huskily.

She gazed into his eyes. Her heart lurched madly and his lips descended deliberately to meet hers. They were warm, soft, his kisses absorbing all of her. Tumbling, aching, her arms went around him.

Coughing came from behind them, made her stagger back, but she wasn't free of those effective arms.

"Hayden. Tim. We were just leaving."

Chuckling, Hayden said, "The way I see things, the sooner the better."

Gage let go, picked up Nicole's coat sliding her into it.

"Goodnight, Hayden. Tim," he said. "It was an exceptional party."

Snatching her stuff off the bar, Gage took her elbow steering her out the front door. Outside, an icy Nor'easter felt subzero. Inside, she was on fire as Gage helped her into his warmed up truck. He jaunted around the front end, the wind whipping at his hair, only the sharp lines of his face detected in the shadows. In that moment, she concluded, tonight would be theirs. He climbed in, reached his hand behind her neck and pulled her into an intimate kiss.

"Where?" she murmured raggedly.

This time he wasn't going to seduce her like a testosterone driven teen doing it his first time, even if his level of excitement was on overdrive. He told her he was going to show her how much he loved her and one way or another hoped to capture her love, hoped she couldn't escape his.

"Is this where you've been staying?" she asked once inside Joe Hamlin's house. Then blurted, "You brought my luggage here."

"Mac felt sorry for me sleeping at the station. I'm more inclined to think he'd had enough of my cussing the cot and yes, I brought your luggage here."

He sensed she fought urges to question his actions. After removing her coat, he went to the kitchen, filled an empty milk carton with water to stuff her roses into it. He knew she didn't want to discuss *why* he was staying here when she started yammering a blue streak about the night's events. He searched and found a large pitcher for Travis' bouquet.

"Are you hungry? You didn't eat dinner tonight."

"I'm fine. Was it good?"

"Very."

"How much did Caitlin really eat? Why did you let her drink all that pop? That's not good for her especially at night."

Gage stopped what he was doing. Although she kept avoiding his, distress filled her eyes. "You *really* do love her. Nikki, come here."

Extending his arm, he waited until she took his hand. She shivered a little and reached. He dragged her in. "I'm sorry you heard her."

He brushed his mouth over her cheek, her lips, and she quivered in his arms. "Baby, I'll kiss away your pain."

Tenderly, he nibbled the corner of her mouth. A slight bite on her bottom lip coerced a deep guttural croon. Shivers followed every caress and when her arms came around him, he saw her eyes. Dark, glazed, exciting. He tugged her closer, tasted her bare shoulder, slid his arms down hers.

It wasn't fast. It wasn't quick. He merely kissed her as her knees went feeble. The instant heat sucking the chill out drew her breath away. She tightened her grip on his shoulders. The more he simply skimmed her flesh, the larger her ache to feel his vigorous kisses.

Gage lifted Nikki, carrying her to the bedroom and linked their hands when she started wrenching at his shirt.

"Let me."

His actions were gradual, deliberate the way he peeled away and broke down the layers of her emotions, and her gown. He controlled the evening's end. Her last thought went wandering in her trembles as his mouth manipulated and stroked her tenderly. The slower he moved the more her control slipped away into the night, drowned somewhere in its shadows. She couldn't disguise her body's reaction—electric, turbulent wanting, and powerless to return the pleasure. She tried, but the heat of his mouth seared through, disabling, breaking her down.

She expelled a strangled moan. He held her hands, progressed sinuously over her flesh, letting it take him, trying her, seeking to savor. He was getting in deep, losing his reason and sense. The more she arched, pleaded, begged, the more frantic he became. Desperate appetite ruled by domination. He intended the opposite. He'd meant to bend her will, but fell fast as the scent of her flesh sucked him into that tunnel.

The unhurried moves aroused her. Her hands freed as he traced, pursued, tasted her with open mouth kisses. She dug her fingernails into his flesh. The ache of fire burning inside, hot passion rolled smashing waves into her. She couldn't hold on and surrendered to the whirling sensation, crying out for him.

He was alive, soaring and flying with need. Her heated tremors a mass of hot volcanic moisture, she dug her hands into his hair and fisted, dragging her mouth on his. A deep and primitive moan detonated out of her greedily.

"God, Nikki!"

The need and wanting vivid in her eyes. He clutched her hips and drove himself. She fisted around him like a thunderstorm, squeezing everything out of him. He'd never traveled this road. Never felt the power she had this strongly. She clung to him with the natural hunger of a wild thrashing storm. The aching transition he felt in her rocked him. More shock ripped through him when Nicolina wailed loudly overhead.

❦   ❦   ❦

Arms and legs wrapped around each other, in and out of drowsy sleep, Gage played with her hair, kissed her face. The wind howled unmercifully outside. Night had dawned hours before around their third time, maybe it was their fourth surge with heated passion. She was nestled against him, drawing some unknown design on his arm. He actually thought he died the first time. Then discovered himself abundantly vital when she initiated their second go-round, and he let her shatter him once more. The way they hurled against each other was storm tossed—no matter how many times they loved each other, he understood only one thing.

"Baby," he managed hoarsely, "I don't want you to go."

Now, he'd gone and done it. Nicole sucked in a sigh, letting it slip out. She strongly suspected this part of the evening had not been a planned event on his part. Maybe it was. The roses, keeping his distance in the beginning, making her want him more. Dancing with her and making her emotions flutter until he brought her here to show her how much he loved her. *It was an intricate plan.* He was wrong she decided. She never caught his seduction technique, never saw it coming until it hit her with blinding force. This time he not only seduced her in the drowsy scintillating way, he had determinedly done a whole lot more. He stole her heart.

"I have to," she finally whispered.

"I love you, Nikki. I don't care about anything else."

She sat up. "It's late and a two hour drive to the airport."

He followed and snuggled up close, wrapped his arms around her. Kissed her shoulder, ran his hands through her long disheveled hair. The scent of her flesh would be engrained in his memory forever. "You're really gonna go through with this, aren't you?"

She couldn't look at him, nodded lamely.

The suffering was killing him. Forcing her to stay would be another mistake. It wouldn't be right if she didn't want to stay. He had to let her go. "All right. I won't fight you. Just answer one question honestly?"

She looked over her shoulder at him.

"Do you love me?"

When she gulped hard, he immediately saw the answer in her eyes. "Don't say it. I lied. I *will* make you stay."

He scrambled out of bed and headed for the shower. He needed it hot. He needed it fast. He needed it hard. Hard enough to destroy what he saw in her eyes. He didn't want to ever remember. He couldn't relive that distressed look over and over, forever knowing she was in love with him. He couldn't live with the complete misunderstanding of her hidden reasons for leaving. He twisted the handle all the way. Water gushed out of the spout steaming, rapid, cruel. He braced his hands against the wall and hung his head letting the scalding pellets beat against his flesh.

✽   ✽   ✽

The plane touched down at LAX late. Wisely, Nicole had made a hotel reservation for near midnight. Drowsily in and out of sleep most of the flight, she felt a different kind of excitement. But no matter how hard she tried to believe it right, the thrill of her dream come true didn't bubble inside of her the way it should.

She had always known she loved Gage, but she hadn't fallen in love with him until last night. She also knew he saw her response this morning. They parted wordlessly, no arguments, no conversation. Just a succulently intimate kiss to make her always remember him.

Nicole collected her winter coat, purse and carry-on, and followed a handful of groggy passengers through the telescopic corridor. This time, pacing herself, she knew where to find the baggage claim area inside the passenger terminal. It would be awhile before her luggage came down the conveyor belt. Afterward, she'd grab a cab, doubting a shuttle bus would be available, check into her hotel in downtown L.A. and try to sleep.

"Nicole Jarvis?"

She swung around, surprised to hear someone call her name. A man not quite six feet stood a comfortable distance from her. Sandy-colored, his hair receded from front to back. Hazel, tired-looking eyes lacked life. Hollow cheeks misshaped what she thought once gave the stranger's face strength. He was dressed casually carrying a briefcase and she stared at him, wondering who he was.

"I apologize, but it's just that you look a lot like someone I once knew."

"I am Nicole Jarvis, but I don't seem to know you."

"Terry Hunter. I was a couple years older than you."

"Great—" remembering, Nicole stopped. "My God! I don't believe what a small world we live in. Are you coming or going?"

"Just flew in from Green Bay. How about you?"

"Moving out from La Pointe. I'm starting a new job out here on Tuesday."

"Really? Where at?"

"Mackinaw Designs. I'll be designing fashions for Chantilly Mackinaw. What are you doing these days?"

"Own my own computer software company back in Green Bay. I'm here on business. I hate late night flights, but we've got a meeting at seven sharp."

He flushed slightly and it actually enhanced his face to a point age didn't disguise him now. "How long are you staying?"

"At least three days, maybe longer. Can I buy you a cup of coffee while we wait for luggage?"

"I'd like that," she answered.

"Great. There's an all-nighter upstairs."

He picked up her carry-on and they headed toward the escalators. "Terry, it's amazing running into you here. Obviously, you've done something good with your life. Computer software, I never knew."

"We started out small. You remember Ken Bloomberg from Bayfield?"

She shook her head.

"He and I started Hunberg Software together."

She stopped. The computer company he spoke of was world-renowned. "You *own* Hunberg Software?"

His color flushed deeper. But his smile was filled with pride. They walked further, entered the open bar and he ushered her to a table.

"Would you prefer a latte, or maybe a drink?"

"Latte."

"Wait here and I'll get them."

She watched him lope away like he was fighting for his last breath of life. Felt the heat flare in her cheeks wondering if he remembered the incident that had crossed her mind. He returned moments later, and they talked about the future, her new job, his busy schedule, La Pointe, had it changed, how it changed, neither mentioning the past.

Ninety minutes later she checked into the hotel. Two hours later, she tossed and turned in a king-size bed, thinking king an unfitting title due to her discomfort. The pillows were flat, the mattress hard. She got up, robed herself and went to the window staring out on the sea of city lights. Orange haze billowed around the illusive structures. At four A.M. traffic snaked through the streets like the day had no end. The latte had kept her awake.

Liar her brain screamed. What kept her awake were the questions, the doubts of her choice. Questions about Brian's accident, Gage's love for her, the murders, the doubts Gage had caused. Her decision. Had she really done the right thing? She looked up at the sky astute to the first substitution in her new life.

"Twinkle, twinkle little star. I wonder where you are tonight."

Had it been chance or an omen Terry Hunter found her? It didn't matter since he distracted her inner thoughts. When they finally collected their suitcases, he invited her to dinner tonight, and she accepted. He'd call later with where they could meet.

Shifting about, her room was lavish enough. It furnished enough drawers and closets for the few clothes she had, a coffeepot and hairdryer, phone, large-screened TV, an average hotel refrigerator, even an iron and drop-down board.

Desperately needing a hot shower, she headed that way. Dropped her robe and stepped into the tub. She had to find a place to live, but had no desire to look. She needed to do some shopping. A new outfit would lift her spirits. What she had with her wouldn't be enough. Flipping the tub's stopper, it filled with hot water. She terminated the shower and sunk into liquid warmth. She decided to soak until the stores opened later.

CHAPTER 21

Days later, Nicole learned quickly that Samantha Tobias was not just gorgeous, but a gigantic pain in the backside. The high-handed, over-priced model protested and criticized everything. She snarled verbal abuse at the assistants, cussed the waxy cosmetics, and suffered a severe case of expertitis. Wouldn't listen to a thing anyone told her.

Chantilly's dowdy-looking assistant, Becca, harbored strong dislikes for Samantha and now her. Nevertheless, Nicole sympathized with the monotone-speaking associate who rarely made eye contact with humans. Blatant stress produced the hard pinched facial expressions in Becca's face. Nicole also believed that a little work on Becca's underlying beauty the lady who appeared to be in her late twenty's would have the power to manipulate the world.

The head honcho, Chantilly Mackinaw, was out of town. Therefore, Nicole had been shuffled into a cubicle, she assumed for the time being, left to etch and draft and sketch the next line of sellout fashions. It was crowded, noisy, and the middle traffic lane for on-the-go employees of Mackinaw Designs. She heard it all, saw it all, could reach across the traffic lane and touch her neighbor's drawing table, who still hadn't put in an appearance.

An overwhelming conglomeration of cheap toilet water and inexpensive perfumes committed fragrance abuse on the air they breathed. It made Nicole queasy enough to skip lunch. It didn't help that she thought the furnace was working overtime—it felt eighty inside. She didn't understand how everyone could be dressed in wool and sweaters either. These people had to be nuts when it was fifty-five outside.

Despite the clutter and disorder, Nicole pumped out and contrived several fascinating designs, or so she hoped and somehow managed not to note the time of each day.

"Ms. Jarvis—"

She jumped when Becca spoke from the cubicle's entrance.

"I didn't mean to scare you."

Putting on the final changes to next fall's mixture, she now muttered, "Yes, Becca. What is it?"

"It's after seven. Are you—"

"Oh!" She swiveled. "I didn't realize."

"Ms. Jarvis, tomorrow should be a better day. Whenever Chantilly leaves...I...well, I'm not...,"

Nicole set her drawing instrument down. "Becca, I'd really prefer it if you call me Nicole. I'm also going to speculate that you're not the most congenial considering the way everyone misuses you around here. I've been here less than a week but it's pretty obvious without you the place might just fall apart."

"I guess."

"You don't guess. I think you know it."

"I might."

"Becca, I'm not your enemy. I'm the new kid and with what I've seen, I'm gonna need all the help I can get. Will you help me get through my new job jitters?"

"I can do that."

"Good." Nicole grabbed her top sketch. "Then maybe you can tell me what you think of this one."

Becca took the tablet, eyed the ensemble for a longer time than Nicole thought necessary. It actually made her nervous to wait, but cutting through the crap would be worth it.

"Ms. Jarvis, I mean, Nicole. Do you really want my opinion?"

"Your opinion, and your advice. How bad is it?"

"Well, it isn't bad. In fact, I see why Chantilly hired *you*. These lines are new, they're different, appealing to the eye."

"Thank you. Hired me instead of who?" she asked as quickly as she accepted the compliment.

"Nobody," Becca said, shoving the sketch back. "Everyone is usually packed up ready to fly by six."

Nicole noticed for the first time the quiet penetrating the office floor. "How come you're still here?"

"I'm generally the last one out."

The same way she was at the tavern Nicole mused. "By choice?"

"Not always. Will there be anything else?"

"Yes, there is."

Becca's long lashes flew up. Her eyes were the most beautiful shade of gray-blue Nicole had ever seen. A skewed nose added character to pitched cheek-bones. Her frazzled hair, too long and unkempt, would look fabulous in a lay-ered cut, maybe a curled bob. The dark chocolate color would pay tribute to those beautiful eyes. The rest of her, well, it was hard to tell under baggie layers and measuring tapes, wrist pin-cushions, scissors, whatever else she'd stuffed into her spare pockets.

"What I'd really appreciate is for you to tell me who I beat out of this job."

"The best person has the job."

"I doubt you believe that, Becca."

"Okay. So I'm obvious."

"Would you like to get some dinner. My treat, unless it's pricey."

"You don't have to buy me."

"I'm not trying to buy you. I'm trying to con you into sharing a few secrets on the best places to shop for clothes, and how to find a decent place to live in this city. One that won't bankrupt me."

"You don't have a place yet?"

"Nope. Flew in Sunday night with a hotel reservation. I'm still on central time so it's after nine in my body and my favorite late night snack is pizza. How about you? You know a good place we could grab a juicy sausage pizza."

"Do you always talk fast?"

Nicole laughed. "Hon, I managed a bar and restaurant that catered to sum-mer tourists. Sometimes very drunk tourists," she added with another chuckle. "You either kept up or you'd drown in Superior."

"Drown in superior?"

"Lake Superior," Nicole said, quickly decoding her ignorance. "Oh, hon. Fresh blue waters and clear blue skies as far as the eye can see and the largest of the five Great Lakes system. Together they spell *homes*. Huron, Ontario, Michi-gan, Eerie and Superior."

The minute Nicole spoke those two words, she regretted it. Superior had always been her home, always would be no matter how much it lacked in parenting.

"What's wrong?"

"Nothing. Now, how about that pizza? You want to join me or not?"

"Yeah, I think I will join you. I get very few offers around here."

"Well, hon, where I come from help is just around the corner and offers are plentiful. I also don't have a means of transportation to get wherever we have to go."

"Not a problem. The best pizza in the entire city is just around the corner."

"Great! Let's go, I'm starving."

❦   ❦   ❦

Over the next several weeks, Nicole's selfish gesture that night, selfish because she needed someone, had converted into a friendship with Becca. Chantilly's right-hand played favorites with one new designer, and probably for the first time in her life. She revealed trade secrets of the business, Chantilly's plan to expand into menswear next year, and indulged Nicole with clandestine adventures of the Mackinaw Design models. Sam, as everyone called the autocratic top paragon, was a heroin junkie. It was the only way she kept her five-ten height at one-o-seven. Dana Whitfeldt liked her bouncy-bouncy with both sexes, Tobie Rozelle preferred women, Jocelyn Argus, known as Joss, had a 'thing' for married men. The fashion designers taunted each other like the Packers and the Vikes on a Sunday afternoon. Gabrielle, appropriately labeled 'Gabby' behind her back, and Nicole's neighbor on the other side of the runway, instigated most of those challenges

Becca was the gem of the office skyscraper. She exposed Nicole to a hundred and seventy different fabrics along with the designs for each piece, loaded her down with numerous fashion styles, and flooded her with knowledge of clothing throughout the last four centuries, Medieval England and France to Ancient Rome and Greece.

The woman was an educated miracle worker in the complex world of fashion. She knew layout, marketing and advertising, how to calm disputes between designers and models, and could draw and design better than any Chantilly actually paid to do it. She recognized the outlook and the inlook, understood dynamic versus romantic, high-tech with high voltage, and could identify winners and losers. She was a munchkin, could bring home the moola and cook it up in a damn pan. Nicole wondered if Chantilly realized Becca was one in a million.

The drab assistant had one little problem. She desperately wanted to design clothes, and Nicole had taken that job away from her. She knew only two ways to payback the out-of-fashion assistant. Tonight she'd go to work on Becca

Marsh, single woman with so much to offer the world. It would be easy, too, since Becca had offered her a place to stay until she found her own, which was also proving an irksome task. Rent was sky-high within walking and or unreasonable cab distance.

Once Chantilly returned to the office, her days went from eight to twelve hours and Nicole despised early morning *passionately*.

"Hey, Munchkin, it's Friday, whaddaya say we have ladies night in?"

"Why do you always call me that?"

"It's not meant as an insult. It's a person of low status in a corporation."

"Thanks for the vote of confidence."

"Well, on the contrary—"

"Nicole Jarvis what are you stewing in that pot of yours now?"

"You got any plans for the weekend?"

"There's a joke!"

"Good. Because, Becca Marie Marsh, I'm going to change your life in the next forty-eight hours."

"What?"

"And it starts right now. Get your purse we're going home in a cab. The bus takes too long."

So did the cab. A four car pile up had them sitting in downtown traffic. Fortunate for them, Nicole had a nose for department stores and found one right around the corner. She paid the cabby as Becca shrieked out gibberish about her being crazy.

"Come on. We're going in there."

"Why?"

"Because beauty means looking good and turning it into a woman's individual charm. You, hon, are oozing with charm. Deplorably, you've just never learned how to exploit it."

Grabbing Becca's hand, she added, "I'm going to teach you how to wow the biggies. Then Sam and her slew of companions can eat shit on Monday morning."

"Eat what? Nicole, I don't want to wow the biggies."

She stopped and looked into those sinfully sexy eyes. "Oh, no? Hon, you've got more talent and curves than any designer or model Chantilly pays. Trust me, you're wasting your breath arguing with me. I'm a champ at it."

"Yeah, I know. By the way I forgot all about a phone call you got today. Some guy named Terry is in town."

"Terry Hunter?"

"Yeah, who is he? A rejected lover?"

Nicole started laughing and by the time they hit the escalators, she was hysterical.

"Sorry. Didn't know it was that funny."

"I'm sorry. But it felt good to do that. The more I did it, the better it felt. Terry Hunter found me the night I landed at LAX. He's married. Lives in Green Bay Wisconsin. We knew each other from back on the island. He's a couple years older and I hadn't seen him for many years. What'd he want?"

"Said something about being in town for a week and dinner, but he never called back."

"If he calls on Monday put him through to me. Now, for starters we're going in here."

"What for?"

"What do you think they do in here? Serve drinks? I know the perfect hairstyle for your features."

"Nicole, do you know how much this salon charges for haircuts?"

"The first one's on me. Oh! There's the cosmetics. That'll be our next stop. As long as we're here, start thinking about some sexy ensemble you'd like to slink that stunning figure of yours into."

"Bet your girlfriends back home ran whenever they saw you coming."

Nicole ignored the slippery comment to speak with the receptionist. After more-than-the-necessary questions, she felt satisfied and made an appointment. The problem was it would be two hours before Pixie could *do* them. Another quirk about L.A. Everything was 'let's do'. Had they never heard of going to, or, just plain having lunch?

An hour later they left cosmetics and a happy woman who worked on commission. They headed for clothing up one more floor.

"I'm guessing you're about a size six—"

"How did you know that?"

"I *do* clothes for a living, hon. You need flair and color, not too garish, not too subtle. A sexy mini skirt to show off those gorgeous gams will work."

"Gorgeous what?"

"Gams. Attractive female legs, and you've got 'em. Oh, Lord! They're having a sale."

"Nicole, quit drooling."

"Oh, look at this. It's perfect for your summer face."

"My what?"

"Becca, summer is cool colors. It's all in the intensity of the shade. Cool colors lean toward pastels. With those gray-blue eyes, you'd look fabulous in this deep rose. Periwinkle blue, lavender, mauve, fuchsia are other fantastic colors that would suit you.

"Well, okay. But, what if I like green?"

"Medium blue-green or a pastel aqua," Nicole said absent-mindedly as she floated from rack to rack. "Unfortunately, those shades aren't in this year." She stopped, looked at Becca and giggled. "I'll have to do something about that, won't I?"

Nicole tossed outfit after outfit at Becca. With ten minutes to spare they paid for several and hustled downstairs to the Ralph Chiffon beauty salon. It took fifteen minutes to explain to Pixie the hairstyle Nicole had in mind for Becca. After serious corroboration, Pixie had excellent advice and began with a shampoo as Becca snarled and grumbled under her breath with every snip and clip.

"Damn girl! That's one helluva of a haircut and worth every penny! Do you like it?"

Becca admired, cooed, and sighed.

"Okay, girlfriend. Let's go find some dangling bobbles to show off your dainty ears."

❦   ❦   ❦

The long night filled with turmoil, uneasiness and hope. Katharine went into labor a little before one A.M. Mac panicked. Gage did too, and had the ambulance arriving at their home in record time. The ambulance transported Katharine and Mac to the chopper as there was immediate need to airlift her to Duluth. She barely made it, giving birth to twin boys before two A.M. and five weeks early. Mom was good. She'd probably be able to come home in a couple of days.

Gage called Pete, his part timer, to see if he could work for them. When that didn't pan out he tried Alesha who came in to cover while he and Mac were off the island. His parents had driven south to Madison for a sporting show and Gage called them with the news—they were out the door of their hotel before he disconnected. He woke up Travis and Michelle as well. Then he made reservations because he considered this situation an emergency.

Now here he stood with a sleeping Caitlin looking at those tiny little babes lying in incubators. It worried him that there were more tubes than flesh and body. Doc said their chance of survival was ninety percent. They were just extremely tiny and wrinkled and all reddish. Neither weighed quite three pounds, he said a prayer. He figured out which one had been giving Katharine all the trouble, too. The one on the right with number one in front of Dobarchon. He fought his kid brother to make it into the world first. Gage felt sure he would be feisty like his mother.

"Gage."

He turned. "Mac, you doing okay?"

"What a night! Damn, I'm a father! I've got two sons, Gage, and the most beautiful wife in the world."

"How's Katharine" She okay?"

"Yeah. She's great! She's sleeping. Damn! Two boys, Gage! Look at them. I called my parents and my sister. They're coming."

"Mac. Sit down and take a load off. I'll get some coffee."

They both saw a nurse take a direct route toward one of the twins. Moments later a doctor and several others were working fastidiously on Dobarchon number one. The muscles in Mac's face tensed and twisted up all weird like. Gage felt his own stomach contract into a hard ball as both stood watching, waiting. *This can't be happening*, this can't be happening, *this* can't be happening went through his mind a dozen times. But it was and the grief grew inside of Gage, gnawing on his soul like a dog with a bone.

It felt like eternity when the first nurse who rushed to Dobarchon number one signaled thumbs up. Gage wanted to cry. Mac did cry.

"Come on let's go sit down," Gage told him. "I'll get you that coffee now."

"It'll be touch and go, Gage. They told me that."

"Mac, the little guy came into the world first and probably fighting. He'll be fine. They both will."

He returned with two coffees and sat down. Caitlin only snuggled closer. "Here try this. Have you picked out names yet."

He took a sip. "Katharine wants all-American boy's names. We were discussing it when she dozed off. I have to go see her. She needs to know."

"Tell her I'm proud of her."

He stood and went to the window to look at his two nephews. "Come on guys, hang in there," he said quietly. "You mean everything to your parents."

Out of the blue it hit him. The idea hit him so hard Gage jerked making Caitlin whimper. He looked down at her, knowing what he had done was right. "I made you a promise, squirt, and now I'm gonna keep it."

❀   ❀   ❀

Becca wowed everybody on Monday morning. No one recognized her until she fired off her normal flippant comments. Nicole grinned up a storm inside her little cubicle hearing sarcastic whispers from the jealous and quiet compliments from the not so jealous. The weekend had been worth it in some ways. She taught Becca how to style her hair, mix and match her clothes, and walk with confidence.

In other ways, the weekend was lonely. Nicolina cried. She wailed and then cried some more. Katharine and Michelle were on her mind a lot. Did Michelle have the time of her life on her honeymoon? She wondered. Was she having any morning sickness the way Katharine did? Had Ted found a replacement for her, or Nick, yet? The Realty company hadn't found a buyer for the house, either, and she'd never felt lonelier in her life.

Terry Hunter had been in her subconscious, too. He called Saturday and they met for a second dinner together. Their conversation was casual until he shocked her by bringing up Josie. There wasn't much to tell him without sounding snippy, so Nicole stuck to facts.

Then he blew her away and went blood red with embarrassment mentioning that summer day on the beach. He was mortified when she discovered them. He told her he'd decided shortly afterward, Josie wasn't for him. Amongst other things, shame had compelled him to keep that day secret, and buried. Nicole found the courage to ask if the possibility existed Josie's son could be his. Explained her reasoning—Clyde didn't look anything like Curt. No way, Terry told her. He broke up with her a week after the incident, he called it, which was more than a year before Clyde's birth. Years later, it seemed that a shitload of heartache had taken place within that tragic week.

Her nagging thoughts traveled further to the place she had locked up since the day she lifted off the Duluth runway. It had been a wretched uphill battle to fight her memory of Gage, and since she was wallowing in the middle of the week why not get it all over with in one day. The persistent ache inside of her wouldn't go quietly, but at least this job kept her mind on other things.

"Nicole, Chantilly is ready to see you."

"Thanks, Becca."

The new Becca walked around the office very confident and smiling.

"Don't go too far. Plan two is going into effect," Nicole whispered picking up a folder and sliding gracefully around a speechless Becca. She headed for

Chantilly's office having requested a meet with the owner upon her return from a three-day trip.

Tapping the door, Chantilly looked up.

"Nicole. Come in. Becca said you needed to talk with me. Is everything going well?"

They'd cleared up the name thing on her return trip. "Things couldn't be better, Ms. Mackinaw."

"That's exactly what I want to hear. We'll have a better office setup for you soon."

"Oh, I'm adjusting just fine."

"Good. How can I help you?"

"Do you mind if I close the door?" The fashion designer indicated no and Nicole shut it. "I have some designs here I'd like you to take a look at."

"Didn't I make it clear that I don't have to approve everything you do?"

"Yes, you did. But these aren't mine."

Chantilly removed her glasses and rose as if prepping to face off. "Nicole, I hope you're not going to become one of my employees from hell."

"No, ma'am. But I couldn't forget something you said to me during our interview and I think you should really take a look at what I have here."

Chantilly smoothly, re-sat. "Okay."

"First, I apologize for copies, but I have four sets if you would scan them for a second"

Curiosity benching Chantilly's annoyance, Nicole placed two matching sets side by side. Next she laid out the other two mated sets alongside each other. She waited while Chantilly looked through all four sets.

"What's going on here, Nicole?"

She took a deep breath. Picking up the first set, she began. "These as you can see, Gabrielle has her John-Hancock on them." Picking up the second set, she said, "These bare a great resemblance to Gabrielle's, which just happen to be in last year's January issue of *Vogue*."

Pointing to the third set, Nicole indicated, "Gabrielle's." She selected the fourth set, which matched the third on the desk, and said, "This fourth set belongs to Becca."

"How is it you managed to get your hands on someone else's work?"

"Gabby—I mean Gabrielle, believe it or not, showed me this first set she claims to have done. At the time, I assumed she was flaunting her work in my face. But something kept bugging me about what I saw. Oddly enough, I've studied fashion magazines my entire life and recall almost every one. I know that sounds freaky but it's me. Becca happened to show me why she spends more hours here than she's actually paid for. Upon my discovery, I committed the ultimate sin. I copied the sets, returned the originals and thought you should be made aware."

"Have you told anyone else about this?"

Nicole recognized stewing. Pressed lips and a tense jaw were just the beginnings of the owner's deepening anger. "No."

"You and Becca have hit it off. The two of you wouldn't be in cahoots would you?"

"I thought you might ask me that." Nicole opened the file in her hand. She handed over the *Vogue* magazine then another set of sketches. "These," she passed across the desk, "are the real Gabrielle's work. Ms. Mackinaw, there's a drastic difference. If I hadn't found the magazine, I might have had doubts, but since I've thrown myself into the fire, I'm going to say this. I think you should take a serious look at your assistant. You're risking a huge loss to your competition if you don't."

"Have you always been candid and aggressive?"

"Yes. It comes from providing for myself since I could walk and talk."

"I see. Well, thank you for bringing this to my attention. One more thing."

"What's that?"

"Are you responsible for Becca's transformation? I'm narcotized by that girl's overnight transition."

"Beauty's in the eye of the beholder. I think Becca just opened hers."

"I see...," rethinking, she said, "perhaps not. It appears my eyes have been closed to several things. Thank you, Nicole. On your way out, track down Becca. I want to see her immediately. Oh, and keep up the good work."

"Yes, ma'am, I'll do that and find Becca for you. I'm confident you won't be disappointed."

March sixth became another day Nicole would remember. As laymen's clichés went, the shit hit the fan. Gabby Morris hissed, protested and objected, then threatened until finally LAPD was called to escort her off the premises. When Becca returned from lunch ecstatic after having met and been asked out by a 'handsome hunk', Chantilly announced her promotion to Fashion Designer. Congregating for congrats was held in the middle traffic lane near Nicole's cubicle. Becca had blossomed and she stood back happily amused.

"Nikki!"

Everyone went silent, turned. Nicole snapped around, the shock monopolized her. "Caitlin!"

Her little blond cutie ran and leaped. Nicole caught and swung the three-year-old into her arms. They hugged, squeezed, and kissed each other with arms wrapped tight.

"What're you doing here? How'd you get here? Oh, Caitlin, I've missed you so much."

"I miss you more, Nikki."

Then, she looked. Gage stepped into view and Nicole's breath caught quick and sharp. Her heart lurched anxiously. His eyes were haunted by some inner anxiety as he forced a feigned smile. He had a look of knowing everything about her. A million things went through her mind, and all she could do was stare wordlessly at him.

Nudged, she blinked.

"Is that Terry Hunter? Is this your daughter?" Becca asked.

"Um…no. Becca, would you excuse me?"

Gage's eyes shifted from the crowd back to her. He stepped first and Nicole went to him her free arm outstretched. He stroked her cheek and drew her and Caitlin into an embrace.

After several moments, she pulled back. "Gage, what's wrong?"

"Who's that," he asked looking behind her. "Never mind," he said, releasing her. "Nikki, its Katharine."

A rapid gasp plunged out. "What happened?"

"Her water broke last night. She went into labor and was airlifted to Duluth. She had the twins before two A.M. this morning."

That haunting anxiety she first witnessed in his eyes had changed to clouded uneasiness. "Gage, it's too early for the twins. You didn't fly all the way out here with Caitlin when you could have called. Is she okay? What happened?"

"Nikki, they're premature. We don't have your home number, and well, you're two hours behind us. It's touch and go right now."

When Gage glanced at Caitlin without speaking, Nicole knew the situation was bad.

"How's Katharine? What about Mac? I have to return. Just give me a minute to call and get a reservation."

"Nikki, I knew you'd want to come back. I have tickets. Plane leaves at five."

"Give me a second. We'll grab a cab—I'll throw a bag together and we can leave."

CHAPTER 22

❀

They touched down just before eleven P.M. and cleared Duluth International forty-five minutes later. It was after midnight when the three of them arrived at the hospital. Caitlin fell asleep midair from L.A. and stayed that way. Gage carried her and steered Nikki toward maternity.

Coming around the corner Gage's parents, Travis and Michelle greeted and hugged them. Introductions were made to Mac's parents, his sister, Linda, and her husband, Joe.

"Gage, I have to peek in on Katharine first."

"She's that way," he pointed. "Room 310. I'm gonna check in with dispatch."

Nicole found the room and quietly slipped in. Mac opened his eyes, then rose out of the recliner.

"Nicole."

He'd moved toward and embraced her. "How's she doing?" she whispered.

"Tired, but good."

"Hey, you saucy twit," Katharine muttered.

Nicole turned and went to Katharine. "Oh, hon, I didn't mean to wake you." She bent over and gingerly squeezed Katharine. "You're a mom."

"Have you seen my prize boxers?"

"Not yet. I wanted to see you first."

"They're so tiny, Nicole. But I know they're going to make it. They're fighters."

Caressing Katharine's cheeks, she purred, "Just like you, hon. You rest. I'm home now."

When Katharine's eyes drooped shut, Nicole turned away, wiped her tears and followed Mac into the hallway. *Weird, but I haven't had tears since I left.* "How are the babies, Mac?"

"Each hour that passes is good. Come on. Let's go take a look."

"Have you given them names? Gage said when he left you hadn't decided."

They reached the window and he pointed. It was automatic to gasp and Nicole instantly covered her mouth. Their tiny size startled her.

"Its okay, Nicole. They're both hanging on and they *will* make it. Dobarchon number one is Adam and his brother is Michael. Where are Gage and Caitlin?"

"Right behind ya, brother-in-law."

Mac pulled out two cigars. "Gage, my man. Here ya go. One for Adam. One for Michael."

Taking the cigars, he slid them into his shirt pocket. "Nice names. How they doing, Mac?"

"At different times both their hearts stopped once. They're jaundiced, but they keep reassuring us."

"How's Katharine?"

"She's been asking for you. Go see her."

"I'll take Caitlin," Nicole told him.

She extended her arms and Caitlin fussed when Gage passed her then he leaned and kissed both their cheeks.

"She's not the only one that's missed you, Nikki. I'll be back in a few."

When Mac headed back to Katharine's room, Nicole asked, "Gage, have there been anymore—"

"No. No arrest either. We'll talk about it later," he said quietly and walked away. Exhaustion and caffeine were a dangerous combination and a sure-fire way to screw up. He'd been feeding off both to the point his entire body ached with defeat until he saw Nikki inside that L.A. office building. Bottomless peace and satisfaction consumed him in that brief moment of their initial visual exchange. Gage stopped abruptly on his way to see his sister. Something clicked in his mind. Fatigue made him overlook the details. He paced circles in the hallway, started filling in the empty blanks. There was one person who wasn't at the Tavern the night Nikki discovered Stacy White. Maybe when he heard Terry Hunter's name as he stood there gazing at Nikki in that L.A. office building—everything she told him came back with the vivid memory of that long-ago weekend. He hissed under breath, slammed one fist into the other.

Gage rounded the corner and came to another abrupt halt with the intrusion of something Brian once told him. The words replayed in his mind like a very bad song. It didn't make sense years ago, but when Brian didn't offer further explanation, he never questioned it further.

"Jesus," he muttered.

It was coming together in his head and he looked up when Nicolina announced her return. Maybe he didn't have latents or witnesses, but he had the damaging evidence. If what he was thinking had an ounce of truth, he just figured out the crime scene location, too. His adrenaline kicked into high gear. He'd have to talk to Michelle. He'd need search warrants.

His chest ballooning with the adrenaline rush through his body, Gage picked up the pace headed toward Katharine's room and entered. Although pale, both delicacy and strength filled her face. He was proud and felt the curve of his mouth. In the semi-darkness, he couldn't tell if her eyes were open. "Is she awake?" he whispered.

Mac replied with a head shake. Gage inched toward the bed, leaned down giving her forehead a peck. Her eyes fluttered open. "Hey, Pipsqueak. You done good."

"Bro, I'm a mom."

He swallowed a lump in his throat. "I know, Sis. And they're beautiful, like you."

"You went and got Nicole. She's in love with you...make her tell you...make her stay."

Katharine dozed off before Gage could respond then motioned Mac outside.

"I'm going back to La Pointe. I think my trip to L.A. just gave us a break in the case."

"What? How?"

"Terry Hunter is one key."

"Victim five's father?"

"Yeah. I knew I knew him, just couldn't remember how until I heard his name in L.A."

"What?"

"Mac, I'll explain everything later. You take care of Katharine and my nephews."

"Gage, you said one key. Is there another?"

He nodded. "But, family comes first. I'm taking Nikki and Caitlin back with me. Nikki's life is still in jeopardy. The three of us will be at Joe's place. I'll get a hold of Cole. We're gonna need a search warrant and I'll call you when we're ready. We'll make the arrest together."

Revived, Gage hustled down the hall to talk to Michelle and stopped when he came around the corner. Nikki had fallen asleep sitting up with Caitlin wrapped around her torso. *I've been miserable ever since she left.* This time he knew it all, had it all, and he'd never let her get away from him a third time.

Travis waited and watched him. Michelle used his shoulder to rest her head and Gage debated how he would explain everything to her. Travis made her happy and that solitary fact supplied him with the determination he needed. He went to Michelle first and tapped her knee. She opened her eyes, lifted her head.

"Michelle, you guys should get a room so you can rest."

"No. We have to be here with Katharine and Mac. I'm fine."

"Can we talk for a minute?"

"Sure," she said yawning and standing. "What is it?"

Gage led her away to ask her a couple of questions about the Cadotte history and had what he needed after a few minutes. Then he hugged her. Whatever happened, he would tell her everything. She, out of all who had suffered, had first dibs on what really happened to Brian that horrible weekend. Gage peeked at Adam and Michael, and smiled. "Hang in there little guys."

He moved over and squatted in front of Nikki. It all made sense especially *why* she became the killer's ultimate sacrifice. "Hey, Baby," he whispered, nudging her awake. She lifted her head and stared groggily.

"Let's go home."

❧   ❧   ❧

After a couple hours of sleep, Gage had a serious talk with Nikki. He convinced her she had to keep her return to the island quiet. Alesha and Pete took time off from their regular jobs to rotate staying with her at Joe's place and covering La Pointe. It freed him up not to worry, and to work with Cole once he detailed how he knew who the real serial killer was, and why. His sense of conviction convinced Claire Huntington.

Cindy, the front office typist, granted another bitch session. Cole then labored over the tedious language and four search warrants were successfully completed. Two were for physical locations. Two were for medical records. The wording had to convince a judge based on a single piece of circumstantial evidence—one white dress.

Subsequent to discussion, and agreement, Gage and Cole opted to use Tom Coville and his Park Rangers instead of the FBI to execute two of those warrants. First, Gage would deliver one and Cole would affect the second of the two medical record warrants. Mac would definitely be involved in the fourth—the most important—at the location of the arrest of the Green Bay Serial Killer. They were going to execute the location warrants simultaneously or at least try.

With the documents in hand, ready for a judge to sign, Gage headed out after calling the hospital to check on Katharine and the babies. Adam and Michael were still in their incubators, would be until they gained weight, but both were doing better. The shock of defeat had left him numbed until the day he went to get Nikki. His sense of strength returned that day and his despair lessened. *Believe what is, not what you think. Always expect the unexpected.* Gage couldn't explain any of it, but that day in L.A. the pieces fell into place. All he had to do was prove it. The documents he held were a sure-fire guarantee the serial killing that began in Green Bay over three years ago would finally end. Other proof he didn't have Gage felt positive Sully could give, if he could just locate the skipper. Gage put the word out that he was looking for him but no one knew where the old man was.

Sealed by ice and snow, Gage drove the plowed path across Lake Superior enroute to meet Judge Stone. Overnight the entire area had crystallized with lake snow cover. Leafless trees coated with frozen dew painted magnificent images on every side of Bayfield. A mid-afternoon stillness lay beneath a deck of clouds. They hung graphite and shadowy like in a protective shield over the entire area. In between, colors protruded off homes of Victorian flavor, curious shops and several inns and lodges. Each swelled out of snow roofed bluffs. He thought it was peaceful and appealing.

Hundreds of masts at the marina to his left were in dry dock. Nobody would be there and he wondered if Sully might be hanging out at the ferry's office or if anyone connected had seen him around. He'd check there after getting his warrants signed.

Driving onto the mainland, he negotiated his squad through Bayfield and hit the highway. Judge Stone said he would wait, which he did. Gage walked into the Courthouse at half past six. He left fifteen minutes later filled with a new experience. Self-satisfaction. Judge Stone knew the case—most likely, everyone in Wisconsin did. Five minutes after listening to reason, the judge signed the warrants.

Back in Bayfield shortly before eight, his dispatcher radioed him. He picked up his mike responding, "301."

"301 cross over to your City radio. They're looking for you."

His heart kicked like a mule, as he said, "10-4." Switching over, he aired, "301 to 310 on City."

"Chief, we found Sully for you."

The kick in his chest transformed into another kind of charged energy. "I'm in Bayfield. Where's he at, Pete?"

"At the station with us."

"Have him wait. I'll be there in twenty. Everything else okay?"

"Affirmative."

❀   ❀   ❀

Chutes and Ladders was Caitlin's favorite game. Although she preferred the card game of Memory with pictures of animals, that was at the LeNoir house. A deck of Vegas cards broke the monotony of repetitive amusement and being stuck inside all day. It also became the start of Caitlin learning to count. Red hearts and diamonds with black spades and three-leafed clovers made it simple for her until she worked her way up to the royalty.

Nicole learned a lot. Fruit Loops was Caitlin's first choice of cereal, which Joe didn't stock in his house, nor did Gage. The child preferred apple to orange juice, hotdogs to hamburgers, what kid didn't she mused, and chose having a story read to her versus watching cartoons. They played dress-up, painted toenails and fingernails, and sampled perfumes and lotion to pass more time. Alesha thoughtfully supplied the essentials when she relieved Pete.

Chattering up the same blue streak she always did, Caitlin laid a huge declaration and request on Nicole after hearing a second bedtime story.

"Nikki?"

Sitting on the edge of the bed, she brushed Caitlin's cottony fluff off her face. "What is it, sweetie?"

"Gage said you won't know if I don't tell my secret."

"What secret?"

"Are you still mad because I didn't like you?"

"Caitlin Graham, I was *never* mad at you."

"But you left and you said you wouldn't. Remember, in the summer, you said you wouldn't leave me."

She looked at the girl in surprise. *She had forgotten.* Her words had followed the death of the child's mother, Maryann Graham. They were meant to comfort. Looking at the dejection in Caitlin's face, Nicole felt the child's heartache. "Yes I did say that. Sweetie, come here."

Caitlin scrambled out of the covers into her outstretched arms and sat in her lap. "Honey, sometimes we say stuff not knowing—"

"Nikki, am I in your heart like Gage said?"

Kissing the top of her head, Nicole sighed. "You sure are, sweetie. Right here," she pointed to the spot near her left breast.

"Why?"

"Because you are a very special little girl. I have lots of love for you and I keep it safe in my heart so I'll never lose what I feel."

A serious guise replaced a happy face while Caitlin weighed, considered and contemplated her words. She even touched the spot she had pointed to as if she could reach in and pull out the love.

"Remember you said to think of mommy with the angels before I go to sleep?"

"Yes, I remember."

"I still think of mommy, but wish something else."

Tears dribbled down Caitlin's cheeks. "Sweetie, I know you miss your mom. I miss mine some days, too."

Crying, she said, "I don't want you to go away. I wish you'd be my new mommy."

"Oh, Caitlin," she sighed. Nicole squeezed her snug. "I don't know if that's possible."

"I promise I'll be good and always like you."

"I know, darling. Don't cry. Tell you what. You climb back under those blankets and we'll talk about this tomorrow when you wake up."

"Promise," she sniveled.

"Yes, Caitlin. I promise." Yanking out a tissue, she said, "Now let's wipe away those tears and I'll make another promise right here and now." She dried Caitlin's cheeks, tucked her in for the second time and kissed her cheek.

"What?"

"I promise that you will always be in my heart. No matter where we go or what we do. You can promise the same to me if you want to."

"Does it mean you're leaving?"

"What it means is that even when you grow up, fall in love, go off and marry the man of your dreams, or do whatever you want to do, I'll always be there for you no matter where we are."

"Will you stay in my heart if I want?

"I sure will, sweetie."

"Love you, Nikki."

"I love you too, Caitlin. Now close your eyes, think happy thoughts, and dream of sweet things."

Near ten when she walked into the living room, Alesha had dozed off on an over-stuffed sofa in front of the television. Nicole rarely noticed décor, but this room was cozy and warm. She wondered if Joe had put it together. Soft earthy tones surrounded the creamy-white, pillow-cushioned furniture. There was very little in the way of intimate possessions yet the gracious room offered comfort and homey satisfaction. She could smell Gage in certain spots around the house, especially one of the three bedrooms he slept in and in the bathroom. She didn't have the courage to face him tonight whenever he found his way back here and put the thought aside.

She called the hospital earlier to check on Katharine and the twins. So far, so good. Lacking slumber herself, Nicole flipped on a light over the kitchen sink for Gage, left the TV on, Alesha sleeping and prepped for bed.

She felt like crying alongside Caitlin but uncovered a potent strength in responsibility. She couldn't possibly grant the child's wish. Not with her new job. Besides, L.A. was no place to raise a child. She heard Gage come in the back door, heard him talking quietly to Alesha before she went out the door. Then he padded down the hall, checked Caitlin first, and when he knocked gently, opened her door, she pretended to be asleep.

He shuffled in bent and kissed her head, and feeling guilty she shifted and looked at him.

"I shouldn't have woke you."

"You didn't."

He nudged his rear onto the edge of the bed. "Nikki, we're going to Duluth in the morning."

She pushed herself upright. "The twins—"

"No, they're doing good. But you can visit while I take care of business."

"Gage, you said this morning you know who the serial killer is. Are you going to shed some light on this since I'm the one he's after?"

He shook his head and flicked on the bedside light. "It'll be out by late tomorrow night or early the next morning. It's better this way, Nikki."

She blinked—*his words, the card with his roses.* She thought he meant better that they didn't get involved. Never considered the safety issue or *his* responsibility.

"Tell me about your new job. Is it everything you'd hoped it would be?"

She thought about her new friendship with Becca. That was good, but the models were ditzy, the designers were rude and competitive, and the pay sucked for the cost of living in the area. The one point she avoided thinking about all day revolved around being locked up here. The bottom line was this still felt more like home than anywhere she'd ever go or live. Since returning, the barren loneliness she felt in L.A. had dissolved.

"No, it's not," she finally told him.

He looked at her for a long moment. "Nikki, when this is over we are going to sit down and talk. Afterward, if you still want to go back to L.A., you'll get no argument or coercion from me. But, I'm giving you fair warning. When we have that talk, I am going to do everything within my power to convince you that you're all that matters to me. All I want or need is you."

He dropped a gentle and surprisingly persuasive kiss on her mouth. It made the heart she shared with Caitlin flutter inside her breast. She heard Nicolina overhead and felt powerless to challenge the haunting fairytale any longer.

Gage stood and caressed her cheek with the back of his knuckle. She had about thirty-six hours to come up with a way to tell him. She could only hope she did it right.

"I love you, Nikki. Sleep well. You, Caitlin and I will be leaving around seven. What time do you want to get up?"

"Better make it five."

CHAPTER 23

✿

One search warrant for medical records proved ineffectual, one didn't. Mac returned from Duluth with Gage. Travis and Michelle also returned and took Nikki and Caitlin to their home. Gage's mother decided to stay with Mac's family, while his father asked to be part of the warrant execution.

After last minute discussions, they decided to execute the last two warrants one at a time. Tom Coville with six Park Rangers, Claire Huntington, Pete, Alesha, his father, and Mac and Cole backed him up as Gage pounded his fist against the first door. Waited, pounded again. Tom checked the front windows. Pete looked inside the garage.

"Looks like nobody's home."

"I'm after the shed on the back of his property. Let's go. When necessary, we'll get another warrant to boot the door to their house."

With the proper equipment, any structure was accessible. Two Park Rangers had Bert Hanson's shed doors open in thirty seconds. Flashbangs would've been gratifying, Gage thought, but a pair of heavy-duty bolt cutters did the job. Flashlights illuminated the inside of the tin shed and Gage stopped suddenly. Rage almost singed the corners of his control. Instead, the air whooshed out of his pipes.

The inside of the shed was a shrine.

His father swearing he didn't believe it, Gage stood stunned, staring wordlessly. His heart pounding, he gaped at the inside of the heated shed. A white sheet with bronze stains covered a wood altar table. Pictures plastered the wall above the sacrificial platform. Gage gulped harder. Literally hundreds of Terry Hunter alongside old ones of Brian formed a maze around a colored glossy of a mother's womb.

Dozens of rosary pea bracelets were placed on another table in intricate orderly lines. Six bottles of Johnny Walker Black liquor neatly lined a shelf above the second counter. All Gage thought was, *how many more?*

He shifted. Several remaining gallons of what were sure to be the paraquat stolen from the County garage sat on the floor along one wall.

"Secure it!" he snapped. "Gus from the crime lab is on standby. Get a hold of him, Pete. Now! You, Alesha and one of Tom's men wait here. Nobody gets into that house until I say so. I want any who tries arrested! Do you understand?"

They nodded.

"And if Bert Hanson shows up, I want him taken to the station. I don't care how you get him there. The rest of you follow me."

As they drove to the pretentious house, anger poured out of Gage in ragged breaths. He had wanted to be wrong, but knew all along, he was right. Ten minutes later he, Mac and Cole, along with the Park Rangers surrounded Curt and Josie Stewart's house. On a three count, weapons drawn, they forced entry through the front door a little different than the way they entered the shed—they booted the door.

Josie screamed. Curt yelled profanities while Clyde cowered.

Cole took Curt, Mac grabbed Josie, one of Tom's men had Clyde and all three were handcuffed. They quickly searched the rest of the house for others and finding no one else inside, Gage marched over and stood firm while Mac did the honors.

"Josie Stewart, you're under arrest for murder."

Mac read her her Miranda rights as she screamed obscenities and cursed all of them. Curt stopped yelling at them when his wife's voice changed an octave. Her profanity turned to chanting before her voice changed once more.

"It was necessary to squeeze the unclean spirit from their souls. They were sinners. They had to die for what they did to me. The Divine Creator said so. *He* stole my baby. I had to do it. My baby said murder would close the gates of hell. My baby screamed and cried for me."

Each one of them stood rooted to the spot and stunned as they watched Josie. Bizarre feelings of horror and dread filled the atmosphere like a quick-spreading disease. Josie hissed and spat angrily.

"That bodacious bitch thinks she's so perfect. *She will die!* She must die for stealing my Brian away from me. Nikki-wikki has to die. She stole my love from me. I'm going to slay her heart for what she did. I tried once. I *will* get her."

The steely edge in her voice changed. It was lower, huskier, like that of a man but more like the sound of some inhuman creature growling out unintelligible words. She began chanting foreign words that no one understood then stopped. Her eyes glazed over and her head rolled around on her shoulders. Silence followed before more ruthless threats came out cold and bitter. Josie's head bobbed forward and backward, her eyes rolled in their sockets until only the white showed. She chanted in English this time. *"Almighty One, I offer this virgin flesh to absolve my sinful transgressions. To replace the death of my baby. Come forth to receive my sacrifice. Close the gates of my hell forever."*

She jerked, took a quick deep breath and let it out. Her voice changed once more but to that of a child. "Daddy, *please* forgive me. Daddy, don't make me. Don't take my baby! Please, Daddy, don't make me do this."

"You have sinned! Be damned to hell for your impurity!"

Gage stiffened, felt the hairs rise on his neck. He just stared at Josie. He wouldn't have believed it if he hadn't been witness to the changes. The words came out of her angry and coarse, hard and masculine. "Get 'em outta here. We're looking for a *Susan Bristol* white dress and anything else related."

Claire went with Josie as they escorted her out and placed her in a separate squad car from the others. The remainders searched the house before Gage escaped out a back door. Shoving a hand through his hair, he goose stepped snow banks, making circles around them with feelings of navigating a minefield. He no longer wondered when and why everything went wrong. Convulsed with heartache, it sucked to be right, and he glanced up at the heavens. "This one is for you Brian. I'm sor—"

"Gage."

He whirled around and stared at his father. Numb from the years of control, Gage no longer had the time or patience to deal with his father's low tolerance and frustration with him. The lack of trust and disbelief his dad had in him made the disappointment obvious, but he didn't care. The rigid thinking and closed mind his dad had had cast him out long ago, but he didn't care about that either. Right now, he didn't care what his father thought of him. In fact, he didn't care what anyone thought of him. The damage was done and more would still suffer the aftereffects of this case.

"Gage, you were right. I was wrong."

He stood there, his face most likely glazed with shock, as if someone had struck him in the midsection.

"I'm sorry about everything," he said forcing his withered pose to stand tall.

It had to be difficult for him to say that.

"Parents make mistakes," he said. "We're supposed to learn from them. I'm sorry my faith in you fell. You were always good at this job…better than I was. Your mother's wrong. You weren't just born efficient. You are the most stable person I've ever known. Nobody's ever been able to influence you. You never panic under fire and you know exactly how to get your point across. When you started working under me, the latter peeved me, but not as much as the way you always stayed cool under everyone's complaints. I spent years working to get where you were after one week on the job."

"Dad—"

"Wait. I need to get this out. Since it will take longer than we have, I'm apologizing for every misunderstanding we've had, known or otherwise. You did a good job today, son. I've never been more proud of you than I am right now. You believed in yourself and you stuck with your gut and your beliefs."

Standing in the cool air, his muscles relaxed a little. He observed sorrow for all the misdeeds and misunderstandings filling an expression in his dad's eyes, and then he saw love was at the heart of his dad's words. The emotion came through loud and clear before Gage thought about Elisabeth Callihan and how much grief she must suffer because she couldn't admit how the loss of her son had caused more agony in her life. After several silent moments, Gage stepped up and hugged his father. "Thanks, Grandpa."

No matter how brief, his dad reciprocated hurriedly then backed up. Moisture wormed into his dad's eyes and Gage kept a secret smile buried inside of him.

"By the way. I know what your mother's been up to. I believe there's someone you need to stop from getting back on a plane."

Gage latched his thumbs atop his gun belt. He glanced around before he said, "I think it'd be easier to figure out another serial killing."

"She's a feisty one," Frank said with a chuckle.

"That'd be putting it real mild, Dad."

"Maybe. But we both know she's worth it."

"I've loved her ever since the first time I laid eyes on her," he calmly said. "Dad, I've made plenty of mistakes myself. I have to figure out a way to fix this one, too."

"I love you, son."

He spoke quietly, but somehow his dad must have known that saying the words now would make the rest of his tasks a whole lot easier. "I love you too, Dad."

❦   ❦   ❦

Gage had called Travis shortly after bringing the suspects back to the station. Near midnight now, he knocked on the door of the Baines' new home. He still had no idea what or how he would tell Michelle. If she were unable to wait up, he would come back first thing in the morning, but take Nikki and Caitlin home with him tonight.

"Hey, Gage," Travis said. "Come in."

"Are they sleeping?"

"Caitlin is. Michelle and Nicole are downstairs. You want anything? Drink? Something to eat?"

"No, I'm good."

Travis led him down the split entry. The furnishings weren't complete, but their home was nice, big, done with the future in mind. Not too lavish, either. Gage went to Nikki first, tugged her to her feet and gave her a long deep kiss.

He sat down next to Michelle, motioned Nikki to sit on his other side. Travis squatted on the arm of the couch next to Michelle. He'd given Travis brief details over the phone.

"What's going on," Michelle asked.

"Michelle, I'm here because I have to talk to you. This is not going to be easy but I want you to hear from me first what needs to be said."

"Is it Katharine? The twins? What happened?"

Travis placed his hands on her shoulders, and Gage answered, "No. It has to do with Brian."

"Brian?"

He nodded not having a clue where to begin then remembered his dad always said 'best way to say things is just say them'. "Michelle, I'm sorry about Brian. I'm sorrier to have to tell you that Brian's death wasn't an accident. Brian was murdered by the Green Bay Serial Killer."

"*Omigod!* I don't understand. Gage, what're you saying?"

"The serial killings that began in Green Bay actually started with Brian's death."

"*What?* How? Why?" She looked at her husband. "Travis?"

He wrapped his arms from back to front around her. "I'm here, Milady."

"Tonight we arrested Josie Stewart for all the murders, including Brian's. She's the Green Bay Serial Killer."

Stunned by what he just told her, Michelle's face paled and Gage was glad she had Travis. Nicole gasped, more like croaked, as she sat upright.

"Gage, you better start—tell me everything," Michelle strangled out.

"We have proof Josie got pregnant when she was a teenager. In the beginning, all I had was something Brian once said to me, a story Nikki told me, an inkling from a nursery rhyme, and then Sully came forward. Josie confessed to everything on tape after we arrested her."

"*Sully!* Nicole? Gage, you are not making any sense."

"Brian went out with Josie a couple of times, and well, as things happen, fathered her unborn child."

"*Clyde is Brian's child!*"

"No. A long time ago, Brian made a comment to me about being coerced by a wild feline and that he didn't know how he was going to handle it. We never talked about it again, which I now have regrets about. Josie really did follow through with a threat she made, perhaps a promise she made to herself for what she believed was justified revenge. The FBI Profiler is sorting out the details back at the station and believes the serial killings were triggered by Josie's accumulative hostility, her history of frustration, her incapability to work out internal conflict and her abrupt feelings of rejection. That is, Brian's rejection of her."

"Gage, I don't understand."

"When Josie's father found out she was pregnant he forced her to have an abortion she didn't want. That baby was Brian's. Bert confirmed the abortion as well and we have the documented hospital records for evidence."

"But how do you know it was Brian's?" Michelle asked.

"Josie told us in her confession. She also told us Brian dumped her after he got her pregnant. The profiler believes that that combined with Terry Hunter rejecting Josie started her feelings of inadequacy."

"Terry Hunter," Nicole repeated incredulously.

Gage nodded. "Brian was never serious about Josie and told her he had never planned on seeing her beyond a few dates. At the time, when he told me about getting someone in trouble, I didn't know he was referring to Josie. Following the breakup with Brian and before the boating incident, Josie had already hooked up with Terry Hunter. Things got sticky in the days before Brian's death because Brian had asked Nikki out on a date. They were at the beach when he did, and Nikki agreed to go out with him then she went one way while Brian went the other. That same day, Nikki accidentally happened to come upon Terry and Josie at the beach…,"

Michelle's eyes flew up. "Doing it?" she shrieked, looking at Nicole.

Gage held Nikki's hand and kissed it when she nodded. "I don't know how Josie learned of that date yet, but she somehow found out about it. Whether she vowed to get even from that day forward, I don't think we'll ever know the answer. Anyway, Josie incited more trouble the night of their date. I went out to the hangout to look for Brian after I got off work ran into Josie and Terry and Josie told me Brian had hit on Nikki. She said they'd gone off somewhere together implying that the two of them had been at the hangout earlier."

Gage retold Michelle about the fight he had with Brian and everything he and Nikki had already talked about on New Year's Eve. "The next day Brian did take his boat out and here's where Sully enters into the picture."

"But if Sully knew something why didn't he say something back then?"

"It isn't so much what he knew as it was what he saw, Michelle. He ran into Brian and saw the bruises I'd caused. Brian told him how and why he acquired those bruises."

Gage looked at Nikki. "That's when Brian told him you and I were meant to be together. Sully told me Brian felt terrible about what had happened the night before between us. Brian had every intention of straightening out the mess he thought he had created."

Nicole's eyes were dry and enlarged. Gage squeezed her hand once more. Looking at Michelle, he continued. "Sully attempted to make him feel better. He suggested he walk off his frustration and obvious disappointment, but Brian wouldn't hear of it. Sully went about his business at the Marina and a matter of minutes later he heard Josie yelling and screaming. She was involved in a full-blown argument with Brian. Sully said he heard her screaming at him about being dumped and blamed Brian for getting her pregnant then not taking responsibility. She also told him she'd get even with him for going out with Nikki the previous night. That was her initial threat. Little did Sully or Brian know at that moment that she had already carried out the threat."

"But they said Brian was speeding and hit a sandbar," Michelle argued.

"I know and they were half right. I had the report pulled. If your parents had never insisted on having that boat checked, we never would have figured it out. I'm still not sure why they didn't figure it out back then. Anyway, the cause of the accident was documented as a result of a throttle malfunction."

"I don't know what that means," Michelle told him.

"Milady," Travis said. "The throttle gages the speed of the boat. If it malfunctions, the boat races at high speed out of control."

Michelle gasped. Her face paled.

"Michelle, Brian and I worked on his boat all the time. Brain, as Nikki knew, was a mechanical genius. Brian never would have taken that boat out if he'd known of any problem. Because of that, I have received back-up testimony that cotter keys do not *just* jiggle loose. A cotter key fits the throttle and holds it in place so the operator can control the speed of the boat. Josie admitted in her confession that she jimmied the cotter key."

A look of tired sadness passed over her features before tears swelled in Michelle's eyes and slid out. Travis held Michelle providing her with comfort. If that were even possible in this dismal moment, Gage thought.

"That's not easy to do," Travis finally said. "Those keys are solid and tight."

"I'm aware," Gage replied. "I checked into that as well. Josie had two memberships to fitness joints. It's another key to the murders she committed. She worked out every day of the week pumping iron—bench presses a hundred and fifty according to the fitness places. We also found workout equipment at their house, which was seized as additional evidence. She had the strength to move the bodies without dragging them, and as I've been told the proper tool would add to her strength to do what she did to the boat."

"Gage, what does any of this have to do with the serial killings?" Michelle finally asked.

"That's where Terry Hunter comes into this. The guy doesn't even know he paid the price for going out with Josie."

"What're you talking about?"

"Victim number five in Green Bay was Terry Hunter's sixteen-year-old daughter."

"Jesus," Nicole muttered. "Terry broke up with Josie because I caught them doing it on the beach. I ran into him at LAX the night I flew out there." She looked at Gage remembering that Sunday. "He asked me out to dinner because he was in town on business. We talked about many things before he brought up the subject. He wanted to know what happened to Josie. He told me he was as much to blame but he'd never been so ashamed of what she enticed him to do that day. He said he quickly figured out she was not his type after I caught them. He never mentioned his daughter."

"Josie admitted that Terry did break up with her," Gage confirmed. "She claims it was for a sixteen year old Native American girl he dated for awhile."

Michelle just looked at him with a doubtful expression.

"Amelia Rainbird was the first female victim when this began, and the daughter of the girl Terry dated for about a month. Ironically they both live in Green Bay now but never married each other and have both lost their daughters for the same reason. The rest of Josie's victims became random picks she made by race and age. She was obsessed with a concept that sixteen-year-old Native American girls had to die for what one had done—stolen Terry away from her. But, every vicious act was all leading up to the ultimate sacrifice."

Gage looked at the woman he loved more than life. A little surprised, her eyes were dry. "In her mind she believes you stole Brian from her, Nikki. Because you went out with him. He was the one man she claims to have truly loved but couldn't have because of you. She transferred the rejection of two men into her hate for you. In Josie's mind, she believed she had to kill all women who interfered with her love for one man."

He looked back at Michelle. "But, Michelle, there's more."

"How much worse can this get?" she muttered.

Gage glanced up at Travis who gave him a look of reassurance to continue. "Three pieces of evidence with each death were a rosary bracelet, the poison that kills them and a bottle of Johnny Walker Black liquor. We found all of that in Bert Hanson's shed, which is the original location of every crime scene. We also discovered a rosary bracelet off the search warrant inside Josie and Curt's house. According to Josie, Terry gave that one to her. She said Johnny Walker Black liquor was Terry's favorite alcohol. Her plan was to kill all Native American girls with the paraquat she stole from the Ashland County garage."

"Where Curt works," Michelle said.

He nodded. "We don't have the answer yet why she chose to steal the chemical or how she even knew about it. The Profiler said two men dumping her as a teen incited the anger and jealousy, which led to her killing rampage, starting with Brian. The bracelet and liquor she left at each scene were her symbolic mark behind the murdering. She really had little on Brian, or rather Brian hadn't given her anything to remember him by, so there were never any clues to his memory at any of the crime scenes."

"Josie really stole the poison from where Curt works?"

"Yes. We have a report from the County that Curt had lost his key and had to have it replaced. Josie refused to admit to taking Curt's key, but we found it with another rosary bracelet at her house. After stealing the chemical, she mixed it with the liquor and made her victims drink it. But like I said she was working up to her ultimate sacrifice."

He looked at Nikki again and squeezed her hand. "Unfortunately, even with the amount of evidence we discovered I think Josie's too far gone and would have continued killing even if she had succeeded at getting you."

"Oh, God," Nicole moaned. "Michelle, I'm sorry. I'm so sorry about every-thing. About Brian."

"This is not your fault!" Michelle blew out.

"In Josie's sickness," Gage continued, "she honestly believed she was Jozette Cadotte, a real Cadotte daughter—"

"The one we know little about," Michelle said. "Why? How?"

"The Profiler will try to sort it out but we believe at this moment she will be found mentally incapable of standing trial. Josie is telling us that her aborted baby sobbed and pleaded for help, hence some of the voices we suspect she hears in her head. In her statement, she told us the Divine Creator, or another voice that speaks to her, ordered her to kill the girls to rid her of the sin she committed—getting pregnant and having it aborted. We've heard many voices coming out of her, her father, Brian's, a child's."

"Her father, a God-fearing Catholic, made her abort," Michelle whispered now.

"Yes," Gage replied to her statement.

"How did the man Katharine shoot fit into all of this?" Nicole asked.

Gage thought for a second about all the victims over the span of a three-year killing spree. Not just those who had died by the poison, but the ones left behind with families destroyed forever. He was glad Mac and Katharine found each other.

"Josie was having an affair with Patriot. We have witness testimony on that from Janice Anderson. I'll get to her in a minute. Patriot was just as mentally unbalanced as Josie, but he murdered for other reasons," Gage answered, then looked back at Michelle. "From what we have discovered so far Josie hooked up with Patriot somewhere and somehow convinced him to murder with her. Josie's had several affairs. Kevin was another."

"You're going to tell me Derek was one of her affairs aren't you?"

He nodded. "I'm sorry, Michelle. I interviewed Derek as well. Although what I have recorded is distorted gibberish because of his mental state, I'm sure it's all going to match in the end."

"Does Curt know?" she asked.

"Yes, we arrested him, took his statement and released him," he told her.

"What about Clyde?"

"He's innocent. Neither he nor Curt knew what was going on and Curt's only involvement came when Josie stole his key for the County garage. I'm convinced he had no idea."

"What about the Anderson woman in Green Bay and the white dress?" Nicole asked.

"Well, Babe, that white dress became very important in the end. You remember the shop owner was going to fax me a list of customers?"

"I bet you're going to tell us Josie's name was on that list."

"That, and the shop owner had a record of Josie's credit card purchase for the white dress. We didn't find the dress tonight in our search warrant of their house, which is exactly what we were hoping for. She's denying the dress Stacy White had on the night you found her in your backyard was hers but it's circumstantial to the rest of the evidence. Janice Anderson, the woman Josie claimed to be her cousin, has no involvement inside the realm of the murders other than she's dating Kevin Stewart. Green Bay PD has convinced her to cooperate with us in every way."

"Who broke into my house?" Nicole asked him meekly.

"Josie did. I didn't know it was her the day we got back, but I was already suspicious that we were not dealing with a man. We found a typed nursery rhyme on Stacy White. It talked about a baby dying in the woods."

"How'd you conclude that from what happened inside my house?"

"Because every piece of your outer clothing was shredded violently. It leaned toward a personal vendetta. Statistics show that if it'd been a male, there'd have been proof of sexual involvement. Your underwear wouldn't have been shredded the way it was. A man would have stolen them. The fact all the dead girls were virgins also had me thinking it was a female. That it was someone who had to be jealous of you, not someone who worshiped you. Like I said, I already suspected we were dealing with a female, but the first thing that put me onto a woman was the night you discovered Stacy White."

"How?"

"When Mac first arrived here in La Pointe, all clues did point to a man. In fact, after Patriot was shot and killed, and bodies still kept turning up, Mac and I seriously thought Curt and or Kevin was the serial killer. The nursery rhyme is what convinced us both that we were dealing with a female. It wasn't until I heard that woman mention Terry Hunter's name in the L.A. office building that I put all the pieces of the puzzle together."

"That was Becca," Nicole told him.

"Hearing someone else say his name, asking you if I was Terry triggered it. If you'll recall Josie was not at the Tavern the night you found Stacy White. Just a little unusual with their routine and considering the rest of the Stewarts *were* there. Mac and I figured out Stacy was left in your backyard between four and

ten PM. Although many things pointed away from a male killer it was my recollection of what Brian said to me about getting a girl in trouble that pointed
to a local. What you told me about that weekend increased my suspicions but I
had no way of proving anything until I heard Terry's name the day I came to
get you."

Nicole sat upright. "Josie *wasn't* at the Tavern that night. She never came in
after you all left either. In fact, that night when Kevin punched Mike and you
came, Josie was acting very nervous. Was she the one calling me and hanging
up, too?"

"Most likely, yes."

"I had the phone disconnected. Guess we'll never know now."

"Is there anything else, Gage?"

He studied Michelle for a long moment. Mac had been right about her
strength and courage. Although she had Travis, he felt deep down Michelle had
learned everything she needed to know about survival long before anyone
linked to any of the killings. "Nothing that really concerns you, Michelle. The
news is going to spread fast. I'll be making a public statement in the morning. I
wanted you to hear it from me first so there'd be no questions in your mind.
Also, because I—" he took Nikki's hand. "*We* owed you. I've always believed
Brian's death was my fault the same way Nikki did. We're both deeply sorry
and we have to live with our regrets."

"Gage, you couldn't have known what was going to happen. If that were the
case, then Brian's to blame for his involvement with Josie. The bottom line is
Josie made the choice to kill. Unfortunately, many innocent people have suffered for something she wanted and couldn't have."

"Perhaps you're right. Michelle, you know I've always loved you like my sister."

She looked around him at Nicole now. "Is this what you were talking about
that day at your house? When you told us you'd hurt so many people?"

Nicole couldn't look at her best friend, or reply, just nodded.

"Yes, Gage, I do know that," Michelle answered him. "I feel the same. I have
something to say to both of you. Then I want to speak to Nicole alone. What
happened to Brian still hurts me, but hear me loud and clear. If you still called
Brian's death accidental, came and told me what you just did, I'd never blame
either one of you for his dying. Nevertheless, if either of you ever keep anything from me again I'll hunt you down and make your life a living hell. *We* are
family! We always have been and we always will be! Because of that, I'm going

to butt in. You two either get your *fricking* act together or I'm going to lock you both in a room until you do!"

Her point made, Michelle looked up at her husband. "Travis, love of my life, take Gage upstairs, pour him a good stiff drink and close the damn door!"

"Yes, Milady." He kissed her, stood, and smiled at Gage. "See why I love her," Travis said leading the way.

When they were up the steps, Nicole mustered out, "Michelle, I—"

"Shut-up, Nicole! Answer me. Why did you go out with Brian?"

Panic flipped through her. Michelle didn't want to know why she kept secrets from her best friends. No, Miss Meticulously Detailed wanted to know why she went out with Brian. Probably the worst question she could have asked, too. Nicole looked at her. Her vision clear, her eyes were dry as sand. She mustered out. "To make Gage jealous."

"Well, then. You're not only a saucy twit but a bigger dumb jerk than I've ever been."

"Mi—"

"I'm not done!" She heaved herself off the sofa. "You listen to me, and you listen to me good. That man up there has put his whole life on the line for you. The fact that he's been living for fifteen years off the memory of a dead man he believed you were in love with is unthinkable. Do you have any idea what it took him to sit here and tell me everything he just did! No, you don't! You've always been excessively preoccupied in self-pity of a situation you have had absolutely no control over.

Nicole looked away from the pregnant woman pacing, ranting and raving right now. Didn't want to face what was coming. In fact, she wondered what had happened to her meekest best friend.

"Dammit, Nicole! Open your eyes and take a good long look at what's staring you in the face. Gage is in love with you and all he wants is you. Nothing else matters to him. Can't you see that if he isn't with you, kids don't matter to him?"

"I guess," she muttered.

"You guess!" Michelle screeched.

"Okay! Fine! I know."

"Then what the hell are you waiting for? And what are you going to do about it?"

"He found the courage to do what he did. I'll find the courage to tell him…somehow."

"Just do it! Caitlin is staying here for the night and both of you go home and straighten out the mess you've made of your lives."

Nicole lifted herself up. She studied her best friend for a moment. "Mrs. Baines, what did you do with my friend Michelle?"

"She grew up," Michelle told her. "Nicole, I love you with all my heart. All I want is for you to be happy."

"I know you do. That's all I ever wanted for you. I've been afraid of many things for so long maybe it's time for me to grow up, too. When I stood there looking at Adam and Michael it was weird. I saw their fight for life. For the first time, I didn't feel sorry for myself. I think tonight, I've finally figured out what it means to have a family. It started with Caitlin yesterday. That little runt is smarter than she knows. It has nothing to do with blood and biological parents. It's all about love—being there when the other needs you. I didn't have that in L.A. and I certainly didn't know until now how much of it I have here."

Nicole wrapped her arms around Michelle. "I love you girlfriend."

"I love you, too. Katharine's coming home tomorrow. She's gonna need us for awhile."

With a wee, hopeful smile, Nicole responded, "I think I'm gonna be here."

"Good. Now get your butt upstairs and take care of this problem."

When they left, Travis pulled his spunky wife into his arms. "You okay?"

"Ask me in the morning when the shock wears off."

"Those were some speeches you gave."

"Well, *shit*. Somebody had to do it!"

Travis kissed her. "I love you, Milady."

CHAPTER 24

❀

The ghost, neither once believed in moaned and cried during the trip back to Joe Hamlin's house. It was melodious and sad at the same time. The noise drowned out the blowing winds that reliably deluged the month of March.

"Do you hear her now," Nicole asked quietly.

"Yeah, Baby, and it's the best thing I've heard since you left."

Shooting him a curious look, she asked, "Why?"

"Once you were gone, I stopped hearing your ghost. I really started to believe we weren't meant to be together. The day I brought you back and we went to the hospital, I heard her for the first time since you'd left."

"Guess she didn't have the power to be in two places at once. I was hearing her more out there than I did here. Maybe it means because I was the one who needed to be convinced."

"Could be," he responded.

"There's something else," Nicole said.

"What's that?"

"I believe in the meaning of Sully's fairytale for the first time in my life."

"Why?"

"Before I left, I found a book my parents gave me when I was a kid. The Cadotte History. Anyway, my last night here, I sneaked back over to the house. Maybe wishing things were different…I don't know. The book was laying there and I started flipping through it, remembering things."

"What things?"

"I'll get to that. I have this picture of the three best friends. It's my favorite of us because it was taken before Brian was killed. That's when I saw something. I found a picture of three Cadotte sisters in that book. Purely accidental...I think. Gage, it freaked me out. Those three were a match to us. Except for the fact the old one was taken on a different ferry in black and white, it was like staring at Katharine, Michelle and me on the Island Queen. I swear those three women had our eyes—maybe we have theirs. I don't know. I realized Sully's ghost story about jeweled eyes really did refer to the three of us. To all of us. Whether or not the daughters were murdered, or died naturally, the legend isn't about death. Sully's story is about family. It's about living and loving."

Gage pulled into the drive and stopped. He smiled. "Nikki, you aren't the only one who believes in ghosts nowadays." He exited the truck and jaunted around to help her out.

They went through what felt like unnecessary formalities until they were locked inside the house, each holding something to drink. Too wrapped up in thinking, Nicole didn't have a clue what he'd given her.

"Nikki, come and sit with me."

She did, sinking into the cushioned sofa. "Gage, I'm sorry. I'm sorry for everything. That was very brave of you to tell Michelle what you did and the way you did. It must've been very difficult."

"It was the second hardest thing I've ever done."

Maybe in her head Nicole had been saying it subconsciously over and over. But, it was now or never she thought and blurted out. "Gage, I do love you. I have ever since the first time you pulled my hair, but I can't give you what you want. I can't give you a child. That's why I left. That's why I cried when you asked me to marry you."

"Nikki, I know."

"That's why I've been acting like such an idiot. Or as Michelle said, a dumb jerk. I love Caitlin, too."

"I don't care about that."

She stopped. Shot him a pointed looked. A deep chuckle greeted her. "You don't care that I love Caitlin?"

"That's not what I said, Babe."

"Gage, you just said—"

"What I said was, I already know you can't have kids and I don't care."

She sat up, eyes wide, demanding, "*Who* told you?"

A deep chuckle turned into jovial laughter as she sat glaring at him.

"Welcome back, Babe. I've missed disputing every subject in the universe with you."

He leaned over and shattered what little calm she had left inside of her with a hungry kiss. He caressed and teased, traced and tasted before he devoured her.

Sighing, she murmured, "What was the first hardest thing you ever did?"

He put their drinks aside to hold her in his arms. He played with her hair as he looked into her eyes and said, "Tell you, we were through."

Caressing his face first, Nicole ran her fingers through his hair. "Why did you do it? The night of the party when you took Caitlin into the dining room to soothe her tears I was standing there listening."

"I know. I always know when you're around."

She looked into his eyes, totally understanding. "All I could think about after that little scene was what you'd told Caitlin about not being able to make me stay. Deep inside I figured if you really wanted me you would have found a way to keep me here."

"Nikki, I've made my share of mistakes. I kept telling myself it was because I couldn't protect you. That wasn't true. I was angry—hell! I'd never been madder at you then when you decided to leave. I knew you were in love with me yet you couldn't tell me. You wouldn't say it to me and I needed to hear it. That same night before you left the next day, I really thought I got through to you."

"Oh, you got through to me all right. That's when I realized I didn't just love you, I'd fallen in love with you. By then I was too scared to tell you how I felt and have to toss another bomb in your lap. It would've been deceitful. How *did* you find out?"

Giving her forehead a kiss, he said, "I found the card you sent to my mom when I went looking in the attic for a nursery rhyme book. You made it hard for me to figure out what was wrong, until I stood in the hospital holding Caitlin and looking at those tiny newborns wishing you and I could have one together. That's when it registered what you couldn't give me. It's also the night I promised Caitlin you'd become her mother."

Her heartbeat picked up. "You knew that's what she wanted."

He nodded. "She told me the night of the party."

"You've always made it known you wanted a family," Nicole spoke quietly.

"How so?"

"Gage, you love kids and you don't hide it. Brendan and Shalee, now Caitlin."

"Yeah, you're right. I do. But, Nikki, it never meant I didn't want to share my life with you. The moment when I stood there wishing it, something happened.

"What?"

"Having kids meant nothing if I couldn't be with you. Besides, I was already holding our little girl in my arms. Nikki, my love for you is like oxygen. I need you."

Nicole's heart lurched. She sat up, faced him.

"We've got a sweet little thing desperately needing a mom and a dad, grandparents, a lot of love, and a home."

"You really want to adopt her?"

"Nikki, I want to marry you first. I want *us* to adopt Caitlin and several more." Gage added matter-of-factly, "Can't have my brother-in-law outdoing me."

She studied the play of emotions on his face. Since the first time he pulled her pigtails, the depth of his feelings were fully exposed. "I love you madly, deeply, always and forever. You're on."

"No more secrets?" he asked.

"No more secrets," she replied.

Epilogue

❀

The beginning of a new treasure waited for them in La Pointe. The ice had slipped out while they were overseas traveling Rome, Paris, Florence, Nice and Cannes. The ferry snaked along Superior's icy blue waters, too slowly, Nicole thought.

But the air was fresh and pure.

Feathered friends had returned. Trees were tall and blossoms would bud soon from their branches. A brassy sun gleamed with warmth high above forcing a new birth of spring. Nicole gazed at her husband then at their jewel in the Apostles. No other place felt so dear. Nuzzled into the south shore, Madeline Island was the best thing she'd seen in three weeks. The Island Queen approached their rock, finally bedding with the dock.

This was home and she couldn't wait to wrap her arms around one child and the family who had taught her many things. Gage reached over, took her hand as he steered his truck off the boat onto the dock and headed to his parent's house. She sensed he was just as anxious to get home as she was but they'd go to their home later. Joe Hamlin couldn't resist the substantial offer her loving husband made for his place. Her house sold while they were away on the expense-paid honeymoon.

Gage pulled in behind the cars, parked and shut off the engine. "Wonder what's going on?"

"Looks like everyone is here," Nicole responded.

"Mommy! Daddy! You're back!" Caitlin squealed, pushed open the door and ran out of the house.

Gage hopped out of the truck, caught her, flinging her into the air and squeezing her tight in his arms.

"Hey, squirt. Did you miss us?"

"Yes. Lots!"

"Give me a dozen hugs and kisses," he said.

She'd already begun and Gage blew whisker kisses on her belly until she giggled and squealed.

"Mom, help!"

"Not on your life, sweet thing," Nicole said, walking around the truck. "But, I want my share of kisses and hugs."

Gage let Caitlin reach out and wrap her arms tightly around Nikki. Caitlin planted a blowing mushy smack on her cheek.

"I missed you lots my little blond cutie."

"I missed you more."

"Hun-uh."

"Uh-huh."

"Did not."

"Did too."

"Not."

"Too."

"Took thirty seconds for you two to start," Gage teased and tickled Caitlin until she squealed out the magic word. "Uncle!" He propped her upon his shoulders and her chatter began.

"Mommy, Adam and Michael and Brendan and Shalee are here. Grandma says we're having a party. Guess what?" Caitlin didn't wait for an answer. "Adam made Michael cry. And Grandpa took me out in the boat."

Nicole smiled at her new daughter unaware until this moment how good the word mom sounded. "Grandpa took you in the boat already. I bet while Grandpa's having fun, Grandma's pulling her hair out."

"Hey, squirt, we've got a couple of surprises for you."

"You got me something?"

"Sure did."

"Did you get something for Brendan and Shalee and Adam and Michael?"

"Yes. Let's go inside and Mom and I will tell you your surprise."

When Nicole opened the truck, Gage said, "Babe, leave everything. The three of us are going home together tonight."

Gage wrapped an arm around Nicole and they walked into Grandma and Grandpa's house.

"Welcome home," the growing gang hailed and greeted them inside the door with more hugs.

"Nicole, did you take lots of pictures?"

"We sure did. Florence was my favorite, but Gage liked Cannes. Oh, Paula, it was beautiful and romantic. Absolutely the most wonderful honeymoon. Thank you each and every one of you," Nicole said to Travis and his family.

"I want to hear every detail of Paris and Rome?" Paula said. "But later when we have hours to talk about it. I bet you kids are exhausted."

"Never felt better." Gage grinned and kissed his wife. "Now where are those nephews of mine?"

"Grandpa's got them," Caitlin informed him.

"Well, squirt, let's you and me go see if we can nab them away from Grandpa. Duck," he told her and dipped so his daughter missed the header.

"Nicole, we're having our first barbecue of the year. Travis' family flew in a couple of days ago…,"

Paula chattered on happily and Nicole took it all in. Travis had turned into a nervous, loving hen over Michelle's pregnancy. Nearing half term, she had expanded in the middle rapidly. Katharine never looked more radiant—motherhood was good to her as was working at home for Michelle's business. Scenic Landscaping was expanding to the mainland. The twins were coming up on three months old, and thankfully, healthy, happy tykes. Mac still proudly passed out cigars, and Grandpa LeNoir pretty much controlled how long anyone held either of his grandsons. The adoption of Caitlin was in process and finalization would come quickly.

Brendan, Shalee and Caitlin had become great friends—maybe another trio of best friends, Nicole mused. Sylvie and Harvey, along with Aidan sat together observing. Rosemary and Phillip Baines along with Ronson and Grandma-ma, everyone called Julia Grandma-ma now had laid back and truly appeared to enjoy the gathering. In the middle of everyone, stood the man Nicole dearly loved. The one who had given her life's biggest dream and much more than she ever could have believed possible.

But she couldn't help thinking back to the first week in March when she made a phone call to Chantilly Makinaw. She was ready to trade in her fantasy job for family. Instead, the famous model, elated with her illustrations, offered to keep her on long distance as long as she made a trip to L.A. once a month. Nicole felt deep down that Becca had pulled some strings. Turnabout was fair play. Gage readily agreed to the arrangement and while on their honeymoon, they decided a home office was necessary, along with an extra bedroom. They we're going to discuss the designs for the add-on with Travis.

A slice of empathy drifted into Nicole's happiness. Josie had been diagnosed as schizophrenic with major psychotic tendency or something along the lines of those psychological terms. The bottom line Josie and her split personalities were incapable of standing trial, as Gage had thought would happen. Curt had put their house up for sale then he and Clyde moved off the island before it sold. Elizabeth Callihan still denied herself the truth about her son Brian. Guthrie's trial was scheduled to start next week. Gage thought it would go fast. Kevin Stewart had moved to Green Bay, and Bert Hanson, God-fearing man that he was, had drowned himself by cutting a hole in the ice and jumping into the big lake. Too many had suffered at the hands of jealousy.

With the Cadotte ghosts at rest, Nicole wondered what story Sully would tell the tourists now. Somehow she figured he'd come up with a good one though it didn't matter. She was happy. She was home. And this family was the jeweled gift. A kiss brought her back to the moment.

"Where were you, Babe?" Gage asked.

Smiling, she told him, "Right where I belong. I love you, Gage."

"I know," he said with genuine belief. He looked at their daughter then back at Nikki. "Should we tell her?"

Nicole nodded. "Let's tell everyone."

Gage whistled to get their attention. "Caitlin, come 'ere."

She scrambled through the crowd and leaped into his arms. "What?"

"I won't bore anyone with details of how it happened, but while we were in Paris another opportunity passed our way. Caitlin, little squirt and one of the love's of my life, you're gonna have a baby brother in six weeks."

"Oh, Daddy, that's what I wished for!"

Caitlin squeezed her arms around his neck and as the others offered congratulations, Gage observed approval and pride on his father's face.

Mac rallied, "Can't have you catching up. I'll have to get to work."

"Dobarchon, there's no *I* in this partnership," Katharine told him.

Gage smiled. He looked at Caitlin then Nikki. "You know I love you both."

"Me too," both said as though their fate had been preplanned.

Dear Reader

My love is writing. As I begin brainstorming each tale, the story becomes a child to me that I covet and protect until it's complete for each of you to read. While I've had the pleasure of meeting many of you at book signings or guest speaking engagements, I'm frequently asked where my ideas come from. Granted my 15 years in law enforcement and hours of additional research guarantee the police procedure is as close to accurate as possible, but the plot and characters are nothing other than a figment of my imagination created for your enjoyment.

While I am always thrilled to hear from each of you, and do enjoy the attempts to figure out whodunit, I'm more excited to hear that you have enjoyed the first two stories in the Apostle Islands Trilogy so much that waiting for the third book has kept you anxious. I really do prefer to keep the anxiety and suspense in the story and apologize for the extended delay. I want to thank everyone for his or her patience. *Jewel of the Apostles* has been a long time coming! I sincerely hope that the final episode and grand finale was worth the wait.

Thank you for all your support!

Barb Dimich

978-0-595-40136-9
0-595-40136-8

Iune 9-6

Printed in the United States
57969LVS00003B/73-81